FORTUNE'S FAVOR

STOLEN STARS

HEATHER GREYE

For Thom, my number one cheerleader and my favorite problem solver

For my mom, who said this could be the first intergalactic romance on a certain movie channel

For my sisters, for their endless enthusiasm for my books

And for Ripley and Hicks

Stolen Stars

Copyright © 2025 Heather Greye

All rights reserved.

No part of this publication may be reproduced, distributed, or transmitted in any form or by any means, including photocopying, recording, or other electronic or mechanical methods, without the prior written permission of the publisher, except as permitted by U.S. copyright law.

If you would like to use material from the book (other than for review purposes), prior written permission must be obtained.

This book is a work of fiction. Names, characters, places, and incidents are products of the author's imagination or are used fictitiously. Any resemblance to the actual persons, living or dead, business establishments, events, or locales is entirely coincidental.

No generative artificial intelligence (AI) was used in the writing of this book. Without in any way limiting the author's exclusive rights under copyright, any use of this publication to "train" artificial intelligence technologies to generate text is expressly prohibited. The author reserves all rights to license uses of this work for generative AI training and development of machine learning language models.

ISBN: 978-1-963299-07-6 (ebook)

ISBN: 978-1-963299-08-3 (paperback)

Published by Black Sheep Media LLC

Editor: Elizabeth MS Flynn, emsflynn.com

Cover Design: Deranged Doctor Design, www.derangeddoctordesign.com

BOOKS BY HEATHER GREYE

Fortune's Favor Series

Stolen Stars

Stolen Chances

(coming spring 2026)

Stroke of Midnight Series

Midnight's Pawn

Midnight's Captive

Midnight's Queen

1

LACY

I stepped from the freighter's cargo hold onto the docking station, rolling my shoulders and stretching my neck side to side. I'd spent the last few hours checking the repairs I'd made to the portside aft docking door and double-checking the other three docking doors for issues.

When freighter AS4455 had limped into Elegium Station's repair bay two weeks ago, she'd been venting atmosphere through that door. And that hadn't been her only problem. She'd had enough issues to keep me and five other mechanics busy once the owner had reluctantly agreed to a full suite of repairs.

Today, the red and black multistory containership had passed her inspection with flying colors. Soon she'd be loaded with cargo and heading out into the unknown, while I would stay here on the space station.

I swiveled my neck side to side again, working out the kinks, then tilted my head back and looked up.

The dark of space lay just beyond the double layers of shielding that kept the repair dock pressurized. Stars twinkled against the black. From here, they looked like tiny pinpricks of light. The shield distorted the view, but I knew what space beyond the asteroid station looked like. Smaller asteroids tumbled past the station, close enough to make the landing approach interesting, but not dangerous.

A streak of light caught my eye, and my lips curved into a half-smile. Probably another ship, crossing from one side of space to another. What was it carrying? Passengers? Cargo?

A wave of longing swept through me. I hadn't sailed through the stars since I'd arrived on the asteroid station two years ago. After growing up on a ship, always traveling from one planet or station to another, staying in one place had sounded like a new adventure.

And it was . . . fine. The work was steady and the pay was good. And, best of all, it wasn't working for my father.

"You gonna stand there all night, Dupree?" The voice echoed from inside the ship.

"I'm goin', I'm goin'." I shook off the whisper of homesickness as I turned and waved at the crew member. "Safe travels."

I laid my hand on the side of the ship and whispered the same to her. "Safe travels, freighter AS4455."

Hitching my tool bag over my shoulder, I walked slowly toward the airlock doors that led to the station's interior. My gaze swept over the dock. Ships of all shapes and sizes filled the cavernous space.

Not every ship here needed repairs. Some were here to refuel, transfer crew, or pick up cargo. The dockmasters managed it all through an intricate system of colored lights at each berth.

All the colors of a rainbow shimmered at the docks around me. Red indicated repairs needed, while orange showed they were underway. Blue meant waiting for crew and green signaled ready for takeoff.

Freighter AS4455's lights had shifted from orange to blue a few hours ago. They'd shift to green as soon as the crew was back on board and they'd scheduled a time for departure.

The metal walkway that connected each berth to the station clanged with each step I took, the sounds echoing in the massive dock and mixing with the sounds of external repair teams and ships' crews coming and going. It was early evening station-time—and quitting time for me—but the docks never slept. Elegium Station was close enough to the main shipping routes to have steady business.

My route took me past a little Cyclone named *Fortuna*. I glanced up at her light, wondering if she were here for repairs. The yellow light next to her berth signaled she was here for cargo.

I smiled. *Mako*, my first ship and my first love, had been the same class. My father had "acquired" her during a raid. My sister hadn't been interested in owning or maintaining a ship, while I'd jumped at the chance. But she'd never turned down a ride in *Mako*.

My heart panged and I rubbed my chest. I missed my family—my sister, my father, and his crew—but sometimes I missed my ship more. Since I'd planned to be stationary here on Elegium, it hadn't made sense to pay docking fees for a ship I wasn't going to use. Still . . .

My stomach gurgled, reminding me of how long it had been since lunch. The pay for this job should have hit my account as soon as the inspector approved the repairs, so tonight I was treating myself to my favorite noodle shop. Tomorrow, I was going to sleep in and enjoy my day off.

Picking up my pace, I caught up to a group of spacers

and slipped into the airlock with them. I pressed into a corner, holding my tool bag in front of me to protect my personal space. Maybe I should have waited for them to clear the airlock, but I was starving.

Tucked into my corner of the airlock while the pressure stabilized, I studied the other occupants. From the way they argued over whether to visit a bar or a brothel first, I figured they were fresh off one of the many ships.

One of the men noticed me. "You're not part of our crew," he said. His gaze ran up and down the length of me.

Ew.

I didn't let my disgust show, just responded calmly. "Nope, Elegium Station crew."

Now all six of them looked at me, taking in my dirty coveralls and battered tool bag.

I wasn't concerned about my safety. The penalties for harassing station personnel were pretty steep. And really, did you want to piss off the person repairing your spaceship?

"Start at Meecham's," I said. "Their drinks are the cheapest and the least watered down." I'd tried every bar and restaurant on station in the two years I'd lived here, some more than once. Brothels, on the other hand . . . I could make recommendations, but they were based on secondhand knowledge, rather than personal experience. As my father said, you never knew what information might save your life.

"Wanna join us?" the one who'd initially noticed me asked.

"No, but thanks. Got the early shift tomorrow."

The airlocked dinged, the transfer between the outer dock and the inner station complete. With a chin lift and "You know where to find us," the spacers piled out.

I followed slowly, pulling my communicator out of my

pocket. Ordering dinner from my favorite noodle joint took seconds. The restaurant was preprogrammed and my order was always the same: spicy garlic noodles.

That taken care of, I shoved my comms into my pocket and headed into the main part of the station. The commercial zone hummed with activity as people ducked in and out of the shops, restaurants, and bars that lined the corridors. Conversations filled the air, many in English, but I caught a smattering of other languages.

Officially, Elegium Station was home to nearly 800 people, most of whom worked to keep either the station, the stores, or the ships running. The population easily doubled—or more—when the docks were full. The station provided food, fuel, and repairs to the crew and tourists who stopped here.

As I wove through the crowds, it was easy to tell who lived here and who didn't. Spacers lingered outside the bars and strip clubs. Tourists gaped at the many shops and food stands that sold goods from across the galaxy. No one ever expected a station this size to have such diverse food offerings. I rolled my eyes. Everyone came from somewhere. Why would Elegium be any different?

Dodging the visitors who frequently stopped in the middle of the corridor, I bypassed the more expensive touristy places and ducked into my favorite restaurant. It was a little hole in the wall, the kind of place most visitors were too afraid to try because of concerns about cleanliness or whatever other issues they extrapolated from the half-broken neon sign and peeling paint.

But to me, the rich scents of spices, grease, and a hundred other flavors that had seeped into the walls over the years represented comfort.

"Hey, Lacy." The owner pushed a warming bag toward me. "Good day?"

"Long day," I replied as I swiped my credit chip over the reader. "This is a lifesaver." I picked my order up and carefully tucked the meal into my tool bag.

"Thank you," I called and slipped back into the crowded corridor.

2

———

LACY

EVEN THOUGH I did this every day, my shoulder ached from the weight of my tool bag and my breathing was uneven by the time I reached the fourth floor. My tiny one-bedroom apartment was smaller than the restaurant, but the price was right. It was a short walk from the docks and reasonably safe. The biggest complaint I had was the permanently broken elevator.

I swiped my key across the keypad and stepped inside as soon as the automated lights flickered on. Out of habit, I locked the door and set my tool bag on the card table in the small kitchen.

The delicious smells wafting from my bag only made my stomach grumble louder. I was *starving!* Washing the grease and grime of the day off my hands, I grabbed a bottle of water from the small refrigeration unit. I plopped into the lone chair at the table, datapad at my elbow. A hot meal and an episode of my favorite show—maybe even two!—since I didn't have to work tomorrow.

"God, I'm boring," I muttered. I wasn't living the

adventurous life I'd imagined when I'd taken off on my own. I worked too much and had barely made acquaintances, much less friends here. Even my sister, who spent all her free time in dusty libraries and museums, had a more exciting life.

I could always go back.

As soon as the thought crossed my mind, I snorted and shook my head. This may not be the perfect life, but neither was that.

"You got what you wanted, Lacy. You're fixing ships, not stealing them."

Hungry and a little homesick, I queued up the next episode of *Galactic Queens* and plucked chopsticks from the utensil caddy on the table. Noodles and reality TV made everything better.

The jazzy theme song underlaid the "previously on" segment. "Welcome to *Galactic Queens*. I'm your host, Avalon Westerly." The glamorous redhead gestured broadly toward the palatial estate where the scheming queens were living this season.

Before I could pull the takeout from my bag, my doorbell buzzed, interrupting whatever Avalon was going to tell me about this episode.

Weird. No one ever buzzed this late except when I ordered takeout.

I paused the video and changed screens to answer the door. "Who is it?"

A gruff voice responded. "Bob, your neighbor. Delivery guy messed up and left something for you at my place."

I frowned. Had I ordered anything lately? Pretty sure I hadn't. Still, Bob was the definition of surly neighbor and didn't interact with anyone in the building unless he had to, so he was probably telling the truth.

Cranky from hunger, I returned to the door and peered through the low-tech peephole.

Despite the distortion from the fisheye lens, I recognized my neighbor immediately by his close-cropped white hair and permanent scowl. Bob was a cantankerous bastard and I was pretty sure the grouchy ran all the way through.

Apology ready—it never hurt to be nice to the neighbors—I opened the door. "Sorry. I wasn't expecting anything."

"Don't care," Bob said. "Some courier left this for you." He held out his hand.

When I opened mine, he dropped a packet into my palm. My fingers had barely curled around it before he turned, disappeared into his apartment, and slammed his door.

"Thanks," I mumbled to the empty hallway.

I slipped back into my apartment, studying the packet. Yep, that was my name and address on the front, along with the logo of a data transmission service in the upper right corner.

Hmmm.

"Who sent you?" I whispered. It felt like a data chip, but where did it come from?

Since there was no way I was putting a random data chip anywhere near my computer system without disinfecting it—twice!—I tucked the mystery package into my pocket. I'd deal with it after dinner.

The door buzzed again when I was halfway back to the table. A quick glance through the peephole revealed it was Bob again. "Another package?" I asked with a laugh as I opened the door.

He didn't laugh. His face was pale, his expression tight with pain.

I barely registered the figures behind him before he was shoved in my direction.

I dodged, but the unexpectedness of the intrusion took me by surprise. My back slammed against the door and my breath caught as I tried to get out of the way.

Ignoring the pain radiating from my shoulder, I shuffled sideways and stumbled into the living room. A masked figure pushed Bob deeper into the room and slammed the door closed. Bob collapsed onto the floor with a whimper and then was silent.

Though I hated to get farther from the door, I moved back, keeping distance between the intruders and me.

"Where's the map?" the larger of the two men demanded.

Both wore nondescript dark cargo pants and long-sleeve shirts. I didn't see any identifying marks on their clothing.

That was all I had time to process. My brain whirled, trying to make sense of his question. "What map?"

I looked at Bob lying still on the carpet—was he *dead?*—and then at the two men behind him. Heart pounding, I struggled to understand the nightmare I'd suddenly found myself in. What the fuck was happening here?

Bob lay between me and my unwelcome visitors. All three of them blocked my access to the door.

Think, Lacy, think! Panic wouldn't help right now, but knowing that didn't stop my heart from racing. *What would Dad do?* He'd probably say something like if you can't talk your way out of it run, and if you can't run, fight.

Fear threatened to overwhelm my ability to reason, so I shoved it back as much as possible. I may not have my father's charm, but maybe I could buy time to think.

"What map?" I repeated. Hands spread to indicate I

wasn't a threat, I backed farther into the kitchen. "I don't know what you're talking about."

My gaze bounced around the room and between the two men as I sought a way out. They didn't seem inclined to negotiate and I couldn't take them in a fight.

Run it was.

Another couple steps put me even with the table which held my tool bag and the utensil cup.

My run options were limited. The only way to the door was past them. I might be able to dodge one, but both? I bit my lip. Not great odds. My stomach churned, more nauseated than hungry now.

The kitchen window behind me was the only other potential exit. Not ideal from the fourth floor, but it was the best of my bad options.

Another wave of nausea rolled over me.

"I don't know anything about a map." I had to keep them distracted while I cobbled together my plan. Chopsticks might not do any damage, but the few kitchen knives I owned were in the utensil cup too. "Maybe you've got the wrong address?"

I took a half step to my left. Then another when neither man noticed.

"We traced the data broker to this station. To you. Give us the map, bitch!"

Crap. They were angry instead of distracted. Inhaling deeply, I rolled onto the balls of my feet and forced my shoulders to relax. I'd only get one shot.

I visualized my movements. Then, with another deep breath, I lunged for the table.

My fingers curled around the tool bag's strap before either of them could react. Muscle memory drew it over my head, while my other hand reached blindly for a knife.

The utensils rattled, but I never took my gaze off the bad guys.

My fingers curled around a wooden handle just as the bad guys lunged.

Bob pushed to his knees with a groan and lurched into the path of the man on the right. He shoved Bob into a chair, which slammed into the table. Silverware clattered with the impact. Neighborliness demanded I check on him, but my instincts screamed to take advantage of his assistance.

Distracted by the sound, the man on the left looked away from me. Exploiting his moment of inattention, I threw the knife at him. It hit him in the shoulder with a squishy thud.

"Fuck!"

He staggered, then groaned as he pulled the knife out.

That bought me a couple more seconds. Would it be enough?

I darted to the table long enough to grab another knife, then backed toward the window. Brandishing the weapon in front of me, I stepped backward until I pressed up against the plasglass.

Both men advanced on me, a bit slower than before. Maybe it was because I'd fought back, maybe they thought I was trapped, since they remained between me and the door.

"You can't get away," the one on the right said. "Give us what we want and we'll let you go."

Liar!

Shoulder Guy glared at his partner. "Bullshit. She stabbed me. She pays."

"I don't think so." In one move, I threw the knife at the uninjured guy's stomach then pivoted toward the window. I wrapped my arms around my bag, tucked my shoulder, and launched my body at the plasglass window.

Shouts echoed behind me as the entire window broke free of the frame. "You bitch!"

I tucked my body into a ball as I launched through the window.

Fuck. This was going to hurt.

3

LACY

Stomach in freefall, I dropped three stories, vaguely aware of the window clattering to the ground. I really hoped that I wouldn't do the same.

I hit the awning of the ground floor shop. The taut material didn't have much give so I hit hard when I landed. Agony shot through my left side. A low moan of pain escaped my lips as I rolled to my knees. I barely heard the shouts of the people on the walkway below over my thudding pulse.

"You won't get away!"

That made it through the haze and I glanced up. Both men leaned out the window, masks still in place. Shoulder Guy gripped his wounded arm. Even from this distance, I knew his gaze promised retribution. I felt bad about leaving Bob up there with them, but my safety had to come first. That was a lesson from my childhood.

I had to keep moving.

Ignoring the pain in my left side, I scrambled to the side of the awning. Hooking my hands on the edges, I flipped over the side. The weight of the tool bag threw me off center and I swung wildly. Between the pain and the uncontrolled swinging, my left shoulder couldn't hold steady and I lost my grip. I dropped awkwardly onto the walkway below. The impact jarred my already battered body.

"Watch it!" Someone stepped abruptly around me.

"Sorry!" I took a moment to catch my breath. A few people rushed toward me, exclaiming about security and paramedics and wondering if I was okay.

I embraced the pain, using it to make myself seem fragile. "Those men . . . they broke into my home. I was so scared."

Some of the bystanders looked up. The men scrambled away from the space where the window had been.

An older woman patted me on my left shoulder and I flinched away. "Ow."

"You're safe now." She offered me a reassuring nod and pulled her comms out of her pocket. "We'll get security here to take care of you—and them," she added with a dark look.

"Thank you," I said and meant it. Mostly. I truly did appreciate perfect strangers coming to my aid. But that was the problem too. They *were* strangers and any of them could be working with my attackers.

Maybe everything was fine. But I didn't trust it. Couldn't trust it. I wasn't wired that way. What I needed was a place to hide. Catch my breath. Eat my cold noodles. Figure out a plan. Maybe then I'd be willing to talk to security.

But not right now.

As more people stepped forward, sharing what they'd seen or heard, I tucked my tool bag close and stepped back. When it didn't seem that I was recognizably the center of attention, I melted into the stream of people on the walkway.

Maintaining a steady pace and not limping was difficult. Somehow, I needed to move fast enough to get away, but not too fast to draw attention, all while not screaming in pain as my hip and side and basically everything yelled at me for jumping out the window.

Gritting my teeth, I increased my pace long enough to join a large group of people. I hovered on the edges, hoping there was safety in numbers. They were heading back toward the commerce center. It was still dinner time, so maybe I would be able to lose myself in the crowds until I could find a place to lay low.

Grateful that someone else was making decisions on where to go for the moment, I focused on steadying my breath and stopping my hands from shaking. The adrenaline rush from diving out the window—*oh my god, what was I thinking?*—was wearing off.

Distracted, I didn't realize my group had gone into a club until I came face-to-face with the bouncer. "Dress code," he growled, looking me up and down with a sneer.

Shit.

I looked down at my coveralls. They'd been covered in grease and grime even before I went out the window. Now the blue-gray fabric looked worse for wear. Heat flushed my cheeks. I definitely wasn't dressed for the club.

"Sorry, wrong turn." I stepped out of line and quickstepped until I was out of sight of anyone who'd witnessed my rejection.

Turning a corner, I sagged against the wall and considered my options. I couldn't go back to my apartment, not with those guys hanging around. While the station was technically open at all times, most people and shops hewed to a regular day and night cycle. I could lose myself in the dinnertime crowds and maybe a bit later, but eventually, the commerce center of the station would empty and I'd be mostly alone.

I shifted my tool bag and searing pain flared in my left side. I needed food and sleep—not necessarily in that order—and I needed it soon.

The station housed a couple of med clinics where I could get patched up, but those felt too exposed. Maybe I could lose myself in the station's service tunnels? I shook my head at the ridiculousness of that thought. Surely that was something that only happened in the movies.

Outside of my apartment, the only place I truly felt at home was on the repair docks.

My breath caught. Was that the answer?

Did the men who'd broken into my home know that I worked on the docks? Would they expect me to go there?

Did it matter if they did? I'd spent most of my time on those docks. I knew them better than they ever could.

My stomach gurgled, its discomfort battling my left side for supremacy. I needed to make a decision and this was the best plan I had. Now I just had to get back to the docks without being noticed.

The main drag—the one where the club was located—was the shortest, most direct route to the docks. Usually the busiest too. Hopefully I could lose myself in the foot traffic all the way back to the airlock.

It took a few minutes until a group of drunk spacers passed my corner. They were going the right direction and I prayed that they were headed to the docks.

My heart jumped as I left my hiding place and fell into step alongside them.

I tucked my bag close to my body and kept my eyes on my surroundings and the people around me.

We made it all the way back to the airlock before the spacers finally noticed me.

"You followin' us?" The spacer who challenged me was big. Built-like-a-tank big.

He was also slurring his words. Maybe I should have thought twice about stepping into an enclosed space with a bunch of drunk strangers. I obviously wasn't firing on all cylinders right now.

There was nowhere to run and the last thing I needed tonight was another problem, so I tried to defuse the situation.

"Naw, man. Heading back to my ship, same as you." I raised my hands to show I was harmless. My left shoulder stung and I bit back a wince. "I'm not looking for trouble."

Just another spacer coming back from a night in port. Hopefully he'd ignore me.

His eyes narrowed. "Which ship?" Suspicion coated his voice.

By this time, his friends had turned around too and studied me with expressions ranging from goofy drunkenness to angry suspicion. I counted quickly. Seven including the big dude.

Fuuuck.

I felt the weight of his friends' gazes, but I never took my eyes off him. It took supreme effort to keep my muscles loose and tension from my voice.

Could I brazen my way through this?

The spacers could have come from any of the ships currently docked at Elegium Station, but since they were a big group, I guessed it was one of the big ones. Hoping I was right, I took a deep breath and blurted out the name of the first small ship that came to mind: the little Cyclone.

"*Fortuna.*"

4

———

LACY

THE AIRLOCK FINISHED its cycle and pinged, the door to the dock opening.

For a long moment, no one moved. I shifted to the balls of my feet and held my breath.

The drunk spacer leaned past me, so close I could smell the alcohol. He sneered and pointed over my shoulder. "That piece of shit?"

We were still pretty far away, but I knew what he saw.

Sure, she was smaller than most of the others in the dock. A sleek, mid-bulk transport ship, not a huge cargo ship. Room for cargo, crew, and maybe a shuttle, depending on her internal configuration. Maybe she was a little rough around the edges, but I'd bet that was mostly cosmetic. Her vibe wasn't that of a down-on-her-luck ship.

"Hey! Don't talk crap about my ship!" I defended *Fortuna* the same way I would've defended *Mako*.

The spacers chuckled and the tension in the small space eased a smidge.

The big guy snorted and stepped back, out of my

personal space. "Good luck out there in that tin can." He shook his head and took off, followed by his friends.

And then it was just me in the airlock. I braced my hands on my knees and sucked in the first deep breath I'd taken since they'd noticed me. Then, despite the pain that was getting worse the more the adrenaline wore off, I straightened and stepped back onto the dock. In case the spacer and his friends were still suspicious of me, I ambled over toward the *Fortuna*.

My brain raced as I tried to sort out what I knew. I was in the middle of the spaceport with basically the clothes on my back, my tool bag, my hopefully still-edible dinner, and whatever credits I had in my bag. And the data disc that Bob had delivered.

I patted my pocket. The small packet was still there. Was that what they'd been looking for?

I had no idea who'd sent it, much less what was on it. A map of . . . something?

Time and a safe space. That's what I needed. That was the only way I could figure out what was happening. A place where no one would think to look for me.

Stopping in front of the *Fortuna*, I studied the ship.

Though the Cyclones were designed with a full crew in mind, they *could* be piloted by a single person. The ships had capacity for a dozen crew, maybe a few more if they doubled up. Their size made them perfect for running smaller cargo loads.

I bit my lip and stared at the ship. What I was thinking was crazy, right?

The final dregs of my adrenaline rush chose that moment to wear off and a wave of exhaustion rolled over me. That decided it—I'd sleep on the ship tonight. I knew that model inside and out; there were plenty of hidden nooks and crannies I could tuck myself into.

Tomorrow, after I'd gotten some sleep, I'd come up with a better plan.

The freighter next to *Fortuna* cast an immense shadow over the smaller ship. Hopefully my dark coveralls and dark hair—and my I-belong-here attitude—would prevent anyone else from questioning my presence.

From the darkness, I studied my surroundings. The docks were never truly silent, never really empty. Repairs, loading and unloading cargo, arrivals and departures, the docks were a source of constant activity. Fortunately for me tonight, none of that was happening around *Fortuna*.

The lights at the end of the docking station indicated she was there for cargo, not repairs. She wasn't waiting for crew either.

I swallowed hard. If the ship was carrying a full complement, this could be the dumbest thing I'd ever done. But to me, this ship—this *style* of ship—represented safety.

That was what I needed right now.

With my reserves fading and that safety a guiding light in my mind, I steeled my resolve and stepped out of the shadows. Right up to the main entry hatch. As far as I was aware, *Fortuna* didn't have external security sensors. They weren't standard on the Cyclones and anyway, my presence would have already set them off.

Setting my shoulders, I placed my hand on the right side of the hatch, then measured two palm widths further to the right. There was an easy way to break into a Cyclone and a hard way. This was the easy way.

"Here goes nothing," I muttered. I slammed the base of my palm against the hull. Pain radiated up my arm from the impact, but it was worth it when the hidden panel popped open.

The access panel was an open secret. Originally

designed to allow military pilots quick access to any ship with a single access code, all Cyclones had been built with them. I knew the original military code. I'd always assumed that was how my dad had acquired *Mako*.

Sometimes private owners changed the codes. Sometimes they didn't. Frequently that depended on whether they were dealing with an honest ship broker or not. I was about to find out how much *Fortuna's* owner knew about his or her ship.

Angling my body toward the door, I entered the access code. The hatch opened with a faint whisper and a puff of air. Every muscle tensed and ready to run, I stood to the side of the entrance, waiting for someone on the ship to come investigate.

No one appeared.

I exhaled slowly.

Now or never.

Stepping through the hatch, I held my bag close to my body and pressed the inner latch to close the door.

Dim lighting illuminated the corridor. The ship was probably set to station standard time, which changed the interior lighting with the time of day.

If I followed this corridor to the rear of the ship, I'd pass the crew cabins, then the cargo hold, and shuttle bay. The engine room was down a level. The bridge was forward. I went that direction.

As I walked, I kept my steps light and my body loose. What would I do if I encountered any of *Fortuna's* crew?

My best chance would be a version of the truth: I'd been attacked and was looking for a safe place. I saw the open hatch and ran in here for safety.

Certainly, my clothes would support that. They were ripped and covered with dirt and grime from my window exit. That was on top of the grease and grime from a day spent in the engine room. Believable. Except for the last bit. I tried not to think about how my dad would respond to a stowaway. He'd either keep them as crew or drop them at the next habitable planet. Usually.

The corridor was empty as I approached the bridge, so I didn't have to test my story. The lights flickered as I neared my destination, reminding me of every haunted derelict ship movie I'd ever seen. I shuddered. Dammit, that was the last thing I needed to think about.

The bridge stood open and empty. I stepped inside and another pang of longing swept over me. It looked so much like my beloved *Mako*. And yet . . . it didn't.

The stations were tidy, while the equipment showed signs of wear. Nothing drastic, just the wear that came from regular use. Nothing indicated that the ship hadn't been well taken care of. Taken care of, but not loved. There were no tchotchkes placed lovingly on the dash, like my bobblehead shark or the air freshener my sister had stuck to the console as a joke.

I moved closer and studied the setup. None of the standard equipment—radar, comms, and holo table—was missing, but I didn't see any of the fancy add-ons I'd expect if the ship had seen better, more prosperous days. The captain's chair was the most modern piece of equipment in the small space.

I smiled. The military-standard seats had been so uncomfortable, I'd upgraded *Mako*'s pilot chair within a week of receiving her.

Turning slowly, I scanned the rest of the bridge. A quartet of small video screens near the auxiliary pilot station caught my attention. I drifted closer to get a better look. "Tricky tricky," I murmured. Each screen captured a wide angle of the space around the ship, one for each direction. Including the main hatch.

The ship had to be empty because my entrance surely had been captured on the video feeds. If the captain or a crew member wasn't on the bridge, where were they?

Movement on one of the screens caught my eye and I leaned closer. Another group of spacers, wobblier than the pack I'd attached myself to, made their way down the docks. I released a ragged breath when they turned in the opposite direction of *Fortuna*.

As I was about to leave the bridge, more movement onscreen caught my eye. Two figures staggered around the dock, though without the boneless grace too much alcohol gave you. I peered closer. Were those my pursuers?

Crap. The only way I'd know for sure would be to come face-to-face with them again. No way in hell was I risking that by leaving the ship.

My heartbeat quickened and the not-quite-formed bruises from my window exit begged me not to get in another fight.

If fight was out, what about flight? I bit my lip and looked at the console in front of me, then at the captain's chair. Everything was the same as my *Mako*.

I considered my options.

The ship was empty.

I knew how to fly it.

Ignoring the tiny voice that warned that doing this would make me just like my father, I placed my bag on the navigator's seat. Pliers in hand, I sank to my knees and wriggled beneath the master console.

Seconds later, it opened, revealing the mechanical heart of the bridge. Motor memory guided my hands as I bypassed the security and initiated engine start.

After I closed up the system I'd just performed delicate surgery on, I dropped into the captain's chair and called up the command screen.

I took a deep breath and flipped the communications switch.

"Elegium stationmaster, this is *Fortuna*. Requesting immediate clearance for liftoff."

The comms crackled to life. "*Fortuna*, this is Elegium stationmaster. You're not scheduled for departure for two days."

No way was I waiting around two more days.

"Stationmaster, we have a coolant leak and request immediate departure." Even as I said the words, I winced. Coolant leaks were the worst, especially when you were docked. Elegium Station was equipped to handle leaks, but every mechanic I knew—including me—hated them. Coolant failure could lead to explosive results and it was much easier to replace coolant—or clean up debris—in the vacuum of space.

"Stand by, *Fortuna*."

Tense seconds passed while I waited for clearance. Antsy, I swiveled in my chair, my attention bouncing from the comms to the video screens. The two indistinct figures hadn't moved.

Maybe I was overreacting. But, a tiny voice whispered, they hadn't left yet either, so could I really take that chance?

"*Fortuna*, this is Elegium stationmaster. You are cleared for immediate departure through Zone 4. Good luck."

"Thanks, stationmaster. *Fortuna* signing off." I turned off the outbound communications. My stomach rolled and I blamed it on fear from the earlier attack rather than lying to the stationmaster and what I was about to do.

I ran through takeoff procedures quickly and efficiently. Then, with a wish and a prayer, I stole the *Fortuna*.

5

DAX

My eyes snapped open as I shifted from a dead sleep to fully awake. I blinked up at the ceiling—where was Finn's bunk?

Where the hell was I? And what had woken me?

Sitting up, I swung my legs over the side of the bed and scanned the room. I didn't feel hungover, but I didn't immediately recognize my surroundings. On the rare times I'd gotten that drunk, I'd never passed out in a place this nice. The room was way bigger than any of the berthing compartments on the *SMTC Evenrude*, not to mention it lacked the government-issue bunk beds.

"You're on the *Fortuna*, idiot." I exhaled slowly. Not just on the new ship, but in the captain's quarters. A room I didn't have to share with anyone.

How much longer was I going to wake up thinking I was still in the space corps? My team and I had left the military behind. Wilson's death eight months ago—his fucking senseless death—had been the last straw. We'd all left as soon as our enlistments were up, one after another.

Finn had been out six months. I'd been the last to muster out three months ago.

And now that we had a ship, the squad would be getting back together. Our ship, *our* rules. Wilson's last wish had been that we make our dream of running a cargo company a reality and he'd left us his life savings to make it happen. Now here I was with our brand-new ship ready to pick up our first cargo.

"Miss you, man." I rubbed the space over my heart, though I knew from experience that it wouldn't alleviate the sadness.

The ship vibrated under my feet, snapping me back to the present.

I surged to my feet, ridiculously grateful that I didn't need to duck to avoid the rack above me. I might still be learning all the ins and outs of the *Fortuna*, but I was certain she shouldn't be moving. Especially not when we were docked.

What the hell was going on?

Fortuna and I weren't due to depart for two days. We'd docked at Elegium Station because I had a line on a high-value cargo job, one we needed to get our new venture off the ground. The plan was to load the cargo onto the ship then rendezvous with the rest of the crew. We'd deliver the goods and make some easy money.

"Lights." The room illuminated gradually, highlighting the clothes I'd stowed on a chair last night. Such disorder wasn't like me, but I'd been up late studying the ship. My brain had been exhausted from trying to cram a lifetime of knowledge into a few hours. I was ecstatic that I'd managed to dock her without any problems.

Dragging on yesterday's clothes, I rubbed a hand over my blurry eyes, then grabbed my weapon from the locked desk drawer. It fit easily, comfortably, into the holster at the small of my back.

The door to my quarters slid open with a whisper. I stepped into the passageway cautiously, scanning from side to side, taking in as much of the corridor as I could each time.

The lights in the hall were set for simulated nighttime, not quite dark enough to create shadows where intruders could hide, but not wide open either. "Lights to full."

No signs of intrusion or forced entry.

No signs of anyone, but the steady hum of the engines beneath my feet told me that something was going on. Ships didn't fly themselves.

As I slipped into combat mode, my breath slowed and my other senses snapped to attention. I hadn't expected to feel this way after I'd left the service. Hadn't expected the hit of adrenaline that came with each mission.

Focus sharp, I continued down the corridor, clearing the crew quarters methodically and peering into the cargo hold. Every time I entered a room, I prepared for an attack that never came.

What the hell kind of operation was this?

The empty corridor and the running engines were starting to well and truly creep me out. Navy ships were never quiet. I'd only had the *Fortuna* for a week and still wasn't used to being alone on her.

Had that asshole at the shipyard sold me a haunted ship?

Get a grip, Dax.

The engine room and the bridge were the only places I hadn't checked. The bridge made the most sense. It was easier to fly a ship from there. If you wanted to disable one, it was easier to do that from the engine room.

Still at high alert, goosebumps still crawling up my skin

from the apparent emptiness, I approached the bridge carefully.

The door to the bridge was sealed. I'd left it open on my rounds last night. I was sure of it.

Who the hell was on my ship?

Whoever it was, they were about to learn that you didn't mess with a member of the space corps.

My right hand pulled my blaster free, while my left palmed the sensor by the door. It flickered green and the door slid open.

Blaster ready, I stepped onto the bridge, already scanning for hostiles. A quick step left put the wall to my back and gave me my first view of the intruders. *The* intruder.

My jaw dropped.

Whoever I'd expected, it wasn't the woman in the pilot's seat. *My* seat.

Head draped over the back of the chair, a dark braid hanging behind her, she didn't move when I entered. Didn't even stir. Was she dead? That was the last thing I wanted or needed.

Steps light, my weapon still out, I circled the entire bridge. My attention returned to her again and again, even when I was checking under the ship's consoles and behind the holo table. The *Fortuna's* bridge was so small, there really was nowhere to hide.

The woman was the only one on the bridge. Which begged the question, who the hell was she? Why was she here?

My mystery woman hadn't woken while I moved around the bridge and she didn't now while I studied her. The logo over her left breast marked her as station crew and a sewn-on patch said her name was Dupree, but neither of those facts explained what she was doing on my ship. They didn't explain the half-eaten container of noodles that smelled garlicky and delicious and made my stomach rumble either. And they sure as hell didn't explain why I saw stars outside the ship's windshield when I should have been looking at the docking platform on Elegium Station.

Once I'd verified that her chest continued to rise and fall, I tackled the more pressing question: Why the hell had my ship left Elegium Station?

I wasn't supposed to leave until I had my cargo. Turning my ship around was the only way I could salvage this.

Giving my unwanted passenger a dark look, I holstered my blaster and settled into the navigator's seat. Flipping the comms on, I reached out to the station.

"Elegium stationmaster, this is *Fortuna*. Requesting docking access."

There was garbled static on the other end before an incredulous voice came on the line. "*Fortuna*, this is Elegium stationmaster. That's a negative. There's no way you got that coolant leak taken care of that quickly."

Coolant leak? What the fuck? I choked back the words. Surely I hadn't slept through the alarms for a coolant leak.

"Ah, thanks, Elegium stationmaster. Understood. *Fortuna* out." There was no way I was going to reveal my ignorance to the station. They probably already thought I was an idiot.

Coolant leaks could be catastrophic. Like ships-go-boom catastrophic. Praying we didn't have one, I searched through the system for any leaks or alarms. While I still didn't know everything about how this ship worked, I'd spent every free moment learning what made her tick. I'd even downloaded a manual or two as soon as I'd docked at the station.

I still wasn't sure why the team had tasked me to buy the ship and fly her. Once the squad was back together, we'd all be learning new skills, but apparently I was up first.

Which was fine. Except no one had told me what to do in a situation like this.

I shoved my hands in my hair as I studied the search results. I read every chart and report twice until I was absolutely sure that there was no leak. That discovery ratcheted down my stress level just enough for it to bounce right back up as I read Elegium Station's protocols for a coolant leak: get the ship as far away from the station as possible as quickly as possible. As if that weren't bad enough, the safety protocols required a four-day window to ensure that the ship no longer presented a danger to the rest of the vessels docked at the station.

Fuck!

My meeting with the client was tomorrow. I couldn't miss it. If we didn't get that cargo, I'd have to start the search all over again.

I stared at the vastness of space just outside the ship. Day after day, night after night, we'd dreamed and planned and plotted for a life after the space corps. One we'd make the decisions for. Wilson's death had only strengthened our resolve.

I wasn't about to be the one who fucked it up. I *refused* to let my team down.

Before I made any decisions, I had to know what happened. And the only person who had the answers was passed out in the chair next to me.

6

———

DAX

IT TOOK effort to tear my gaze from the stars outside the ship. In the space corps, my squad all talked a big game about making our own choices, but now, faced with nearly as many options as there were stars, I worried if I was making the right one.

My most immediate need was information. I shifted forward in my seat and grabbed the tool bag from where it rested on the command console. It barely missed the open noodle container as it slid toward me. I frowned.

New rule. No food on the bridge, no matter how delicious it smelled. There was too much delicate—and expensive!—equipment up here to risk an accident. I placed the bag on my lap while I closed up the noodles and tucked them on the floor under the console.

That problem taken care of for the moment, I rifled through the woman's tool bag. The front pocket held an ident card, a few credit chips, and a fuzzy mint. I grimaced and dropped that back into the bag. Fingers on the edge of the ident card, I studied it, turning it this way and that to catch the holographic features.

The picture matched the woman in front of me, although she didn't look nearly as disheveled in the photo. "What the hell are you doing on my ship, Lacy Dupree?"

She didn't answer, but her head tilted toward me. Had she recognized her name?

The credits and card rejoined the mint in the front pocket. Opening the main compartment, I pulled out tools. Like the bag itself, the tools were clearly used, but well taken care of.

Lacy Dupree's mechanic rating was on her ident card, so I assumed they belonged to her. But why was a mechanic and her tools on my ship at all? I hadn't requested any repairs for the *Fortuna*.

Sealing the tool bag up, I placed it on the floor next to the noodles, then swiveled to face the captain's chair.

Her coveralls bore the grease stains and dirt that I would expect from someone who worked on engines and other repairs. Now that I was looking closely, I noted rips and tears that weren't what I would expect from a competent mechanic.

In fact, it looked like she'd gotten into a fight.

A glance around the bridge confirmed that there were no signs of a struggle here. Whatever had happened to her, it hadn't been on the *Fortuna*.

Hoping I wasn't making a mistake, I reached over and shook her left shoulder.

She whimpered and curled away from me.

Dammit. As frustrated as I was, I didn't want to hurt her. "Hey, wake up!"

Her eyes fluttered open. "What? Where am I?" She put her forearms on the arms of the seat and leveraged to a more upright position. Her lips pinched and she bit back another whimper.

Her eyes—a deep green a man could get lost in—were hazy with exhaustion.

Focus, Dax. This wasn't the time to be noticing shit like that.

"You're on the *Fortuna*," I replied. "And I'd really like to know why."

I leaned back in my chair, arms crossed over my chest, seeking a balance between intimidating the crap out of her and letting her walk all over me.

"I needed a place to hide."

Of all the things I'd expected her to say, that wasn't one of them. "And you chose my ship?"

She nodded, her gaze holding mine.

"Why? And how?" The ship had been locked down tight. Hadn't it?

"Some guys broke into my apartment. They chased me and I ran." Her voice wavered.

A protective instinct that was wildly unexpected—and completely inappropriate given the situation—flared up. I tamped it down violently. This conversation was about my ship, not her private life.

"What did they want?" Dammit. That was *not* what I'd intended to ask.

"I don't know." Lacy wrapped her arms around her middle. "They said something about a map, but I have no idea what they were talking about. One minute I'm about to eat dinner . . ." She glanced around, her brow furrowing.

I pointed to the container of noodles on the floor.

She nodded. "I was about to eat dinner and the next thing I knew, two thugs knocked on my door. They pushed their way in, using my neighbor as a shield. So I ran, looking for a place to hide." She shivered.

An attack shed new light on her ripped clothing, but

her story was missing some pieces. That didn't stop me from asking, "How did you get away?" My voice was low and growly.

"I threw knives at them, then jumped out the window."

She said the words so matter-of-factly, I waited a few beats for the punchline.

When she remained silent, my jaw dropped. Holy shit, she was serious.

"You what? Are you hurt?"

What was I saying? Of course she was hurt—she'd jumped out of a fucking window. She was virtually passed out when I entered the bridge—completely unaware of her surroundings—and had flinched when I touched her shoulder.

She was either brave or stupid. Maybe both. And now she was my problem. "All right, Lacy, let's go."

"How do you know my name?" Something like fear flared in her eyes before she shoved it down and raised her chin.

People often feared me, rightfully so. The space corps had spent serious money and time breaking me down and building me back up, creating a dangerous soldier. But seeing fear in her eyes when she looked at me? Unacceptable.

I gestured toward her bag. "It's on your ident card. 'Lacy Dupree. Mechanic.'"

Some of the tension in her shoulders eased, but not enough. I wished Mercer, the team's medic, was here. His bedside manner was miles better than mine. But he was off dealing with family stuff. He was one of the later rendezvous scheduled after we picked up the cargo.

At least, that had been the plan.

Sparing another glance at the stars that weren't supposed to be surrounding my ship, I knew that I had to ensure she was healthy before I could get answers from her.

I stood. "C'mon, let's go."

Lacy tensed and stared up at me. "Go where?"

"Med bay."

She shook her head. "I'm fine. I don't need it."

"It wasn't a request. We can do this the easy way or the hard way." Damn, never thought I'd see the day when Mercer's words came out of my mouth. I crossed my arms over my chest and gave her my best basic-training glower. She didn't even flinch.

She glared right back. "I'm fine," she insisted.

Maybe I would have believed her if she hadn't winced when she sat straighter. Or if she hadn't told me that she'd jumped out of a window. But right now? Nope, I wasn't buying it.

"Fine, we'll do it the hard way." Mercer had dragged my ass to med bay on more than one occasion when I'd insisted that I was fine. So that's what we were going to do.

I bent over the chair, slipped my hands under her thighs, and picked her up.

"What are you doing?" she squeaked and grabbed my shoulders.

"I told you, taking you to med bay." She'd been favoring her left side, so I carried her so her right side rested against my chest. Her weight was somehow comforting. Her braid draped over my arm and was as soft as it had looked.

Dammit, Dax. Not the time for noticing things like that.

"What about my bag?"

"The one with all the tools?" I shook my head. "It's staying here."

"But I need it."

"You don't need it for a checkup. Unless you're a cyborg and we need to unscrew you?"

She scowled at me like a fierce kitten. A feral one, with her mussed hair and dirty clothes and sharp claws. I bit the inside of my cheek to keep from smiling. The image made me want to keep her.

"I told you, I'm fine." She pushed against my chest and winced.

Yeah, that's what I thought.

"Then this will be a quick trip."

Her lips thinned and stubbornness radiated from her, but she didn't argue further.

7

———

DAX

Lacy didn't fight me as I carried her to the medical facilities. It wasn't a long walk and we reached the small room located amidships quickly. Two patient beds took up most of the room, with cabinets for scanners and other medical supplies tucked along the walls.

I set her down on the first bed.

When I'd purchased the ship, it had been important that it *have* a med bay, but once that item had been ticked off the shopping list, I hadn't spent additional time here. That was a mistake. Now that I needed it, I didn't know where anything was. Or even if I had the necessary supplies.

I tried to recall the ship broker opening and closing cabinets on our tour. My shoulders loosened with relief. Yes, there were supplies. Now I just needed to find the right ones.

When I opened my eyes, Lacy was watching me closely. She tilted her head and paused, as if she was considering her next words carefully.

Then she gave a brisk nod. "Center drawer on the right-hand side." She pointed.

My eyes narrowed. "What are you talking about?"

"You're looking for the handheld diagnostic scanner, right? It's so much easier to use, compared to the full-body scanner."

How would she . . .

Curious, I followed her instructions. There was nothing on the outside of the drawer to indicate its contents, but when I opened it, there it was, nestled in a formfitting case. Extra supplies, from batteries to probes, each in a designated spot.

I grabbed the scanner and turned back to her slowly, curiosity morphing to wariness and suspicion. "How did you know where the scanner was? Were you in here earlier?"

"What's your name?"

Her out-of-nowhere question distracted me. "What?"

She laughed softly. "It's not a hard question. You know my name. It's only fair I know yours."

I wasn't sure there was such a thing as fair with a woman who knew more about my ship than she should. But there was a kernel of truth in her statement too. It was only civilized to know the name of one's . . . enemy?

"Dax," I said. "Dax Cooper." I didn't offer my hand.

"Captain Cooper." Her nod was as regal as a queen. It should have been out of place on a stowaway, but somehow . . . it wasn't.

Then my brain caught up to what she had said. "Dax," I corrected quickly. *Captain* didn't sit quite right. Was that what I was now?

I'd been a sergeant in the space corps. Captains were the brass. Part of the command hierarchy. The title felt heavy, especially since the squad hadn't decided on roles. Or anything past buying a ship, really.

"Okay, Dax. Call me Lacy."

I hid a smile. It was cute the way she thought she had any control over this situation. I held up the scanner. "Ready, Lacy?"

With a sigh and an eye roll, she nodded. "Fine."

She sat perfectly still as I ran the scanner over first her left side, then the right. Then I passed it over her head, neck, and back. Her front torso and over her legs.

The machine processed all the data, then spit out a diagnosis. "Good news," I said, reading off the screen. "Nothing is broke—"

"I told you I was fine," Lacy interrupted.

I glared at her and went back to the diagnosis. "Nothing is broken—it's mostly bruises. *But,*" I said loudly when she looked ready to interject again, "your left shoulder is partially dislocated."

"Oh," she said in a small voice. "No wonder it hurts so bad."

"Yeah, that would do it." Sympathy warred with exasperation. I'd dislocated my shoulder in training and it hurt like a motherfucker. The fact that she was still standing, rather than moaning in pain, was impressive. "We need to pop it back into place."

She paled. "Shit."

I didn't envy her the next few minutes. "Yeah, it's going to hurt, but then it will get better."

She swallowed audibly. "Fine. Do it."

I winced, hating what I was about to say next. "We'll need to get your coverall top down. It could get in the way of resetting. You're, um, wearing something under that, right?" *Way to sound like a creeper, Dax.*

"Do we have to?"

I nodded.

"Fine, let's get this over with." She braced her left arm on her stomach and grabbed the zipper with her right. The dark fabric of the coveralls parted, revealing a white undershirt. When the one piece was undone to her waist, she started to shrug out of it but gasped in pain.

"Do you want help?"

"Yes, please." Her words were clipped.

I circled to her right side. "This side shouldn't hurt as much." I grabbed her right sleeve and pulled it away from her body. She bent her elbow and pulled her arm out, revealing smooth pale skin and subtle muscles.

Easing behind her, I gently moved the fabric as close to her shoulder as I could get. "I'll go as slow as I can," I warned her as I moved back into her line of sight, "but getting the sleeve over your elbow and wrist is probably going to hurt."

"Stop talking and just do it. The anticipation is making it worse."

"Gotcha." Keeping my touch light and my actions professional, I slid my fingers under the sleeve at her shoulder and guided it down her arm. She tensed as I dragged the fabric over her upper arm, but didn't complain.

When it reached her elbow, I braced it with my other hand and, as gently as I could, scooted the sleeve over the joint. Still holding her elbow, I grabbed the fabric at her wrist and guided it over her forearm, until only her hand was still covered.

Keeping tension on the empty sleeve close to her wrist, I shifted her elbow back slightly.

A pained sound in the back of her throat was her only outward sign of discomfort. I was impressed, because I'd seen marines cry with the same injury.

"And done," I said as I guided the last of the sleeve over her hand. Grabbing the two empty sleeves, I double-knotted them around her waist.

"You okay?"

"Just peachy."

"Perfect. Now on to the fun part. Lay back," I directed.

Her brows furrowed and she studied me uncertainly.

"It's the easiest way to do it. I promise."

"What about the autodoc?"

I shook my head. "If we were on one of the big hospital ships or a troop carrier, they might have the med tech to take care of it. We're kind of limited in a med bay this small."

Her lips pursed. "Right. I forgot."

Wondering what exactly it was that she'd forgotten, I only said, "Do you need help?"

Though she winced, she shook her head. Shifting her weight, she swung her legs up onto one end of the bed. Right hand hooked behind her right knee, she lowered her upper body down to the exam table slowly.

"Ready." Her voice was steady.

Not wanting her to be surprised, I talked her through the next steps. "I'm going to hold your wrist and slowly bring your arm out to shoulder height." I raised my arm to demonstrate. "Then I'm going to bring it closer to your head. At about this point," I held my arm out at about a third of the way between my shoulder and head, "your shoulder should pop back into place. Any questions?"

Lacy stared at me with wide green eyes. "No," she whispered.

"Great. After we've popped it back in place, I'll put it in a sling for you, then get you some pain pills and some nanos. Any allergies?"

She shook her head.

"Great. Let's get started."

When her arm was in a resting position at her side, I wrapped both hands around her wrist and started to shift her arm, all the while moving it in small circles.

Her breath hitched, but I didn't let up. I couldn't, not until we'd taken care of her shoulder. After a minute or two, her arm was up to shoulder level. I glanced at her to see how she was doing.

Her eyes were glassy with unshed tears, but she hadn't said a word.

"You're doing great," I said. "This part is going to hurt, so we're going to go on three, okay?"

"Okay." Her voice was as tense as the rest of her.

"One." I kept my movements slow and steady, continuing the circles as I brought her arm up further.

"Two." Rather than wait for three, I shifted her arm the last bit. I barely heard the soft pop as the shoulder settled back into place because Lacy screamed.

"Fuuuuck!

"You okay there?" I gently settled her arm over her chest.

Her eyes glared daggers at me. "You said three!" She tried to sit up.

"Stay down." I glared right back at her. "You were too tense."

"I hate you." Her eyes drifted shut.

"Fair enough. Let's finish getting you taken care of." Hopefully it wouldn't take me too long to find the supplies I needed.

"Slings are in the bottom drawer on the left," she told me. "Meds and nanos should be in the wall cabinet."

"Thanks." The only reason I didn't think she had read my mind was that I *had* mentioned next steps. But once again, her instincts on where to find everything were eerie as fuck.

It took me a moment to gather the supplies, pausing every moment or two to glance over at her. She was a mystery . . . and a problem.

When I was back at her side, her eyes flickered open and she stared up at me. Tension lines still bracketed her lips, but she didn't complain. "Pills or bots first?" I held up each label so she could read them.

"Bot shot first," she said.

I pressed the nano dispenser against her left biceps and slowly pulled the trigger. There was no way to see the bots being dispersed, but a little green light on top of the dispenser flicked on when the nanos had been delivered.

The pain pills were the dissolvable type, so I handed her the sealed packet.

She studied it a moment. Smart.

It took her two tries and I was just on the verge of offering to help when she ripped the package open with her teeth and tilted the pills into her mouth.

"Guuuhh." She grimaced and made a choking sound. "I can't believe you gave me the fake grape flavor. That's the nastiest." Lacy handed me the crumpled packaging for disposal.

"Second worst," I argued. "The fake watermelon is grosser." Though beggars couldn't be choosers. I'd been in enough hairy situations that I could tolerate any of the lab-made flavors.

Not wanting this to devolve into an argument, I held up the sling I'd found in the supply cabinet. "Ready for this?"

"How long do I have to wear it?"

"The system says overnight to give the bots time to

work without having to continually repair the same injury over and over as you move the arm."

Her sigh echoed around the room. "Fine."

It was easier to maneuver her into the sling than it had been to remove her coveralls. Easier for me, at least. By the time we got her arm in place and the sling secured, she was yawning.

I wasn't letting her fall asleep just yet. My quest for answers kept being put off as I handled the problems caused by her presence. "So, Lacy Dupree. Why did you steal my ship?"

8

———

LACY

I'D JUST STARTED to doze, swaying slightly to the side, but his question jolted me awake. "What?" *Super smooth, Lacy.*

Dax leaned against the cabinet next to the bed, his very fine backside propped against it, his arms and legs crossed. The casual pose belied the tension radiating off him. When I continued to stare at him, he sighed and repeated the question.

"Why did you steal my ship?"

"Borrowed. I *borrowed* your ship." The words slipped out and I slapped my hand over my mouth. *Shit.* That was not what I'd intended to say. I wasn't going to say anything at all.

I wished I hadn't handed him back the pain pill wrapper; I was acting like he'd given me some kind of truth serum instead of the pain meds.

Then I remembered the taste—the one that still lingered at the back of my throat. Nope, those had been standard-issue grape-flavored pain pills. Gross.

"That's not a thing," he countered. "You took my ship without permission. That's stealing."

Okay, technically that was true. That was why I'd really hoped that the *Fortuna* was empty. My getaway would have been so much easier.

I didn't have an immediate counter to his claim and the awkward silence between us grew. My gaze darted around the med bay, looking everywhere but at Dax. Like the rest of the ship, it was almost a twin for the one on *Mako*. The clinic wasn't the smallest room on the ship, not by a long shot, but the walls were still closing in on me.

Until Dax had demanded I get a checkup, I'd successfully ignored the pain in my apparently dislocated shoulder from the impact with the window and the ache in my left hip from the landing. The meds hadn't quite kicked in yet and now both injuries throbbed in time with my pulse. I didn't know which I was more aware of: my aching body or the captain's presence.

He was hard to miss, really, standing there glowering at me like he was.

Dax Cooper was ridiculously good-looking. Dark hair, adorably tousled. Dark eyes that tried to see into my soul. A body that said he hadn't left his military PT behind him and a hint of five-o'clock shadow, perfectly matched to his tanned skin. I wanted to brush my palm against his cheek.

Compared to him, I must look like hot garbage. Self-conscious and exhausted, my control slipped and bluster came out.

"I was going to bring it back." Probably. I actually hadn't gotten that far in my plan.

"Oh yeah, when? Was that before or after you 'fixed' the coolant leak?"

Right. I'd forgotten about the supposed coolant leak. "After, obviously. That's why I took the ship, because there was a coolant leak and we were all in danger."

Oh my god. I was such a liar. And I was pretty sure he

knew I was lying. One corner of his mouth quirked up, softening his stern expression. My stomach did a funny little swirl. Probably from not being able to finish my dinner.

"Why didn't you call security?"

"Why? I didn't need them to get on the ship." I blinked at him. Why would I call security when I was borrowing a ship?

The sound he made was half sigh, half growl, and all sexy. Dammit.

"When the men broke into your apartment. Why didn't you call security when you got away from them?" Curiosity filled his voice. And was that . . . concern?

I stared at him blankly. "Honestly, it never occurred to me." Given my dad was wanted on a number of planets and in one entire sector, calling security wasn't something we were taught. I shrugged and only half wanted to scream in pain.

"How the hell could it not occur to you? That's what they're there for!" Of course, the former military guy would believe in authority and security. Probably a whole bunch of other -ity-s, too.

"It happened so fast." The attack replayed in my mind as I spoke and I shivered.

"Why did you jump out the window?" His voice was surprisingly gentle, lulling me into sharing. Or maybe it was exhaustion.

"The men were between me and the door. My neighbor's a big guy and they tossed him to the side like he weighed nothing. How was I supposed to fight against that? So I did the only thing I could think of—I jumped out the window."

"You could have been killed." Horror coated his voice, but the tone was still gentle.

That startled a bitter laugh out of me. "Stay, go, could have been killed. There were no good options. At least I'd planned for the window."

My eyes closed. I was so tired. That had to be the reason I was talking so much.

"You planned to jump out the window?"

Sure, when he said it like that it sounded kind of crazy.

"No, just how I would get out of my apartment in an emergency. Dad said always have more than one exit."

"Sounds like a smart man."

Barking out a laugh, I opened my eyes and stared at him. "You could say that." If only he knew.

My eyes drifted closed and sleep beckoned. Instead of giving in, which every damn molecule of my body was demanding, I shook my head and brought it back to vertical.

"So, what now?"

"What?" I was losing track of the conversation.

"You stole my ship—"

"Borrowed," I muttered.

"—so what was the next part of your plan?"

Plan? He thought I had a plan? I managed to keep my hysterical laughter on the inside, but it was a close thing.

"Get as far from Elegium Station as I can." Obviously, that wasn't my whole plan. Once I was somewhere safe, I'd explore the mysterious data drive. Was it the map that the men had demanded?

"That's it?" Dax frowned. "If that's all you need, we could have avoided this whole mess if you'd just booked a trip on another ship."

I rolled my eyes and shook my head. "Yep, totally easy to do when running for your life." He wasn't wrong, though. At this point, any ship would have been a better option than *Fortuna*.

"Easier than stealing a ship?" He studied me and I tried not to squirm. "How did you steal my ship, anyway?"

I shrugged. "The door was open." If he didn't know his ship's vulnerabilities, I wasn't going to be the one to tell him.

His eyes narrowed.

Yeah, he knew I was lying. The question was, what was he going to do about it?

"Since you just want off station, how about I drop you off at the next stop?"

Despite the sarcasm, his gruff voice was soothing. Warmth radiated from him and I leaned closer, my eyes fluttering shut.

"You okay?"

My eyes snapped open. "I told you, I'm fine," I said grumpily.

He looked toward the ceiling. I think he mumbled something about not deserving this. His stubble accentuated his frown. I wanted to run my fingers over those firm, angry lips.

Wow. I was way more tired than I realized. My body swayed forward and it was lights out.

9

DAX

WHEN LACY swayed and pitched forward, I was already moving toward her. I caught her by her upper arms and her weight sagged against me. Her head flopped forward, resting on my chest. A tiny snore broke the silence.

Another, slightly less delicate snore followed. I laughed. I was still pissed at how royally she'd fucked up my plans—with not even a hint of regret—but there was something compelling about her. In any other circumstance, I might have tried to buy her a beer. Now I mostly just wanted to find a planet to drop her ship-stealing ass on.

That was a problem for later. Now I had to deal with my stowaway.

"You okay, Lacy?" When her only response was another snore, I slid one arm under her knees and swept her up into my arms, taking care not to jostle her shoulder. The nanos and the pain meds should be working their magic, but why risk it.

Cradled against my chest, she shifted toward me, burrowing closer. Dark lashes fanned out over pale skin. Asleep she'd lost the pinched, in-pain look, though the dark circles under her eyes still pointed to a rough day. Beneath the smudges of dirt on her face, she was pretty. Not stop-your-heart beautiful, but pretty.

What made her attractive was the way she'd looked me in the eye and stood up to me. I'd met marines who couldn't manage that.

And though I'd never admit it out loud, I was impressed that she'd somehow managed to steal my ship. Not enough to ignore that she'd cost me a valuable cargo deal—I hated that—but the way she'd stolen our ship was ballsy.

When she was awake, I'd demand she tell me how she did it. Otherwise, reviewing the ship's entire security system was going to be a hell of a lot of extra work that I didn't have time for. Not to mention the time it would take to review the ship's manuals beforehand.

For now, what to do with sleeping beauty here? Was she a mystery to be solved or a problem to be gotten rid of?

I hadn't decided yet. Until I did, I needed a safe place to stash her, somewhere she wouldn't cause any more trouble.

Med bay was one option. The patient beds were equipped with restraints, but that thought brought a sour taste to my mouth.

On the other hand, *Fortuna's* empty crew cabins were just down the corridor.

A few minutes later, I stood outside the first cabin. Rebalancing Lacy's weight, I pressed my palm against the entry pad. When the door slid open, I stepped inside.

One of ten nearly identical crew berths, the room's spartan furnishings were closer to what I was used to in the space corps. Sure, it had one bed instead of bunks and an attached bathroom rather than shared facilities elsewhere in the ship, and a dresser, desk, and closet when I was used to a footlocker. Compared to the opulent captain's quarters where I was currently sleeping, it reminded me of the places I'd called home for the last ten years.

I lay Lacy gently on the bed, boots and all, and ensured her slinged arm was draped over her stomach. If the nanos did their job, she wouldn't need it by the time she woke up. I'd let her make that decision. When she was fully on the bed, she rolled onto her side, burying her face in the pillow.

Backing up slowly, I watched the rise and fall of her chest for a few seconds before dimming the lights so she could sleep. Another tiny snore followed me from the room and I stifled my laughter.

No matter how cute she was, I couldn't afford the distraction—or the potential damage—that came from her having free access to the ship, so I locked her room from the outside. Plans months in the making had been blown to smithereens, all because someone had broken into her apartment.

I mulled over that as I returned to the bridge. Lacy hadn't backed down when we butted heads. It would probably take a lot to send her on the run. So, whatever was after her—and now me—wouldn't be fun to deal with.

Just what I needed. Another problem.

Adding that to the end of my very long list of things to deal with, I made my way to the bridge. Dropping into the captain's chair, I dragged my hands through my hair. Getting a haircut wasn't even on the list, though I really should make time for it next time we were in port.

I stared out the ship's windshield. Everywhere I looked, dark space surrounded us, broken only by the flicker of stars and, maybe, other ships. For the first time since our unscheduled departure, I checked the autopilot. Why hadn't I done that before?

The course Lacy had set the ship on didn't appear to actually take us anywhere; it just pointed us away from Elegium Station and through Zone 4. After checking to make sure the external sensors were on—they were—I left it alone. I didn't have a better plan. At least not yet.

We couldn't return to Elegium Station for four days due to the coolant leak quarantine protocol, but that didn't mean we had to hang out in Zone 4. I sighed, feeling adrift.

That cargo load on the station had been the best option for our first run. Transfer machinery to a farm planet. Short term. Easy. Lucrative. And a great way to get our name out there as a reliable crew.

Ha.

Not so reliable since I'd had to contact the client and let him know I wouldn't be able to make the appointment. I hadn't bothered trying to explain that it was a mistake. Who was going to believe "Someone invented a coolant leak to steal my ship"? Instead, I'd thanked him for considering our services, though I may have broken my jaw gritting my teeth as I'd choked the words out.

All those credits lost because of my ship-stealing stowaway.

My anger at Lacy flared again, but I crammed it down. What was done was done. That energy was better spent finding a way out of this mess. I pulled up the ship's network and settled in for a long—night? Morning? Whatever it was, I needed to locate another job for us.

Pulling up the message boards used to advertise jobs, I logged into the ship's account and started scrolling.

10

LACY

SHOULDER GUY and his friend were gaining on me. Their footsteps echoed in the corridor behind me. How had they found me? He grabbed my arm, holding me immobile. I struggled and struggled against his grip, but couldn't get free. What did they want?

My eyes flew open. "Dream," I croaked. "Just a dream."

Heart racing, I scrambled up to sit up, but something grabbed onto my arm and held me down. My dream self's sense of panic bled into the real world and I batted at the invisible forces holding onto me. My wild flails finally brought my right hand in contact with the strap that was holding me down. It took far too long to register that my arm was in a sling.

Why was my arm in a sling?

Ignoring that question in favor of freeing myself, I finally scrambled to a sitting position and swung my legs over the side. I studied my surroundings. Low lights illuminated simple, but familiar, furniture. There was a desk tucked into the corner, between the closet and a door that led to a microscopic bathroom.

"*Mako,*" I whispered. My pulse slowed, now that I was safe on my ship.

No, that wasn't right. Sleep fuzzed my brain.

This wasn't my room. Wasn't my ship.

Longing swept through me. It had been two years since I'd been on *Mako.* When I'd made plans to stay on Elegium Station, Dad had insisted that she stay onboard his ship. Why pay docking fees when I didn't need a ship handy, he'd argued. At the time, I'd bought that argument. I sighed. He'd probably wanted to keep *Mako* to use himself. Sometimes I missed her more than I missed my family.

If I wasn't on *Mako,* where was I?

I rubbed my eyes, as if I could clear the fog from my brain as easily as it cleared away the sleep. It worked; everything came rushing back.

Fortuna. The men chasing me. Dax taking me to med bay.

"Lights, 50 percent." My voice trembled, as the dream became memory.

The lights rose, illuminating the sparse room. Yeah, this definitely wasn't my ship. I'd put my stamp on every single one of the crew cabins on *Mako.*

The simple furniture was similar to what was on *Mako,* but there were no homey touches. No rugs, no pictures. Probably not even soft towels in the bathroom. Everything was probably just as it had been as it rolled off the shipbuilder's station, only a little older. It was sad to see the bare spots that had once held pictures and other decorations. Like echoes of crews past.

That fit with what I'd already discovered, that the ship's codes were factory defaults, too. I'd already used that to my advantage. That was another one of Dad's lessons: factory defaults meant your own ship could be used against you.

Slightly afraid, I rolled my shoulder a few times and

exhaled in relief when it moved without pain. The nanos and pain meds had worked. Without them, I could have been laid up for weeks, unable to work if I couldn't use my arm. There wasn't a lot of demand out there for one-armed mechanics.

Of course, I was pretty much out of work right now anyway. I had rushed onto *Fortuna* to buy time. Beyond that . . . I thought about it. Nope, no plan.

After the four-day quarantine for the imaginary coolant leak was over, I could—probably—go back to Elegium Station. Mechanics were always in demand and I was damn good at my job. And until today, I'd been a model employee. On time, efficient. There was a good chance I could get my job back.

But Dax—Captain Cooper—put a crimp in those plans. He was the true unknown in the situation. He could dump me planetside. Or space me, but I'd put up a damn good fight before I let that happen.

"Nothing's going to happen if you stay in this room, Lacy," I muttered then pushed off the bed. My mouth felt gross, morning breath and the lingering nastiness from the pain pills, so I crossed to the tiny bathroom. After I took care of my most pressing needs, I got the first look at myself in the mirror.

My eyes widened in horror. Sleeping in the sling had left an impression on my neck and across my chest. But that wasn't the worst part. My braid was half undone and my hair was thoroughly tangled. Smudges of dirt were streaked across my cheek and chin. And my coveralls, what I could see of them, were dirty and ripped at the knees. In fact, the cleanest thing about me was my white tank, because it had been *under* the rest of my clothes. I needed a shower and I needed it *now*.

When I'd left work yesterday, I'd already been sweaty

and gross from a day working in the engine room. Even when the ship was docked, those rooms *always* ran hot. My plan had been to shower after I ate, but no, the assholes who broke into my apartment had ruined that.

Jumping out the window had left me even grimier. And I didn't even want to think about the stress sweat. Or that Dax had seen me—had carried me!—while I was so dirty.

Ugh.

I stared at the small shower cubicle and sighed. The captain's quarters, at least on *Mako*, had a much bigger shower. This one wasn't luxurious, but beggars couldn't be choosers.

Grabbing the bottom of my tank top, I started to pull it off, then stopped. "Fuck," I said to my reflection. I'd been wearing the same clothes for more than a day and I didn't have any clean ones to change into.

No way in hell was I putting on yesterday's underwear. Or—*ew!*— going commando in my coveralls.

Nope. No way.

Maybe one of the ship's previous occupants had left behind something useful. I stomped back into the small bedroom and pulled open the drawers and checked the closet.

My search turned up nothing but a small stack of towels. *Dammit.*

My gaze drifted around the room as I considered my options. The ship should have a clothes refresher. *Mako* did. On my ship, it had been located at the end of the corridor, just before the steps that took you down to the cargo hold. *Fortuna* was so like my previous ship, I assumed hers would be in the same location.

Since I refused to wear these clothes again until they were laundered, that was my best option.

My clothes would be a small load, so it shouldn't take too long in the waterless refresher.

Pulling the top sheet off my bunk, I draped it over my shoulder. No running naked down the corridor while I waited. Plan in place, I crossed to the door and pressed my palm to the access panel. It flashed red.

Locked.

"Well, that's annoying." Though not surprising. Dax was obviously ex-military, so he must have done a threat assessment. A smile broke across my face. He saw me as a threat, which was pretty cool.

But it was delaying my shower and *that* was unacceptable.

The master override code had gotten me into the ship's systems. Unless Dax had realized what was happening and changed it, it would get me out of this room too. If it didn't work . . .

I studied the door and the frame closely. Well, there were probably less elegant ways out of my situation. But they'd be a lot easier if I had my tool bag. It wasn't in plain sight and I hadn't seen it on the closet. Apparently, Dax hadn't trusted me enough to leave it with me.

Again . . . smart. If only its absence wasn't a pain in my ass. I'd deal with that later. For now, I entered the code and held my breath. After a torturous moment, the panel flashed green. When I attempted to leave my room this time, the door opened smoothly. *Ha! Take that!*

I glanced down the corridor—it was empty—and I quickly programmed in my palm print, so I would be able to get back *in* the room and wasn't left to wander the ship in nothing but a sheet. Later I'd add my palm print shipwide.

As quickly and as quietly as I could, I hightailed it down the corridor.

11
———

LACY

THE CLOTHES REFRESHER was at the end of the corridor where I'd expected it to be. I slipped into the small utility room and closed the door behind me. The refresher, which was the size of a large tool chest, was mounted along the far wall. The other two walls held mostly empty shelves. On *Mako*, I'd used the extra space to store supplies. Cleaning supplies, extra food, whatever needed a little extra room. My sister had jokingly called it the crap room, but I had the last laugh when I had something she needed or wanted.

I shook my head. Dax and his missing crew didn't seem to have any idea what they were doing. Unless money was tight, he should have laid in some basics before heading out to pick up cargo. You never knew if you were going to be able to find things you wanted or needed, whether it was spare parts or your favorite cookies. No one wanted to get stranded in space with a broken ship or a hangry crew.

Not my problem, though it pained me to see him unprepared. Which was dumb, because his lack of preparedness was one of the only reasons I'd been able to get his ship off the station.

Ignoring that dichotomy and the wave of regret, I crouched to unlace my boots. Something pinched in my hip crease. "What the hell?" I rose and shoved my hand into my pocket.

Withdrawing the small envelope Bob had delivered, now crumpled from my adventures, I stared at it. My breath caught as memories of what happened after Bob gave it to me tried to resurface, but I shoved them back. I'd forgotten about the packet.

Was this what they'd been looking for?

Computer printed across the front was my address on the station. I studied the logo in the upper-right corner. There were any number of data-delivery services across the galaxy; they were located on most stations and planets and even some of the larger passenger ships. This envelope came from one of the largest—and most widespread— companies. Tracking down exactly where it had originated from wouldn't be easy.

The companies transmitted encrypted data across the vastness of space and anyone could use them as long as you could pay for the service. Provide them with your data file and they would send it to your recipient almost instantaneously. The end product was either an electronic file or you could pay extra and get it downloaded to a data chip and hand-delivered to the recipient. Either way, only the recipient could access the data and only if they had the key.

I rubbed my thumb over what was surely a data chip. I couldn't do anything with it here, so I carefully set the envelope and its mystery contents on one of the nearby shelves.

I checked my pockets to make sure I hadn't forgotten

anything else. I pulled out a couple of hair bands and set them next to the envelope. Then I finished unlacing my boots and toed them off.

I stripped off my coveralls and chucked them into the refresher. My tank, bra, and underwear followed. Setting the cycle to deep clean, I shuddered at what I might have picked up along the way.

Snatching up the sheet, I wrapped it around my body twice and tucked the end between my breasts. I shoved my feet back into my boots so I could run if I had to and grabbed the mysterious envelope.

The corridor was still clear on the way back to my room. Inside, I gazed longingly at the shower then stared at the package clenched in my fist. Get clean or satisfy my curiosity?

Cleanliness won.

I dropped the sheet back on the bed, knowing I'd need it for my return trip to the utility room.

The closet held a towel set, so I grabbed that and crossed my fingers that there would at least be shampoo in the in-shower dispenser. I could use it as soap if I had to, but conditioner would be a dream.

I turned the water to hot and crossed my fingers that Dax or the ship broker had filled the system with fresh water. I just might throw myself out the airlock if I couldn't get a shower.

Stretching my hand out tentatively, I slipped it into the water that streamed from the showerhead. Hot water hit my palm and brought a smile to my face. I brought a palmful up to my nose and sniffed it. It didn't smell stale or rusty, like water that had sat too long in unused pipes, so I stepped into the small stall. Water sluiced over my head and body and I moaned in delight.

"Thank you, *Fortuna*," I whispered.

Another dream came true when I tested the dispensers and found all three full. Shampoo, soap, *and* conditioner.

I'd lived almost my entire life on ships and I knew that water was a precious commodity onboard that needed to be conserved. But that didn't stop me from washing my hair and my body twice.

Telling myself that another minute or two wouldn't matter in the grand scheme of things, I braced my hands against the wall and ducked my head into the cascade of water. The hot water pummeled and massaged my neck and shoulders in equal measure. As I rinsed out the conditioner, my hair created a curtain around my face.

I stood there, breathing evenly, as I tried to process the events of the last twenty-four hours. I'd never expected to be here, following my father's footsteps into a life of crime. At the first sign of difficulty, I'd stolen a ship. Was that nature or nurture?

Maybe both? I knew it was my upbringing that made me finally turn off the water and face the day.

I grabbed the towel and grimaced at the rough texture. On *Mako*, I'd equipped every room with quality towels. Crappy towels sucked. Maybe I'd leave that in the suggestion box for *Fortuna's* management. I laughed.

Drying off as best I could with the rough towel, I wrapped it around my hair turban style and then redressed in the sheet.

There was still plenty of time before my clothes were done, so I grabbed the packet and sat at the desk. Opening the envelope carefully, I tipped the contents into my hand. The metallic data chip landed in the middle of my palm, its dull silver coating weakly reflecting the light. Slightly bigger than the tip of my thumb, it loosely resembled an octagon and looked to be intact, despite my adventures.

The chip may still be intact . . . but I didn't have the key.

I pinched two of the chip's corners between my fingertips and turned the little mystery this way and that. It looked like any other data chip. Was this what they had been looking for? "Where did you come from?" I murmured. The chip didn't answer.

No matter. I'd figure it out.

I set it on the desk and picked up the envelope again. There had to be something to indicate who had sent it. I blew into the opening and then turned it over again. A small piece of paper fluttered out.

Unfolding it, I stared at the message that had been delivered with the chip and my stomach plummeted.

Hey, Lace. This is my fail-safe. If you're reading it . . . well, shit, I guess I missed a check-in or two. The logs have the coordinates. Same password as always. Get here quick. Love ya! Layla

My breath came in pants and I felt lightheaded, woozy.

This could not be happening.

I dropped my head to my knees and tried to calm my racing pulse while my thoughts spun out of control.

When I could think without wanting to puke or pass out, I sat up and read the message again, trying to parse another meaning, one that didn't make me panic. One that basically didn't just tell me that my sister was missing.

12

——

DAX

The alarm I'd set on my comms blared to life and I switched from asleep to awake in the blink of an eye. After hours of scrolling through cargo ads, my eyelids had been heavy so I'd caught a catnap on the bridge. Until I knew why Lacy seemed to know my ship better than I did—or until I picked up my team—I didn't want to leave the bridge unattended unless she was secured. Or off the ship.

I stood, rolling my shoulders and running through a series of stretches. The captain's chair wasn't the most uncomfortable place I'd ever slept, but after four days sleeping in the captain's quarters, my body preferred a comfortable mattress.

Despite the time I'd spent reviewing the want ads for cargo haulers, I was no closer to having a plan for cargo than I had been. There were a lot of enticing offers, but some of them appeared too good to be true. How the hell did you calculate what made a run profitable and what made it a waste of time and money?

That was a problem for later—later being a few hours, since I couldn't put this off indefinitely. Right now, I wanted a shower. The question was, did I dare leave the bridge unattended? It should be safe enough with Lacy Dupree locked in her room. She'd been exhausted, so I was hopeful she was still asleep.

I toggled through the screens that monitored the ship's systems. Everything looked stable, except . . . What was that?

The chart showing the ship's energy use was higher than it had been last night. I dug deeper into the data. The unusual draw was coming from the crew quarters. Where, surprise, my uninvited guest was.

What the hell was she doing?

The crew cabins were bare bones, not because I wanted them that way, but because I expected that my team would want to put their own stamp on the rooms. The cabins had come with the basic amenities: bed, desk, chair. The only thing in any of the rooms that drew power, outside of the lights, was the computer terminal. It was a dummy system, tied into the ship's network.

I pulled up the data feed for her terminal. A black screen greeted me. "What the hell?" That shouldn't happen.

I re-entered the command. Same result. Frowning, I pulled out the manual to make sure I was doing it correctly.

Yep, same steps. I drummed my fingers on the console. The ship's captain—that would be me—had access to all aspects of the ship. For her to have cut my access . . .

My stomach dropped. Pretty little Lacy Dupree was proving to be a much bigger problem than expected. I'd underestimated her and I couldn't afford to do that again.

I locked down the ship's primary console and reset the password. When I left the bridge, I did the same.

What a pain in the ass. I hated remembering passwords.

Then I strode quickly down the corridor to the crew quarters to find out what Lacy Dupree was up to.

My steps on the metal floor were loud enough that she should have heard me coming. That didn't stop me from pounding on the door. I may have had the key and a good head of mad, but I still had some manners. Plus, nothing good ever came from barging into a room.

But before I could knock, I heard a distorted voice. Was she communicating with someone? Had she smuggled someone else onto my ship?

Was her story about a home invasion just a complicated con to steal the *Fortuna*?

Yeah, that wasn't fucking happening.

My blaster was still in its holster. I reached back and released the strap that secured it in case I needed to draw it quickly, then pressed my palm to the access panel.

"Coming in!" I warned milliseconds before I stepped through the door in a clearing position.

Lacy was nowhere in sight. I assumed she was in the shower. "Hello? Miss Dupree? Lacy?" I took a step toward the small bathroom and called out again. Then I noticed that the bathroom door was open and I couldn't hear the shower.

What the fuck?

The dummy terminal had been moved away from the wall. A tangle of wires—ones I assumed used to be either in the wall or curled neatly—lay on the desk, shavings of yellow plastic were scattered around them. I spied a twist of wires that looked like she'd done something to the data feed from her room. That was probably why I hadn't been able to see what was on her screen.

The way she knew exactly how to finesse my ship was disturbing.

"Today I found an old archive that had a fragment of

the map. It was in bad shape, possibly the worst shape of any of the pieces I've acquired, but I can feel in my bones that it's important."

I looked around for the source of that voice. The room was empty, so it had to be coming from the terminal. I shifted the monitor so I could see it and studied the woman on the screen. Her gaze never wavered and I realized that this was a recording, not a live video. That Lacy wasn't communicating with someone outside the ship was a relief, but it still didn't explain where she was.

The woman in the video kept talking about old libraries and star maps, but I tuned that out as I studied her face.

She shared the same eyes and nose as the woman who'd stolen my ship, but her lips were fuller and her hair was shorter, worn in a dramatic cut that accentuated her cheekbones, rather than a tangled braid. While the speaker was a generally attractive woman, Lacy was more appealing.

And that was a completely inappropriate thought to be having. I was struggling to push my interest down when the door to the room swung open.

Lacy's eyes widened and surprise registered on her face.

My jaw dropped. I was just as surprised by her appearance. Like her *actual* appearance.

The bed sheet was wrapped around her body like a strapless dress, clinging close and emphasizing the curves I'd worked hard not to notice last night in the med bay. The end of the sheet was tucked into a tantalizing glimpse of shadowy cleavage.

My gaze darted back up to her face. She was watching me warily. "What are you doing in my room?"

"What are you doing *out* of your room?" I countered.

Her constant bypassing of my ship's systems was a huge problem.

Her lips pressed into a flat line. "Laundry." She lifted the stack of clothes that she carried as an exhibit. A stack of clothes I'd completely missed because I'd been too busy ogling.

Now I took in the neatly folded coveralls, with her white tank top resting on top. The fact that she wore her boots with her bedsheet gown. The quirky contrast made me smile. "You could have told me you needed to do laundry."

She shrugged and I tried not to notice the slight sway of her breasts when she did. "I took care of it."

"How?"

"The laundry room is down the corridor. Didn't they show you that when you bought the ship?" Her tone had that overly sweet sound that people got when they were fucking with you.

"I know where the laundry room is," I said with a hint of irritation. "I meant . . ."

She stepped around me and headed into the small bathroom. "I've got to get dressed." She closed the door in my face.

That woman. I'd get a straight answer from her one of these days.

While I waited for her to emerge, I sat down and watched the woman talking on the screen. She was dressed differently, so another video must have started. Once again she was talking about notes and flight paths and star maps.

A hand reached over my shoulder and stopped the video.

"That's none of your business," Lacy said, her voice thick with emotion.

I turned to face her and she was right there. Clad in

clean but worn coveralls. She smelled like the ship's soap and that indefinable, almost lack of scent that the refresher left on clothes. "Who's in the videos?"

She quickly took a step back. "My sister."

There was that emotion again.

"Why were you watching videos of her?" I watched her closely.

She closed her eyes, hiding a brief flash of pain. "She sent them to me."

"Is she—" I paused. There was no delicate way to say this. "Is she dead?"

Her fists clenched and she whirled away from me. "I don't know!" Her shoulders radiated tension.

"Does this have something to do with why you stole my ship?" I kept my voice gentle.

"Borrowed."

I rolled my eyes but let her get away with it this time. "Is this why you borrowed my ship?"

"No. Maybe. I don't know. Not originally."

"What does that mean?" When she didn't answer, I gently turned her to face me.

Her eyes were wide and filled with pain.

"What does that mean?" I repeated.

"It means she's missing and I think that . . ." she gestured toward the screen. "That has something to do with the men who broke into my apartment." Whatever restraint had been holding her back broke. She threw her arms around me and pressed her face to my chest.

Ok-ay.

I slowly, carefully wrapped my arms around her.

Lacy cried quietly but fiercely. She held herself stiffly, shoulders tense, her arms squeezed tight around my waist. We were pressed so closely together that her shudders reverberated through me.

I rubbed her back in soothing circles. What else was I supposed to do while she soaked my shirt with her tears?

The top of her head came up right beneath my chin, the perfect height to tuck her against me. "I'm sure your sister is fine," I murmured into her hair. They were the most comforting words I could think of.

Lacy Dupree was a mystery. A conundrum. A problem. One wrapped in attractive packaging no matter whether it took the form of ripped coveralls or an ethereal bedsheet.

The woman was a fucking puzzle and I didn't know how the pieces all fit.

Hell, I wasn't even sure I *had* all the pieces.

Her crying slowed and her grip on my waist lessened. When she pulled away, her movements were stiff. Her hands dragged along my sides, her left passing close—too close—to my weapon.

I sensed the moment her intentions changed. When her hand brushed the blaster, her breath caught and her head tilted to the side. And I knew—*I knew*—that she was going to try for my weapon.

In one smooth move, I pressed my hand against the blaster, securing it to my side and shifted my right leg back. The blaster now out of her reach, she froze against me, then stepped back.

"I'm sorry. That was . . . I mean, I didn't . . ."

Was she going to say she was just borrowing it?

I would have railed at her for attempting to steal my weapon, but one look at the tear tracks on her cheeks made me temper my tone. Sure, maybe she'd faked it all and I was a sucker. But maybe she hadn't.

"What did you think you were going to do?" I asked gently. "I'm a highly trained soldier with several inches in height on you and probably a hundred pounds. Did you really think you could win against me?"

She took another step back, putting more space between us. "I didn't really mean to. It was a spur of the moment thing."

"Like my ship?"

Her cheeks flushed red. "Look, I think my sister is missing. I have to find her." Her gaze flicked between me, the screen, and the door.

"We're in the middle of nowhere," I reminded her.

"On a ship," she ground out.

"Do you know where to look?"

"Maybe," she said after a long pause, her expression wary.

Why did I have the feeling I wasn't going to like what she said? "Start at the beginning," I demanded. "Why do you think she's missing?"

"Because of that." She gestured at the terminal. Her sister's face was frozen on the screen, caught mid-sentence. "That's her fail-safe. And now I have it. The only way that happens is if she misses two check-ins."

Leaning against the wall, I crossed my arms over my chest. This sounded more like a plot from a spy movie, not real life. Then again, one woman stealing my ship sounded very much like an adventure movie too.

Knowing I was going to regret it, I asked, "Why would your sister need a fail-safe?"

13

LACY

I RUBBED the data chip between my thumb and forefinger like a talisman as I followed Dax onto the bridge. My stomach had made a very loud, embarrassing gurgle while I'd tried to decide how much to tell him about my sister. He'd huffed out a laugh and then ushered me out of my room. *My room.* At least for now.

I'd grudgingly followed him to the dining hall where he'd heated up two packaged military meals. Gross. But beggars couldn't be choosers. If he had a fully stocked pantry, or utility closet, those things would just be for true emergencies, not everyday dining.

He took the captain's chair with a smile. A smile that read triumphant to me, like he'd beaten me at something.

Whatever. Little did he know that I could pilot *Fortuna* from almost any console on the ship. If he did, that smile would be gone in a trace.

He pointed at the navigator's seat and I sat.

"Veggie Surprise or Poultry Party?"

"What?"

"Which one do you want? Veggie Surprise," he held up

a shimmery green pouch, "or Poultry Party?" He held up the shiny pink pouch.

It was impossible to keep the grimace off my face.

"Here, take the veggies."

I grabbed the bag he extended toward me. "Um, were any actual vegetables harmed in the making of this?"

He shrugged, his broad shoulders shifting up and down under his black shirt. "Would you really want to know?"

"Good point." I opened the pouch gingerly, then sniffed the steam that escaped. It didn't smell too bad.

He handed me a fork and then tilted a bottle of hot sauce toward me in offer. "It helps," he said with a smile. Just a little half-smile, but it was enough for me to see the hint of a dimple.

Dax Cooper was really fine. His clothes hinted at a nice body, but when I'd had my arms around him? Well, it had felt like heaven. I'd felt warm and protected.

Dashing away those thoughts, I accepted the hot sauce, our fingers brushing in passing. I sighed.

"Something wrong?"

"I can't believe you ate the rest of my noodles! Those were my favorite."

A hint of pink colored his cheeks and that dimple winked at me. He must have been adorable as a kid. "I was hungry. And they smelled amazing." He looked at his meal pouch and it was his turn to sigh. "Bottoms up."

After seasoning the pouch with a few generous shakes of the hot sauce, I took my first, tentative bite. It was . . . not awful. Not good. Especially not *nearly* as good as my noodles, but edible. I wouldn't want to live on these. Then the hot sauce hit, eradicating my taste buds and I didn't taste anything else.

My lips were on fire and my nose was running by the time I finished my pouch, but at least my stomach wasn't growling any more. "Why did you stock up on these instead of regular food?"

Dax reached over and took my pouch, folding it up into a tiny square. He'd obviously done this a lot. "I didn't know what to get."

I stared at him, confused. "Food," I said. "Real food."

"But what kind?" He looked lost.

"Whatever you like to eat." It wasn't that complicated.

Dax looked away, that hint of pink staining his cheekbones again. "For the last ten years, I've served in the space corps. Three hots and a cot. Meal pouches when we were deployed."

Ah. Gotcha. He didn't know how to cook. "How long have you been out?"

"Three months."

That made sense. The hair. The vibe. The reflexes. And the lack of knowledge about civilian spaceships. "I can help. Teach you to cook. How to stock a ship."

The look he gave me was disbelieving. "Don't worry about me, I'll figure it out," he said sharply. "Sounds like you should worry about your sister."

Asshole. I was just trying to help.

But he was right too. He was a stranger. What did I care that he didn't know what he was doing? I needed to focus on my family. "Fine. What do you want to know?"

After a long beat, he said, "Everything."

Everything? I didn't think so.

Ignoring the way he was watching me, I swung my legs up so I was sitting cross-legged in my chair. "Layla's a year younger than me, so we're pretty close. But where I'm more mechanically minded, she got all the book smarts. That girl always has her nose in a book."

"She was talking a lot about books and libraries in those videos. And star maps."

My breath caught. I forced it back into a normal rhythm and hoped Dax hadn't noticed. "Yeah, whenever we were in port, she'd beg and plead to go to the library or a book shop or a museum. If she could learn something, she wanted to visit."

"You grew up on a ship?" He sounded surprised.

"Yeah, my parents weren't the homebody type." That was an understatement. I'd been back and forth across the system half a dozen times by the time I was ten.

"And yet you were living on an asteroid station."

His question was unspoken, but I answered it anyway. "I wanted to try something new. And, for me, new was a permanent station."

"Interesting. So, you ended up stationary and your sister ended up the space-faring one."

This was the easy part of the story. "Ever since she was little, my sister has wanted to be an archaeologist. She loved tales of lost civilizations. Lost treasures. That kind of thing."

"So that's what she does?"

"Not exactly," I said, trying to figure out how to describe my sister's occupation. Obsession? Our dad wasn't really supportive of her dreams, so it's more like she dabbles." And *boy* did she dabble.

"What about your mom?"

I rubbed the space over my heart, the place with a permanent hole. "She died when I was thirteen. Caught some exotic bug from one of our cargo runs."

"Crap. I'm sorry to hear that." His smile was gentle.

I gave him a wan smile. "That was a bad time, a really bad time." My father had held us close—suffocated us, really—while he meted out the justice he thought appropriate to those he held responsible. "I spent more time in the engine room after she died. I studied hard and tested for my rating. Layla buried her nose in her books."

"And that's why you left?"

Another carefully calibrated shrug to hide how much that decision had hurt. "Eventually. Dad's ship had a master mechanic and a full mechanic crew. If I wanted to learn and grow, I'd have to do it somewhere else." It was the same reasoning that I'd given Dad.

"Your sister did the same?"

"Last I knew, she was back home, working for my dad."

"Then what's she doing out there?"

"I don't know!" I couldn't sit still any longer. I untangled my legs and shot to my feet. Dax shifted in his chair to watch me as I paced back and forth.

14

——

DAX

"WHAT WAS YOUR SISTER WORKING ON?"

She froze mid-step. It was the tiniest moment of stillness. I only noticed because I'd been watching her so closely. Lacy Dupree was a woman of secrets, and whatever her sister was doing was another one.

"I don't know for sure." She was turned away from me when she spoke, but her body had already given her away.

"Liar."

Lacy spun around, her wavy hair echoing the move like a shampoo commercial. Her expression was the perfect picture of shock and outrage. I'd be impressed if I weren't so tired of the lies and half-truths.

I leaned forward, resting my forearms on my knees. "Let's cut the bullshit, Lacy. You didn't borrow my ship, you stole it. You cost me a valuable cargo, practically stranded me out here in the ass end of space, and now you're telling me your sister's in trouble, but you don't actually know what she does. She's probably a thief like you and she got caught, just like you."

Apparently I was really tired of her shit, because the

words just kept coming. "I'm pretty sure I'd be well within my rights to space you here and now for the piracy, but I'll be nice and settle for leaving you on the next inhabited planet unless you give me a damn good reason not to."

Whew. The rush of letting that all out was amazing.

Her jaw dropped, but as soon as she saw me noticing, she snapped her mouth shut and glared at me.

"Fine. Next planet it is." I swung back to the console and pulled up the star map. Zone 4 was the ass end of space when it came to Elegium Station, but it was only a few days from several other stations and a few planets. I'd just go to the one closest to where I was supposed to pick up one of the other squad members and drop her off without even a wave good-bye. Or I could space her. Sure, I might feel bad, but she had only herself to blame.

She retook her seat, but I didn't even look at her. We sat in silence for several long minutes as I pondered which would be the best course.

Finally, in a voice so quiet I barely heard her, she said, "She's looking for the *Queen of Stars.*"

Eyes focused on the star chart, I dismissed her claim. "That's a fairy tale. A myth."

"But is it?" Lacy asked softly. "Which side was your family on? Baronite?"

My shoulders tightened. "Good guess."

Her laugh was soft, but sad. "Not much of a guess if you don't believe the story of the *Queen of Stars.*"

I swiveled around in my chair to face her. "The story? More like the lie. A lie the Polarians told when they didn't pay for the supplies the Baronites provided." My voice was harsh.

Everyone who grew up in space knew the story. During the hardship of early settlement outside the core planets in each system, ships had landed on what they had assumed were habitable planets similar to Earth, but most of them had faced unanticipated problems. Untillable soil, unbreathable atmospheres, unfriendly native species. Some of the early settlers had gotten lucky, with either abundant mineral wealth or strong growing seasons, but none of the planets had both.

In exchange for food, the miners—the Polarians—on Swansea Prime traded ore, but when they got further and further behind on payments, their trading partners—the Baronites—had slowed the trade. The ore carried on *Queen of Stars* had been intended for payment—what the settlers had owed and more. But the ship never arrived and no trace had ever been found. The Baronites had stopped trading after that.

The missing ship had exacerbated tensions between the two systems and had been the catalyst for each side building and expanding their military capabilities in space. Now, generations later, the boundaries between the two sides had blurred and the *Queen of Stars* had been relegated to history books and fairy tales.

"Let me guess, you're a Polarian," I snapped.

She smirked. "Not even close. My dad preferred to be, uh, unaffiliated."

I studied her. That was an interesting word choice. Most of the people who claimed to be unaffiliated operated outside the law. Did that mean her family was—

Lacy scattered my thoughts when she stood and stared out at the vastness of space. I turned my chair at an angle so I could watch her.

"When we were little," she said, "I was seven and Layla was six, our ship was on a job at the edges of what had been Polarian space. Layla discovered that fact years later. All I remember was a lot of time in space and *a lot* of stars."

"Layla couldn't sleep, so she slipped out of our room. We had the run of the ship." Her mouth curved into a gentle smile. "The only places we weren't allowed to go by ourselves were the engine room and the cargo hold."

Having been in both cargo holds and engine rooms, I thought the prohibition made sense. Still, I couldn't imagine raising a child on a ship. I'd grown up planetside. I'd had a very generic upbringing—my mom was a teacher and my father was a mailman. As close as they and anyone else in our family had come to space, until the moment I'd joined the space corps, had been the delivery of an occasional package from a distant planet. "That sounds like an interesting childhood," I said. Unspoken was the part where I didn't understand what that had to do with anything.

"Layla loved the stars. Loved learning their names, loved identifying them. So, she wandered out to one of the big windows to watch the stars. She saw something that night. Something no one else did. Ever since then, she's been convinced that she saw the *Queen of Stars*."

I waited for her to laugh, to let me in on the joke. "You're kidding."

She faced me fully, her expression perfectly serious. "No. She's held onto that belief for more than twenty years. It's her, I don't know, passion project. Her obsession."

Her ticket to the psych ward, but I didn't say that. "Do you believe her?"

She shoved her hands into her pockets and sighed. "I don't *not* believe her. Space is vast. It would be easy to overlook a ship that got lost."

"It didn't exist," I countered. "It was a government coverup."

Her eyes widened. "You're a conspiracy theorist?"

I scoffed. "No. I'm a realist. There was no ship. There was never a ship."

Turning back to the stars, Lacy said, "That night she drew a picture of a ship. It looked like a typical five-year-old's work. Unsteady lines, wonky perspective. When my parents asked her about the ship, she said it was the *Queen of Stars*."

"Let me guess, your parents had told that as a bedtime story."

Lacy shook her head. "No. Layla and I had never heard of the ship." She looked toward me and sent me a gentle smile. "Telling little kids about ships that disappear into space, never to be seen again, isn't really conducive to getting them to sleep through the night."

I blanched. Even as an adult, as a member of the space corps, I didn't like to think about ships getting lost in space.

"My mom called up all the information she could find on the missing ship. One of the stories included an image." She paused, letting the tension build. "My sister's drawing was a damn good representation of the ship for her age."

"So your parents believed her?"

"They did. Until there were no records of the ship on our sensors. According to all our systems, we had been all alone out there. My dad decided to focus on the payday from delivering our cargo and that was that."

"But your sister still believes?"

Lacy nodded. "Yep. Nothing anyone said, or did, convinced her otherwise. She's determined to be the one to find it."

"And the chip is what?" I had a good idea, but needed to hear her say it out loud.

She swallowed hard. "As far as I can tell, the chip is the record of all her research. Everything she's collected until a few days ago when she didn't make the check-in for her fail-safe."

I still couldn't quite wrap my head around what Lacy had just told me. Such determined belief in a ghost ship—in an *imaginary* ship—really was an obsession. "So she's out here looking for the *Queen of Stars*?"

"Apparently." Lacy sounded annoyed, but I didn't think it was directed at me. "Usually she stays on my dad's ship and visits libraries and museums for her research while he's in port. I didn't expect her to be out here. Especially not alone."

"Why not?" So far Lacy had proven herself adept—more than adept—at surviving on her own. If her sister was anything like her . . .

"I think I've mentioned that Layla is more likely to be found in a book than in an engine room."

"So?" If my time in the space corps had taught me anything, it was that people were capable of far more than we gave them credit for, good or bad.

"I just didn't expect it. My father taught us both to fly, but she never seemed to care, one way or another."

Interesting.

I turned my attention back to the star chart and considered what Lacy had told me. I'd told her the truth: I didn't believe in the *Queen of Stars* tale. If it had really existed, if it had really been sent, someone would have discovered it by now. The early search teams would have at least found a debris field. Later explorers would have found a trace as they'd pressed farther and farther out into the unexplored edges of the galaxy. Someone would have found it. And yet . . .

"You think she found something."

Lacy gasped. "What? No, I . . ." She trailed off, which

was just as well, because I wasn't sure there was an argument she could make that would change my mind.

I dismissed the star chart with a flick of my wrist. This wasn't more important than picking up my team, but it felt . . . momentous. Like it deserved my full attention. "You think she found something," I repeated.

Lacy started pacing again, her fists opening and closing at her sides. "I don't know. She could have taken off for any number of reasons. A library, a pickup for our dad, a . . . a date!" She threw her hands up in the air. "I. Don't. Know."

"What does the chip say?"

She shrugged, reached the far side of the bridge, and whirled back to face me. "I haven't watched until the end. It could just be her research." Her worried tone said she didn't believe that.

"Then let's find out," I said.

15

──────

DAX

LACY STARED AT ME, indecision written on her face. She shoved one hand in her pocket. That was probably where she was keeping the data chip.

"Look, Lacy. You've told me a lot of stories since you stole my ship. And you've cost me a lot of money. If you want even a chance of me believing anything you've told me, show me what's on the chip."

Her stare turned into a glare and she stomped over to the navigator's seat. She dropped into it with a huff and flashed a silver data chip at me.

I grabbed her wrist as she reached toward the data port. "Wait. How do I know you aren't trying to plant a virus or something?"

"You don't." Her eyes narrowed to slits and her lips curved up in a mean smile.

Damn if I didn't find that attractive.

When she tugged her arm free, I let her go. I didn't trust her, but I was confident that I'd be able to keep an eye on her and make sure she wasn't screwing up my ship.

"Fine. Use that one." I pointed to an unused console in

the corner of the bridge. It was connected to the ship's system, but it wasn't as crucial a station as the navigator's. I hoped.

"You're the boss." With a deep sigh, she moved from one chair to another gracefully. She was definitely comfortable on my bridge.

I followed her to the station, wanting to watch every move she made. Lacy glared up at me. I stared back.

Her gaze flickered over my biceps as I crossed my arms and I thought I saw a flare of interest there. I allowed a small smile, then smoothed my expression again.

Lacy turned her attention to the console and flashed the data chip again. She made a big show about slowly inserting it into the slot. This woman was such a pain in the ass.

I braced my hands on the back of her chair and her spine snapped ramrod straight. Leaning closer, I said, "All right. Let's see this evidence." My breath feathered the hair around her ear.

She shivered.

My gaze wandered to the pulse point by her ear. It fluttered beneath her skin.

My attraction to her was damned inconvenient and couldn't go anywhere, but I was glad that she wasn't immune to me.

The system accepted the chip and then, with a few keyboard commands, the chip's directory appeared on the screen. It was there and gone before I truly had a chance to study it, but I was left with the impression of folders organized by year. Her sister really had been chasing the *Queen of Stars* for a long time.

Lacy's fingers flew over the keyboard.

Fuck. She was good. Good enough that I might not catch her if she decided to screw me over.

Pay attention, Dax! No more watching her delicate pulse.

I focused on the screen, hoping to catch whatever she was doing.

A video file opened. Lacy paused it before it played. "This is her last recording," she said. "It's time-stamped four days ago."

Was four days a bad thing or was the delay usual for her sister's videos? "Are there other gaps in the timeline?"

"I only looked at the folders for this year and last. There are other gaps." She stopped me when I would have spoken. "But it's not the gaps that matter. The data file requires regular logins from her. When she missed two, it sent the data to a broker, who sent it to me."

Lacy pulled a piece of paper out of her pocket. She smoothed her fingers over it before offering it to me. Even then, she almost didn't let go.

I read her sister's message. Then read it again. The "get here quick" part was concerning. "This is why you stole my ship."

Lacy shook her head vehemently. "I didn't even open the package until this morning."

"Um hmm." That seemed way too coincidental to me.

Instead of responding, Lacy advanced the last video two thirds of the way to the end.

Yep, that wasn't suspicious at all. "Let's watch it from the beginning."

The muscles of her neck flexed in tension. "No. You don't need to go through her research. The important part is at the end."

On the one hand, I understood her desire to protect her sister's project. On the other, it was hard to trust her when I didn't know everything.

Lacy pressed play. "I think that asshole on the forum

played me," her sister said from on the screen. "He claimed to be descended from the *Queen of Stars* crew."

I snorted and Lacy whipped her head around and glared at me.

"It sounded fishy from the start, but he *knew* things," Lacy's sister continued. "Things that corroborate information I've uncovered. No one has ever mentioned *credible* survivors before now, though, so I took a chance. Turns out it was just a waste of time. I'm out of here tomorrow." She glared at the screen before the recording ended.

"That's the last entry." Lacy sat back in the chair.

I swiveled it around so we were face-to-face. "I understand why you're concerned," I said. "But it's a big leap from a last entry a couple days ago to missing. Maybe she got lucky and missed a couple of check-ins."

Lacy kicked my shin.

"Ow. Okay, maybe she didn't get lucky. We don't know that there isn't a perfectly good reason for her to miss her deadlines."

"Are you even listening to yourself?" Lacy launched from the chair and got in my face. "What if one of your friends was potentially missing? Would you just write it off to a random hookup?"

Okay, she had a point. "We don't even know where she was."

Lacy's fingers skimmed my chest as she brushed that argument away. "The date and coordinates were at the start of the video."

Her eyes begged me to agree. I was tempted. Who wouldn't be? The chance to hunt for a ghost ship, a legend. A fantasy.

That was what decided me. It was just a fantasy. And right now, I needed tangible cargo if I wanted to keep my promises. To my crew and especially to Wilson. I placed my hands on Lacy's shoulders. "I can't. I'm sorry. I need to pick up paying cargo and my crew. I can stop at the next spaceport. I'm sure you can hire a ship and a crew to find your sister there."

My stomach churned as I spoke. It felt wrong, so wrong, to refuse to help.

She shrugged my hands off violently. But instead of backing up, she stepped closer. "Thanks for nothing." Hands on my chest, she shoved with enough force to move me back a couple of steps.

Then she popped the data chip out of the console and tucked it back into her pocket. She brushed by me, her elbow whacking me in the stomach, then stomped off the bridge. "Asshole."

Well, that went well.

16

____

LACY

Too AGITATED to go back to my room, I stomped around the ship. I couldn't believe he'd just refused to help. A woman was missing. It wasn't like he didn't know where all his crew was. What was one little detour?

My steps carried me past med bay, past my room, and down the steps leading to the engine room. I was pissed enough that sabotaging the engine would serve him right—but I couldn't do that. Wouldn't do that. *Fortuna* hadn't done anything to me. She just had an ass for a captain.

Still, I was curious to see the engine room. It was one of my favorite places to be. Sure, you couldn't see out into space, but it was the heart of the ship. The engine room got you from point A to point B and deserved all the love and respect for doing that.

While my annoyance at Dax didn't fade as I neared the engine room, my pulse slowed and my tension eased as the sounds and smells of the ship's heart worked their magic. The throaty purr—and occasional clank—of the engines. Oil and exhaust and that frisson of electricity that shouldn't have a smell, but did if you were around long enough.

It smelled like home.

I'd missed this. Some nights on the station I would walk through the docks just to try and catch a whiff.

Reaching the upper deck of the engine room, I unlatched the door and stepped over the raised entry and onto the metal grating that ran between the engines at top-of-the-engine height. A second walkway ran parallel to this one, one floor down. Closing the door behind me, I tucked my hands in my pockets and closed my eyes.

At first I let the hum just wash over me. The longer I stood there, the more I could pick out the sounds the different engines made. Nothing sounded wrong. Dax hadn't bought a lemon. Good for him, I guess.

Still, while I was here, I should take a look.

Dammit! I didn't have my tools. Honestly, I wasn't even sure where they were. Had Dax left them on the bridge? I hadn't looked for them, that was how distracted I'd been by my sister's message.

Had any tools been left on the ship? Had Dax even considered that he would need tools? Did he have a mechanic lined up already?

My eyes popped open. "That's it!"

Dax was over his head and didn't even know it. I had all sorts of useful skills that I could bargain for his help.

Feeling lighter than I had before—*Mako's* engine room had always brought me clarity too—I practically skipped down to the lower level.

There was a small alcove behind Engine 1, which was where I liked to keep a set of tools. I followed the tiny walkway behind the engine and voila!

Tools were scattered haphazardly over the small workbench built into the wall and there was no tool chest to store them in. My lip curled. That wasn't great. Improperly stored tools were a hazard in an engine room. A sudden change in gravity would turn any of them into a projectile.

I sighed and shook my head. There should be a little cubby beneath Engine 2 where I could store these until I could properly batten them down.

Gathering up the tools, I slipped them into pockets and tucked them into my belt. I grabbed the rags that had been left on the bench too. Those would come in handy as I inspected the engines.

The Cyclone class ships had four engines. While there were redundancies built into the system, and a ship could limp home on one engine, vessels like *Mako* and *Fortuna* performed best when all four were in peak condition. I wanted to verify that *Fortuna*'s engines were up to the task.

Losing myself in the routine of engine maintenance, I didn't have a great sense of how much time had passed. But based on the amount of work I'd done—tidying the workspaces and inspecting each engine—it had been several hours.

I'd poked around every nook and cranny of each engine, making small tweaks and bringing each part back to as close to pristine condition as I could. I was under Engine 4, taking one last look, when the light clang of boots and the vibrating metal grates warned me that I wasn't alone.

Stilling my movements, I waited to see what he would do.

"You breaking my ship?" Dax sounded friendly enough, so I assumed it was a joke, rather than an accusation.

"The opposite, actually." I tested the last few bolts, then

wiped them with a cloth. Rolling the tools into a bundle in the grease rag, I slid out from underneath the engine.

He stepped back to give me room to maneuver.

From my vantage point on the ground, I had a view of his well-worn black military-issue boots. My gaze traveled up his long legs, clad in cargo pants, also black. A gray waffled henley hugged his chest and arms. A firm jaw, roughened with dark shadow, which was definitely not regulation.

Full lips, strong nose, and chocolate eyes that held a hint of amusement when I finally reached them.

I shot him a big grin. What could I say? I appreciated the view.

"Something was broken?" His lips pressed together in a grim line and his voice hardened.

I hurried to reassure him. "No. Everything is fine. I gave her a thorough inspection, tightened a few bolts here and there. All four engines are good to go."

The tension leached out of his shoulders. A tingle of warmth spread to my belly.

Ignoring it, I braced my feet and tightened my stomach muscles to roll up to sitting. When he offered his hand, I placed the bundle of tools on the ground and grabbed his hand with both of mine.

It felt almost effortless as he pulled me upright.

I stopped just inches from him. He didn't release my hands right away and I didn't try to free myself.

I liked being in his space.

The top of my head came up to his lips, so I had to tilt my head back just the tiniest bit to look at him.

This close I could see the tiny scar just below his bottom lip. It would have been practically invisible except his scruff didn't grow there. My fingers itched to trace it.

Before I could check the impulse, I tugged my hand

free and traced that thin white line with my fingertip. "What happened?"

"Bar fight." His mouth curled into a smile and the move brushed his lips against my fingertips. My skin tingled.

I smiled too and shook my head. "It's always a bar fight. Never anything as mundane as running into a bulkhead."

He laughed and the sound teased my insides.

I brushed my thumb over his stubble. The tiny whiskers rasped against my nerve endings like sandpaper.

"What are we doing?" he asked.

"I was tinkering with the engines until you got here. What are you doing?" *Was I flirting with him?*

His warm hand cupped my cheek. "You know what I mean."

I stared at him a long moment, my gaze never leaving his. "I don't know. But I like it." Too much. I kept that part unspoken.

A half step was all that separated us, so I took it, invading his space and pressing my torso against his. My other hand, the one that had been gripping his, now grasped his shirt.

Using that anchor, I shifted to the balls of my feet, needing those precious inches to match my mouth to his.

His lips were firm. Full. Everything a man's lips should be.

I brushed my mouth over his. Once. Twice. Three times. Teasing little air kisses.

Dax didn't react.

My stomach plummeted. Had I just made a horrible mistake?

My body froze while my brain frantically sought an escape plan.

Maybe I'd just faint. Drop to the floor and pretend I hit my head and didn't remember this.

Yes, that seemed like a perfect plan.

Just as I commanded my muscles to relax, to step away, Dax's hand, the one that had rested on my cheek, cradled the back of my head. His arm wrapped around my waist.

Instead of melting to the floor, I sort of melted into his chest.

While his touch was gentle, his lips pressed firmly against mine. He nibbled on my lower lip and I groaned.

He took advantage of the moment, encouraging my lips to open a little more.

Not that I needed any encouragement. My fingers threaded through his hair, giving me something to hold on to as I pressed closer. I tilted my head, seeking an angle that gave him—gave me—better access to the kiss.

The arm around my waist tightened, not only pulling me closer, but lifting me a few inches so we were level.

I would have marveled at his strength, but I was already lost in his kiss.

So many physical sensations to process. It had been so long since I'd been kissed this well. I gave into the tsunami of feelings raging inside me and threw my whole self into his embrace.

As if he sensed my surrender, his hands gripped my thighs and he hoisted me higher. His mouth swallowed my gasp. My legs wrapped around him automatically, pressing us closer together.

Damn, could this man kiss.

He devoured me. His fingers tangled in my hair and he tugged my head back, breaking the kiss.

A low whine escaped me, but then his lips were on my neck. His stubble rasping my skin with a combination of tickle and torture.

My panties dampened and I rocked against him.

He growled against my skin and nipped my neck.

"Oh!" That little bite sent another layer of sensation racing through my body. My arms tightened around him, holding him close as he continued to nip, suck, and nuzzle my neck.

"More," he demanded with a deep rumble. He moved then, sure, confident steps that rubbed his hard body against mine.

I'd never done this before. Never made out in an engine room— "Ow!"

"What is it? Is it your shoulder?" Dax shifted from interested party to alert soldier in the blink of an eye. He released me and I slid down his body, wobbling as I tried to regain my balance. My equilibrium.

His hand on my shoulder steadied me.

"I'm fine," I assured him. "We ran into the engine."

I pointed to the offender, a pipe that extended out a few inches, then curved around the engine.

He looked at the pipe then away, shoving a hand in his hair. Color tinged his cheeks. "Shit. I'm sorry."

"I'm fine," I repeated. Sure, it might bruise a bit, but I wasn't going to tell him that. Instead, I tried to lighten the mood. "Now I know why I've never fooled around in an engine room before."

No need to tell him that I wouldn't be caught dead making out with any of my father's crew and there had never been an opportunity on *Mako* either because I was always around my sister or on my father's ship.

"Yeah, me neither." He laughed and that killer smile spread across his face. It lit up his eyes and revealed that crooked little dimple in his right cheek.

Heat flared in my belly again. *Down, girl!* You just

learned why you do not engage in hanky-panky in the engine room.

Tension still saturated the air around us and I desperately needed to clear it before I jumped him again. "So, uh, this is the engine room," I said inanely.

"Good to know," he said just as somberly, though there was still a hint of gravel in his voice.

"There were some tools that apparently came with the ship." I pointed to the bundle I'd left on the floor. "It's a start, but it's not everything you'll need. And they'll need to be stored properly."

He raised a brow and looked at the bundle pointedly.

I straightened indignantly. "I was using them until a few minutes ago."

"Gotcha." He smiled and my urge to throttle him transformed back into the urge to jump him.

Swallowing hard, I forced down the desire. "Why don't we discuss the care and feeding of *Fortuna*'s engines somewhere else?" Somewhere the air wasn't heavy with desire.

His fingers swept across my cheek and tucked a loose strand of hair behind my ear. I shivered. Heat flared in his gaze and I was glad to see I wasn't the only one still affected by our encounter. Our kiss.

"Good idea."

"Let me finish cleaning up and I'll meet you out there," I said, when he didn't leave.

After one last, long look, Dax turned and walked away. It wasn't until I heard the clang of the door sealing shut behind him that I was able to take a full breath.

Ohmygod, that kiss!

There'd been a few interesting men on Elegium and I'd taken full advantage of the situation, but they hadn't revved my engine the way Dax Cooper did. How the fuck was I supposed to survive on a ship with him?

Alone in the engine room, I took a few minutes to recenter myself. Breathing in the oil-scented air cleared Dax's fresh scent from my nose, but did nothing to erase the memory of his taste.

"Get it together, Lacy," I muttered. I still hadn't convinced him to help me find Layla, but I had an idea now. A good one.

I stowed the tools in the cubby under Engine 2 while crafting my argument. Then, when I'd procrastinated as long as I dared, I made my way back to the main section of the ship and checked the mess. No Dax. My next stop was the bridge.

Determined to be on my best behavior, no matter how much I wanted to just stroll onto the bridge, I stopped outside and knocked on the open door. "Can I come in?"

He turned away from a data screen to face me. "You're asking this time?" Humor laced his voice.

My cheeks warmed, but I didn't argue because I deserved it. "I can play nice."

"C'mon in."

He was sitting in the captain's chair, which was *fine*, it was his, but I still was drawn to it after my time on *Mako*.

I took the navigator's seat. He studied me a long moment and I tried not to squirm. "You've got something . . ." Trailing off, he gestured to his cheek.

Dammit. I wrapped my sleeve over my wrist and scrubbed at my cheek. "Better?" I prayed I hadn't made it worse.

"Better," he confirmed. "You're sure the engines are running smoothly?"

"I'm sure. I gave them a little extra TLC, but they would've been fine until your mechanic got here and inspected them." Would he take the opening and tell me that he didn't have a mechanic?

"Good. When I saw you working on them, I got worried." He stared at the stars outside. "Some days I worry that I bought the wrong ship."

My eyes widened and I gasped at his blatant blasphemy. "He doesn't mean that, baby!" I patted the console. "You're a wonderful ship and he's lucky to have you." I continued to pet *Fortuna* so she didn't get offended.

"Are you talking to my ship?" His voice was dryly curious.

"Yes! And you should too. She's the one keeping you safe from the wonders of space. Didn't they teach you anything in the space corps?"

He didn't respond right away, so I glanced at him sideways. Was he going to laugh at me? I'd never met an engineer who didn't speak to their ships and their engines.

"They taught us that our armor and our weapons provided that protection." He paused. "Well, maybe not from space. But they taught us that our odds of survival were only as good as our gear."

It was a smaller, colder way to put it, but yeah, I

agreed. "Think of *Fortuna* as the biggest—and best—piece of gear you own. If you love her and care for her, she'll do the same for you."

"That a lesson from growing up in space?"

"I don't think anyone ever said it out loud, but yeah, our ship was our home. Why wouldn't we love her and care for her?"

I felt his gaze on me. "What's the name of your family's ship?"

I swallowed hard. No way I was telling him that. He'd drop me on the next planet. Sure, right now he was *considering* that move, but if he learned I grew up on one of the most infamous smuggler ships . . . Yeah, that wasn't going to happen.

Ignoring his question, I said, "*Fortuna* was a good purchase. She could probably use some upgrades. I'm happy to give you recommendations. Hopefully you got a good price and have money left for modifications?"

He rubbed the back of his neck. "I spent everything we had saved up on the ship, fuel, and enough supplies to get us to our first cargo run." He glared at me. "The cargo run I was supposed to start from Elegium Station."

I ignored the flicker of guilt his words caused. I could —would!—fix that. He just needed to agree to keep me on. "But you got a good deal, right?"

He shrugged and mumbled a price.

I couldn't have possibly heard him correctly. I repeated the price.

"Yeah."

"For this ship?" I rubbed the console again, letting *Fortuna* know that I wasn't being judgy.

"Yeah."

How did you tell a man that he'd been screwed by someone who knew ships better than he did? "Oh. Uh.

Wow." I exhaled. "You've, uh, gotta watch those used-ship dealers."

He frowned and I felt like I'd kicked a puppy. "That bad, huh?"

I thought about soft selling it. Then again, I'd hate it if someone did that to me.

"It's not great. You probably could have bargained it down maybe a third, more if she has any issues."

"One of the cargo-hold doors sticks. The dealer raised one to show me the interior. I didn't think to test the other."

I winced, couldn't help it. "I can fix that."

"You can?" The hope in his voice was promising.

I placed my hand on his arm before I remembered how dangerous that could be. The muscles in his forearm tensed under my touch. "Don't panic. She runs. Maybe we give her a little extra lovin' on our way to get cargo. Do you have a job lined up?" He'd obviously been looking for one. I recognized the posting board he had pulled up.

Dax shook his head.

"Okay," I said brightly, "this is what we're going to do."

18

———

DAX

BASED ON LACY'S COMMENTS—AND her pained expression —I'd fucked up big time and I had no idea how to fix it. The squad had trusted me with Wilson's savings, sure that I would get us the best ship. And I'd completely blown it.

"Dax, are you listening to me?"

I looked at Lacy. She was watching me with concern in her eyes. Unbidden, memories of our engine room kiss came to the forefront and my eyes dropped to her lips. Then back up.

She smiled. "Everything is going to be all right."

I didn't believe her, but since I had no idea how to fix this, I smiled and nodded and waited to hear her plan.

"In its original configuration, the Cyclone class can hold nearly 75 metric tonnes of cargo. More if you install additional cargo mods, but that fucks with the fuel efficiency and sometimes with the ship's balance. While 75 tonnes isn't much when compared to the big bulk carriers, it's a good size for making a living at this."

Was she some kind of witch? Those were the same

numbers that the ship dealer had rattled off when I'd visited the off-planet shipyard.

I spun her chair until we were facing each other. My hands clamped around the arms of the chair. This time I wasn't letting go without getting answers. "Who sent you? How do you know so much about my ship?"

Her surprised blink gave way to understanding. "When I was a teenager, my father gave me a Cyclone. *Mako.* I lived and breathed that ship and learned everything I could about her. After a year, I could fix anything that broke. After a few years," she said with a shrug, "I knew every corridor and cargo hold, every fact and figure about my ship."

Her voice radiated love for her ship. Dax understood her talking to his ship now. Kind of. "What, um, what happened to *Mako*?" Surely if she still had her ship, she wouldn't have stolen his.

Her sigh echoed around the bridge. "When I decided to move to Elegium Station, my father convinced me that it was better to leave her with him rather than pay the exorbitant docking fees for a ship I wasn't going to fly. I've never regretted that more than these last couple days."

I laughed. "Tell me about it."

She shrugged sheepishly. "That's how I know so much about your ship."

About to pull back, I realized that her answer didn't account for everything. "How did you get on my ship? The doors were sealed. Locked." I may not know much about cargo, but I damn well knew security.

Her lips pinched like she was biting into a lemon. Like she had something to hide. Something she didn't want to tell me.

I leaned closer, giving her my best drill-sergeant stare. The one that made new recruits tremble.

She didn't even blink.

Impressed despite myself, I needed an answer. I'd already fucked up once. I couldn't let my team down further with a ship that could be stolen out from under us at any moment.

I was willing to wait her out, as long as it took, but she appeared to come to a decision.

"Factory settings."

"What the hell does that mean?"

"Exactly what it sounds like," she said, exasperation clear.

When I stared at her expectantly, she continued. "When every Cyclone rolled off the assembly line, their systems were coded to a default, factory setting. Every ship got the same code. Since the ships were originally built for the military, it made sense for the ships and the pilots to be interchangeable. One code, many ships."

Okay, that made sense. The military liked to do things the easy way, until they didn't. But . . . "*Fortuna* isn't a military ship."

"Sure. But no one changed the default code. Not you, not the dealer, not even the previous owner."

Flummoxed, I sat back heavily. "So you just entered a code and waltzed right onto my ship?"

"Basically."

My jaw dropped. "How did you get it started?"

She raised her brows and gave me an *Are you an idiot?* look.

"Let me guess. Factory settings?"

She nodded.

Air whooshed out of my lungs. "Holy shit."

"Pretty much," she agreed.

"Does every ship come with factory defaults?" I couldn't get over the horror of so many unsecured ships.

She shrugged but didn't look at me.

"C'mon, Lacy. Just tell me."

Her green eyes swiveled toward me. "Honestly, I don't know, but I'd assume so. I know codes for five ship types, including the Cyclone."

Five codes. That meant . . . "You could have stolen someone else's ship." Dammit.

"Stealing a ship wasn't my first choice. I just wanted to lie low until I figured out what was happening. Then the thugs who attacked me entered the docks." She looked away.

"Sure. I could have entered a few other ships, but they were deeper in the docks and I couldn't have flown them by myself. I would have needed an entire team to take any of the other four ship classes."

Her explanation made perfect sense, but Lacy's familiarity with boosting ships was worrisome.

"Are you a pirate?"

"What?" She choked out the word. "No. Of course not. Piracy is illegal in most known space."

"That sounds like something a pirate would say."

"I. Am. Not. A. Pirate," she ground out. "I'm a mechanic. You've seen my ID. I can prove my skills if I have to."

She paused, tilting her head like she was considering something. "And I'm pretty sure I have a way to solve your cargo problem *and* my sister problem."

I rolled my eyes. "Let me guess. If I help you find your sister, you'll tell me where I can get some cargo." I made an exasperated sound. "I think that helps you more than me."

She narrowed her eyes and glared at me. "No. My plan will help us both. At the same time."

It sounded too good to be true and I wasn't sure I believed her, but still . . . "How?" I asked cautiously.

She gestured toward the holo table tucked in the back of the bridge. "May I?"

I nodded. When she approached the table, I followed her.

With a flick of her hand, she pulled up the star chart on the holographic table, twisting and turning the image until she was satisfied.

It took my brain a moment to adjust to seeing the usual two-dimensional maps in 3D instead. "You'll have to show me how to do that," I said, while I studied the new terrain.

"This is us." She pointed to a glowing blue dot on the edge of the current view.

Fortuna looked so small amongst all the glowing white stars and planets.

"Where are you picking up your crew?"

I looked over at her sharply. This was the first time she'd mentioned my crew. As I rattled off the locations, little green lights sprang to life on the map. "Very cool."

"I know, right?" She smiled at me and my breath caught.

I'd thought she was pretty when I first saw her, here on my bridge, but when she smiled . . . Her smile outshone any of the stars on the map or out the windshield. She was obviously in her element working with *Fortuna* and I hated to admit that I was jealous of the attention she was paying my ship.

She programmed additional commands into the table and some of the existing lights changed colors, subtly glowing pink. "This overlay shows the locations of cargo requests."

"How did you . . ." The question hovered on the tip of my tongue.

"You've been visiting Floyd's Freight Forum looking for cargo jobs." She didn't even have the grace to look ashamed at knowing every move I'd been making. "It's a decent start," Lacy said, patting me on the arm, "but I know better places for cargo. We'll get to that later."

I shook my head. Damn her for being as frustrating as she was intriguing.

She rotated the map, changing the view until she was satisfied it met some unspoken criteria. "That's Elegium Station."

The little pink dot she pointed to looked very far away. We'd traveled quite a ways from the asteroid station in our day in space. Going back now would be a waste of time and fuel.

"This is our current trajectory." A blue line appeared on the map, spearing through the 3D space all the way to the edge of the map. "Obviously we'll need to change course to pick up your crew." Dotted blue lines radiated from *Fortuna's* blue dot, creating a fractured pattern on the star map.

No matter which dotted path we took, we'd pass a number of cargo opportunities. I reached out and "touched" one of the pink lights we were approaching. The screen zoomed in and data exploded on the map. Cargo type, job timeline, payment. "This is amazing, Lacy."

It wasn't just amazing. It could be a game changer for us. No more scrolling the forum. All we'd have to do was click on the nearest point on the map and go.

Her fingers wrapped around my wrist and pushed my arm down. "You do *not* want to transport cows, Dax. Trust me. *Fortuna's* cargo hold is not configured for that shit. And I mean literal shit."

"Oh," I said, feeling dumb. "How did you learn all this?"

She shrugged. "Experience."

Once again, I had the feeling she was leaving a lot out. I pressed another dot and watched the data expand.

Lacy cleared it quickly and keyed in more data. Two purple dots appeared on the screen, farther out than any of my crew, though they weren't far from one of the blue dotted lines that represented one of our potential routes. "Layla's last known locations, based on the geotags on the data chip."

"Lacy—" I started, but she held up her hand.

"You said to show you my plan. That's what I'm doing." She poked her finger at the map and three dots lit up orange. "There are three planets out near her last coordinates: Justin, Kottke, and Pignum. They're so far out, it might as well be a different galaxy. I think she's on one of them."

I opened my mouth to argue, but she hurried on. "I can get you cargo all the way out there. You'll be able to make money, pick up your crew, and help me out."

"That's days of travel, Lacy." I wanted to help her but by the time we reached hell-and-gone space, her sister could be gone. "It might be a wild goose chase."

Her jaw clenched and she didn't reply at first. Her voice was tight and controlled when she finally said, "It's days of travel anyway to pick up all of your crew." A long, tense pause. "Okay, tell me *your* plan." She shoved her hands in her pockets, her expression slightly taunting.

I stepped closer and studied the map. This was supposed to be easy—pick up cargo then start picking up my crew. Based on the way the dots had lit up when I told her the rendezvous points, Burn was first.

"Pick up Burn here." I pointed to the closest green light. "Then Finn." The next closest green light.

"Where are you getting cargo?"

On its face, it was an obvious, innocent question, but I was pretty sure it was a trap. I studied the pink lights. The closest option were the cows that she'd told me to avoid. I'd take that advice. I pulled up the data for the next pink dot. "What the fuck are thermo-blinders?" Whatever they were, there was good money in hauling them.

"Netting that blocks thermal scanning."

Well, that sounded easy enough. And the payment would keep us in the air for a while. "We'll get cargo there." Maybe this wasn't so hard.

"Where are they going?" Lacy asked quietly.

I studied the data again. "Caldon." Where was it on the map?

While I was searching, she lit up the dot. It flared orange, its glow nowhere near any of the other colored dots.

"That's a ways away," I said.

She nodded. "You'll probably need to get fuel here or here, based on what we have now and our current burn rate." Her finger lightly touched two dots in the middle of that route.

"How do you know all this?"

She huffed out a sigh. "I've been trying to tell you. I grew up with this. I know space. I know cargo. Most important, I know this ship." She stepped closer, getting right in my face. "It's easier and a lot less expensive to learn the ropes from someone, rather than trial and error."

She laid a palm on my chest. "You need me for this. And I need you to help me find my sister. It's a win-win."

I looked down at the hand on my chest, then back up

into her eyes. Hoping I was doing the right thing for my crew and not being influenced by her touch, I agreed. "Fine."

19

———

DAX

AFTER EXPLAINING everything to me several times, Lacy had finally gone to bed. Her story hadn't changed and by the third time through, I believed her. As much as I hated to admit it, her plan to pick up my crew—and visit her sister's last known location—made sense.

Left alone on the bridge to stew, I stared glumly at her map. The colored dots flickered among the white stars and planets, mocking me. Her competence with my ship and everything related to it was preying on my insecurities. In the space corps, I'd known my role and I'd been damn good at my job. Lead a squad or turn a bunch of recruits into a cohesive fighting machine? All day, every day. Arrange cargo and transportation? I hadn't felt so lacking since my own recruit days. It sucked and I didn't like it one bit.

In the space corps, there had been three types of cargo: marines, munitions, and supplies. Everything else was just details.

But here in civilian space, those details mattered. Hence the mind-blowing number of cargo classes.

According to Lacy, understanding those tiny details was the difference between a successful crew and one that scraped by. My squad and I definitely planned to be on the successful side of that line.

My squad. We were supposed to be a team, but here I was making decisions for everyone. Why the hell had they voted for me to buy the ship?

Oh, right. Because I had nothing else going on. I'd visited my family after my discharge, but only for a few days. Any longer and they would have started getting ideas about me putting down roots.

I shook off the self-pity. There was no time for it and I had a call to make.

According to Lacy's calculations, *Fortuna* would reach the rendezvous point with Burn in just under two days. Thirty-six hours after that, we'd reach Finn. Once he was onboard, the next stop would be a mid-sized station to refuel, restock, and pick up cargo.

I picked up the radio and tuned it to the comms frequency for the team.

"*Fortuna* Prime calling *Fortuna* team."

We were so far apart that there would be a lag. The radio crackled as I awaited their responses.

"*Fortuna* One here." That was Burn. Our resident adrenaline junkie, she was on an uninhabitable planet doing an adventure race of all things. "'Bout damn time you called. I was beginning to think pirates got you." She laughed.

I flinched. She didn't know how close to the truth she was.

"*Fortuna* Three." Mercer's cool controlled voice picked up next. Our medic was seemingly unflappable. "Good to hear from you, Sarge."

Mercer had headed home to deal with his family—and

the family business. Despite ten years in the space corps, his family was still pressuring him to be a doctor at one of their fancy hospitals.

It felt weird to be called by my old rank. But what the hell was I going to do? Demand they call me captain now? I shuddered. That was a title I wanted no part of. Most captains I'd met in the corps were assholes.

"Finn here." I rolled my eyes. He'd dropped the military conventions faster than any of us and I had no idea what he'd been up to since we got our walking papers.

"Hey guys, good to hear from you all. Any word from Orion?"

"I think he's still at home," Mercer said. "Visiting his mama."

My lips curved up. Orion was taller than my own six-two and outweighed me by at least fifty pounds, but he was a mama's boy through and through.

"It's pretty late there, I think," Burn added.

Damn. I'd forgotten about the time differences. But with everyone scattered right now, there was no finding the perfect time for a check-in. Things would be so much easier once everyone was on board.

"Glad I at least got most of you," I said into the expectant silence.

"How's the ship, Sarge?" Burn asked.

"She's great," I said. They didn't need to know that she had been stolen. Or about the fucking factory defaults. Those wouldn't be an issue by the time they were onboard, because Lacy had promised to change them tomorrow and I was going to watch her do it.

"And the cargo? We get our first payday yet?" Finn asked.

"No, that's why I'm reaching out. Change of plans." *Please don't ask for details.*

"Something wrong?"

"Everything's fine, Burn. The first cargo job didn't work out, but I've got a line on a few others. Wanted to give you and Finn a heads-up to be ready for rendezvous in the next few days. You're the first pickup, Burn. Then Finn. Then we'll hit Rigel Naught for cargo and fuel."

Silence met my words. I stared out at the stars.

"This isn't what we planned," Finn said.

Mercer spoke up before I had to come up with a half-truth. "The civilian world is a lot messier than the military, Finn." His voice was tired. What kind of mess had Mercer been dealing with?

His family owned an interplanetary medical system and they had hated the fact that he'd joined the space corps. I'd never known if it was because he'd enlisted or that he'd dared to not follow the plan his family had laid out for him.

Personally, I didn't give a fuck what Mercer's family wanted, because that man had saved my life on any number of occasions and I was damned glad he'd enlisted.

"Whatever," Finn said.

Well, shit. That wasn't good, but I couldn't fix whatever Finn's deal was from a distance. I'd have to wait until he was onboard.

"Burn, you still on Pangaea?" I turned my attention back to the star map. If she'd moved on, our plan would need to pivot again.

"Yep, just waiting for you to come get me."

"Finn, we picking you up on Holyoke still?"

There was a drawn out pause until Finn said, "Um, no. How about I just meet you at Rigel Naught?"

I frowned at the unexpected change. "Sure. We'll let you know when we're on our way. Mercer, you good waiting a few more days? The plan right now is to make the first cargo run and pick you and Orion up after."

"Ready and waiting," Mercer said. The exhaustion in his voice was still there.

"I'd rush this if I could, but *Fortuna* can only fly so fast."

Unless . . . I'd have to ask Lacy about fuel mods or anything that could make us faster.

"Don't worry about me, Dax. Come get me when you're ready."

We all spent a few more minutes catching up, then signed off.

It was good to talk to everyone, but this time it felt different. Was it because we'd all gone our separate ways, even if it was just for a short while? Or was it because I was hiding things from them?

20

DAX

THE NEXT MORNING, Lacy met me in the mess. "You really need to pick up more supplies," she said between bites of toast.

I ignored her long enough to pour myself a cup of coffee and take a sip. The hot liquid was bitter on my tongue, but I ignored the taste for the hit of caffeine. When we finally made money on the cargo runs, I'd splurge on better beans.

"Sweetener, too. That coffee could fuel the ship."

I stared at her over the rim of my cup. "Maybe I like my coffee black."

"Maybe you do, but you can't tell me your whole crew does."

"True. But they're not here yet."

She scowled. "I am."

"You're not crew." The word "yet" hung in the air between us, which was ridiculous because she hadn't been part of the squad. We had a full crew contingent. Not to mention she'd stolen my ship! There were many reasons for her not to be part of the crew—but part of me liked the idea of her being around. It had to be her knowledge, I decided. That's why I liked her presence. Not because of that damn kiss.

She gave me a long, charged look, then changed the subject before the tension in the air was unbearable. "You said something about a broken door in the cargo hold?"

"Yeah. The internal one. You want to take a look now?" My stomach grumbled in protest.

She laughed. "Get breakfast, while I get my tools. Where are they again?" Her voice was light, but was that a thread of accusation?

"On the bridge, right where you left them." I'd felt safer knowing where they were. And since she hadn't asked, I hadn't bothered to give them back.

"Excellent." She dumped the rest of her coffee in the sink, quickly washed and dried the cup, then brushed past me as she left the room.

What was I thinking, wanting her to stay on board? It didn't matter how intriguing the packaging, the woman was trouble. Not to mention, Finn had already claimed the mechanic's spot. He wasn't trained, but where Mercer had been the one fixing up our bodies, Finn had patched up and jury-rigged our equipment when we were in the field. I was sure he'd do fine with *Fortuna*.

I heated up two breakfast pouches and ate them in quick bites. Reconstituted powdered eggs weren't my favorite, but they were high protein and filling. Lacy wasn't wrong about the need for supplies. I'd initially only stocked enough food for one and had planned to pick some up on Elegium Station. We'd definitely need to purchase more food at the cargo stop, since we were adding two more people

I was recycling the meal pouches when Lacy appeared in the doorway. "All set?" I asked.

She lifted her tool bag. "Lead the way."

When we reached the cargo hold, Lacy asked, "So what exactly is the problem?"

"The internal door. It's stuck a couple feet from the ground. I can't get it to go up and I can't get it to go down all the way." I gestured for Lacy to go first into the hold.

"Do you mean the one that separates the space into two distinct spaces?" The lights flickered on automatically when she crossed the threshold. She clambered down the steps into the hold with sure, easy steps.

"That's the one." I followed her into the cargo bay.

It was a big space, obviously not as big as the hold of a troop transport ship, but big enough for what we wanted to do. Maybe even space for a shuttle. Was that even a thing for cargo ships?

Currently empty, the regularly spaced beams on the floor, ceiling, and sides to lash cargo to were visible and our voices echoed in the space.

She stopped in front of the rolling door and placed her tool bag on the decking. When she reached for the hanging switch that controlled the door, I growled. "Tried that. It didn't work." Seriously, I wasn't that dumb.

Her lips curved just barely, like she was holding back a smile. "I believe you," she said. "I still need to test it for myself. Go do something else and let me work." She made shooing motions.

I crossed my arms and leaned against the railing. "Nope. I want to make sure you take care of my ship."

Her smile faded. "I promise, I'm not going to harm her. I told you I would fix the door and that's what I'm going to do."

"You're the one who said I needed to know *Fortuna* in and out. So I want to see what you're doing."

"Fine, if you want to play voyeur, knock yourself out."

With a huff, she turned away and hit the button to raise the door. Something above us made a grinding sound, but nothing happened.

"Okay, so that doesn't work," she muttered to herself.

I was so restrained, I didn't even say I told you so. But it was a hard-fought battle.

Next she crouched and grasped the edges of the door. Pretty sure this wasn't going to work, but I took a second to enjoy the view, then focused on her form, to make sure she didn't hurt herself.

She pulled up. The door didn't budge.

"I tried that, too." I couldn't help it.

She tossed a glare over her shoulder. "Hit the button, would you?"

"Should we trade places?" I asked as I grabbed the controller. "Me lift and you press the button?"

She rolled her eyes.

Okay, then.

"On three," I said. "One. Two. Three." I hit the button.

The sound of gears grinding against each other filled the space, but nothing happened.

Lacy released the door and stood, arching to stretch her back. "It's jammed. Pretty sure I can fix it, but I'm going to have to cut the power to the cargo hold while I do it."

"Won't cutting the power kill the gravity?"

She raised a brow. "No. The cargo hold power is completely separate from the gravity controls. And life support. And the pressurization."

I held my hands up in front of me. "It was an honest question."

"I need you to wait outside while I reroute the power."

What the hell did that mean? "*Outside* outside?"

"Relax. I need you in the hallway, outside the cargo hold. I may need you to manually restart the power to this sector and it would be better if we both weren't in here."

A new, worse thought occurred to me. "Is this dangerous?"

She looked up from the tools she was pulling out of her bag. "I'm playing with electricity and hundred-pound doors. What do you think?"

"Beyond that." I didn't want her to get hurt. I could hire another mechanic . . .

She stood and approached me, not stopping until she was right in my face. "Do you want this fixed or not? I can back off right now if you don't want me to work on this."

Torn between fixing up *Fortuna* or protecting Lacy, I hesitated too long.

"I. Am. A. Fucking. Professional." She poked me in the chest with each word. "I'm more qualified than you to fix this. You don't need to protect me. I've been working on ships since I was a kid and I know this class of ship inside and out. Now act like a goddamned captain and make a decision."

I looked down at the finger poking into my chest and then back up to meet her gaze.

She was completely serious. And worse, she was right. I had to do my goddamn job. "Fix it. Please."

"About time," she muttered.

"What do you need me to do?"

Lacy walked me through the process, explaining each step quickly but clearly, giving estimates of how long the repair process should take. I appreciated the details.

"Approximately two minutes after I cut the power, the lights in here will go out and the emergency lights will kick on. Okay?"

I nodded.

"Now go out into the hall and close the door."

"Be safe."

"Always."

Turning her back in a way that clearly signaled dismissal, I reluctantly took the stairs out to the corridor. Once I secured the door behind me, I planted myself outside the tiny porthole window in the door.

Just as she'd described, the lights inside the cargo hold went out and the emergency lights kicked on. They weren't bright enough to allow me to see inside. I could just barely hear the clang of a tool against the door.

My breath fogged up the window. Though I knew it wouldn't help, I rubbed the glass with my sleeve. What was she doing in there?

It wasn't that I doubted her experience or her capabilities. It wasn't even worry for Lacy, specifically. I'd have the same concerns if Finn were in there.

Liar.

I could tell myself it was worry for a teammate, the same worry I had when we were on a mission, but that would be a lie. I trusted my team to do their jobs and there was no room for worry on a mission. I needed to do the same for her.

Stuck out here waiting for Lacy to let me know when things were back up and running, I started to pace. It was that or enter the cargo hold against her orders.

The door to the cargo hold creaked open—finally!—and I whirled around to see Lacy standing in the doorway.

At least, I assumed it was Lacy. Grease liberally streaked her face and her coveralls were more grime than fabric at the moment.

I burst out laughing.

"Asshole," she muttered.

"Sorry." I swallowed my laugh. "I was not expecting . . . that." I waved my hand up and down.

"Neither was I." A tiny smile slipped out and she shook her head. "Want to come see your door?"

"Yes." Though I was dying to see the repairs, I kept a careful distance from Lacy and her grease-covered, well, everything.

She stood next to the door that now reached all the way to the floor.

"May I?" I reached for the controller.

"It's your ship," she said innocently.

I hit the button and, with a slow creak, the metal door rose up, disappearing into the track at the top.

I hit the button again. It rolled back down with fewer creaks this time. Another press and the door started its upward journey again, smoother and quieter.

"I swear," Lacy said, "if you hit that button one more time I'm going to break the damn thing."

"Fine. Funsucker."

She raised a greasy hand toward me and I dropped the controller and dashed back up the steps. Her laughter echoed around the cargo hold.

21

———

LACY

"We're going to Pangaea?" My voice rose and I probably sounded slightly hysterical as I stared at Dax.

"Yep." He spared me a glance, then whipped his gaze back toward the little green planet in our view that was getting bigger and bigger. "I told you that."

Okay, fine. He *had* given me the names, but I'd been so focused plotting a path to Layla, they hadn't really registered. Staring at the verdant planet, everything I knew about it came rushing back. "One of your crew is down there?"

He nodded. "Yep, Burn."

What the hell kind of name was Burn? But that wasn't my most pressing question. "You know that we can't land on Pangaea, right?"

Named after the primordial land mass of Earth, the planet was lush and green, with exotic flora and dense forests.

And that was the problem. Pangaea was too lush. Too green. The minute a ship set down, the biosphere overtook the technology. Vines wrapped around landing gear. Bugs infested air ducts. Mother Nature was usually the winner: only one in three ships that landed on Pangaea made it back off the planet.

"We're not landing. Burn will come to us."

What the hell did that mean?

"Hold on," Dax warned, just before we dropped out of space and into atmosphere.

My stomach jumped into my throat and my hands clasped the arm rests. We dropped through cloud cover into blue sky that nearly seemed to be eaten up by green trees. "Wow. I never knew trees could get so big." We'd never had any reason to visit Pangaea.

I turned to look at Dax. "Are you sure you can do this? I can take over." I really didn't want the trees to be the last thing I saw.

"I've got this, Lacy. Grab the radio, would you?"

I picked up the radio and held it out to him.

He shook his head and gave me the comms frequency.

Keying in the frequency, I held the radio near his mouth.

"*Fortuna* One, this is *Fortuna* Prime. You ready for pickup?"

There was a crackle of static and then a wild yelp. "Hey, Sarge!"

"Give me your exact coordinates. We're coming in hot for you."

She rattled off her location and I programmed it into the ship's navigation. "'We'? You got Finn with you?"

"Not exactly," Dax said. "See you soon. *Fortuna* Prime out."

He gave me a nod and I cut the transmission. "Am I going to be a problem?"

"Probably," Dax said after a pause. "I'll handle it, all right?"

"Sure." This was going to be great fun.

"I'll take care of it," he said again. "Now I need you down in the cargo hold to pick up Burn."

"THIS HAS GOT to be the dumbest plan ever," I muttered as I triple-checked my safety harness and the lines that tied me to the ship. When Dax and I had set up the lines and harnesses earlier, I thought this was like a backup plan or something. Like in case of emergencies.

I'd argued with Dax that I should be the one to pilot the ship and he should meet his friend in the cargo hold. He'd refused.

Apparently, we were going to scoop Burn right out of the trees. The only way this was a plan was if he planned for me to fall out of the cargo hold. That would *not* be happening if I had anything to say about it. I tightened my harness again.

When my lines were as secure as I could make them, I checked the others.

The intercom chimed and I pressed the button to answer. "Cargo bay."

"We're approaching the coordinates. There's nothing but trees here. I want you to open the cargo hold door and keep an eye out. Do you have comms?"

"Just the intercom. I can leave it on."

"Do it. Let me know when the doors open and if you see anything."

"Got it. Cargo bay out."

My steps echoed ominously as I crossed the empty cargo hold and my stomach lurched as I approached the external bay door. With each step, the harness bit into my thighs, torso, and shoulders. It was attached to the cargo hold with flexible but strong metal tethers. They had enough slack that I should be able to lean out the door and snag our newcomer but short enough that if I fell out I wouldn't hit the trees we were flying over.

Wasn't that a happy thought?

I tugged on my tethers, giving a few good yanks to make sure they stayed attached. Not that my strength compared in any way to the intensity of the wind outside.

"Here goes nothing," I said quietly. I slapped my hand on the button to open the outer cargo door and grabbed onto the wall for dear life.

As the metal slid upward, the wind increased and the straps rattled throughout the cargo hold. Wisps of hair slapped my cheeks and my braid fluttered out behind me.

"Doors open," I shouted, hoping Dax could hear me over all the noise.

I left my hand on the inner hull as I made my way to the gaping door. Praying my tethers would hold, I gripped the side of the door and leaned out.

Wind battered my vision and made me blink. Why hadn't I thought about a helmet and visor?

I squinted against the stinging wind and studied the surface below us.

A solid field of green passed under the ship. The only breaks in the unending green were caused by elevation changes. This planet was crazy alive.

"We should be coming over the coordinates in thirty seconds." Dax's voice was low against the high whistling wind and clanging metal.

One one thousand, two one thousand. As the numbers neared thirty, I leaned a little farther out the door.

Twenty-five one thousand, twenty—"Holy shit!"

"What's that? Do you see her?" Dax's voice was almost drowned out by the rush of wind.

Dammit, I wished we had better comms.

"I see her!" I yelled. "She's on top of one of the trees! She's got something bright yellow on."

"Shit, we missed her," Dax growled. "Coming about."

Moving as fast as I dared, I grabbed additional tethers and dragged them toward me. Then I dropped to my knees and peered out the door again.

"Do you see her?"

It was hard to reorient myself with all the never-ending green, so I was thankful for that splash of yellow. "See her! Starboard side."

I draped the tethers over the side of the cargo door. Then I lay flat on my belly, with my chest and arms hanging over the side. I focused on the yellow, since focusing on the constantly moving green threatened to upend my stomach.

"We're getting close!" I heard Dax say.

God, I hoped I could do this. Dax would have the upper-body strength for this.

"You should have let me pilot," I muttered under my breath. Then it was too late to do anything but reach for the fast-approaching yellow.

A hand wrapped around my forearm and suddenly I had the weight of the world on my shoulder joint.

I wrapped my fingers around the forearm and prayed I could hold on.

"Woohoo!" One of the extra tethers pulled taut beneath my belly as she crawled up and over my body. The weight on my arms lessened, then it was gone.

A shadow loomed over me. A thud followed. Then my arm was free and dangling over the side. I snatched it back into the ship.

"That was awesome," a voice yelled by my ear.

I could barely hear it over the pounding of my pulse.

Rolling onto my back, I watched our newest crew

member bounce to her feet. My stress lessened just a smidge. It wouldn't go down all the way until that external door was closed.

She leaned over with her hand extended. I reached up and wrapped my fingers around hers.

One minute I was flat on my back, the next I was standing. It was so fast and unexpected that I stumbled. She caught me by the shoulders and held me steady.

"Easy there." She laughed.

A gust of wind hit me. "I, uh, I need to shut that door."

"Oh, I got it. You seem a little unsteady on your feet."

My eyes widened as she walked toward the door—completely untethered.

"Wait, you're not hooked in!" I lunged for her, but she was already moving.

Burn rolled her eyes. "Don't worry about it." She sauntered to the door like we weren't hundreds of feet above the ground, moving at a speed that would probably leave us a smear on the surface if we fell. Slamming the button to close it, she stared out at the green planet until it disappeared, the cargo hold sealed once again.

"That was amazing!" If her daredevil moves hadn't telegraphed her status as an adrenaline junkie, the glee in her voice would have.

I shook my head, impressed and horrified in equal measure. I loved being on ships, but preferred to at least mostly adhere to safety protocols.

Now that the door was closed, I could hear Dax yelling over the intercom. "Dammit, Lacy, answer me! Did you get her?"

"Aw, did you miss me, Sarge?" Burn's smile lit up the hold.

"You're okay?" The concern in Dax's voice kicked up

something in my system. Not jealousy, because that would be ridiculous, right? We barely knew each other.

"I'm fine, Sarge. That was one hell of a ride."

As I moved around the cargo hold, unhooking my tethers and ensuring they were properly stowed, I studied Burn. She was tall. Taller than me by a good few inches. Probably as tall as Dax.

Her olive cargo pants and a high-tech black shirt hugged muscles and curves. With her smooth dark skin, cheekbones that I'd kill for, and hair pulled into a series of tiny topknots, she looked more like a model than a soldier.

My gaze dropped to her boots. At first glance they looked like typical combat boots, but then I noticed the chunky high heels. Even her sleek yellow backpack—that's what I had seen on the approach—looked like it came off a runway.

Damn. I wanted to be her when I grew up.

"Lacy? You okay?"

Burn replied before I did, curiosity coloring her voice. "Oh, is that her name?" I looked up and she smiled at me. "Despite how up close and personal we got, we hadn't gotten around to exchanging names."

I blushed at the innuendo in her voice. Was she fucking with me?

"She's fine, too. Very fine."

Yeah, I was pretty sure she was fucking with me, given how dowdy I felt in the sweats and long-sleeve shirt Dax had lent me while I laundered my coverall. Again. I gave my hips an extra shimmy as I wiggled out of the harness.

Her grin widened and she let out a loud, boisterous laugh.

I laughed too.

"Yeah, she's fine. You wanna talk to her?"

I missed Dax's reply, but Burn said, "Sounds good.

We'll be up to the bridge as soon as things are squared away here."

I stowed the harness with the rest of the gear.

"Anything I can do?" Burn asked.

I swiped my hands on my hips and shook my head. "That's about it."

Burn studied me for a long moment, then looked around the hold. "I hear we're going after some cargo."

I nodded, not sure how much to tell her. "Yep, next stop."

She tilted her head. "Didn't expect Sarge to have a bed bunny help out with this, but don't mind it either."

My jaw dropped. "Excuse me, what?"

Burn gestured at my clothes. "Don't deny it. I recognize the shirt. Our squad all received one when we won an interdivision training exercise."

"It's not like that," I protested. "I'm a mechanic."

Her gaze and her voice turned frosty, so different from her earlier welcome. "Yeah, right. Finn's going to be our mechanic."

"Look, Dax can explain it all." That was so far above my pay grade at the moment. Plus, I did not want to mess with a woman who wore high-heeled combat boots to an adventure race.

"Why are you calling Sarge 'Dax'?"

I shrugged. "Because he told me to."

"You must be one helluva piece of ass."

I stiffened and straightened. "I am," I said archly, "but that's not why I'm on the ship."

"Right." Her words dripped with disdain.

I opened my mouth, closed it again. Nothing I could say would convince her otherwise. "Ready to see the rest of the ship?" I asked instead.

"Yeah, let's get out of here. I need to have a conversation with Sarge."

"After you." I gestured for her to precede me.

She gave me a hard look, one that said she didn't trust me.

Ditto.

She stomped toward the door that led to the rest of the ship. "Enjoy your free ride. I'm sure we'll be dropping you off at the next stop."

I followed several feet behind her. I'd known it was going to get messy when Dax's crew arrived—and that was before they'd learned about my unauthorized taking of *Fortuna*.

22

DAX

WE WERE ACCELERATING out of Pangaea's atmosphere when the clomp of footsteps announced my visitor. I swiveled in my chair and waited for her entrance. Burn appeared in the doorway looking like a badass space pirate from the movies I used to watch as a kid.

"I see you made it," I said with a smile.

"Hey, Sarge."

I stood to greet her, hand extended. She took me by surprise and pulled me in for a hug.

Behind Burn, Lacy's eyes widened in surprise. She stood rooted outside the bridge. I wanted to beckon her inside, but my arms were pinned to my sides by the hug.

"It's good to see you, Sarge! And our ship! She's a beauty."

"Good to see you too, Burn." Gently pressing out with my upper arms, I nudged Burn to release me. "How was Pangaea?" I asked when I was finally free.

"Amazing!" Burn dropped into the navigator's chair.

Hurt flashed across Lacy's face before she smoothed

out her expression. Blank faced, she stayed outside the bridge and leaned against the doorway.

Shit. I didn't know what to do about that. I'd felt the same way when I'd first seen her in the captain's chair, the one I considered mine. But Lacy wasn't crew. Except, for the time being, she sort of was.

Dammit.

I decided to ignore it for the moment. Lacy may consider it her seat, but to kick Burn out of it right now would only lead to questions. Questions I wasn't in a hurry to answer.

Currently, no one had an assigned seat but me.

I took my seat and waved Lacy into the bridge, but she shook her head.

Okay, up to her. I'd find Lacy later and explain. Not that I owed her any explanation.

I turned my attention back to Burn. She was already describing some of her adventures on Pangaea.

Lacy turned on her heel and marched away.

I clenched my fist. Then, after a deep breath, I focused on Burn's words.

"Scaling that last tree . . ." She shook her head. "I heard you coming and I wasn't sure I was going to make it in time."

"We would've circled around a few times. I'm just glad we had the coordinates. Otherwise, finding you would have been like finding a needle in a forest."

"'We,' huh?"

Hiding a wince, I realized I couldn't brush off her question the way I had over the comms.

"Yeah, not sure how this pickup would have gone without assistance." I felt bad about minimizing Lacy's contributions.

Burn looked at the now-empty hallway like she was

worried about being overheard. "Assistance? That's what we're calling it these days? I mean, I get that you have needs and stuff, but I didn't expect you to bring some random woman on board."

"Watch yourself. She's a passenger and a temporary mechanic." I bristled at the implication. Sure, Lacy and I had shared an amazing kiss, but there was nothing between us. "I picked her up at the asteroid station."

"Picked her up? Like in a bar?" Her tone radiated disapproval.

I scowled at Burn. "Even if I did, that wouldn't be any of your business. I've seen you slip out of a bar with a stranger or two in the past." When she looked affronted, I added, "No judgment. I don't give a fuck who sleeps with whom, as long as it's safe, sane, and consensual. You should do the same."

She didn't say anything for long enough that I turned my attention back to the ship's controls. I wanted to double-check our course tonight before I set the autopilot for the night shift. I was too exhausted to take another evening and Burn didn't know the ship. If Burn hadn't reacted the way she had, Lacy would be an option, but I wanted to deescalate this before bed, not set Burn off again.

"I'm sorry," she said finally. "It's just . . . This is our dream. You, me, Finn, Mercer, Orion, and Wilson. The ship is *ours*. We scraped and saved and planned and Wilson died for it. And to have a stranger be the first person I saw, a stranger wearing *your* clothes . . . Well, it was a lot. I'm sorry."

"Apology accepted." I gave her a smile and a light punch on the shoulder so she knew I really meant it. "How badly did you insult her?"

"Who?" Burn tried for light and playful, but I could tell

it wasn't good. "Fine. I flirted with her, then I called her your bed bunny."

"Fuck, Burn." I winced. "You definitely need to apologize to her too."

She sighed. "I know. I will. Did you really pick her up in a bar?"

I checked the programming one last time, then swiveled to face her. "No. I picked her up at the spaceport on Elegium Station after she ran into some trouble. She needed help."

That was skirting the truth, but Lacy and I hadn't had time to concoct a good cover story. I wasn't going to tell Burn that Lacy had stolen our ship, at least not right away. Burn could probably rip the other woman in two with her bare hands.

I waited for the next question. She surprised me when it wasn't about Lacy.

"What about the cargo?"

I sighed. Lacy had fucked that up for me, too, but I felt this urge to protect her. To make sure that my crew saw her as one of them. I couldn't explain it, except tension between crew members on a ship this size would be awkward, if not uncomfortable.

"That was a misunderstanding," I told my former squad mate. "Lacy helped me identify Rigel Naught as a good source for cargo. We'll meet Finn there and pick up a shipment or two."

Burn's dark eyes drilled a hole in me. "First, she's a mechanic. Now she's a fucking cargo master? I think you've been conned, Sarge."

Because Burn poked at a worry I still had, I responded harsher than I intended. "She grew up in space. Knows ships like *Fortuna* like the back of her hand."

Burn shook her head. "Okay, Sarge. Whatever you say."

With that, I snapped. "No. None of that 'okay, Sarge' bullshit. Like you said, this is our *dream!* Everything we worked for the last few years. You got concerns, you tell me. You got a problem, you tell me. You assholes might have decided to make me captain, but it's not a one-man show."

"Fine, I don't like it, but I'll trust your judgment. For now." She stood and stretched. "You got a bunk assigned to me?"

I shook my head. "Wherever you want. I've got the captain's quarters, the only damn perk of this job, and Lacy's got one of the cabins, but you're free to pick any of the others."

"Gotcha."

As she started past me, I grabbed her wrist. "It's really good to see you, Burn."

"You, too, Sarge. You, too."

23

LACY

After I'd stormed away from the bridge, I'd stomped around the engine room, cursing, for a little while. It made me feel a bit better, but it didn't take away the sting of seeing Burn in the navigator's seat, the space on the bridge I thought of as mine, or Dax basically ignoring me.

It hurt, dammit. And I was pissed that it hurt.

When I finally calmed down, at least a little, I made my way to the utility room. After Burn's disdainful comment about me wearing Dax's clothes, I'd feel better in my coveralls.

I really needed to pick up some new clothes when we stopped at Rigel Naught. I was so sick of that damn jumpsuit!

And yet, here I was, pulling it out of the clothes refresher. I shimmied out of Dax's sweats and shoved my legs into the blue one-piece. As I pulled his shirt over my head, I caught his scent, that subtle, earthiness that I'd snuggled into when he carried me to the med bay.

"Dammit!" I tossed his clothes into the refresher and programmed a new cycle. My nerves felt raw, exposed.

Used to having a plan in place, I felt adrift and I didn't know what to do with myself. What I really needed was a big repair job, but unless I broke something myself, I was out of luck.

Hauling the front zipper up, I escaped to my room. If I couldn't fix the ship, I could try to fix Layla's situation. I'd already watched the videos a few times, but maybe this time would be the charm.

I slipped inside as soon as my door opened, then pulled up short. Burn was leaning over my small dresser. "What the hell are you doing in my quarters?"

Burn stood up straight. "Your quarters?" She shut the drawer and looked around. "There's nothing in here."

Straightening to my full height, I shifted to the balls of my feet. She was taller than me and probably weighed more too. Not to mention she was a trained soldier. But that didn't mean I wouldn't fight for what was mine. "My tool bag's in the engine room." Now I wished I'd kept it in my room. There were plenty of tools I could use as weapons. What I wouldn't give for a big, hefty wrench right now.

"That's all you've got?"

"That and the clothes on my back." And the data chip. And, technically, the clothes that Dax lent me.

"Sarge said he picked you up in the spaceport. That you'd run into a little trouble." Her brows furrowed together. "But why don't you have any stuff?"

"Why don't you?" I snapped back before I could corral my inner child. All she had was that yellow backpack. The one currently draped over the chair in *my* room.

"Contest rules," she said. "I got a change of clothes and a few pieces of gear." Her brow furrowed as she studied me. "Seriously, though, what's the story?"

I gritted my teeth and held back another sarcastic

comment. Burn was officially part of *Fortuna*'s crew and I'd need them on my side. Or at least not hating me when the whole story came out. So I closed the door and sat on the edge of the bed, pulling my legs up to sit cross-legged.

"Two thugs broke into my apartment right after I got home from work. I got away, but all I had was my tool bag and the takeout that I'd picked up for dinner." My mouth watered just thinking about those noodles.

Burn had flipped the chair around and straddled it. "How'd you get away?"

"I jumped out the window and ran." I absently rubbed my left shoulder. The memory lingered longer than the pain had.

"Holy shit." Was that admiration in Burn's voice?

"Yeah." I'd do it again if I had to, but I really hoped my window-jumping days were behind me.

"Why the spaceport?" She sounded genuinely curious, but for now I needed to treat this like an interrogation, no matter how friendly it might seem.

"Elegium is an asteroid station. It's more spaceport and docks than anything else. Plus, that's where I spent most of my time."

"Why not go to security?"

I laughed. "Dax asked me the same thing. It honestly didn't cross my mind. Fight or flight," I said with a shrug. "I chose flight." Literally.

She whistled. "That's some story. You got any proof?"

And there it was. The interrogation.

"Med bay should have a record of my injuries. Dax took me there to get fixed up." I didn't think she'd have access to the med bay files, but if Dax asked, I'd share my records.

"What did the men who broke into your place want?"

Deciding to stick as close to the truth as I could, I

shared what I'd told Dax. "I didn't know at the time. Since then, I think they were looking for a data chip."

"Do you have it?" Her gaze never left me.

"I do."

I let the silence between us grow, while I determined how much else I was willing to share. I held her gaze and watched her wrestle with whether to ask.

Curiosity got the best of her. "What's on the chip?"

"My sister's research. And an indication that she's been kidnapped." Though I spoke matter-of-factly, my stomach clenched with worry. It had been four days since I'd received the chip and I was no closer to knowing what had happened to Layla.

"Holy shit! What are you going to do?"

"Working on it." What else could I say? Telling her that Dax had agreed to help seemed like something he should tell her.

She slapped her hands on her thighs and stood. "Let me know if we can help. Sisters should stick together." There was something in her voice, sadness, maybe, when she said that.

Her offer was the last thing I expected. "Oh. Thanks."

She gave me a small smile. "Look, I'm sorry about what I said. What I called you. But don't get comfy here. We're picking our mechanic up at the next stop, so we won't need you anymore."

Something else I'd let Dax tell her. I just nodded.

"I better go find another room." Burn grabbed her bag off the chair and let herself out.

I stared at the door long after it had closed behind her. I'd told Burn the truth or at least as much as I could right now.

24

LACY

THE VIBE on the ship had changed since we picked up Burn. It was no longer me and Dax, trying to figure each other out. Burn's presence tipped the scales toward Dax.

I got it. They had history. They were already on the same team. Spoke the same language and had the same inside jokes.

But it made me feel like the outsider I was. *Fortuna* may have been Dax's ship, but she felt so much like my *Mako*, that I guess I'd gotten lost in the fantasy that she was. With thirty-six hours to kill before we met up with Finn, I'd holed up in either the engine room or my cabin, making lists, making plans. As long as Dax's team didn't convince him to kick me off the ship, I intended to keep my end of the bargain and identify lucrative cargo opportunities.

Rigel Naught, where we were meeting Finn, was a hotbed of trade. The moon station orbited a dry, barren planet. Normally the moon of a dead planet wouldn't be a good place for trade because the planet below had nothing to offer, but Rigel Naught was extraordinarily lucky: it was almost perfectly equidistant from three inhabited planetary systems.

Need engine parts? You could probably find them on Rigel Naught. Rare spices? Anything your heart desires—for a price. High-value trade goods? Opportunities so thick on the ground you'd trip over them.

The opportunities for cargo were endless. Navigating it all—the legal, the shady, and the dangerous—was tricky for a newcomer. I'd outlined the best of the cargo options available online and added a few that were invitation only. With the right word in the right ear, I was pretty sure I could get an invitation for *Fortuna*.

I was finishing a different kind of shopping list when Dax's voice crackled through the intercom. "All hands to the bridge. We're on approach to Rigel Naught."

Show time. Nerves fluttered in my stomach. Burn hadn't been very welcoming and I was afraid I'd face the same from Finn. Add in worry about my sister, and my anxiety threatened to boil over. These last few days in space, putting distance between me and what had happened on Elegium, felt like stolen time.

No time for worry. I had a job to do. Shoving the tablet with my lists in my pocket, I slipped out of my room and approached the bridge.

Dax and Burn were already seated. He had his hands on the controls, but as soon as we got closer, the station's automatic docking system would take control and pull the ship in.

"Have you been here before?" Burn asked, her attention never straying from the console in front of her.

"A few times. With my sister and our father. It's been a few years, though."

Burn hmmed. "And you think your information is still good?"

I rolled my eyes since she couldn't see me. "Haul cargo long enough and you'll learn that things out here don't change quickly. Sure, the technology might get a little fancier and the names may change, but the work stays the same."

There was a clunk and then a shudder ran through the ship as Dax steered us into the docking mechanism. I held my breath as he bobbled the controls a tad, but his oversteering was quickly corrected by the automated system.

"Where'd you learn to drive this thing, Sarge?"

"Trial and error."

Burn laughed, but I saw the way Dax practically peeled his hands off the controls. I didn't think he was joking.

"So what's the plan?" Burn asked. She swiveled in her seat. "Can we go meet Finn now?"

I shook my head. "We won't be cleared to leave the ship for at least an hour. Docking takes time and there's registration paperwork to take care of. Once you're in the system, it will be a little shorter next time."

Dax turned to face me. "Paperwork?"

I nodded. "Yep. You'll face it on most stations. The more legit ones, at least. The shadier ones don't tend to care."

He sighed. "I guess that's what I'll be doing."

"I need to place a supply order." I pulled my tablet out of my pocket and opened up the master list.

"What's your favorite meal, Dax?"

He shot me a startled look. "What?"

"What's your favorite meal?" I asked again.

"Spaghetti and meatballs," Burn said.

I looked at her in surprise then back at Dax. "That's your favorite food?"

"No, that's my favorite," Burn said. "I assumed you were going to ask me too."

"Good to know," I said evenly.

"Why are you asking?" Dax wanted to know.

I held up the tablet. "Making a supply order. Figured you all might like something other than ready-to-eat meals. We can probably get the ingredients here on Rigel Naught."

"Hell, yeah." Burn snatched my tablet out of my hand and ignored my protest. Her finger scrolled over the list. "Veggies? Yeah, I suppose we might as well. Chocolate? Thank god. Coffee. Good, good."

Annoyance spiked as she continued to check my work. I didn't see *her* thinking ahead and making a supply list.

"Oil? Spare parts?" She peered up at me from *my* seat.

"Never travel without replacement parts if you can help it. We should be able to get what we need at a good price here. Which is better than spending too much later— or not being able to find it at all."

"Okay. That makes sense."

Oh goodie. So glad she approved. I tried to grab my tablet back, but Burn moved it to her other hand, farther away.

"Underwear? Clothes?"

Color flared in my cheeks. "I've had one outfit for almost a week now. I want—no, I *need*—a change of clothes." I just might burn my whole outfit once I purchased replacements.

"Oooh," Burn said. "That's why you were wearing Dax's clothes. Not because you were banging him."

My cheeks blazed hotter.

"That's enough, Burn." Dax finally reined her in. "Give Lacy her tablet back."

Burn handed it over. "Make sure you add spaghetti and meatballs for me."

I dutifully added the ingredients to the ship's order.

"My favorite meal is pizza," Dax said.

I looked at him. "That's pretty vague. What kind of pizza?"

"Any kind."

"Seriously?"

"He's telling the truth," Burn said. "He's never met a pizza he didn't like."

"Pick one, please." I was not shopping for whatever pizza.

"Meat and veggie."

"That I can do." Those ingredients went on the list.

"Add the ingredients for your favorite meal, too," he added.

"Oh, no, that's okay," I stammered.

"No arguments."

I nodded.

"Now, Sarge," Burn tried to interject, but he ignored her.

"Add steak and potatoes," Dax said. "That's Finn's favorite."

I typed in the ingredients for noodles for me and Finn's steak, though I added a price limit for that. Dax and Burn had no idea what fresh meat could cost out here.

He grabbed my wrist to get my attention. Tingles danced over my skin where we touched. "It's a good idea. Making a list, I mean. I wouldn't have thought of it," he said. "Or even ordering supplies."

I smiled back at him. "Little things like that can make the time in space feel not so bad. Some stuff will be fresh, some will probably be frozen. Once we have cargo loaded and booked, we can plan the meals out."

"How do we order supplies?"

"It's easy. You log on to the station's system and send your order. The software will direct it to the appropriate sources. They'll send a quote and once you approve it, they'll deliver the supplies to the ship."

"Show me." He stood up and gestured me into the captain's chair. "Enter the order and show me how I accept a quote."

I sat slowly. This had been my seat on *Mako*. Part of me missed being in charge, making all the decisions. Except for when my sister tagged along, I hadn't had a crew on board. Long term, I preferred spending my time in the engine room rather than on the bridge.

I walked Dax through how to safely connect to the station's network, then showed him how I connected my tablet to it.

"First we need to create an account." I swiftly keyed in *Fortuna*'s name. "Now create a password."

He leaned over the back of the chair, arms going around me to the keyboard and typed one in. His breath feathered over my ear and I shivered.

His shoulder brushed mine and I fought the ridiculous urge to lean into him. If I turned my head, I could sink my teeth into his meaty biceps.

Wait, what the hell was I thinking?

I shoved that thought away and tried to find a semblance of professionalism. That struggle wasn't helped when his hands brushed over my upper arms.

Or when Burn muttered, "Just when I believed you weren't sleeping together."

Dax rested his hands on the back of the chair. I kept my back ramrod straight so I wouldn't accidentally brush against them. "What now?" he asked, his deep voice sending butterflies through me.

"Now we just transfer our list." With one click, the list on my tablet populated on the screen. "Sorry. Let me remove my clothes from this. I'll place that order separately."

"Leave 'em," Dax said.

"What?" I swiveled my head to look at him. "I've got an account. I can order them from there." I'd just have to be careful that they didn't see it. I couldn't afford the questions they would have.

"Consider it payment for the work you've done on the ship. I noticed the sink in the mess isn't leaking anymore and the air purifier is running smoother, too."

My cheeks warmed. I'd wondered if anyone had noticed the tweaks I'd made while keeping my distance from the two of them. "Ah, thanks."

"Does that mean I can order clothes too, Sarge?"

I sensed, rather than saw, Dax draw up to his full height. His hands released my chair. I tilted my head back to watch him. He glanced at Burn. "Are your clothes covered in grease from making repairs?"

Burn shook her head.

"Then buy your own damn clothes," he said with a laugh.

"It was worth a try," Burn said. "What's the shopping like?"

I thought back to the times I'd wandered the station with my sister. When my father hadn't been in a hurry. "It's fine, I guess. Pretty utilitarian. You're not going to find much fancy stuff." I gestured toward her high-heeled combat boots. "What you do find will probably be either legit but expensive, or a cheap knockoff."

Burn rubbed her hands together. "Good hunting, then. I can't wait."

"Burn . . ." Dax dragged out her name with exasperation.

"It was one time, Sarge. I've never been late for a shuttle since you left me on Sardo."

While the two of them negotiated, I removed my clothing from the master list. It felt weird—intimate, even —for Dax to purchase my underwear. I subbed in a dozen coveralls in a range of sizes and requested customization with the ship's name on the breast pocket. I figured that was something neither of them would have thought of.

Then again, maybe they were tired of uniforms. Either way, they'd probably be grateful to have them at some point. I finalized the order and sent it. I could show Dax that part later.

"I'll reach out to Finn and find out where he wants to meet us," Burn said. "Can we get dinner on the station?"

Dax nodded. "I could definitely use some time to stretch my legs. Is it better to arrange cargo online or on-station, Lacy?"

"I'd go in-person, since you're a new outfit. Put a face to a name and people will remember you. Once you've established a reputation, either should be fine."

Burn slapped her hands on her thighs. "It's a plan. Let me know when it's time to go." With that, she exited the bridge, leaving me alone with Dax.

I stood too and found myself standing closer to him than I expected. Close enough to feel the heat of his body. "I, um, placed the order. You'll be notified when there's an offer. Once you accept it, you can enter payment details and arrange delivery. You can log in on your comms. You'll want to keep an eye on it when we're on the station and at dinner."

"Thank you," he said. His voice rumbled through me

and his gaze held mine. "You've taken care of issues we didn't even know about."

"You're new at this. You'll get the hang of it."

I didn't want his thanks. I wanted . . . him. My body leaned toward Dax.

His head dipped toward mine. "Lacy," he whispered, his lips brushing over mine as he said my name.

The radio crackled to life. "Welcome to Rigel Naught, *Fortuna*. We see it's your first visit to our fine establishment. Please take some time to acquaint yourself with the rules and regulations."

"Dammit." Dax stepped back.

"You should take care of that," I whispered regretfully. I moved out of his way, so he could resume command of the ship.

Tablet clutched to my chest, I left the bridge to finish my own preparations.

25

———

DAX

Lacy hadn't been exaggerating about the paperwork required to dock at Rigel Naught. After acknowledging the rules and regs of the station, there were questions about our cargo—none—and the length of our stay—unknown. I was able to fill in the crew information at least, grateful that I'd seen Lacy's ID that first night.

I stood and stretched, more than ready to explore the station. The ship's small gym took the edge off my restless energy, but it wasn't enough. And as much as I wanted to ask Lacy to help me burn off the rest, that felt inappropriate. I was used to the massive decks of the battleships I was stationed on. Running the length of them took twenty minutes. I could walk from one end of *Fortuna* to the other in less than two. I hadn't considered the inactivity when we'd made our plan. I didn't think any of us had. Would hauling cargo from one star system to the next be enough? Or would we need something more? Something like helping Lacy locate her sister?

"Hey, Sarge." Burn popped her head into the bridge.

"Finn's got a table at a bar near the docks. Moya's Place. Said it's easy to find, just look for the giant alien head."

"Great. I've got to change. Let Lacy know, would you? Meet me at the main hatch."

"Can't you tell her yourself? You guys were so close before I left you up here all alone."

"She was placing the order for the ship."

"Sure, Sarge. Sure."

She disappeared back down the hall before I could reply. Which was fine, since I had no idea how to respond. There'd been that moment, that barely there kiss. The station's interruption had been a good thing. At least that was what I tried to tell myself. Because I was pretty sure that was a lie.

My comms pinged with a message as I crossed the threshold of the bridge, locking it behind me. I'd learned that from my visit to Elegium Station. Though I couldn't swear that a locked door would stop Lacy. Before we'd picked up Burn, she'd shown me every backdoor into *Fortuna's* systems and I'd changed the passwords. But would that be enough?

The quote from a place called Pop's Deli appeared on screen. I scrolled through it, absently noting the ingredients for Burn's spaghetti and my pizza. I frowned at the cost of Finn's steak—that was robbery!

Several items looked like they could be turned into a spicy garlic noodle dish. I smiled. That had to be Lacy's favorite. The other items looked pretty standard for stocking groceries for a ship.

The number at the end, on the other hand, was big, bigger than I'd expected. If that was only enough food for four people, what would the bill look like when we were feeding six?

I'd check with Lacy before accepting it. She'd have a better sense of what was standard than I would. Right now, that was just something else I needed to learn. When our squad had dreamed this plan up, none of us had considered the logistics.

The others were in for a rude awakening, because I wouldn't be the only one tackling all this paperwork.

"Everyone ready?" I asked several minutes later when we met at the main hatch. I'd stopped by my quarters to change clothes. Burn had obviously done the same, pairing a black tactical shirt with purple cargo pants. The heels on her boots looked lower too. Based on that, and the blaster snugged against her back, she was ready for anything.

My blaster was strapped to my side. "Are weapons allowed?" I asked Lacy suddenly.

She nodded. "Yes, but if you use it on the station, you'll need an extraordinary reason. Rigel Naught takes safety and security very seriously."

"Are you bringing a weapon?" Burn asked her.

Lacy shook her head, her ponytail swaying behind her. "No. I don't have one."

Burn looked concerned. "Where's the armory, Sarge?"

I blinked at the question, the looked at Lacy. "Do we have an armory?"

"Yes and no. The space for the armory has been incorporated into the cargo hold. I can show you where it used to be." She started walking toward the rear of the ship.

"Wait," I called after her. "You can show me, show all of us, after dinner. We've got to meet Finn."

I studied her as she walked back toward us. Her coveralls were clean, but had definitely seen better days. She hadn't worn the clothes I'd lent her since Burn arrived.

I wanted her to mesh with Burn and Finn so that they accepted her as one of the team. I wasn't trying to replace Wilson, no one ever could, but she'd more than earned her passage in the last two days. Parts of the ship I hadn't even known were broken now worked better and smoother.

For an attempted pirate, she was handy to have around.

"Let's roll!" Burn slapped her hand on the palm reader and an unhappy beep sounded. "What the hell?"

I rubbed my hands over my eyes. "We'll need to add you to the reader. Can we do it after dinner, though? I'm starving."

"Fine. But right after dinner. It's *our* ship, remember?"

I pressed my hand against the sensor and didn't look at Lacy. If she'd granted herself access when Burn didn't have it? Big problems.

The hatch opened and station-flavored air rushed in. It was at once stale and flat, but also alive with all the little things that made up a station: ships and exhaust and people and food.

Mostly, it made me appreciate the fresher air on the ship.

"Let's go." I ushered Lacy and Burn out first, then waited while *Fortuna*'s locks reengaged.

Burn took point position. In addition to the blaster, she also had a knife tucked into her boot. I wouldn't be surprised if there were other weapons I didn't know about. Next time I'd put her in charge of reviewing the weapons policies wherever we landed. I crossed my fingers that everything she was carrying was legal on Rigel Naught.

Lacy, on the other hand, was quiet.

"I need to talk to you about one of the quotes." I matched my stride to hers.

"Sure, which one?"

As I relayed the order and the price that they'd quoted me, Lacy nodded. "Yes, that sounds about right."

My jaw dropped. "You're kidding. It feels like robbery!"

She started to speak, then snapped her mouth shut and gestured for me to turn around.

Annoyed, I turned and realized we'd arrived at the customs desk.

"Purpose of your visit?" The bored customs officer on the holoscreen looked straight through me. It was eerie.

"Arrange for cargo pickup." I used my best command tone.

"Name of ship?"

"*Fortuna.*"

"Number of crew?"

I looked at Lacy and shrugged. How was I supposed to answer that?

"Arriving with three," she said, "adding one for departure."

Apparently that was the right answer because it next asked for our IDs.

We held them up to the screen and a blue light washed over them, cataloging the data in the chips.

There was a long pause and I felt more than saw Lacy hold her breath. Then the gate opened and we were on the short walkway to the station.

The closer we got to the main part of the station, the louder and more crowded it became.

"This place is busy," I said, looking this way and that to take it all in.

Next to me, Lacy nodded. "I told you. This is a major trading center. It's a great place to pick up cargo."

"Sarge, I see the bar." Burn was already several feet

ahead of us. She pointed to a neon sign depicting a large alien.

I lifted my chin, indicating that she should go ahead.

She nodded, then wove her way through the crowd.

Stepping close to Lacy so we wouldn't get separated, I placed my hand on the small of her back. Her muscles stiffened beneath my palm. Then she exhaled and they relaxed. I ducked my head so she could hear me. "Is Elegium Station like this?"

I'd spent a few minutes off my ship, but I didn't remember it being this busy.

She turned her head, her lips inches from my ear. "Rarely. Maybe if we get a flotilla or a military ship docked there. This station is easily three times the size of Elegium." Her words fluttered the fine hairs near my ear and a shiver ran through me. "This is one of the station's spokes. If we take the exit on the far end, we'll end up in another corridor and then the heart of the station."

I raised my head and looked for the exit she mentioned. This section of the station appeared to be a large oval and I finally saw what looked like another passage at the far end.

People moved this way and that all around us. Some seemed to have a destination. Others appeared to be taking it in, the same as us.

Neon signs like the one that hung over our destination crowded the walls, advertising everything from lodging and food to supplies and company. I'd been on shore leave often enough that I wasn't usually overwhelmed in situations like this.

But this time was different, I realized. In the past, I'd had my orders—be back on the ship by a certain time or else. Now I was the boss. The orders came from me . . . and I had no idea what they were.

While I'd been gaping, the crowds had moved us farther away from our target. "Burn and Finn are waiting," I said. "We better catch up."

Lacy nodded, but when I stepped in that direction, she didn't move.

"Lacy, c'mon."

She took my hand, lacing our fingers together. Then, with startling grace, she started to move.

Lacy wove us through the crush of people like it was a dance, occasionally muttering "Excuse me" when we cut too close, but we never hit anyone.

Content to let her lead, I kept my elbows tucked in and matched my stride to hers. One minute we were dancing through the crowd, the next I nearly plowed into Lacy when she stopped in front of the bar.

"Sorry," I murmured as she placed a hand on my stomach to stop my forward momentum. My muscles flexed under her touch.

Heat flickered in her eyes.

"Finally," Burn said, interrupting the moment.

Lacy's hand dropped, but her fingers trailed over my abdomen before falling away. She shot me a bright, mischievous smile before she looked away. One of these days, we wouldn't be interrupted. And I wasn't sure my heart would take it.

Burn held the door open and ushered us inside.

It took my eyes a moment to adjust to the dim lighting. The interior of the bar was loud, but compared to the crowd outside, it was bearable. The bar itself was tucked along the back wall. Tables were scattered around the main room.

Some ceiling-mounted screens advertised specials and the on-tap offerings, while others streamed a variety of sports and news channels. The air was thick with the scent of fried food, warm bodies, and spilled beer. The combination should have been revolting, but instead it immediately put me at ease. This could have been any of the bars on any of the stations we spent our leave on.

"I see Finn!" Burn grabbed my hand, dragging me away from Lacy and toward our teammate.

26

———

LACY

Burn dragged Dax toward a table near the back wall. I took a minute to breathe and get my bearings. Competition for spacer cash was fierce. Good food drew them in and good fights kept them coming back. Moya's Place had the best of both on Rigel Naught.

It had been a few years, but I'd been here before with my dad and his crew. I didn't expect anyone to recognize me, especially since my larger-than-life father tended to draw every eye in the room, but my nerves flared to life anyway.

Once my eyes adjusted to the light, I sought out my companions. Dax and Burn had reached their friend. A white guy with blond hair, Finn had a hint of shadow on his jaw, circles under his eyes, and a smirk on his lips. Burn greeted him enthusiastically, but his greeting didn't seem quite as effusive. Dax shook hands with Finn then did that hug–back slap combo that men did. When they separated, Dax turned and searched the crowd for me. He tilted his head, a concerned smile on his face.

I'd intended my smile to be reassuring, but whatever he saw on my face made him frown deeper.

Crap. Might as well get this over with.

I found that same loose-hipped swagger, the one that said I belonged here and that I'd used to cut through the crowds, and made my way across the much smaller space to *Fortuna*'s crew.

Every step felt like I was walking a tightrope. Dax and his comrades were tight and I was obviously the outsider. But being on *Fortuna* and now on Rigel Naught felt right. I'd *missed* this. Missed ship life and adventure and exploring new ports of call. Dax's ship—hell, Dax's presence —felt more like home than Elegium Station ever had.

Finn had staked out a booth near the back of the bar. It was curved, allowing everyone to sit with their back to the wall. Smart.

"Lacy, Finn." Dax made the introductions. "Finn, Lacy."

"Hi, Finn."

"Hey," he said in return.

I offered my hand. He took it, but I got the sense he only did so because it was expected.

We dropped hands after two pumps, almost like we'd choreographed it.

"Have a seat." He gestured toward the booth and indicated all of us.

At first no one moved. Then Burn slid in first. Finn followed, sitting on the outside edge of the booth.

Dax stood silently and I knew he was waiting for me. Hating the thought of being trapped in the middle, I didn't have much of a choice, unless I wanted to cause problems right off the bat.

I slid across the seat toward Burn.

Dax slid in next to me. The press of his outer thigh

against mine was a warm, welcome weight, but it didn't counter the feeling of being trapped.

"We're getting the team back together!" Burn's exclamation was loud enough that nearby tables looked at us.

"She's not part of the team," Finn grumbled.

Burn slapped his arm. "She's temporary crew. Dax said he picked her up on Elegium Station, but I'm still not sure if they're sleeping together or not."

My jaw dropped and I tried to melt into the shadows.

"Burn," Dax said.

"Sorry, Sarge," Burn said, though she didn't sound sorry at all.

He just sighed and shook his head. "Burn's right, though. She's crew for now. A combination of mechanic and consultant."

Finn didn't look like he was buying it. "I'm supposed to be the mechanic."

His declaration dropped into dead air, as a waitress approached and conversation stopped. "What can I get you folks?"

While everyone else ordered, I studied Finn. While mechanics came in all shapes and sizes, he looked more like a down-on-his-luck spacer than any mechanic I'd ever met. And I'd met a lot of them.

When the waitress looked at me expectantly, I ordered a cider—something crisp and clean, that I'd drink slowly—and fries. "What?" I asked, when everyone stared at me. "They have good fries."

"You've been here before?" Suspicion dripped from Finn's question.

"A few times with my old crew."

That drew the waitress's attention and she studied me closer. Dammit. There was no spark of recognition on her face and that eased some of my tension, but not all. She could just be a damn good card player.

After she left us to get our drinks, the conversation started again.

"You hear anything about cargo?" Dax asked Finn.

"I've got a few leads," he said. "Not sure which is the best."

"What are they?" I asked when no one made a move to fill the silence.

Finn glared at me then looked at Dax.

"Go ahead." Dax answered Finn's silent question. "She's got more experience with cargo than the rest of us combined."

Finn's lips pursed. He didn't like it, but he followed Dax's order. "Someone's got a shipment of pukka berries to be delivered a few planets—"

"No." I started shaking my head the moment he said "pukka." "Absolutely not."

He glared at me for interrupting. "You may have the knowledge, but you're not the boss."

What an asshole. "Do you even know what a pukka berry is?"

He shook his head.

I looked at Dax and Burn. They were just as clueless.

"They're small delicate berries that have a window of three days when they're perfect to eat. Before that, they're hard as a rock—"

"Who cares?" Finn interrupted.

I pretended he hadn't spoken. "Outside that window, they start fermenting and let off a gas that smells like rotten eggs had offspring with a corpse." I paused and made a face. I'd only smelled it once, from a distance, and that had been enough. Elegium Station had charged hazard pay if a ship reeking of pukka berries needed service. "Once that gas gets into your ship's vents, you practically have to vent the entire ship to space. And that only works 80 percent of the time."

"You're lying," he said.

I shrugged. "Look it up yourself."

The waitress returned with our drinks, while Finn pulled his comms out of his breast pocket. "Pukka berries," he said to the AI interface.

I sipped my cider as he scrolled through the results.

Burn moved closer and read over his shoulder.

I'm not sure how many results it took to convince them, but finally Burn said, "Damn, she's telling the truth."

"If we can't haul pukka berries, what kind of cargo should we take?" Even if his tone hadn't carried his belligerence, his body language did. Arms crossed over his chest, he glared at me.

I sighed on the inside. His type were always a pain in the ass. Especially when they didn't know something.

"Saber fish. They're—"

Finn interrupted me again. "You say no to berries but want us to take on fish?" He sneered. "Talk about stinky cargo."

I took a deep breath. Keeping my cool with Finn was gonna be hard.

"They're not fish at all. They're actually spools of highly specialized wire. Not many industries use it."

This time even Dax stared at me. "Seriously?"

"Yeah." I nodded. Inside I was trying not to laugh. Or cry. Dax and his crew seriously had no clue what they were doing when it came to cargo. What had he planned to pick up on Elegium Station? At this point, I was starting to think I'd saved them a lot of trouble by stealing the ship.

"Saber fish are easy cargo, but there just aren't that

many places you can offload them. We're pretty close to Raddech, which tends to have a high demand."

I paused to take a sip of my cider and study them. No one looked that interested in the saber fish. I didn't blame them, but they'd soon learn that not all cargo was created equally. And some days, they'll be thankful for any cargo at all.

Time for the big guns. "Big payoffs require big risks. Is that what you're looking for?"

"Now we're talking," Finn said.

Dax and Burn were slower to respond, but she finally said yes. Dax nodded.

"Stupid shooters are probably the biggest bang for your buck here on Rigel Naught."

"Well, why didn't you lead with that one?" Finn asked belligerently.

"Stupid shooters?" Dax asked at the same time.

"Because these literally are the biggest bang. The payout is big because stupid shooters are fucking dangerous." I left it at that, curious what they would ask next.

Burn was the first to break the silence. "What are they then? Bombs?"

I nodded. "Basically." I shared a little more information. "Stupid shooters are filled with a specific particle that is attracted to the atmosphere. In 99 percent of space, the particles are completely inert. But once you hit Harrier's atmosphere, or another planet like it, that changes. Stupid shooters will rip through the walls of ships to get to the atmosphere."

They all stared at me in silence.

"Why the hell would we risk our ship for that? Why would they want them? How the fuck do you transport them?"

There was no way to give them the master class in hauling cargo that they needed, but Dax's questions were a good start. "They're used for mining the planet. Because of their affinity with the upper atmosphere, the miners bury the stupid shooters in the earth. They break through the rock as they try to reach the upper atmosphere."

"That's . . . crazy," Burn said. "How do they get them to the planet?"

"Very carefully. There are special boxes designed for stupid shooters. As well as special delivery routes. It's a very specialized, very dangerous cargo route."

"You're serious?" Burn asked.

I nodded. "This isn't cargo to joke about."

"How do you know so much about it?" Finn asked.

"I grew up on cargo ships. I learned this at my father's side."

Finn was staring at me in dislike again. "Why aren't you running cargo then?"

"Because I'm a mechanic."

The waitress arrived with our food, providing a break in the tension. I bit into a fry, then added ketchup to the side of the pile while I waited for their decision. I was 90 percent sure that they'd decide on the stupid shooters. Personally, I thought they should do those and the saber fish. We could fit both in the cargo hold—and empty space didn't pay for itself.

If they did go for the dangerous job, I knew people here on Rigel Naught who knew people. New crews weren't usually tapped to carry something this dangerous, but I was pretty sure I could get them the job. The question was, how much would I have to reveal to Dax and his crew to make it happen.

No one spoke, but I was absolutely sure that a

conversation was happening between the three of them based on the long looks and facial expressions.

"Assuming we want to take on the stupid shooters, what do we have to do?"

"The first step is easy—we make contact with the client. Then we need to convince them that we're qualified to take the job."

"'We'?" Finn said with a sneer.

"Do you know anyone else with connections here?" Shit. That came out harsher than I intended.

"Both of you behave." Dax used his I'm-in-command voice.

I probably shouldn't have found that as hot as I did.

Fine. I would play nice. Hands raised in an I'm-not-starting-anything position, I turned to Finn. "You got a current map?"

"Of the station?"

"Yeah." I kept my tone carefully neutral.

He pulled out his comms and projected a map of the station onto the table.

I slid my fingers over the projected screen and turned the city this way and that. It had been years since I'd been here, but it didn't look like all that much had changed.

I turned the station back to its original orientation and zoomed in. "This is where we are." My finger jabbed into a cluster of dots that represented buildings. I pointed to another section several inches away. "This is where we docked."

"Duh," Finn said.

Ignoring him, I pinched my fingers together and spun the map a quarter turn. "Pukka berries are here."

Another quarter turn spin. "Saber fish are here."

Another spin, whirling the station upside down. "And stupid shooters are here."

That deep into the station, the map was fuzzy and less substantial.

"Bullshit," Finn said. "There's nothing there." He turned to Dax. "Why are you listening to her, Sarge? She's got nothing."

I raised my eyes from the map to him and kept my voice cool. "Have you been down there?"

He smirked. "No. No point. There's nothing there." He spoke slowly, like I was a child . . . or an idiot.

"Finn—" Dax started but I shook my head, cutting him off. There was only one way to deal with this.

Our waitress was at a nearby table, so I flagged her down when she left them. With an easy smile, I asked, "Is Bolton still working out of Sub3?"

Her eyes widened and her skin paled. "I don't . . ." She broke off and swallowed. "I don't know anything about that. Let me get my manager."

She bolted from our table.

"What the fuck was that?" Burn asked. "Who is Bolton?"

I studied Dax and his crew before responding. Burn looked intrigued, Finn was pissed—at this point, I was pretty sure that was his whole personality—and Dax was obviously weighing everything he heard.

"Sublevel 3 is where the stupid shooters are, as well as a whole array of other dangerous and unsavory shit. They keep the explosives as far away from the main station as possible."

"Bullshit," Finn repeated.

I shrugged and ate another fry, though I was only half as nonchalant as I projected. It was possible things had changed since I was last here, but I didn't think so. If a huge shakeup in the shadier side of Rigel Naught had occurred, trickles of information would have reached Elegium Station.

A shadow fell across the table and I camouflaged my smirk by sipping my drink.

A redhead stood next to Dax. At least two decades older than me, her pale skin glowed in the bar's dim light and her body radiated displeasure. Moya of Moya's Place. "You upset my waitress."

"It was her fault." Finn was quick to point at me. "She's trying to feed us some bullshit story about some big explosives and spooky sublevels to scare us into doing things her way."

What an asshole. I'd roll my eyes, but I didn't want to piss Moya off when I needed her help.

Moya turned her disapproving gaze on him. "Bolton isn't a story."

Her gaze swept slowly over our entire table. Burn's hand dropped below the table. I wanted to wave her off, but I wasn't sure she'd listen to me. Next to me, Dax tensed.

Then I was the one pinned under her gaze. She studied me for a long moment. Did she know who I was? "Y'all don't look like folks who have business with Bolton."

"We—"

She cut Finn off with a slash of her hand. Damn, the number of times I'd wanted to do that and I'd just met him.

"We need cargo," I said.

Her finely arched brow raised. "There's plenty of cargo on the station. Have you considered pukka berries?"

My lips curved into a half-smile until I caught it and smoothed it out. "Looking for a something a little richer."

She didn't say anything. Just waited for one of us—me —to fill the silence.

I relented because I wasn't sure how much patience my companions had. "Stupid shooters."

The words hung in the air. Then she laughed. A deep, rich belly laugh.

"Oh, you're precious."

Both Burn and Dax tensed beside me. I just prayed Finn didn't do something stupid.

"Assuming you can even get a meeting with Bolton, what makes you think you're qualified to run stupid shooters?"

The tension around the table ratcheted up and I knew things were about to go to hell. And Finn would be the reason.

Best-case scenario: we'd get kicked off planet and lose our cargo . . . and my chance to go after Layla. Worst case? We died in a bar fight.

"I've done it before." I focused on Moya and ignored the other three. Their stares were a weight on my shoulders.

"Sure, sugar," she drawled. "Who'd let a pretty young thing like you run dangerous cargo like that?"

I knew she was baiting me. I still didn't know if she'd recognized me. *Fuck.* I didn't see any other way out.

I took a deep breath and blew my current situation up. "Orpheus Blazer."

27

LACY

Moya gave me a barely there nod. Yeah, she'd figured out who I was. Blazer didn't talk much about his daughters and those who knew kept their mouths shut. I had to trust she'd keep doing so.

But I didn't have time to dwell on that now. Now, I had to deal with the fallout of my announcement.

Finn reacted the most predictably. He practically tripped over himself in his hurry to get away from the table and accuse me. "You work for Blazer? Did you know about this?" he demanded of Dax.

I cringed at his volume. The last thing we needed was to draw more attention.

Burn was quick to slide away from me. That she didn't jump out to follow Finn was a win. Maybe.

But it was Dax's reaction that I was most interested in. I held very still, waiting for it.

He shifted in his seat but didn't rush to get away from me. He turned to study me.

"Are you working for Blazer?"

My stomach did a nervous little flip. He was asking, not accusing.

"No. I haven't in years." I shook my head vehemently.

"Are you working for anyone else?" His gaze never left mine.

"Just you." The words slipped out.

No surprise, Finn erupted again. "No fucking way she's working for us."

Support came from a surprising source: Burn. "She's been doing some repairs around the ship. Earning her keep."

He sneered. "Jesus, you must be a lousy lay if you can't even earn your keep in Sarge's bed."

"Stand down, Dancy."

I'd never heard Dax sound so cold. Not even when he'd discovered I'd stolen his ship. This was the ice-cold marine he'd been. I'd been damn lucky that the kinder, gentler Dax discovered me on his ship.

"She's the one fucking everything up!" Finn pointed at me.

Every eye in the bar was on our table. I wanted to sink into the shadows, but that would be a retreat and I refused to give Finn the satisfaction. He'd think I was afraid of him and his accusations.

Yeah. Like that would ever happen.

I didn't know how Dax would react to Finn's refusal to obey his orders. As much as I'd like to see Finn get his ass kicked, nothing else good ever came out of a bar fight.

Moya took that decision out of Dax's hands. "Sit your ass down and shut up or get the fuck out of my bar."

Finn, the idiot, glared at her and crossed his arms over his chest.

Fuck. This was not going to end well.

With a flick of her fingers over her shoulder, the owner summoned two burly security guys. "Take out this trash."

They each wrapped a big fist around Finn's upper arms and picked him up.

Finn struggled, but the bouncers held firm. He might have been part of the space corps, but at the moment, drunk and pissed off, he was no match for the two men. With coordinated moves that spoke of lots of practice, they pivoted and carried Finn to the door. His feet didn't even touch the ground.

"Fuck!" Burn slid out of the booth to follow him. "I'll stay with Finn." She glared at me. "You two finish up whatever the fuck we're doing."

Moya was watching me, so I swallowed my response.

"You planning to carry stupid shooters on the same ship as that one?" Her tone indicated that we were the stupid ones.

"He'll calm down," Dax said. The "or else" was unspoken.

With the booth open now, I tried to put some distance between Dax and me, but he wasn't having it. His hand clamped down on my thigh. Okay. Guess I wasn't going anywhere.

What would my dad say in this situation? "We need fast, high-value cargo."

Moya looked between us. "Who's running this show? You or him?" She directed her question at me.

"He's the captain." I jerked my head toward Dax.

She glanced at him, then back at me. "Un-huh."

"She's the cargo master," Dax gritted out.

"I am?" Dax squeezed my thigh. "I mean, I am."

"Lord save me from amateurs," Moya muttered.

I opened my mouth to argue, then snapped it shut. She

wasn't wrong. We *were* amateurs. I'd never done this on my own and Dax hadn't done it at all.

"The only reason I'm giving you this information is because of your Blazer connection. I take no responsibility for anything that happens as a result of this information."

"How do we know it's not a trap?"

Moya ignored Dax's interruption and kept her focus on me.

"It's not a trap," I reassured him when she paused to let me do so. "That would be bad for business."

Dax mumbled something that sounded an awful lot like "fucking smugglers," but Moya and I both chose to ignore him.

"If you get blown up, I'm not responsible. If you anger the men you'll be working with, not my responsibility."

She continued to list her non-responsibilities. None of them were a surprise, but listening to her rattle them all off was boring. Finally, she came to the most important piece of information. "Fifteen hundred credits. Upfront."

"For what?" Dax asked.

I winced. I hadn't expected negotiations to start quite like this, so I hadn't warned him beforehand. Nothing was free on Rigel Naught, not even information.

"For the location I'm about to provide."

"Why the fuck didn't you lead with that? Then you wouldn't have wasted all that time keeping your hands clean."

Fuck, this could get messy, fast. I placed my hand on Dax's thigh, not gripping it the way he had mine. Just a gentle, soothing touch. His quad tensed and flexed under my palm. "That's how it works, Dax."

"It's bullshit."

"Yep, it is." I flashed Moya a placating smile. She rolled her eyes and shook her head, but let me continue. "Bullshit is everywhere. I bet you dealt with your share before this, right?"

"That's why I got out."

I shrugged. "Welcome to life."

Well, shit. That sounded just like my father. Except he usually added "baby girl" to that pearl of wisdom. It was annoying as fuck.

I took a deep breath and completely overstepped my bounds as cargo master. "Information now, 3 percent later?"

Moya's light laugh was out of place in a spacer bar. "Talk about bullshit," she said. "Twenty percent. Stupid shooters are dangerous business. You walk out of here without paying me, I may not see you again." She pressed the fingertips on one hand together, then forced them open, mimicking an explosion.

I shuddered at the thought.

Releasing Dax's leg, I leaned back against the booth, keeping my muscles loose and relaxed despite the tension riding me. "Pfft. That's too high and you know it. Five percent and we'll throw in Finn as collateral."

"The one I just had escorted from the bar?" She shuddered delicately. "No thanks. I'm happy to take the captain off your hands, though, if you're looking to abandon crew."

My teeth ground together. The thought of bargaining Dax away bothered me a lot more than getting rid of Finn had. "No deal."

She smirked at me.

"I think we're done here." Dax released my leg and stood.

What the hell was Dax doing? This was the best place on the station to get hooked up with cargo. But he was the captain, so I had to back his play. I slid to the other end of the bench and stood as well.

"Oh, sit down." Moya waved her hand at us. Humor and exasperation threaded through her voice.

Dax looked down at her a moment then took his seat.

I followed suit but perched on the edge of the bench. Trying to look relaxed while remaining ready to move was a difficult balance.

"I recognize cash strapped when I see it," Moya said.

Jaw clenched, the tendons in his neck tense, Dax said nothing.

What had given it away?

She probably had people all over the dock, but from the outside *Fortuna*, as new as she was, wouldn't look like cash was a problem. Had Finn been running his mouth?

"Ten percent and a future favor," she said finally.

I sucked in a breath. Owing favors wasn't an unusual payment option on the more distant planets and space stations, but it was a dangerous one. Agreeing to this was above my paygrade.

Dax considered her offer for what felt like forever. "Eight. No violence. No drugs."

Her lips curved up in a slight smile. "Done."

"Give me your comms," she said, holding her hand out.

I guess we were really doing this. It would be a waste of time to argue. Dax placed his communicator in her outstretched palm. She touched it to hers, transferring the information we needed for our meeting. A tiny chime confirmed the data transmission.

"Bolton will meet you in two hours on Sub3 to arrange for the cargo transfer. I highly recommend you do not bring your excitable friend to that meeting with you. He's been making a name for himself in the betting halls on the station—and not in a good way."

"Understood."

Dax's curt response gave no indication of what he thought about Moya's tidbit of information. But she wasn't wrong about Finn being a potential problem. I could only hope that Dax could either rein him in or recognize the need to cut him loose.

She handed Dax his comms, but kept her gaze on me. "Are you sure about this?" she asked quietly.

"I am," I said with more confidence than I actually felt. It brought me one step closer to finding my sister.

"Good luck, then," she said. She leaned closer, her voice dropping low, husky. "If you see Blazer, tell him to come see me. It's been a while."

My eyes widened when her meaning hit me. I knew my father hadn't been a monk since my mom died, but ohmygod, I did *not* need to know that. "I'll do that," I managed to croak.

I scrambled out of the booth. "I need to pick up some clothes before we meet Bolton," I told Dax. Clothes and brain bleach.

28

———

LACY

"C'MON, LAYLA, PICK UP!" I stood in a shadowed corner in Rigel Naught's central spoke. In one hand I gripped one of the new comms devices I'd picked up at one of the stalls after I'd left Moya's Place. I'd bought two, so I had a backup, just in case. The second device was tucked in a drawer back on the ship.

I barely resisted the urge to hit something when the system urged me to leave a message. Not that I had actually expected Layla to answer. I'd spent the length of my shower rehearsing what I would say.

"Hey, sis. Got your message. Waiting on some cargo right now, but thinking we'll have time to catch up soon. Call me when you get a chance. Miss you."

I hung up and my head dropped to my chest. Defeat and worry were a toxic mess in my stomach and in my heart. I had no idea what was happening to my sister. Ever since we'd plotted a course to Rigel Naught, I'd clung to the foolish hope that Layla would have access to her phone.

I sighed.

Okay, Lacy, what next?

I stared at the burner comms in my hand. There was one other number I knew by heart. But calling my dad was like . . . well, it was like bringing out the nuclear option.

Orpheus Blazer was an amiable scoundrel. A charming rogue. Until you messed with his family. If I called my dad about Layla's disappearance, my sister and I would never be let off his ship again. As for whoever had taken my sister . . . It wouldn't end well for them.

My father's love was a weapon to be wielded very, *very* carefully.

Not yet willing to choose the most drastic option, I shoved the device into the pocket of my new pants. After leaving the bar, I'd indulged in a little retail therapy. Every piece of clothing on my body was new and I loved it.

Between the new clothes and the long, hot shower I'd indulged in back on *Fortuna*, I felt like a new woman. Despite regularly laundering them, after a week in my Elegium Station coveralls, I'd seriously considered jettisoning them out the airlock. Instead, I'd tossed them in the clothes cleaner for another round. If nothing else, I'd use them for the really grimy work in the engine room.

Hands stuffed in my pockets, I studied the ebb and flow of people. Dax and I were due to meet in a few minutes. While I'd showered, he'd faced off with Burn and Finn. Poor bastard.

Both crew members had wanted to accompany us to the meeting. I didn't know for sure that Dax had told Finn that he was explicitly not welcome, but a slamming door in the crew quarters while I was changing had pointed to yes.

Claiming errands, I'd slipped out of the ship early to make my call. Now I had a few minutes to kill before Dax and I were to meet. Lingering in the shadows, I watched people move through the center spoke. Some stopped and looked around, while others knew where they were going and moved with purpose.

Dax was one of the latter.

He strode through the crowd like a man on a mission. I smiled slightly. Even in civilian clothes, there was no denying his military training.

I let him reach the bar ahead of me, while I scanned the crowd for anyone who looked too interested in him. When I was satisfied that he didn't have a tail, I slipped out of the shadows and glided to his side.

"Got the map?" I asked.

Dax didn't show any surprise at my sudden presence so I guess I hadn't snuck up on him.

"Yep. It was in the data packet Moya transferred over." He wiggled his comms. "Any reason why you're lurking in dark corners?"

I shrugged. "I had a few extra minutes."

His gaze skimmed over my body like a caress. "I see you found some new clothes."

I smiled up at him. "Yes. Finally." My pants were black with a lot of pockets, similar to the ones worn by Dax and Burn. My top was a sleek hooded shirt in a dark blue. I currently had the hood up, covering my clean and freshly braided hair. I wasn't hiding per se, but discretion wasn't a bad choice. And I wasn't alone—plenty of the crowd around us wore cloaks, hoods, or hats. "I was tempted to burn my old coveralls."

His snort made me laugh. "Why didn't you?"

I shrugged. "There's still some life left in them. They'll be perfect for the really dirty jobs, like deep cleaning the engines." Realizing that sounded like I would be there long term—which really I wouldn't mind—I quickly added, "Not that I don't appreciate the loan of yours."

Dax dipped his head closer. "I liked seeing you in my sweats," he said.

Goosebumps flared to life all over my body and my cheeks warmed. What was I supposed to say to that?

"Me too," I admitted quietly.

The air between us pulsed with unspoken longing.

Fuck. The timing of this conversation couldn't be worse. Why couldn't he have said *those* words in *that* tone when we were alone on the ship? My cabin, his cabin. There had been plenty of space to explore this attraction.

"We should go if we want to make the meeting with Bolton in time." Before I did something stupid like drag him back into that dark corner with me.

His lips quirked up in a roguish smile that tested my resolve. "If you say so."

I swallowed hard. "I say so."

He pulled the map up on his comms. "Looks like we go that way." He pointed toward one of the spokes.

"Great!" I reached for his comms unit, but he held tight and shook his head.

"Follow me."

He took off through the crowd.

I hurried to catch up, grabbing his hand to stay close.

His fingers laced with mine.

I stumbled, momentarily overcome by the simple nature of the move. *Don't be an idiot, Lacy.*

Dax paused, his dark eyes concerned. "You okay?"

I nodded vigorously. "Yep, fine. Totally fine."

He squeezed my hand and then we were off to meet Bolton.

29

DAX

THIS HAD BEEN A MISTAKE. It wasn't the first time I'd had that thought as we approached this meeting. Wouldn't be the last.

After descending three levels to Sub3, we'd passed through an underground market and into a rowdy bar. None of this had been on Finn's map. There was no way we would have found our way through the twisty corridors without Moya's directions. If this turned into actual cargo, and I still wasn't sure it would, the bar owner would have earned her percentage. And her favor.

I stared at the three men—probably pirates—who awaited us at the designated meeting spot, a game room at the back of the bar. A fourth man had ushered us into the room, then closed the thick metal door behind us, cutting off the noise from the main bar area. The hum of the lights was the only sound as we studied each other.

If only I'd been able to bring Burn and Finn. We wouldn't be outnumbered. But Moya's instructions had been clear. And I couldn't afford to lose another cargo.

The man in the middle—the one I assumed was Bolton

—was maybe six foot and slender. I didn't for a moment confuse slender with weak. Wiry guys could be deceptively strong. He wore his hair in a bun and a smirk on his lips that made me want to punch him in the face.

The two men on either side of him could have been from Mercenaries-R-Us. Slightly taller than the middle man, slightly wider. The only difference between them was a scar that ran across one man's right cheek. Their aggressive postures made me want to roll my eyes. It was possible to be a threat without needing to be so obvious about it.

Busy sizing up our opponents and wishing I had a weapon, I didn't notice Lacy pull out a chair at the game table until it was too late.

"Good evening, gentlemen," Lacy said as she pushed her hood back and took a seat at the table. "I'm Lacy. This is Dax. Moya said you could help us with a shipment of stupid shooters."

"Bolton." The man in the middle confirmed my guess. He took a seat opposite Lacy. The other two stood at his shoulders, watching me with what I was sure were supposed to be intimidating glances.

Whatever. I took a position behind Lacy. Expression neutral, I crossed my arms over my chest. I had her back and would do whatever it took to keep her safe. Walking hand in hand through the tunnels with her had tugged at something fiercely protective down deep.

"After my conversation with Moya, I asked around about your ship—the *Fortuna*, isn't it?" There was that smirk again. "No one has worked with you. In fact, no one on Rigel Naught has ever heard of you. So why would you be looking for such dangerous cargo? This isn't a kiddie toy."

The downside of my position was that I couldn't read

Lacy's expression. On our way to Sub3, she'd asked me to let her do all the talking. Which was fine, except . . . what if there was a time she needed me to speak up? I'd have to trust that she knew what she was doing.

The realization that I did was like a kick to the chest. It couldn't have come at a worse—or maybe it was better—time. I trusted her to do right by the ship. By me and my crew.

"You're right," Lacy said in that smooth, confident way of hers. "*Fortuna* is new to running cargo. However, she has a capable crew, including someone who has hauled stupid shooters in the past as well as even more dangerous cargo."

When she paused, Bolton's eyes flicked up to me. I shook my head.

"Me," she said. If it bothered her that the men had assumed it was me, nothing in her tone gave it away.

Bolton and his men laughed. "You can't expect me to believe that a pretty little thing like you would be dealing with such big, dangerous bombs. Where would you learn something like that?"

"*Eternal Nocturne,*" Lacy said quietly.

Their laughter died the moment she named Orpheus Blazer's ship.

"No shit," Bolton said after a long pause. His gaze turned speculative. The same way Moya's had.

What was I missing?

"Now that you know my credentials, what do you say?" Lacy kept the conversation on business.

"Not so fast," he said. "Maybe I should do some due diligence. Reach out to Blazer and verify your claim."

Lacy's back stiffened. "Be my guest," she said coolly. She pulled out her comms device and slid it across the table. "You can even use mine. Need the code?"

Damn, she was impressive.

"No, no need." Bolton's gaze flickered from her to me again.

I kept my face impassive. I still hated that she had been part of Blazer's crew. Orpheus Blazer had made his name as a smuggler decades ago. Rumor had it, he worked for whoever could afford him. He wasn't number one on the space corps' most wanted list, but he was in the top ten on any given day.

Interestingly, none of the crimes he was wanted for were violent ones. I'd always assumed that was because someone was covering up for him. Now that I knew Lacy had crewed for him, I couldn't help but wonder if it was the truth.

Seemed unlikely. No one had such a long career, had so many people willing to protect him, by charm alone.

But the legend of Orpheus Blazer wasn't why we were here today. Valuable cargo was, so I tuned back in to the negotiations.

"What's your cargo max?"

Lacy launched into *Fortuna's* specs. I understood most of the stats, but I wouldn't have been able to rattle the numbers off like that.

I stifled a sigh. Another thing to learn. Maybe I could convince Lacy to become our cargo master if Finn took on the role of mechanic.

Even as that thought took hold, I realized it was unlikely. Lacy was in her element in the engine room. Finn had been the one to keep our gear working on missions, but would he be able to keep a ship the size of *Fortuna* running? The biggest projects I'd ever seen him work on were repairing vehicles when we were on missions, cobbling together fixes so we weren't stranded planetside.

"Do we have a deal?" Bolton asked.

"We have a deal." Lacy extended her hand.

Bolton shook it, then they touched their comms devices together. "That's the contract," he said. "Funding will be released upon delivery. *Successful* delivery."

"Got it." Lacy scrolled through something on her comms. "Looks in order. We'll see your team for loading tomorrow morning."

She stood from the table. "We have a few other arrangements to make. Pleasure doing business with you." She nodded to each man then left the room without a backward glance.

I backed out of the room, keeping my eye on Bolton and his crew, still not sure they were trustworthy.

"You're damned lucky to have her on your ship," Bolton said before I reached the corridor. "We wouldn't be doing business with you without her."

I nodded to show I understood, then met Lacy in the hall. The door closed behind us.

Ducking my head low, I leaned close and asked, "Back to the ship?"

"Yes."

I placed my hand on the small of her back and escorted her through the crowd.

30

———

DAX

WITH TWO MORE CREW ON board, we'd been able to implement round-the-clock watches. I didn't expect trouble, but handling it would be a whole lot easier if at least one person was running on a good night—or day's—sleep. Once we had a full crew, we'd reevaluate and reassign.

I grabbed a cup of coffee and what looked like fresh pastries from the mess hall and made my way to the bridge.

"Morning," I said as I entered.

Burn turned around and flashed me a smile, then turned back toward the monitors. Her shift was just ending. "Morning."

Curious what held her attention, I glanced out the windshield, then looked at the monitors. A handful of men and a number of loaders waited outside the cargo hold. "That the cargo?"

"Yep. It arrived a couple of minutes ago."

"You're not dealing with it?"

Burn spun around in her seat. "Me?" She shook her

head. "They asked for the cargo master. I decided that meant Lacy, so I went to wake her. But she was already up." She gestured at a plate that held a few crumbs. "I think she'd already gone out to get us breakfast too."

I'd wondered where the pastries had come from. "So what's the holdup?"

"Relax, Sarge. There's no holdup. Lacy just took a few of the workers into the cargo hold."

I bit into the flaky pastry while I pondered Burn's words. So far yesterday's realization still held. I trusted Lacy. Trusted her to make the right decision for the ship and the crew. But I also needed to know how this worked. As much as I'd like her as a permanent asset, I should know how to load cargo on my ship.

"You okay to hang out here, while I check things out in the cargo hold?"

"You think there's a problem?"

I shook my head. "Not at all. First cargo load for *Fortuna*. I need to see how this works."

Burn nodded. "We had no fucking clue what we were getting into, did we?"

My laugh was heartfelt. "I'm still not sure we do, Burn."

I shoved the last of the pastry in my mouth and waved at Burn as I turned to leave. Coffee in hand, I made my way to the cargo hold. The closer I got, the more I could hear voices.

Lacy was in the hold with a couple of men. "Mornin'." I lifted my cup in greeting as I joined the trio.

"Good morning." Lacy sent an apologetic look toward the delivery team. "Need something?"

I shook my head. "Just observing."

She sighed. "Fine. Just stay out of the way. This is dangerous cargo."

"Be careful," I said.

Her smile was fleeting. "Thanks," she said. Then I was dismissed as she and the others returned to their conversation.

I stepped back so I was along the wall. Everyone's warning about the cargo rang in my ears as the cargo loaders started entering the hold. Each and every box that was placed in our hold was stamped with multiple warning labels. The delivery crew worked quickly and quietly. There was none of the jovial chatter that I expected.

Its absence made me feel both better and worse. Better, in that these men were professionals who took their job and their safety seriously. Worse, because what the hell had I gotten my ship into?

In the middle of the delivery ballet was Lacy. Her coveralls looked fresher and cleaner than usual. Maybe she'd gotten a new one. It fit her well, highlighting her curves. But they were barely noticeable under the air of authority she wore like she'd been born to it.

She was in charge and every single one of these men knew it. Knew it and respected it.

Watching Lacy work was a lesson in cargo handling. And coming from someone who'd *been* cargo, it was damn impressive.

And it raised a lot of questions.

"That's everything, boss."

She rewarded the speaker with a big smile. "Thanks. You guys did a great job."

"It's a pleasure to work with a pro. Let us know next time *Fortuna's* in port."

"Will do," she said with a bittersweet smile. Was she thinking about not being with the ship?

Just the thought made me unhappy.

Frowning, I studied the cargo hold while she escorted

the dockworkers off the ship. It was tidily organized. The straps lashing the boxes to the base were anchored through bolts in the flooring.

The stupid shooters took up three quarters of the cargo hold. The warning labels caused me a few heart palpitations, but I reminded myself that Lacy and the dockworkers were pros. The cargo was as safe as it would get. It was up to me to deliver it safely.

No pressure.

Lacy closed the external cargo-hold door. The hold was darker with cargo, with deeper shadows.

"Problem?" Lacy asked as she skirted the stupid shooters and made her way to me. Even the sounds in the hold were different, muted.

"What's all that?" I pointed to a small stack of boxes near the door that led to the rest of the ship.

"Supplies," she said. "*Fortuna* wasn't stocked for a full crew. I picked up shelf-stable supplies that should last you a while and fresh food that will need to be consumed over the next few days. The perishable stuff is already in the mess."

"Sounds like you've thought of everything."

A blush tinged her cheeks and she looked away.

I slipped my finger under her chin and gently lifted until she faced me again. "Thank you. We wouldn't have gotten this far without you. We'll learn, but I appreciate you picking up the slack." I shifted my hand so my palm cupped her cheek. "I couldn't have asked for a better ship thief."

"Borrower," she said with a laugh.

My thumb ran over her cheek and she leaned into it.

The door to the corridor opened and someone stepped heavily into the cargo hold. Lacy stepped away from me. I dropped my hand to my side.

"Everything's locked down," she said, her voice slightly husky. "You want to check it out?"

I shook my head. "I trust you. But while we're in transit, I'd like you to walk me through the process. We'll need to know in the future."

If I had my way, it would be nice to know the process, but we wouldn't *need* to know because we'd have her. Now I just had to convince my crew.

"Anytime," Lacy said.

"Well, I want to check her work." Finn's belligerent tone and combative words came from the shadows.

I'd known he was there. His heavy tread gave him away, but I hadn't expected the vitriol.

"Knock yourself out." Lacy curled her fingers into fists. "The stupid shooters are tied down as required. If you do anything, if you touch them, anything that happens is on you." She pointed at him in emphasis.

He'd stomped toward the cargo, but at her words, he tucked his hands in his pockets. I exhaled the breath I didn't realize I'd been holding.

"C'mon, Finn. Let's go. We've got a departure time soon."

Ignoring me, Finn walked from one end of the stacked boxes to the other and back again. Thankfully he didn't touch anything, but my worry didn't stop until he was back at the door.

"He doesn't do well with change," I told Lacy quietly as I followed Finn to the stairs.

"He doesn't do well with me," she countered.

"You're new," I said.

"Pfft. Make as many excuses as you want. That won't stop him from being an asshole."

"No, he's definitely being an asshole." This wasn't the Finn I knew. The one I trusted to have my back no matter what. If I didn't find out what was going on with him, this trip was going to be a nightmare. I changed the subject. "Are we ready to leave Rigel Naught?"

Lacy stared at me like she was going to say something. Then she nodded and looked away. "Yeah. The cargo is secured. We can stow the supplies while we're underway. You have the delivery coordinates?"

I nodded. "All that's left is to request a departure time."

"Great," she said.

Silence fell heavily between us. Finn's presence—Finn's anger—had effectively killed the ease between us.

"You should go to the bridge. Get the ship ready for takeoff. I want to take one more pass through here and then make sure the engine room is secure." She turned to go.

I caught her hand and she faced me reluctantly. "Are we okay?"

She sighed but didn't look away. "My sister is missing, your crew hates me, and we're surrounded by deadly cargo. We passed okay a long time ago."

I tucked an errant hair behind her ear. "Everything will sort itself out."

"I hope so, Dax. I really do." Lacy tugged her hand free. "You're needed on the bridge, Captain."

"Let me know when the ship is secure." She wanted distance, so I'd give it to her. For now.

31

────

DAX

Burn was still on the bridge when I returned. "Everything good with the cargo?" she asked.

I dropped into the captain's chair. "It's fine. Strapped down solidly. Shouldn't move at all during this trip." Man, I really hoped it didn't.

"You're not worried about this, are you, Sarge?"

Shifting in my seat so I faced her, I said, "In my head, I know that we flew with munitions a thousand times more dangerous than what we have in our cargo hold right now. But now that it's *our* ship, our *small* ship, it's kind of terrifying to have that much explosive power just one level away."

When we'd discussed having our own cargo-hauling business, we'd never actually talked about what the cargo would be. We hadn't discussed a lot of the realities that we now faced.

Burn smiled wryly. "It's probably too late to get out of this contract, isn't it?"

Remembering the stacks of crates strapped in below, I laughed and shook my head. "Yeah, definitely too late."

We couldn't afford to lose another cargo. Our accounts were running low. Food, fuel, and other necessities were expensive, especially out here on the farther reaches of space.

"Even after Moya's cut, our finances should be pretty solid. Enough that everyone could take their share and still have enough in the ship's account to hold us over a few months if we need it."

"How big a cut?" Finn dropped into the chair behind us. Both Burn and I swiveled to face him.

I shrugged. "I haven't done the math. We need to ensure that *Fortuna* has enough in reserve to hold us through any dry times."

"Lacy definitely earned her keep getting us this contact and loading the cargo," Burn said. "She gets a cut, right?"

Burn seemed to be coming around to having Lacy on board. I don't know if she was friendly, but she definitely wasn't as antagonistic as she'd been.

"No! What the hell?" Finn's outburst was unexpected, but par for the course since he'd been on the ship. Whatever was going on with him, that shit needed to stop.

"What the fuck, Finn?" Burn said. "Without her, we wouldn't even have this cargo. She deserves a cut."

"What the hell does this woman have on you? You're both all 'Oh, Lacy should get some of our hard-earned money.' She isn't one of us. She doesn't belong here." Finn's tone was darker than I'd ever heard him use.

Burn placed a calming hand on his arm but he shrugged it off. "I don't know what the fuck is wrong with you, but you need to cut this shit out right now. You've been an asshole since you got on board. Lacy's a perfectly nice woman whose sister is missing. We're going to help her find her. In return she's teaching us a bunch of shit we didn't know when we started this business."

Finn surged to his feet. "What kind of bullshit story is that? She fed you some sob story about a missing sister and now she has free range on the ship? Engineering. Cargo hold. Captain's bed. Has she been in your bed yet too, Burn?" He sneered. "You're a bunch of suckers. She's here for the ship. Probably some mission for Blazer. Hundred percent she's still on his crew. We're probably gonna get boarded and our cargo stolen before we even reach the mining colony."

I stared at Finn in shock. That was quite an imaginative story. Where the hell was all this coming from? "Stand down, marine."

"Fuck you, Sarge. We're not in the corps anymore. You may be captain, but you're not the boss here." He stormed off the bridge, leaving Burn and me staring after him in shock.

Finn was no longer visible, but I still stared at the corridor outside the bridge. I could only hope that he'd gone back to his quarters rather than stomping off the ship. We were on a timeline now and I still had to request a departure slot.

We'd come here for cargo and crew and I didn't want to have to chase after my crew. We stuck together and didn't leave a teammate behind.

I closed my eyes. If we left Finn behind, it would be his own damn fault. But he wouldn't see it that way.

Activating the intercom, I winged it. "This is the captain. We will be departing the station shortly. All crew on board?" It wouldn't be the worst thing to have a protocol for when we had a larger crew.

Lacy responded immediately. "Here."

There was a long pause, then the crackle of static. Finally, Finn's voice came over the system. "Here."

"Great. Burn and I are on the bridge. Everyone stay on

board. We're taking off as soon as we're cleared for departure."

"Copy," Lacy said.

"Sir, yes, sir." Finn being a total asshole.

"You got any idea what's going on with Finn?" I asked Burn once I'd switched off the intercom.

"I haven't seen him this on edge since . . . you know." She paused. "The accident."

The accident that had killed Wilson and injured Finn. He'd been laid up for a few weeks, getting crankier and crankier.

Hell, we'd all been cranky, drowning in our grief.

"That's what I was thinking." I looked over at her. "One of us should corral him and find out what's bugging him."

"Not it," Burn said immediately.

"If I can't talk some sense into him, you're going to have to try."

Her lips curled up in a moue of displeasure. "Fine. But make sure you try really, really hard first, okay?"

"Always. Ready to get out of here?"

"Ready when you are."

Switching to an external channel, I picked up the comms. "Rigel Naught stationmaster, this is *Fortuna* requesting clearance to take off."

32

———

LACY

It took *hours* to get clearance for *Fortuna* to leave Rigel Naught. Hours where I had nothing to do. I'd tried to pop into engineering, make sure everything was stowed properly, but Finn had met me at the door and refused to let me enter. I could have argued, maybe even dragged Dax into it, but tensions were high and Finn already disliked me, so I didn't push it.

When I walked away, his angry muttering followed me down the corridor. I was obviously some Blazer plant and they were all going to regret letting me on board, blah, blah, blah.

I'd left him down in the engine room, though it nearly killed me to do so. Over the last week, I'd come to think of it as my domain. Plus, I was pretty sure he had no idea what he was doing.

Whatever. Not my decision.

Being on the outside looking in with Dax and his crew was lonely. Some moments, like when I'd been loading the cargo, it was easy to fool myself that I was one of the team. But the in-between hours, like waiting for launch with nothing to do, made it clear that I was not part of *Fortuna's* crew.

"Ladies and gentlemen, this is your captain speaking." I chuckled as Dax's voice came over the intercom. "We've exited the atmosphere and have set a course for the mining station Harrier. You are now free to move around the cabin."

Finally!

The past few hours had been torture. I'd paced my room, I'd showered, and I'd rewatched so many of Layla's videos. And I was starving!

I may not be allowed in the engine room and wasn't sure I'd be welcome on the bridge. So I went to the next best place: the mess.

The kitchen was fully stocked now, thanks to the orders I placed on Rigel Naught. I'd purchased enough fresh groceries to feed the four of us for several days, as well as enough dry goods and shelf-stable foods to last several weeks.

Dax had hammered out watch crew schedule for the three of them, but no one had thought about a cooking schedule. Did they even realize that would be something they needed? Based on the number of pre-packed rations we'd eaten on the way to Rigel Naught, I didn't think so.

Technically, it wasn't my problem. Practically, though, my stomach was grumbling and I needed something to do.

Thirty minutes later, the kitchen smelled garlicky and delicious. I dipped my fork into the bowl and dangled a single noodle over my open mouth. Bursts of garlic and chili hit my tastebuds as I chewed. Maybe not quite up to my favorite restaurant, but they were damn good.

Before I could second-guess myself, I put out four place settings, as well as extra chili oil. Then I took a deep breath, steeled myself, and pressed the intercom. "Dinner's ready."

Would anyone even show up?

The thump of boots down the corridor sounded like Burn, so I wasn't surprised when she was the first into the dining room.

"That smells amazing. Did you cook?" She stood by the table and stared down at the bowl of noodles with a hungry look.

"Yeah," I admitted. "We didn't really talk about cooking schedules, but I was hungry. There's enough for everyone."

"Not if they don't get here soon." Burn dropped into one of the chairs and with a quick look at me for permission, served herself. "I *can* cook," she said, "but it's not my favorite thing."

Something that looked like regret flickered over her face. "It's one of the things I miss about the corps. They fed us three squares a day."

My nose wrinkled. "I've tried some of your meal pouches. You ate those three times a day?"

"The meal packs?" Burn grimaced and shook her head vehemently. "Oh no. Not those. Those were for missions only. Or this last week, since Dax didn't buy proper food."

I laughed and took a seat across from her.

"When we were on the ship, we had actual food. Proper meals with a meat, a vegetable, and a dessert. Not those horrible heat-and-eats."

Burn took a bite, smiled, then liberally added chili oil to her bowl.

Maybe I should have bought more. Good thing I'd purchased a variety of hot sauces.

Dax and Finn entered the mess hall at almost the same time, though they came from opposite directions. Dax looked good, excited. Finn looked like the miserable asshole he was.

I sat at the table with my bowl of noodles studying the others as they took their seats and served themselves.

Finn just glared at the bowl. I ignored him and watched Dax from the corner of my eye.

He took a few bites, then added the chili oil, too.

Looks like I should probably up the spice a bit next time.

"Thanks for making dinner, Lacy." He smiled at me.

My answering smile practically cracked my face. "You're welcome."

Twirling the noodles on his fork, he said, "These are really good. Almost as good as the ones you had the night you stole the ship."

My smile faded and I stared at him in shock. *Had he just . . .*

A look of absolute horror crossed his face. That answered *that* question.

The room was silent for a moment, then filled with a chorus of "what the fucks" from Burn and Finn.

I carefully placed my utensils on the table next to my bowl, waiting for the explosion that was sure to come.

"You stole our ship?" Finn practically bellowed.

Someone should teach him about inside voices, I thought randomly. I didn't say anything, just waited to see what Dax would do. He'd created the problem—well, *we'd* created the problem—so I was going to let him take the lead. He knew his crewmates far better than I did.

"Well," Dax said, rubbing his neck. "It's not as bad as it sounds."

"Gosh, that makes it okay, then," Burn said sarcastically.

"What. The. Fuck. Happened?" Finn asked.

I watched Finn carefully, not at all sure that he wouldn't resort to violence. He seemed on that edge all the time.

The silence around the table grew longer. More tense.

Fuck it. I owned my mistakes.

I started at the beginning. "Then after the men broke into my apartment, I ran. I was looking for a safe place and ended up at the docks. I just wanted to hide out for a while, so I boarded *Fortuna*. When I saw the men searching the docks for me, I panicked and launched the ship."

Burn seemed to be mulling over the story, but Finn was sending me a death glare.

"And what? You just let her take off with our ship?"

Pink tinged Dax's cheeks. "I was asleep," he admitted. "We were already off the station when I woke up."

Finn lurched up from the table with a scowl. "I told you she was a fucking Blazer thief, but no one wanted to listen to me."

I had to give it to him. He was 100 percent right, just not the way he thought.

"I want her off the ship. Now."

Burn and Dax looked alarmed. "We're not going to space her, Finn. That's not how we do things," Burn said.

"Then let her off at the next stop. She's got no business being on our ship."

Fuck.

If they dropped me off on the mining colony, it could be weeks or even months until I could get a ride on another ship. I'd never learn what happened to Layla.

Burn turned to me, hurt and betrayal in her gaze. "Was it all a lie? The story about your sister?"

I clenched my fists under the table. Somehow, I had to convince them to keep me on board. The truth was a place to start. "No," I said softly. "That all was true. The only lie was how Dax and I met. We met on the bridge when he came to see why the ship had left Elegium."

"Why didn't you just turn the ship around?" Burn asked Dax.

I winced and answered that too, even though she'd asked him the question. "I'd called in an emergency so that we could get priority takeoff. Because of that, they wouldn't let us back."

"So that's why Dax couldn't pick up cargo on Elegium Station."

"Yes. It was my fault he couldn't make his meeting." I leaned forward, trying to convince her of my sincerity. "That's why I've been working on getting you well-paying cargo runs. To make up for it."

"Bullshit!" Right on cue, Finn was there to cast doubt on my every word. "You're here for Blazer, aren't you? You want to steal our ship, steal the cargo and leave us hanging."

"I don't work for Blazer." I spoke slowly, constantly studying his posture, his movements, so I could be prepared if he attacked me. "I'm not here for your cargo. I just want to find my sister. Dax said you all would help, but you needed cargo too. That's all." I held my open palms out in a placating gesture.

Finn ignored everything I said. "I vote we drop her off with the cargo on Harrier." He turned to Burn.

She sighed. "I don't know, Finn. I see your point. But if she's telling the truth, she's done nothing to harm us since that night."

"She stole our ship! Isn't that enough? How can you believe her?"

"I don't know if I do." Burn's tone was tinged with sadness. "But I'm not making a big decision like this on the spur of the moment." She stood, grabbing her bowl.

"Thank you for dinner, Lacy." Then Burn left the mess hall, her steps subdued.

Left with just Finn and Dax, I sat quietly, aware that my fate was still up in the air.

Finn sneered at Dax. "I suppose you're going to vote to keep her on the ship."

I didn't dare look at Dax. My hands curled into fists again, my nails digging into my palms.

"You're right. I told her we would help her find her sister and I'm sticking with that."

"You're sticking something, all right," Finn said, his expression as cruel as his words.

Dax stood, drawing himself up to his full height. "Stand the fuck down, Finn. I don't know why you're acting this way, but it fucking stops now." Military command coated his words.

Finn flinched, but he didn't back down. "She's getting off the ship at the next stop. Burn will agree with me." His chair hit the floor with a clatter as he stormed off.

The tension in the mess pulsed for several long moments, until Dax sighed. "I'm so fucking sorry, Lacy." He retook his seat, but stared at the empty space where Finn had sat. "I didn't mean for it to slip out like that."

I patted his hand. "Neither did I. But maybe it's better that it's out there." I didn't really believe that, not when I didn't know whether I'd still be on the ship in a few days, but for Dax's sake I pretended.

His hand flipped over and he laced his fingers with mine. "Maybe. I honestly don't know how Burn will decide. And I may be the captain, but they have equal votes when it comes to the ship."

I understood, but I hated it. "Maybe they'll come around." We had three days after all.

"Maybe." He gave my fingers a quick squeeze. "After we finish dinner, I need to confine you to your quarters."

He squeezed my hand a little longer, a little tighter, until I looked at him. "And I need you to stay there. For real. I know you can probably still get out if I lock you in, but Finn will take that as more proof that you're a threat, and I'm not sure what would happen in that situation."

"I'll stay in my room." It would drive me stir crazy, but I'd do it, because Dax was asking.

"Is there anything else I need to know?" he asked. "Anything else that will come back and bite us in the ass?"

I shook my head. "No." I wouldn't—*couldn't*—tell him about my dad now.

33

———

DAX

I finished my noodles and wanted seconds, but it didn't seem like the time since Lacy was just pushing the rest of hers around her bowl since the conversation had blown up. "Thank you for making dinner."

She nodded but didn't look at me.

"Let me get dinner cleaned up and I'll walk you to your room."

Finally meeting my gaze, she reared back. "What, you don't trust me to walk all the way to my quarters by myself?" That was the most reaction I'd gotten out of her since I'd fucked up and mentioned her first night on the ship.

"Don't be ridiculous. Of course I trust you." I covered the big bowl of noodles and placed it in the fridge. "I wanted to spend more time with you before I have to go and face the music."

I was actually surprised that the others hadn't come to chase me out of the mess hall. They'd be itching for an explanation—probably even a fight. All I wanted to do was spend more time with Lacy.

"Let me put that away." I slowly, carefully placed my hand over hers, stopping the endless noodle circles. "You're not going to finish that, are you?"

"No." With a sigh, she released her fork and pushed her bowl away. "Not hungry anymore."

"It'll be in the fridge if you are. You can . . ." I trailed off, remembering that I didn't want her roaming the ship alone right now. "You can let me know and I'll bring it to you."

"Yippee."

I don't know what she saw on my face when I looked at her, but she apologized immediately. "Shit, I'm sorry. I can't believe we just fucked everything up."

"It's my fault. I was the one who said you stole our ship."

Lacy's laugh carried a hint of tears. "I'm the one who stole it, though."

"Then it's both our fault." After I put away her leftovers, I stood by her seat and offered my hand. "I'll do what I can to rectify the situation."

"Sure, whatever." She sighed, placed her hand in mine, and stood.

Hand in hand we walked the short distance to the crew quarters. Her body radiated tension, like she was waiting for another attack. This one physical.

I'd protect her if that happened, but I was pretty sure that both Finn and Burn were waiting for me on the bridge.

When we stopped in front of her door, she looked up at me. "I bet you regret the night I came on board."

"Never." I squeezed her hand and pressed my forehead to hers. "We'll figure it out," I said again. Then I lowered my voice. "I'm leaving your access in place, but please, *please*, stay in your room, unless there's an emergency."

"Okay." Her agreement was a whisper of sound.

"Thank you." I brushed a kiss over her temple then waved my hand over the door lock. Her door whooshed open and, after the briefest hesitation, she stepped through.

"I'll be by soon." I reluctantly released her hand. The door whooshed shut between us. I pressed my palm against it, for just a second. Drawing up to my full height, I straightened my shoulders and braced for a fight.

As expected, Burn and Finn were waiting for me on the bridge.

"You should have told us!" Burn was still pissed.

"I know." I ignored both of them to check our course. The last thing we needed was to screw up on our first delivery. Once I was satisfied everything was as it should be, I turned to face them.

"I understand your anger," I said. "I've been there. Lacy stealing our ship was a problem, a big one. We lost the chance at cargo. But things are turning around. We've got this delivery." I gestured vaguely in the direction we were going.

"If she stole our ship and cost us cargo, why the fuck is she still here?" That was the first non-accusation question Finn had asked.

"She's useful. Lacy has made minor repairs. She's taught me—and Burn—about the ship and about cargo. She has more knowledge about this business than our whole crew combined."

"And you want to fuck her," he muttered.

"Watch it," I warned. No matter how Lacy had come to be on the ship, there were only so many insults I could take. "Yes, I'm attracted to her. No, we haven't slept together." I was so fucking tired of justifying my love life. "Like I told Burn, even if I were, it's none of your goddamned business."

"Attracted to her?" Finn sneered. "She's a fucking honey pot."

Burn gasped at Finn's vile words.

My fists clenched and my shoulders tensed. I wanted so badly to take a swing at Finn. But doing so could fracture our whole team and destroy our business before we even got started.

Gritting my teeth, I counted to ten, then twenty, until I had calmed enough to speak clearly. And to not hit him. "No. More. Lacy is not a honey pot. She is not a plant. She's a talented mechanic and a resourceful woman who got herself out of a troubling situation."

Finn's mouth opened, no doubt to spew more disgusting comments, but Burn spoke before he did. "Have you told us everything?"

"Have a seat."

Burn sat in the navigator's chair. Finn remained standing, his arms crossed over his chest. His expression was dark like a thundercloud. "So you can tell us more lies?"

"So I can bring you up to speed."

No way was I going to be sitting when Finn exuded such threatening vibes. I wanted to be able to move if I needed to.

I quickly recounted everything that had occurred, from the moment I woke up to find Lacy had taken our ship to the scene in the med bay to leaving Rigel Naught. Even the kiss that we'd shared in the engine room.

When I finished, I studied my team. Burn looked troubled. Finn looked just as pissed as he had before.

"Nothing needs to be decided tonight," I told them. "We've got a few days until we reach Harrier."

34

———

LACY

I'D BEEN "LOCKED" in my room for nearly forty-eight hours and I was going stir crazy. I'd practically worn a path back and forth across the small space. I'd tried sit-ups like they did in video montages, but quickly decided that was *not* for me. My sister's videos had played on a near-constant loop, in case I finally caught something I had missed. And none of it was enough to keep my mind off the fact that I was trapped in a room that I technically could get out of but shouldn't because someone had it out for me.

So much for *Fortuna* being my safe place.

There was a knock on my door. I sighed. Probably Dax or Burn bringing me another heat-and-eat. Better them, because I wouldn't trust anything that Finn brought me.

But the heat-and-eats pissed me off too. I'd purchased a lot of nice, fresh supplies and apparently no one on this crew could cook. Or they weren't feeding the prisoner the good stuff.

"Assholes," I muttered. I paused Layla's video and then crossed to the comms system by the door. "Yes?" At least they didn't just barge in.

The door slid open, revealing Burn. Empty-handed Burn. Apparently it wasn't feeding time at the zoo.

"Can I come in?"

"Sure." I stepped back and gestured broadly. Not like I had a choice, right?

She stepped inside, then waited until the door had closed completely before moving again. Like always, she wore cargo pants with a long-sleeve top and boots. Her hair was up in those little knots again. Her shoulders radiated tension. And her expression, with pinched lips and tired eyes, said she was either mad or didn't want to be here.

Probably both.

"So what brings you by?" I asked in a perky voice as I sat on the edge of the bed. That left her with the desk chair.

She didn't say anything as she sat down, though she swiveled to study the screen. "That's your sister?"

"Yep, that's Layla."

"And she's missing?" Burn looked directly at me, her gaze never leaving my face. Like she was weighing the truth of my statement.

"Yes, I believe so." Was she waiting for me to tell her the whole story? "I can walk you through it if you like."

She shook her head. "Dax filled us in."

I nodded, unsure what else to say then. Why had she come?

"You and Layla, you're close?" She leaned forward, her forearms resting on her knees, and studied me.

I sighed and crossed my arms over my chest as I pondered my answer. "Yes and no. We're only a year apart, so we grew up together. Obviously. And played together. Got in trouble together. But we have our own interests too. Mine was engineering. Hers was archaeology. We talk every few weeks, but I haven't seen her in a couple of years." My heart squeezed. I should have made time to see her more often. "Do you have any sisters?"

Burn swallowed. "Yes, one."

"So you know what it's like." I missed Layla. But we could also drive each other crazy.

Something dark and painful flashed in her eyes before her expression smoothed out. "We're not close," she said.

There was obviously a story there. "Where did you grow up?"

"Some backwater planet you've never heard of." Her tone shut down any further questions. "Why this ship? Why *our* ship?"

We were having a moment and I knew how easily those could shatter. I chose the bald truth. "I was scared and it reminded me of a ship I used to have. *Mako.* She was the same class as *Fortuna.* I thought I would be safe here."

"Why didn't you hide on your ship?"

I smiled ruefully. "I left her at home with my dad. Didn't think I would need her while I was working on the asteroid station." A soft laugh escaped. "I was wrong."

"I don't like you much right now," Burn said, shifting the conversation again.

Ignoring the unexpected hurt her words caused, I nodded. "I know." Last night had made it perfectly clear.

"*Fortuna* is our ship. Ours!" She thumped a fist to her heart. "We spent years in the space corps, following orders, going where they sent us. Ten years and I—we!—finally had a chance to be our own bosses. Our team. Our crew. *Our family.*"

"And before we even had a chance, you were here first. On our ship, with Dax. Nothing was like we planned."

When she looked at me, I just nodded.

She dropped her gaze to the ground. "Then you were

nice to me and I told myself it was okay for a short time. You fixed stuff without even being asked. Little things like the squeak in my door." Her gaze flicked back up and her lips curled in a sad smile. "Thank you for that, by the way. You treated *Fortuna* well. You treated us well, and I started to like you. Even after I found out you had been on Blazer's crew. And then I found out it was all a lie."

She paused. Was this my chance to defend myself?

As the silence grew, I decided to fill it.

"I think my sister's been kidnapped." I looked over at Layla's frozen face. Her smile was crooked from being paused, but I could still see the twinkle in her eyes. "I didn't know that when the men broke into my apartment. When I broke into your ship. I was only thinking about my safety."

And now I was thinking about my sister's.

"I'm sorry I messed up the cargo job on Elegium Station. I've been trying to make it up to Dax—to make it up to all of you—ever since. That's why I recommended the stop on Rigel Naught and our current cargo."

"But you're not just helping because you feel bad, are you?"

Her words pricked at my conscience, but I'd been upfront with Dax. "You're right. Dax said he'd help me find Layla. I said I'd help your team make money. I still think it's an even trade."

"Dax wasn't authorized to make a decision like that." Burn's tone was hard. I'd lost her, assuming I'd ever had her support.

Too many captains ruined the business. If they really intended to make all decisions equally, they'd find that out soon enough.

"I'm sorry about your sister. I really hope you find her. But I don't think it can be on this ship."

"Thank you for your candor." How I kept my tone even I'll never know. I wanted to beg and plead and rage. She obviously had a tight bond with her team—her family! —why couldn't she understand that all I wanted was to protect mine the same way?

With a long last look at the computer screen, she stood and left the room. The sound of the door closing behind her was like a fist closing around my heart.

I slid off the bed, dropping to my knees on the floor. Tear streamed down my face.

Harrier was off the main shipping corridors. Sure, ships like ours — I shook my head. Ships like *Fortuna* brought supplies, but they didn't run on a regular schedule. We were already more than a week behind whatever had happened to Layla. This would set me back longer. Assuming I could find a way off the planet.

I don't know how long it was until I had cried myself out. My body felt dry. Dehydrated. My nose was runny. Wiping the remnants of tears from my face with the bottom of my shirt, I slowly, reluctantly, stood up.

So they were stranding me on a mining planet, were they? Assholes. I'd find a way off. I'd find my sister. And we'd find the *Queen of Stars* and I'd rub it in their faces.

That's a really nice plan, Lacy, but first you have to get off the planet.

Shit. Shit. Shit.

That was the main problem, wasn't it?

I could call my dad—as a last resort—but that would still take time, depending on where he and his ship were. I'd rather solve this myself.

I mentally cycled through my options. Usually, I'd hang out in the engine room and work on something until an idea came to me.

Yeah, that wasn't an option this time.

My dad would fight. I hated that option. Sure, I'd take on all three of them if they tried to space me, but short of a threat to my life, I didn't want to hurt any of them. Didn't want to hurt Dax.

My emotions regarding Dax were all over the place. He said he would fight for me and I believed him, but with what Burn had just told me, it was two against one. And he either couldn't or wouldn't override them as captain.

I shoved that mess to the back of my mind. Mooning over him wouldn't help me come up with a plan.

Staring at the computer screen, at my sister's image, I realized that Layla always started with research. Dad and I were more of the do first, ask questions later variety. Layla was the opposite, more like our mom had been.

Research. Was that the answer?

Dax hadn't mentioned anything about cutting off my access to the ship's systems. He'd just asked me to stay in my room.

Taking the seat Burn had vacated, I closed out the data disc and lay it carefully on the desk. I practically had it memorized, but I would need it for the last set of coordinates. She'd met up with a guy from a forum. A guy who said that he had physical proof from the *Queen of Stars*. The data chip had been sent from a service near their meeting point. But I was betting on her being taken back to his planet. Back to either see this proof or to combine their research.

"What have you got for me, baby?" I whispered as my fingers practically caressed the keyboard as I carefully explored my computer access.

Yes! Turned out, all of my access was still in place. I slipped into the cargo job database and looked at the options from Harrier, the mining colony. However thin, it was the start of a plan.

35

—

DAX

THE ATMOSPHERE on the bridge was tense as we approached Harrier. Burn sat to my right in the navigator's chair and Finn was hunkered down in the engine room. I would have been more comfortable with Lacy up here on the bridge with us, but that had been vetoed by the others, no matter how hard I argued for her expertise.

Finn was still adamantly against her involvement with anything to do with *Fortuna* and Burn seemed to be supporting Finn, albeit reluctantly. I had convinced them to let her listen in on our communications with Harrier, in case we ran into any problems. And I'd spent several hours with her going over what we needed to know.

She had still been generous with her knowledge, but her eyes had lost their sparkle and her expression lacked her usual animation. It was like the spark had gone out of her.

Even before I'd told her of the crew's decision, she'd known that we would be leaving her on Harrier. I'd felt like the world's biggest asshole asking her about our destination, but we couldn't afford a mistake, not with such dangerous cargo.

The comms crackled to life. "Unidentified craft, please be advised that you are entering Harrier airspace. State your name and business."

"Harrier control, this is *Fortuna*. Be advised we have a load of stupid shooters from Rigel Naught."

"Well now, that's useful cargo. 'Course, if you'd said you had fresh fruit, we mighta had to throw you a parade."

That surprised a laugh out of me. "I'll keep that in mind for next time."

Burn waved to catch my attention. *Next time?* she mouthed.

Why not, I mouthed back. Regular, well-paying cargo would be damned handy. Depending on how this delivery went.

"Appreciate it," the gruff voice on the radio responded. Then it turned business-like again in the next breath. "Land at the auxiliary spaceport and we'll offload that cargo for you."

"Auxiliary?" I asked.

"We keep those stupid shooters away from the main populated areas. Those things don't mess around."

"Got it."

I verified the coordinates after Burn entered them into the navigation system. "Course is laid in."

"Roger. *Fortuna*, you are cleared for that flight path. Safe flying."

"Thanks. Appreciate the assistance." I signed off, wishing Lacy was on the bridge with us. Her experience would be invaluable.

"Next time?" Burn asked again.

I shrugged. "If we're gonna run cargo, it never hurts to start making connections. This could be a valuable run."

"That makes sense. Holy shit! Would you look at that?"

Once just a dot on the radar, the auxiliary spaceport suddenly appeared out the front windshield.

"That's one ugly base," Burn said.

I don't know what I had been expecting, but it was not the floating, twisting tangle of shapes ahead of us. Part circle, part pyramid, part . . . I had no idea. The whole thing looked cobbled together. A pit formed in my stomach as I wondered if my skills were enough to land *Fortuna* on the floating structure. And if the structure was solid enough to support our ship.

With a confidence that I didn't feel, I contacted the controller on the base and confirmed our dock number.

"Should I get Lacy?" Burn asked as soon as I cut the call.

Wanting nothing more than to take her up on that offer, I shook my head. I needed the experience. And after this stop, we wouldn't have Lacy to fall back on any longer. "No, I got it."

Burn raised her brow but didn't say anything other than "Aye aye, Captain."

I eased the ship into the docking station, hoping that Burn didn't notice my white-knuckle grip on the controls. A combination of autopilot and either luck or skill got us safely into our assigned dock.

"We're attached," Burn said after she verified our position. "And the atmospheric shield is stable."

Only when I'd cut the engines and the ship slowly settled into the port did I finally release my grip.

"Welcome to Harrier auxiliary spaceport, *Fortuna*."

"Thanks, glad to be here."

With the atmospheric shield in place, we wouldn't have to put on spacesuits to unload the cargo.

"Are you ready for this?" Burn asked.

I blew out my breath before responding. "Completing our first job? Yes. The rest of it?" Leaving Lacy here? "No. Not really."

I really fucking hated the idea. I'd wrestled with options all night. Sure, I could probably enforce my will, or try to at least, but it would either lead to physical violence or destroy my crew. Either way, it was a step that my team would never come back from.

My job. My responsibility.

I shoved out of the captain's chair, wishing again that the circumstances were different.

Burn followed me with a sigh as I left the bridge. She went to corral Finn, while I stopped at Lacy's door.

I knocked, then opened it. "We're here."

Lacy logged off the computer, then stood up from the desk. She looked subdued. Her hair was pulled back into a high ponytail, the braided end draping over her shoulder. She wore her worn Elegium Station coveralls.

My heart raced, knowing this was likely the last time I would see her. I hated that thought.

"How will this work?" I asked to break the tension that hovered between us.

"Depends," she said. "Am I allowed to help?"

"Yes." My response was immediate, even though it wasn't technically what Finn and Burn had agreed to.

"Okay. Someone will need to meet the unloading crew on the cargo deck. Someone else should open the cargo hold. The team will let us know if they need help. Most likely, they'll instruct us to stand back and stay out of their way."

"Sounds easy enough."

Lacy laid her hand on my forearm. "Dax, nothing about this delivery is easy. The stupid shooters are essentially massive bombs. They're no less dangerous now that we're on the spaceport than when we were in transit. It's not easy until we're—you're—well away from here."

I covered her hand with mine. "Thanks for the reminder." I hated knowing that we would be leaving her here, in danger.

"Want to meet the station crew with me? We can get Burn to open the cargo hold."

After a beat, she nodded. "Sure. Can I come back for my gear later?"

The excitement of embarking on a new adventure with her fizzled out. "Yes. Of course." I'd noticed her tool bag when I'd entered, but I'd either missed or ignored the duffle that sat next to it on her bunk.

Lacing my fingers with hers, we exited her room and made our way down the corridor. Burn stood near the internal cargo-hold door. Her gaze flicked down to our clasped hands, but she was smart enough not to say anything.

"Where's Finn?" I'd expected him to meet us here too.

She shrugged. "Said he'd be along in a minute."

It was just as well. I didn't need another one of his explosions. "We're going out to meet the base team. You're in charge of opening up the cargo hold."

"Got it, Sarge."

The three of us slipped into the cargo hold. Burn lowered the ramp. Flood lights flickered to life outside the ship. I blinked several times to clear my vision. When I could see, I started down the ramp, Lacy close behind me. When we stepped out on the station's platform, half a dozen crew waited at the bottom. They were dressed in protective gear. Their loaders were parked a few feet from the ramp.

The work crew leader stepped up and introduced

himself as Bruce. "Hear you got some stupid shooters for us."

I nodded. "Got a cargo hold full of them." I gestured back toward the ship.

The work crews lead whistled. "That's ballsy. Those fuckers are dangerous if you don't transport 'em right. You see that debris field out there approaching the auxiliary station?"

I frowned. I didn't recall seeing any debris field on our approach. "No, must have missed it."

The other man slapped his leg and laughed. "That's cuz there ain't none. When those fuckers blow up, there ain't nothin' left."

Damn. That was some dark humor. "Got lucky," I said. "One of my crew's got experience with them."

"Handy," Bruce said. "Every once 'n a while, some amateur gets hold of some and tries their hand at delivering them. Only goes well about a third of the time."

There was no hiding my wince. Damn, was I grateful that Lacy had worked with the loading crew. Her experience and theirs had probably saved us from blowing ourselves to smithereens. Another reason to keep her on the crew.

"Who do I talk to about—" Lacy's hand on my arm stopped me.

She'd stepped to my side during the conversation and I looked down at her with a question.

"Captain, don't forget to ask about the fruit," she said. I had no idea what she was doing, but followed her lead.

"You got fresh fruit?"

I shook my head in real regret. "No, but we heard that would be welcome. Got any preferences, in case we make it back this way?"

A jumble of voices answered my question. Apples, kiwi

berries, the slimy pears from one of the watery worlds. Basically, everyone had an opinion and I could see where this could become a profitable run if we figured out the logistics of transporting fresh fruit.

Finally, Bruce spoke over the rest of his crew. "Honestly, whatever you bring we'll eat. Just don't go cheatin' us. We'll pay a fair price but no more."

He paused then continued, "Now let's get this cargo unloaded."

I looked back at the ship. Burn waited in the cargo hold doorway. "Show these folks the cargo, please."

She nodded. The crew started up the ramp, an almost militaristic precision in their movements. Several guided the carts that would make the process of getting the shipment off *Fortuna* easier. The wheels rattled lightly against the metal.

"Why'd you stop me?" I asked Lacy. "It wasn't really to ask about fruit, was it?"

She looked around and pulled me farther from the ship and the ramp. We were completely alone on the platform. She leaned closer, her hand still on my forearm. "You were about to ask about payment, right?"

I nodded and looked at her. "Well, yeah. We need to get paid for these things. That's the whole point of running cargo, right?"

"Yes, of course. But you don't ask about it here."

I didn't understand whatever she was trying to tell me. "Here, as in in this moment? Or here, as in on the spaceport?"

"Both."

"That makes no sense."

She looked at the ship for a moment, seeming to consider her words. "Did you have superstitions in the space corps? Things you didn't do? Things you never said?"

I nodded. "Of course. There's a long rich history of those in the military."

"It's similar here. Asking about payment is considered disrespectful. The explosives we brought here—the ones he joked about vaporizing ships—those things cost lives. You don't talk about money when the cost can be so much higher."

I rubbed my forehead. There were so many nuances to this business that I never would have guessed. "Then how do we get paid?" I winced as I asked, her words already having taken root.

"Someone, probably the crew leader but maybe not, will bring out a tablet. He'll enter the amount; you enter the account. The money will be transferred without anyone saying a word."

"What would have happened if I'd asked?" I needed to know the worst-case scenario.

Her serious gaze met mine. "You would have still gotten paid. But they would have taken note of the question, the ship. Maybe you stop here again, but it doesn't go as smoothly. There's no joking around." She shrugged. "And maybe it's more widespread. Someone leaves the mining colony, they remember the ship, mentions the question to someone on another station. Word spreads."

I stared at her, hoping she was kidding. Seconds ticked by as I realized she was dead serious.

Fuuuck. That would have been a disaster. "Thank you."

She smiled then and her whole face lit up. "You're welcome."

There had to be a way to keep her on the ship and

keep Burn and Finn happy. "How am I going to learn all this without you?"

"You'll figure it out."

Whatever she said next was drowned out by the sound of unloading cargo.

The crew leader led the way, with his team and their cargo lifters staggered behind him. I shuddered as I watched the highly dangerous cargo leave my ship. The risk would be well worth the payday, but I'd sleep easier at night with the explosives off my ship.

Burn and, finally, Finn followed the crew down the ramp.

The first pallet of stupid shooters rolled past Lacy and me, the crew members carefully guiding it from the ship to the loaders.

The rattle on the ramp got louder and faster. I looked up in horror as the figure in the back lost control of his cart. "Fuck! Watch out!" he yelled.

Gravity and the angle of the ramp pressed it down against the man at the front. No matter how strong he was, there was no way that he would be able to stop the cart full of heavy explosives.

I shoved Lacy behind me. Even knowing I wouldn't get there in time, I raced toward the ramp.

Vaguely aware of everyone around me stopping what they were doing, I prayed someone would stop the tragedy about to happen.

I didn't see how the other man could survive.

36

DAX

A BATTLE CRY tore through the loading dock. My head whipped up and everything appeared like snapshots.

Finn shoving past Burn.

Finn bracing a hand on a cargo pallet.

Finn vaulting over the pallet.

Finn flying through the air.

Finn wrapping his arms around the man in danger.

Finn shoved him hard enough that he cleared the cart's path and stumbled along the deck. Several of his team members caught him and pulled him to safety.

All of that happened in the blink of an eye. I kept my attention focused on Finn. He was so close to clearing the cart.

Come on, buddy.

But the same momentum that launched the other man forward caused Finn to lose his footing on the steep ramp.

He dropped to one knee, his hands catching the rest of his weight.

The cart caught his ankle. Rolled over his shin.

The sickening crunch of bones echoed around the loading dock.

"Aahhh!"

"Finn!" Burn and I yelled his name at nearly the same time and raced toward him.

The cart slowed but didn't stop and ran over his right hand. Another anguished cry split the air until it was cut off abruptly.

"Finn!"

Was he dead?

Burn reached him before I did, so I joined the scrum of men trying to stop the runaway cart.

It slowed, stopped, but the damage was done. And Finn was still trapped beneath it.

"Finn?" His name was a prayer and a question.

"Still . . . here . . . Dax." Every word sounded like a struggle. I hated that he was injured and in pain, but I was so glad he was still breathing.

Next to him, Burn was sprawled on the deck, her hand reaching for him under the cart. Her murmured *nonononono* broke my heart. Finn had been injured in the same accident that killed Wilson. This incident, while completely different, threatened to dredge up memories of that horrible time.

I shoved those thoughts as deep as I could and channeled my fear and anger into command mode. One of my team—my brother—was injured. I couldn't afford to lose myself in the moment.

"We need medical help, stat!" Damn, I wished Mercer was here with us.

"On its way." Bruce already had his comms in hand and was communicating with someone, presumably medical.

That sorted, I focused on the next problem. Finn's position.

At Burn's side, I dropped to the ground and peered under the cargo sled. Finn's face was ashen, every feature caught in a rictus of pain. As far as I could tell, the cart wasn't actually pinning him down. It would just be almost impossible to move it without some part of Finn being in the way.

"Help is coming, Finn. Just hold on." Sitting back on my knees, I found Bruce in the crowd of people on the deck. "How long 'til medical is here?"

"The spaceport's medic will be here any minute now. The planet-based medical transport has launched. ETA on that is twelve minutes."

"Hang on, buddy."

"I . . . hate . . . our new . . . gig."

I laughed the way I was supposed to. "Yeah, this wasn't a great start."

A shadow appeared at my side. I looked up to find Lacy next to me. "I grabbed the ship's med kit." She set it down next to me.

I stared at the kit longingly. I didn't know what to do for Finn. "I'm afraid of hurting him more."

Her hand settled on my shoulder, a warm, comforting weight. "The medic is almost here. They'll take good care of him."

She kept speaking, her voice a calming counterpoint to the thud of blood rushing in my ears. "Bruce has his crew clearing the stupid shooters that they managed to unload out of the area. They'll be safely stored and that will free up the space around *Fortuna*. They won't be able to unload the others until we've helped Finn."

"I want them off my ship," I rasped.

She rubbed my shoulder. "The team will take care of

them as soon as it's safe to do so. Right now, everyone is focused on getting Finn to safety."

"And that's what I'm here for." A breathless voice joined our conversation.

A figure clad in a dark jumpsuit dropped to his knees next to Burn. Despite the white armband emblazoned with a big red cross, his shock of red hair and the freckles scattered over his cheeks made him look twelve.

"I'm Jefferson," he said in a calm, soothing voice. "Your friends call you Finn, but everyone here on the station is calling you a hero."

"Damn . . . straight," Finn wheezed from beneath the cart.

If the sound concerned the medic, he didn't show it. The ginger medic's calm, easy manner and steady movements eased some of my concerns. As did the gentle, almost magical way he urged Burn—and me—to move out of his way.

Lacy helped Burn to her feet and wrapped her arms around her.

I felt a rush of affection for her. Even after everything my team had said about her and done to her, she was still here, willing to step up for them.

I stood too, ready to help however I could, but Jefferson shooed me out of the way. While understandable, I hated being sidelined like this. All I could do was watch as Bruce and his team, directed by the unflappable Jefferson, slowly and carefully disassembled the cart from around Finn.

I nearly darted forward when the cart gave an ominous rattle, but Lacy grabbed my wrist. "Let them do their jobs, Dax," she whispered.

"But I can help!"

"They're a well-trained team. Used to working together. Let them do their jobs."

I understood her message. I wouldn't want someone interrupting my team. Except her. I shook my head. *Not the time or the place, Dax.*

Time had no meaning as we watched them work. Watched Jefferson stabilize Finn and get him loaded on a hover stretcher.

Jefferson carefully removed his gloves and disposed of them. "The medical transport is at the next dock. You can have a minute with him, but then we need to get him to the hospital immediately."

"He's coming with us." Burn dashed past the medic, stopping at Finn's side. She reached out to touch him, then pulled her hand away.

I followed more slowly and put a hand on her shoulder. "Burn, we can't."

"He's one of us. He belongs with us." Her voice was thick with unshed tears.

"I want that too. But *Fortuna's* med bay is small and we don't have the proper tools. We can't help him the way he needs, can we?" I looked over to Jefferson.

He shook his head, regret stark on his face. "It was touch-and-go there for a minute. We've got state-of-the-art facilities down on the planet."

"The planet you use those bombs on?" Burn was shaking now. Shock probably. Maybe rage.

The medic took her question in stride. "The hospital is well away from the active mining sites. We take safety very seriously in all aspects of life here."

"What about the emergency medical pod?" Burn asked.

From her position behind Jefferson, Lacy shook her head.

"You don't know that," Burn said. "You're not a doctor."

Lacy flinched from Burn's verbal blow, but she didn't try to convince her.

Jefferson stepped into the emotional fray. "A Palaminto?" He looked at me.

"I don't know." I looked at Lacy and cursed my blind spots and the huge amount I had to learn still.

"Yes. Model 458."

"Yeah, that's standard on most smaller ships." He directed his next words to Burn. "The emergency life pod is for when the only option is to get the patient to a medical facility as soon as possible. It keeps them alive—usually—but it can't heal them."

His tone gentled. "You don't have to rush him to a medical facility and hope you make it in time. Our clinic is minutes away. We're ready to take care of him. Will you let us do that?"

Staring down at Finn, Burn didn't answer for a long minute. Finally, she nodded.

"Great. You can come with us while we strap him in. It might make you feel better about his treatment."

"Yes. Thank you."

Several more figures dressed like Jefferson had appeared during our conversation. They had to be the staff from the medical transport. They grabbed the sides of the hover stretcher, but before they could roll him away, I leaned close to Finn. "Your job is to get better," I told him. "We'll be back to get you when you're back on your feet. I promise."

When I stepped back, one of the medics gave me a solemn nod, then they took Finn away.

Bruce stepped forward. "We'll take care of him. He's one of ours now."

Although I was glad that someone else would be looking after Finn, I battled a sense of failure that we couldn't help him. If Mercer had been here, would he have been willing to risk bringing Finn on *Fortuna*?

"If you need anything for his care—" I let the words trail off. That was as oblique an offer to pay for his treatment as I could make.

The other man shook his head. "Your guy was injured saving one of my guys. We've got him." His words were as solemn as a vow.

"You'll contact us if you need anything?"

"I promise." He pulled a tablet out of a pocket. "We've unloaded the rest of the cargo. Ready for funds transfer?"

I nodded. Now I understood what Lacy had meant about not talking about payment. I felt incredibly uncomfortable after what had happened to Finn. It took a couple times clearing my throat to be able to say yes.

He handed the tablet to me and I swiftly entered the ship's account number.

"Thank you." I handed the tablet back.

He pressed another button and we both watched the numbers change between accounts. I nearly whistled through my teeth. That much money would keep us in fuel for quite a while.

Once we were back on the ship, I'd verify payment and transfer the finder's fee to Moya. Then Burn and I would figure out next moves. Picking up Mercer and Orion was a priority.

Bruce pocketed the tablet then studied me. "You'll be back for him?"

"As soon as he's ready. Maybe before then, if we can swing a visit."

"Wasn't sure about your team when you got here. Working with a bunch of first-timers is always a crapshoot.

But you've got good crew members since they know how to transport these damn stupid shooters. Jumpin' in to save others? That's above and beyond. Feel free to put Harrier on your route any time." He paused. "We'll have your guy back on his feet, next time you're here. Might even try to keep him."

I managed a slight smile. "Thank you." My feelings about leaving Finn here—trusting complete strangers with his care—were complicated, but if they could get him whole and healthy? I'd be forever grateful.

"Safe travels." We shook hands, then he headed toward the medical ship.

I stayed where I was, staring at the sky all around us. From here I could just barely see the stars through the atmospheric shield. Beyond that, the planet floated in a sea of darkness.

When we'd first planned to come here, I'd just wanted easy money.

Now we'd made connections. It would be both easier and harder to come back in the future. Easier because we knew the protocols and harder because we'd always be wondering about Finn.

"You okay?" Lacy asked.

For a moment, I'd forgotten she was there. Forgotten I wasn't alone in the vastness of space.

"Not really." When the adrenaline rush wore off, the shakes would begin. So far I'd staved it off. Hopefully I'd keep them at bay until I'd plotted our next course. Damned if I knew where that was going to be, though.

"That was— What Finn did was amazing. I hope he's okay." Her voice was soft.

"Me too."

We stood there in mostly comfortable silence until Burn returned. The tear tracks on her face shimmered, reflecting the pale light around us. I opened my arms and she stepped into them, pressing her face against my shoulder. Fuck. I knew exactly what she was feeling.

"I'll go grab my bag and then get out of your way," Lacy said quietly then walked away.

I nodded absently, my attention on Burn. "We don't have the facilities to give him the care he needs."

Her voice muffled, Burn said, "Leaving him behind feels wrong. What if he needs us? What if we never see him again, like Wilson?"

Wilson's name was like a punch. One day he'd been standing next to us, making us laugh the way he did with his jokes and impressions. The next we'd been shellshocked when he and several other marines were killed and Finn injured in a vehicle crash planetside. His death broke something in our team and we still hadn't managed to get the pieces put together quite right.

"He'll get better," I whispered. "We'll come back as soon as we can to check on him."

She nodded against my neck. "Promise?"

I didn't even hesitate. "I promise," I said, hoping I wasn't a liar.

Burn released me and stepped back reluctantly. "What now?"

I tilted my head back again, studying the sky like it had the answers I needed. "Not sure. We pick up Mercer and Orion. Get some cargo." I shrugged. "Find Lacy's sister?"

"Are you kidding? You can't be thinking of letting her back on the ship." She punched my shoulder.

Rubbing my hand over the shoulder—Burn hit fucking hard!—I said what I'd been thinking since we arrived. "I think we need her."

Scoffing, Burn crossed her arms over her chest. "I can't believe you're serious about this."

"Dead serious." I filled her in quickly about the superstition about talking money. And the potential consequences if you did.

She whistled long and low. "Did you ask him about it?"

"No, Lacy stopped me before I could." I paused to gather my thoughts. "She knows a lot about the cargo business. Knowledge we don't have."

"We can learn," Burn said petulantly.

I nodded. "We can learn. And we have the perfect teacher."

Burn's scowl said she wasn't buying it. "Look, we wouldn't have gotten the cargo on Rigel Naught without her connections and knowledge," I pointed out.

Brow raised, she countered, "We wouldn't have *needed* that cargo if she hadn't stolen our ship."

"Sure. I'll give you that. But without her, we might have a fat bank account for the moment, but our reputation for jobs like these would be trash before we even started."

"How long would we have to put up with her?"

Permanently, I wanted to say. "How about until we rescue her sister? Then the two of them can go on their merry way."

"Promise?"

Though I hated to do it, I agreed. "Promise."

"Fine. Just until we find her sister. And we have to tell the others what happened up front. No more keeping it a secret."

"Okay."

Eyes narrowed, her scowl deepening, Burn glared at something over my shoulder.

I turned around, knowing I would see Lacy. She stood at the top of the ramp, the duffle I'd seen on her bed slung over her shoulder. Her other hand gripped her tool bag.

For a moment, she looked lost. Then she stood straighter, lifting her head, drawing her shoulders back, and started down the ramp.

I looked back at Burn. "We good?"

Lips pursed, she nodded.

"Thanks," I said and whirled to catch Lacy.

We met at the middle of the ramp.

"Yes?"

"We've got a proposition for you," I said.

She studied me suspiciously. "Okay."

"We need your help. Teach us what we need to know to succeed in this business. Things like stupid shooters and not talking about money, and we'll help you find your sister."

Her breath caught, but she still stared at me with mistrust in her eyes. "How do I know you won't dump me on the next planet when one of the crew gets a bug up their ass about me?"

"We won't."

"But once we get your sister, you're off the ship." Burn had come up behind me. "That's the deal."

"Will you at least take us off the planet where she's being held?" Snark and a bit of anger colored her question.

"That's fair," Burn said. "The next planet."

"The next planet with reasonable transport," Lacy countered. "I don't want you to leave us on some ship-eating planet like Pangaea."

"Deal." Burn thrust her hand past me.

Lacy slowly, carefully set her tool bag down and shook Burn's hand. "Deal."

Then she offered her hand to me. Tingles raced up my arm and I fought the urge to slide my thumb over hers. "Deal."

"Now let's get off this fucking spaceport." Burn brushed past us both.

Once Burn had disappeared into the cargo hold, I turned to Lacy. "Ready?"

Her shoulders lifted in a barely perceptible shrug. "Sure. I guess."

I picked up her tool bag, but she immediately took it from me. "Don't jerk me around, Dax. No more votes about my presence. No more treating me like the devil incarnate. Let's get my sister, then we'll get off your ship."

Pain shot through my heart and I rubbed my chest. "That's the plan." I nearly choked on the words. "After we pick up the rest of the team."

Her eyes widened in betrayal before she whirled away.

"Lacy, it's not like that. I promise." Dammit, there I went making another promise. Would I be able to keep them all? Or would I let someone down? "We're going to need more support to rescue your sister. Especially since we don't know what we're facing."

"Whatever you say." She didn't look at me, just strode back into the cargo hold.

I released my breath. At least she was still on the ship.

37

DAX

"Just pull the bandage off, Dax."

I stopped fiddling with the comms and swiveled in my chair. Burn lounged in the bridge's doorway. "What?"

She rolled her eyes. "You're calling Mercer and Orion, right? So we can pick them up?"

"Yeah." It had been one of her conditions to leaving Finn and bringing Lacy with us. I'd agreed. Not just because I wanted Lacy with us, but since we had no idea what we'd face when we found Lacy's sister, more people—and more skills—were better.

"Then just do it. Sitting here all wishy-washy won't make it any easier."

I winced at her words. I'd always considered myself a man of action, but she was right, dammit. "What if this turns into a clusterfuck?"

She opened her eyes comically wide. "More than it already is?" With a shake of her head, she continued, "Then who the fuck would you rather have at your back? No one?"

"You're just full of little wisdom nuggets today, aren't you?" I groused.

She flashed me a mischievous smile. "Today? I think you mean always."

I laughed and gestured toward the seat. "You want in on this call?"

"Sure, why not." She dropped into the navigator's seat, while I steadied myself and pulled up the comms.

I keyed in their codes and waited while the system connected.

Mercer picked up first. "Hey, Dax! How'd the delivery go? I saw the bank numbers. Nice job!"

"It was a hell of a learning experience," I said as I stared out into space.

"That sounds like a story," Mercer said. "Everything okay?"

Blowing out my breath, I answered the best I could. "More or less."

"What's more or less?" That was Orion joining the call.

"The delivery," Burn said.

"What's that mean?" Orion growled.

"We made good money, but Finn got hurt, and we ran into a problem."

I hated Lacy being categorized as a problem.

Mercer immediately slipped into medic mode. "What do you mean, Finn got hurt? How badly? Where is he? I'm on my way as soon as we end this call."

I tried to keep up with the questions. "He was crushed by a piece of cargo. It looked pretty bad, but the medical staff at the mining planet assured me they would give him the best care. And we want you to join us. You and Orion. But not for that."

"Then for what?" Mercer's tone was clipped.

"For the problem," Burn drawled. "Dax acquired a stowaway and we haven't been able to get rid of her yet."

What the fuck? I mouthed to Burn, but she turned away.

"A stowaway?" Mercer asked at the same time Orion said, "She?"

"Dax likes her. Even though she stole our ship." Burn had wanted Mercer and Orion to know the truth from the start, but I hadn't expected it to come out like this.

"What the hell, Dax?"

Glaring at the side of Burn's head, I recounted everything that had happened since Elegium Station, up to and including a longer account of Finn's accident.

"Dammit, Dax! You're supposed to be the coolheaded one of the squad," Orion said. "And you just let some woman waltz off with our ship?"

Swallowing the urge to growl, I shoved my hand through my hair and wished for patience. I was getting damn tired of defending myself. "What's done is done," I said with finality. "We lost one cargo, but we picked up a new, more profitable one."

"We lost one crew member, but it's okay because we picked up another?" Mercer asked like an asshole.

"That's not what I'm saying. And we'll get Finn back. After he has time to recover." Suddenly, I was done with this conversation. "Look, the plan is to pick you both up and then go rescue Lacy's sister. After that—after we've delivered them somewhere safe and sound—that'll be it. End of story." The words tasted like ashes in my mouth. "You two coming or not? We can pick you up after otherwise."

I'd miss them if they decided not to help. Burn was right, we could definitely use backup. But I couldn't— wouldn't—order them to do this.

"Hell yeah, we're coming, Dax," Orion said. He

dropped his voice to a whisper. "I gotta get out of here. My family is driving me nuts."

"Hey, Orion, weren't you planning on going to Parcival Prime rather than home?" Burn asked.

There was a heavy pause. "Yeah, that didn't work out."

Before Burn could ask another question, we heard in the background, "Orion, dinner!"

"Was that your mom?" Orion must be blushing from the top of his buzz cut all the way down his neck.

"Yeah, shit. I mean, dangit, I gotta go. Momma made my favorite tonight."

"Lucky," Burn said wistfully.

Orion's laugh was subdued. "She's on a mission to remind me how good life is here. The food is great, but she keeps inviting the neighbor girls over for me to get a look at."

I smiled. "Is it working?"

Another long pause. "No, uh, not so much."

Sounded like there was a story there, but before I could ask, he said, "Let me know when and where and I'll be there."

He dropped off the line, leaving just the three of us. Me, Burn, and Mercer, who'd been silent for the last few minutes.

"You in, Mercer?"

"Yeah, I'm in. My family's driving me nuts too."

I wasn't surprised. His family had been pressuring him to join the family medical practice since the day we met. Not that it was really a practice. More like an interplanetary hospital system. He'd really pissed them off when he joined the military. Their only solace was that he'd gone in as a medic. Now that he'd mustered out, the pressure must have exponentially increased.

"Great, thanks." The tension in my shoulders eased. "Are you with your folks? We can pick you up there."

"No, that'll take you too far out of the way. There's no time to waste if this sister really has been kidnapped."

I wasn't going to get into it about whether Lacy was telling the truth. I'd seen the videos, Mercer hadn't. "Where then?"

"Where are you heading?" I heard him typing in the background.

"Cluster of planets on the edge. Most likely spot is a place called Kottke. As far as we can figure, it's a dusty outpost. No industry that I can find. Just a shitty little planet on the edge of nowhere."

"I thought we were done with shitty little planets," Burn said.

She was right. We'd seen too damn many during our tour. It was pure luck that our assignments on planets like Kottke had only ever been temporary. Long-term duties would have been mind-numbing.

"Looks like there's a planet called Justin nearby—"

"What the fuck kind of planet name is that?" Burn asked.

I shrugged and Mercer kept talking. "We can meet you there in three days."

"Three days?" I asked incredulously. We were maybe that distance from Kottke, but Mercer and Orion were much farther out. "How do you plan to get there that quickly?"

"You let me worry about that, Dax. We need supplies?"

I thought for a moment. "We're good on food and the like, but the armory is empty."

"Orion and I will take care of that too."

Burn pumped her fist in the air.

"Make it three and a half days," Mercer said. "See you soon," he added and dropped off the call.

I reached over to close the channel.

"See, Sarge, told you it would all work out."

"You were right." If it all really worked out, then this was the beginning of the end of Lacy's time on the ship. The thought tied my stomach up in knots.

38

LACY

AFTER SPENDING MOST of the afternoon in the engine room making sure Finn hadn't broken anything—he hadn't, which left me with nothing to do—I slipped down the hall and into my room. Setting my tool bag on the desk, I stared at the bare walls of my temporary quarters. If I were staying, I'd do some decorating, make it my own. But this wouldn't be my place for long. In the not-too-distant future, this room would be filled with someone else's stuff.

I walled off the rush of emotions tangled up with that thought. Yesterday had been a lot and my feelings were all over the place. I'd gone from persona non grata on *Fortuna* to . . . what? Persona grata?

I laughed softly. I was hardly a welcome guest. And with nothing to do in the engine room, I felt useless on top of everything else.

The only silver lining in the whole damn situation was that Dax and his crew were going to help me get my sister back.

My hands flexed. I needed something to do. Anything

to get out of my head. Since tinkering in the engine room wasn't happening, I was left with one option.

Dammit! I hated working out.

My duffle lay in the corner, where I'd tossed it after coming back on board yesterday. There was no point in unpacking since I wouldn't be here that long. I dropped to my knees and rifled through its contents. I dug through my clothes until I found the sweats and T-shirt that Dax had lent me. They were the closest thing to any type of workout gear I owned. Stripping down to my underwear, I struggled into a sports bra and then donned my borrowed clothes. I'd planned to take them with me, a souvenir of my time onboard this ship. My time with Dax.

I swirled my hair up into a bun and grabbed the sneakers I'd purchased on Rigel Naught.

Fortuna's gym was tucked into the belly of the ship, between the cargo hold and the currently empty armory. *Mako's* gym had never been an actual gym. I'd used it for storage. Sure, weightlifting and cardio were a part of life in space, necessary to counter the effects of different gravities and maintaining the muscle needed for most jobs, but I'd never enjoyed them.

I stood in the doorway of the small gym, staring unhappily at the limited options. A small collection of adjustable weights and a treadmill. A big multipurpose mat covered the rest of the floor.

Ugh.

Nothing appealed to me. Working out *never* appealed to me. On Elegium Station, my daily walk back and forth to work and the constant repairs provided all the exercise I needed. But onboard *Fortuna?* I hadn't done anything.

Deciding the treadmill would be closest to what I was used to, I stepped onto the track with caution. The screen blinked to life and I studied it carefully, choosing a moderate level.

The tread moved and I concentrated on keeping pace. I tried to clear everything else—all the anger, all the fear, and especially all the stress—from my mind.

Easier said than done.

My sister. Dax. Engineering. Finn. My dad. From the moment Bob had handed me that data chip, my life had gotten so *complicated*. So tangled and confusing.

As the workout picked up, it became easier to clear my head, until finally, I slipped into that elusive headspace where I didn't think past my next step, past the next hit of adrenaline.

39

DAX

Our plan, running cargo on a ship that we owned, had not survived contact with reality fully intact. We had a successful cargo run under our belt, but the cost had been Finn. Even though he'd been acting like an extreme ass, he was one of us, one of our squad, and leaving him behind hadn't felt right.

But leaving Lacy behind hadn't felt right either. Despite our rocky start, she fit in. She felt like one of the crew. If only I'd been able to get Finn and Burn to see that.

In just a few days, the rest of the team would be on the ship and we'd rescue Lacy's sister. And then she'd disappear from my life.

Dammit!

In the space corps, things had been hard, but in some ways they'd been easier too. Big decisions were made by the brass. Now we had to make them ourselves. Had I made the right ones? Was it my fault Finn had been injured?

Burn had argued that we were all adults, all in charge of our own decisions, and as much as I felt responsible for everyone, she was right. The only one I could really help was myself.

I'd skipped PT today and, though it was late, I knew it would help get me out of my head. In my quarters, I quickly changed into high-tech, high-performance shorts and a tank top, then made my way to the gym.

Off-key singing filtered into the hallway before I reached it. I recognized Lacy's voice, though I'd never before heard her sing. She was really, really bad.

Would sharing the gym with her be worth the torture?

Yes. Despite the truly awful singing, any time I spent with her was worthwhile.

Wincing, I stepped into the gym.

"Hey." I must have surprised her, because she jerked her head up and bobbled a step. She caught herself and slowed the treadmill.

At least the singing had stopped, but I was halfway across the small room before I realized it. "Are you okay?"

"Yeah, I'm fine. I mean, hi." Cheeks flushed from exertion, skin glowy from sweat, she looked amazing.

"I didn't think anyone would be down here. I mean, I've never seen you here before." I hid my wince. That sounded like the world's worst line and I'd meant it as a serious conment.

"Yeah, not a fan of gyms, but needed to work off some energy."

Her words and the way she was dressed, in my clothes, flooded my brain with much better ways to work off excess energy. Turning away so she wouldn't see the effect she had on me, I studied the mat in the center. Weights wouldn't burn off the energy buzzing through my system, but movement might.

I removed my shoes then stepped to the center of the mat. My position provided a clear view of the entry and allowed me to watch Lacy in my periphery. With one last look around the room, I settled into my stance and closed my eyes. Bowing to a nonexistent opponent, I moved through the first kata.

The first set of movements were a warmup of sorts, getting my body and my brain to work in sync. They also provided the building blocks for later combinations. Muscle memory guided my hands and feet through one sequence and into the next.

As I slid deeper into my practice, executing the moves over and over again, I became more attuned to the sounds around me. The shush of the treadmill belt. The steady beat of Lacy's feet. The rush of my pulse in my veins. The hum of the ship's electrical system.

Fortuna vibrated beneath my feet, and I'd never felt so connected to a ship before. To *my* ship.

That rush of pride sent another pulse of energy through me and I channeled that last burst into the final, and most difficult, combination.

My arms sliced through the air, battling unseen opponents. I ducked, dodged, spun, and kicked. Every ounce of power I had, I fed into the movements. Until the series ended, the energy spent, and I was once more grounded to the mat and the ship beneath me.

As I slowly returned to awareness, I noticed the lack of sound in the gym. No more treadmill. No more footfalls.

No more Lacy?

My eyes flew open. Expecting to find myself alone in the workout room, my startled gaze met Lacy's slightly glazed one.

She leaned against the treadmill's handrail, a towel hanging loosely from one hand. Her skin shone with perspiration and sweat dampened the edges of her hair. Her chest rose and fell rapidly, almost as fast as mine.

"I thought you'd left," I said.

"I was going to. When I finished my workout, but then . . ." she paused and swirled her free hand through the air. "Then you were doing that and I didn't want to get in the way."

I studied her. Everything she said could be the truth, but she seemed too affected to have just been waiting for me to finish.

"Good workout?" I had to distract myself from how good she looked all messed up. It was too easy to imagine another reason for her to be flushed, sweaty, and breathing hard.

"Good enough." She jumped off the treadmill. Her breasts shimmied slightly beneath her T-shirt. *My* T-shirt.

"Just good enough?" I stepped closer. Close enough to see little drops of sweat beading at her temples.

"I'm restless," she admitted. "It took the edge off, but I needed to do something . . ." Her voice trailed off. She gestured to the treadmill. "It's all yours. I'll get out of your way."

"Do you know how to fight?" The question slipped out. It wasn't a bad idea, though. I'd be happy to teach her. I wanted her to be able to protect herself if she ever faced men breaking into her home again.

"Some," Lacy said with a shrug.

"Seriously?" My surprise must have shown because she smiled.

"I've picked up a few things."

"Want to spar?" I didn't disbelieve her, but this also gave me an excuse to spend more time with her.

Head tilted, she studied me. "Sure, why not."

I jolted. I hadn't actually expected her to agree. "Ground rules?" It would be very, very easy for me to hurt her, which was the last thing I wanted.

"No hits to the face," she said.

"Agreed."

"Nothing hard enough to bruise."

"Okay." I'd already planned to pull my punches.

"And no blood." She looked at me. "What about you?"

"Those sound good."

"Best of three?"

Surprised again, I nodded. "Whenever you're ready."

She bent and unlaced her shoes. Hands pressed to the floor, she held the stretch. My sweats hugged her ass and I enjoyed the view for a moment, then looked away.

Her arms went wide as she stood, interlacing her fingers over her head. Arms extended, she tilted from side to side, then arced her back. The movement lifted her chest, accentuating her breasts.

I swallowed hard. This was torture.

She released her arms, swinging them back and forth, criss-crossing them in front, then in back. Stepping out of her shoes, Lacy padded onto the mat. "All set."

Moving together, we positioned ourselves near the center of the mat, leaving roughly four feet of distance between us. Lacy shifted her body so she faced me sideways, her left foot in front, her right foot back, hovering on the balls of her feet. Her hands came up to shield her face.

I studied her position, looking for weaknesses, but it was a strong starting stance, well-balanced. She'd definitely had some training.

"Ready," she said.

"Go," I said.

We circled each other slowly, our relative distance not changing much.

My gaze drifted over her form again, studying her movements before I made my first move.

I knew how the rest of my crew fought; we'd trained together for years. Lacy was an unknown entity. A mystery. A challenge.

I liked challenges.

A wide smile on my face, reflecting how much I was looking forward to our session, I stepped toward her, throwing an experimental punch with my left hand, to test my range and to see how she reacted.

She swayed back easily and my hand swung harmlessly past her face.

Quicker than I expected, she darted forward. Ducking under my swing, she popped her fist just below my ribs.

"Fuck."

Lacy slipped out of range.

"That would do some serious damage if you hadn't pulled your punch." Admiration in my tone. I honestly hadn't expected her to get that close.

"Oh, I know. One for me." She shot me a bright smile.

That smile was a challenge and a turn-on rolled into one. *Game on.*

I danced sideways, forcing her to turn as I circled her. A few jabs that she easily dodged or blocked.

Left, left, right.

Left, left, right.

Left, left, leg sweep.

Instead of a jab, I reached out and grabbed her shoulder with my front hand. My other hand grabbed her other shoulder almost immediately. Then I pulled her toward me.

"Shit."

She leaned back, just as I'd expected. I was ready. My back leg swept around and I planted it right behind her feet. Then I let go of her shoulders.

She'd put a lot of force into pulling backward. As soon

as I freed her, there was nothing to counter that momentum. She couldn't step backward because my leg was there.

It was a controlled fall. She'd hit the ground, but it could be worse.

While I was busy picturing my point, she threw her arms forward and wrapped her hands around the back of my head.

Shit! I'd been distracted and now I was going to pay.

Using her grip around my head, she stepped in close and planted her foot in my abdomen. She fell backward, taking me with her.

I expected her to throw me over her head, but she maintained her grip. I flipped over her head and she used our momentum to roll with me. We landed with her on top, straddling my hips. Her hands quickly released my head to pin my wrists to the ground.

That was more than picking up a few things. That was training.

"My point," she gasped.

"Hey!" I was breathing too hard to make a coherent argument. "I got your legs."

Her hands pinned my wrists down. "But I'm the one who came out on top."

I'd been really trying to ignore our position. She straddled me, her knees pressed into my sides. Her lower legs bracketed my hips and outer thighs, leaving her center hovering over my pelvis. If I arched against her, she'd feel my rapidly stiffening cock.

I lay on the floor beneath her. There were half a dozen moves I could use to unseat her and change positions. But why would I?

Her quick breaths pressed her breasts against me. The

only way our positioning could be improved would be if we were both naked.

"You've definitely had some training." I stared up into green eyes that gleamed like emeralds.

"I told you so." Her breath whispered over my lips.

"I'm impressed. I didn't expect you to hit me, much less take me down." I'd known the woman had hidden depths and I'd *still* underestimated her.

"I know." Eyes dancing, she released my wrists and used my shoulders to lever up to sitting. The shifting angle rocked her pelvis against mine.

"Oh!" She sucked in a breath as her center ground over my cock. Paused, shivered.

The pressure was excruciatingly delicious. I didn't say a word, just held her gaze.

The air around us felt heavier, as if all the oxygen had been sucked out of the room.

She shifted her weight again, rocking forward, back.

More blood raced to my cock. I held her gaze the entire time. Saw when her eyes went slightly out of focus.

She wiggled against me and released another throaty groan.

"You're killing me," I growled.

"Do you want me to stop?" Her voice was low. Husky. Dangerously sexy.

"God, no." It might kill me, but what a way to go.

Lacy stilled her pelvis and let her hands wander over my chest. They drifted down toward my waistband and my stomach tensed. We were moving pretty quickly . . .

Then her hands grasped the bottom of my shirt and tugged it upward.

I curled up into a sit-up.

"Oh!" Lacy gasped again.

My smile was hidden as I dragged my shirt over my head, then tossed it next to my shoes. Slowly, with control, I eased my torso back down. Every inch was torture as Lacy dragged her fingers over my bare skin, her smile wicked.

Once she reached my abs, fingernails replaced fingertips as they scraped down my stomach.

I sucked in a breath and my stomach concaved away from her touch.

She stilled. "You don't like that?"

"I like it too much." Desire turned my voice gruff.

"Oh good." She teased her fingers back up my stomach and dragged them back down.

I growled and arched my hips into her.

"You do like that," she purred and ground down on me.

I groaned and gripped her hips. "Okay?"

She nodded.

I rested my hands there, letting her get used to their weight, their pressure, my touch. I channeled restraint when all I wanted to do was grind my erection against her.

"Kiss me," I blurted.

Her smile left wicked in the dust. She tilted forward slowly, so damn slowly.

I felt every damn millimeter of movement along my dick. Her muscles flexed and released under my hands and it took everything I had not to dig my fingers into her ass and pull her close.

Her hands shifted from my chest to the mat beneath my shoulders and her breasts pressed flat against my chest. Right back where we started. Her feet curled around my knees and her mouth brushed over mine. A whisper. A tease.

"That kind of kiss?" she asked against my lips.

I groaned. "No. More."

She hmmmed. The vibrations tickled and teased the oversensitive nerve endings in my lips.

"More like this?" She licked her lips then mine. She blew lightly on the damp skin.

Fire raced through me. "Kiss me!" I couldn't for the life of me find the right words, so I pressed up against her. Bringing my erection against the sensitive cradle between her legs.

"Oh. More like this," she purred.

Her mouth pressed against mine, seeking the best angle. Seeking more.

Her tongue darted out, teased my lower lip until she nipped it.

When I groaned, she captured my mouth.

She tilted forward to get better access. The movement shifted her hips against mine, rocking her pelvis against my rock-hard erection.

Just a few layers of clothes separated us. Too many layers.

My hand skimmed from her hip to the small of her back. My fingers slid beneath the T-shirt—*my* shirt—and rested on her soft, soft skin. I growled into our kiss, primitively pleased that she was wearing my clothes.

Of course, she was. She was mine.

That thought firmly planted in mind, I tightened one arm around her waist and slid the other up so I'd be able to control our landing. I raised my knee, making her gasp, then tightened my abs and flipped us.

She tore her mouth from the kiss to make a sexy surprised sound. Her eyes flicked up to meet mine just nanoseconds before her mouth was glued against mine again. Her eyes fluttered closed.

All her focus was on kissing me.

It was so fucking hot.

She dragged her knees along my sides until her feet rested on the floor and her thighs were clamped around my hips.

I nipped her bottom lip and she strained against me. I pulled my arm from beneath her back and braced my elbows on either side of her head.

She made a mew of pleasure and curved her hand around my neck, pulling me closer.

Slowly, giving her time to object, I lowered my weight onto her, settling into the vee of her thighs.

My cock throbbed and I rocked against her in time to the rush of my pulse.

Hip to hip.

Pelvis to pelvis.

Every little movement now pressed us closer—harder—together.

Her mouth devoured mine. Her legs lifted and wrapped around my waist.

She lifted up. I pressed down. And together we found a rhythm that made her dig her fingers into my back.

As I increased the pressure and the timing of my thrusts, Lacy started to shake in my arms. Her kisses became more frantic until finally she tore her lips from mine and pressed her face into the crook of my shoulder. Her nails dug into my back as she came in my arms.

Holy. Shit.

Her muffled moan threatened to trigger my own orgasm. But this one was for her.

Her body continued to shiver against mine, every little spasm pushing me a half step closer to the edge I was trying to walk back from.

"Oh my god," she whispered against my neck.

I smiled against hers.

Slowly, tentatively, her legs loosened from around my

hips and found purchase on the floor. It took longer for her to release her grip on my shoulders, so she once again lay beneath me.

Her breath came in rapid pants. "I can't believe we just . . . I mean, anyone could've . . . wait, did you?"

"That was for you." Bracing my weight on my knees and elbows, I dipped my head down to nuzzle her neck. I was still rock hard, but seeing her like this, gazing up at me with pupils blown wide and a hazy expression, was enough.

"I could . . . We could . . ." The flush that had started receding from her cheeks flared again.

I'd never seen her so flustered. Endearing and strange, it tugged at emotions that I wasn't ready to explore. So I kissed her. Unlike our earlier lust-driven kisses, this one was tender, slower.

And infinitely more dangerous.

40

———

LACY

When Dax ended the kiss and pulled back, it took me a moment to regain my bearings. That kiss . . . I reached up and pressed my fingers against my lips. They were tender to the touch and sensitive. So sensitive.

"Um, hi." My brain was too scrambled, my breath too ragged to say much more.

"Hi," Dax said with another one of those panty-melting smiles.

We stayed there, in that moment, for what felt like forever.

Dax brushed a soft kiss over my forehead, then sat back on his heels. His body had been a furnace against mine and now I felt surprisingly chilled.

I scrambled up to sitting. What had just occurred . . . It had been magical. And I wanted more. I wanted to strip him bare. Feel him against me. In me.

But this wasn't the place. And given how his crew felt about me, this probably wasn't the time. Maybe all we were meant to have was this stolen moment.

"That was unexpected." I'd intended the words to sound humorous, but they came out serious.

He nodded.

Gaze steady on his, I asked, "Where do we go from here?"

"I don't know." Heat blazed in his eyes.

Was he thinking the same thing I was? That we should explore this further, behind the closed doors of a cabin? Despite how intense my orgasm had been, I'd never been an exhibitionist. I wanted Dax, but I wanted him in a bed.

"Will this cause problems? With Burn and your crew?"

He closed his eyes briefly. "My love life is my business."

I laughed softly. "That's great in theory. But Finn and Burn have already proved that they won't leave it there." They'd kicked me off the ship once. I was too close to finding my sister to let them do it again.

Dax sighed. "Yeah, it'll probably create some tension."

Because that was exactly what this ship needed. More tension.

"I guess we know the answer then. We pretend it didn't happen." My throat tightened and I could barely say the words.

Dax stood, the movement easy and smooth, then held his hand out for me. I grasped it and, for a moment, considered tugging him back down to the ground.

Instead, I let him pull me up. As soon as I was upright, he pulled me against his chest and wrapped his arms around me. "We don't have to decide anything right now." He lowered his lips to mine and I rolled up onto tiptoe to get closer. Wanting, needing, another taste of him.

This kiss was slower, less frantic, but no less powerful.

I pressed my hand against his chest and slowly pulled away. Desire burned in his eyes and his heart raced beneath my palm.

"You're right. There's no need to be hasty." I pressed harder on his chest and his arms dropped to his sides. I took two big steps back, because I didn't trust myself that close to him.

"I should go do . . . stuff." Not that there was anything to do, but staying here, in the small gym that smelled like sweat and man and sex . . . That wasn't a great idea. I needed some distance if I was going to be able to leave this ship after we rescued Layla.

"We'll figure it out." He spoke softly and dragged his finger over my cheek in a soft caress. "I'll see you later."

"Okay." I nodded, then ducked to grab my shoes and socks. I left the gym quickly, needing the comfort of my room to process what had just happened.

Closing the door to my room, I leaned against it. My heart was racing and it wasn't all from speed walking down the hall.

I pushed off from the closed door and stared in the mirror. At first glance, I looked pretty much the same, so maybe no one passing me in the hallway would notice.

But if you looked closely, my puffy lips, mussed hair, and flushed cheeks couldn't be written off as a post-workout glow. Not even a good sparring match would leave me looking like that.

Except this one had. I pressed my fingers to my lips again.

Oh my god. I'd just rolled around on the floor with Dax Cooper and gotten off doing it. The orgasm had been fucking *amazing*.

I still felt a little bad that he hadn't come. But honestly, I wasn't sure I'd want to get down, dirty, and *naked* in the gym.

I eyed my bed. It was small, but I knew from experience that it could work if you got creative.

The captain's bed, on the other hand, would be plenty big enough.

Was this really happening? Me and Dax? Did I want it to?

I stared at the woman in the mirror, wanting an answer.

"Yes," I said with a short nod. "I want Dax."

Finn would be a problem, but he wasn't here right now. Burn might be. But Dax was a grown-ass man. He should be able to decide who he wanted in his bed without input from his crew.

Crew.

That was another problem. Not for fucking him. I wasn't crew.

I was still in the same place I was pre-orgasm, pre-workout. There was no role for me here on *Fortuna*.

41

LACY

"THAT'S STUPID!" Burn broke into my explanation of how cargo hauling on Yarty worked. Small planet, known mostly for their beers, they had very specific requirements before they allowed you to take on any of their precious beers as cargo.

"Yeah, it is," I agreed. "But they make the beers, they make the rules."

We were sitting in the mess going over the unspoken rules of interplanetary cargo. The reason Burn had agreed to let me back onboard *Fortuna*. She was proving to be a good student who took meticulous notes on her tablet, but every once in a while, the more arbitrary rules confounded her.

She stared at me wide-eyed. "But . . ." She stopped, started again. "How do people get things done?"

I shrugged. "I honestly have no idea. Magic?" It was as good a reason as any.

She leaned over her tablet, making notes of this latest crazy custom.

I watched her with a half-smile. There really was no

method to my madness when it came to sharing my knowledge. Sometimes I stared at a map and let planet names tickle my memory. Other times, Burn or Dax asked about a specific planet.

They seemed almost disappointed when I had to remind them that I hadn't been everywhere. That was when I pulled out some of the more outrageous customs.

I wasn't the world's best teacher—I liked engines better than people, so I could never do this for a living—but I was having a lot more fun than I imagined.

Plus, it kept my mind off my sister. And the upcoming rescue. And the new crew members who would be joining us.

Oh yeah, and yesterday's sexy times with Dax.

I definitely needed the distraction.

"Maybe it's some religious angle. Or the reason could be lost to time. It doesn't matter why. What matters is not doing it will unravel any deal on Yarty and probably cost you any goodwill you may have built up. It's rude," I repeated.

"It's stupid," Burn echoed.

"Okay, fine. It's a dumb superstition, but it's the way it works. I'm sure your planet has customs that seem backward."

"That's because they are," Burn muttered and shoved away from the table to start pacing.

Her reaction reminded me how little I knew about her. She was an adrenaline junkie. She'd been in the space corps. But I knew nothing about where she came from. Her reluctance to discuss it told me there was a story there. Same as me.

When Burn rounded the room and passed in front of me, I caught the look of distress on her face. Crap. I hadn't meant to cause her pain. "I'm sorry. I shouldn't have pried." I turned my attention back to my coffee.

Burn made another circuit of the room then dropped into the chair opposite me with a thunk. "You've probably never even heard of my planet," she said, "which is completely fine, because it sucks."

I put down my cup and focused on her. I wasn't going to interrupt.

She took a breath and started picking at her nails. I'd never seen her express anything but extreme confidence or righteous anger. To see her obviously bothered . . . Whatever she had to say, it wasn't going to be pretty.

"I grew up on Octavius Prime." She paused, waiting to see if I recognized the name.

I shook my head.

"It's a planet filled with misogynistic, small-minded people. Where the men are men and the women are . . ." Her words trailed off and she redoubled her efforts on her poor cuticles.

I covered her hands with mine. She tensed, then the muscles under my palm loosened and the picking stopped.

"Women are baby makers and food preparers and that's pretty much it. No education, no other skills. From the cradle, they're taught to aim for the best men—the wealthiest and the oldest—and to treat other women like competition."

"That's awful!" I blurted, then realized how it might make Burn feel. "Sorry."

She gave me a grim smile, her eyes haunted. "No, you're right. It's awful." Her hand curled up to grip mine. "The fact that you want to go after your sister? That's awe-inspiring to me."

"She's my sister." I didn't understand why that would inspire awe.

"You love her, right?"

I nodded.

She pulled her hands free and rolled up one sleeve. Her hand traced over a long scar. "My sister gave me this because I refused to marry Old Man Weather. It was my 'duty' as the oldest daughter," she said robotically. "I ran away and she was forced to marry him in my place. Instead of his son." She rolled down her sleeve and pushed her shirt up to reveal another scar on her stomach. "When they caught me and brought me back, she tried to kill me."

"Your sister did that?" Horror coated my voice. Layla and I had our moments—some of our more violent fights had involved throwing things—but we'd never intentionally tried to harm each other.

"With our mother's favorite carving knife." Tightly leashed pain was barely discernible in her tone.

I squeezed her hand. "That's awful. I'm so, so sorry."

She gave me a bleak smile. "I'm not. It was the final push I needed to leave that godforsaken place."

"How?"

"I learned from my first escape. I was sneaky, careful. And I knew my timing had to be perfect." She laughed bitterly and I glimpsed the deep well of pain and suffering that Burn kept hidden. "I smuggled myself out on a supply ship."

I waited for her to say more. When she didn't, I ventured one more question. "How did you get into the space corps?"

"There weren't a lot of job opportunities for a woman with no education and no idea how the world worked. But I was strong and willing and they promised me hot meals and a place to sleep."

"I'm glad you're safe now."

"And I'm glad you've shown me that sisters can fight

for each other, not just with each other." She gave me a tight-lipped smile and pulled her hand away.

I'd always fight for my sister. I couldn't imagine it any other way.

A tiny voice inside added that I'd fight for Dax now.

"Anyone else need coffee?" Dax's arrival broke the silence between us. I was grateful, because I had no idea what to say or how to offer comfort. Or if Burn would even accept it.

Both of us murmured no.

"What's going on?" Dax asked, having picked up on the tension. "We're not kicking her off the ship yet, Burn."

Burn laughed, but I caught the edge to Dax's voice. Like he would fight to keep me onboard.

I tried not to read anything into that and did my best to ignore the rush of warmth that came with the thought of staying here. Staying with him.

"It's fine, Dax," Burn said, her gaze holding mine. "I was just asking Lacy how she ended up a mechanic and her sister became an archaeologist."

Since I wasn't sure exactly what each of them knew, I started at the beginning.

"We grew up on a ship." I wasn't sure if Burn knew that or not. When she nodded, I continued. "There's not a lot to do when you're in space. I was fascinated by the engines, so I spent a lot of time there. My sister spent a lot of time in books. And on the rare occasions we had time to explore the planets or the stations, she was always in the museums or libraries. She still is," I added with a smile.

"It doesn't sound like you and your sister are much alike," Burn commented.

I shrugged. "We're close anyway." There wasn't a lot I could add to that without revealing more about our family than I liked. Though I wanted to know more about Burn's family, I didn't want to poke at that wound again, so I looked at Dax. "What about you? Any siblings?"

He settled in at the table with smile, his lips quirking. "Three of each. I'm smack dab in the middle."

My mouth dropped open. "Spacer?" There were spacer clans who had big families to help with the upkeep of their ships. Keeping it all in the family.

"Naw," he said. "Horny parents."

My face flamed and Dax laughed at me. Burn just shook her head. I guess she already knew this.

"I can't imagine having such a big family," Burn said. Was that a hint of wistfulness in her voice?

"It was just me and my sister and my parents, until my mom died," I said. "But growing up on the ship was like having one big extended family. Except the crew members were more like aunts and uncles than siblings." I wouldn't say the crew of *Eternal Nocturne* had been one happy family —except when it came to me and Layla. The crew hadn't coddled us, but they'd protected and taught us and somedays I missed them almost as much as I missed my sister and dad.

"Did you have other kids to play with?" Burn asked.

I shook my head. "My dad always said it wasn't a great environment for kids. My sister and I were the only exception."

Dax studied me over the rim of his coffee cup, his gaze intense.

I swallowed. Why was he looking at me that way? I reviewed the conversation and realized I may have said too much. Why would Layla and I be the only kids allowed onboard? Only someone high up would have the authority to make that call.

"Where did you grow up?" I asked Dax, both to get his

attention off me and because I was curious about the man I'd practically slept with.

"Mandarina," he said.

I rifled through my mental files. "Hybrid economy, tech and agriculture, but ag is the biggest export."

He nodded. "You've been?"

"Not on planet. Maybe the spaceport." We'd visited a lot of places growing up and I didn't remember them all. If I'd been planetside, would I have met Dax? Remembered him? I thought about his kisses. Our time in the gym. Yeah, he was definitely memorable. A rush of heat colored my cheeks.

"Now I understand what you meant, Dax, when you said it was awkward walking in on your parents with their googly eyes," Burn said conversationally. "I'm going to go." She set her mug down, then started to stand.

"Wait, Burn. Tell her the rest, Lacy." He leaned back in his chair, his legs extended beneath the table, bracketing mine. Was he asking me to share about yesterday? My face flamed in mortification. What the h—

"About your sister," he clarified.

"What?" I tried to keep up, but I didn't understand what he was asking.

"About why she's so interested in archaeology and history."

"Oh." I paused, searching his face. "Are you sure?"

He nodded.

Burn dropped back into her seat, her voice tight when she asked, "What are you talking about, Dax?"

"We said no more secrets. So tell Burn about Layla or I will."

I glanced at Burn, unsurprised to see a hint of distrust returning to her questioning gaze.

"When we were kids, my sister thought she saw the *Queen of Stars*. She's been searching for it ever since."

I was ready for the questions. The excitement. The accusations. What I hadn't expected was the blank look on Burn's face. "The what?"

"The *Queen of Stars*. The missing treaty ship."

"The fairy tale ship," Dax chimed in so helpfully.

Burn shook her head. "Sorry. I have no idea what you're talking about. If they didn't teach it in the military's remedial classes, I didn't learn it." She leaned back in her chair, arms crossed defiantly.

I remembered what she said about the lack of education for women on her home planet and my heart ached for the little girl she'd been.

Instead of making her feel bad about her lack of knowledge, I quickly told her the story. Dax chimed in, repeating his belief that it had never existed.

"So it's full of treasure?" Burn asked, a gleam of interest in her eye.

"No one knows for sure," I admitted. "It's more likely to be ore, maybe other supplies for building. Or maybe it doesn't exist," I added, shooting Dax a sharp look. "Regardless, my sister has spent her adult life looking for it and I think that's why she was taken."

Burn leaned forward, utterly engaged in the story. "Because she found it?"

"I don't think so." Based on everything I'd read in her files, I didn't think she had the location yet. "But someone might think she did. Or is about to." My money was on the second option. "She'd agreed to meet with someone from a history forum who said they had new information."

"So we're going treasure hunting?" Burn's excitement bled into her words. She leaned over to give Dax a one-armed hug. "You take me to the best places, Sarge!" Then she bounded to her feet, pausing to look at me. "I'm glad we're going to rescue your sister and all, Lacy. But you really should have led with this. A treasure hunt is badass."

She left the room and I swear I heard her say, "What do you wear to a treasure hunt?"

I shook my head as Dax and I watched her leave.

He shifted to face me, his hand grasping one of mine. "I'm going to tell the others when they come on board, Lacy. I meant it when I said no more secrets."

Exhaling slowly, I nodded, while still mulling over his words. "Do you think it will be a problem?"

Dax didn't say a word and I started to worry.

"Not as much of one as Finn," he said finally. "If we're upfront with them, everything should be fine."

Famous last words, I thought, and gave him a weak smile.

42

LACY

A COUPLE DAYS LATER, Burn, Dax, and I were gathered on the bridge, going over my latest lessons. We'd fallen into a routine since our discussion in the mess hall: we'd come together several times a day for meals and lessons. Dax and Burn would do some kind of workout in the small gym. Sometimes, but not always, together. I made sure to stay away from the gym when Dax was working out. The temptation was too great.

Then Dax would cross-train Burn on running the ship. The woman was a sponge, absorbing whatever lessons Dax or I threw at her. Knowing her background now, it made sense. My parents had supported whatever my sister and I wanted to learn. I couldn't imagine growing up in a world where the opposite was true.

Burn was on her way to becoming a competent pilot, which was why we were all on the bridge. Giving her a chance to work in the controlled chaos that could occur in transit.

The radio crackled to life. "*Fortuna*, this is *Red Ranger*. Please respond."

All three of us stared at the comms. "*Red Ranger?*" I asked.

Both Dax and Burn looked surprised. Then Burn said, "That sounds like Mercer."

We were a few hours away from Justin, our rendezvous point with the rest of their crew. "Do you think it's them?"

Burn had already grabbed the radio. "*Red Ranger*, this is *Fortuna*."

"That you, Burn? Good to hear your voice."

She smiled. "You, too, Mercer. So, uh, *Red Ranger?*"

"Commercial transport would have taken too long, so we rented a courier ship. She's sleek and red and fast as hell."

"You sure it's not a woman, Mercer? Sounds like you're in love," Burn teased.

"You know his thing for redheads," another voice said. I figured it must be Orion, their heavy artillery guy, since as far as I knew we were only expecting two new crew members.

"Remember that time on Proxima?" Burn asked. She and Dax and the voices on the other end all laughed. I felt a tinge of jealousy.

"We can reminisce in person," Dax said, putting an end to their casual conversation. "We're still a few hours out. What's your ETA?"

"We're already here on Justin," Mercer said. "Thought we'd do a little shopping, stock up the armory and whatnot while we wait. You all need anything?"

Burn and Dax looked at each other, then at me. I shrugged. "We're pretty set on supplies, but fresh food is always good. Weapons-wise, that's not my area."

There was a long pause on the other end of the line. "That your stowaway, Dax?" Mercer's lighthearted tone had been replaced by a harder one.

Fuck it. "Yep, that's me," I said before Dax could. "My name is Lacy."

There was a muffled laugh on the other side. Then the second voice, Orion, said, "I like her."

"Don't buy into that damsel in distress shit, Orion. She stole our ship," Mercer said.

I dropped my head back. I was so tired of the accusations. Layla damn well better appreciate what I'd done for her. "For like a whole few hours," I muttered, not caring who heard me.

Dax set his hand on my back, rubbing small, comforting circles. I leaned into his touch. We'd avoided any overt displays of affection the last few days, though that didn't mean we hadn't snuck kisses and a little heavy petting in the hidden corners of the ship.

"Look, we can discuss this later rather than take potshots now. Mercer, you and Orion go shopping. Get weapons, fresh food, and whatever medical supplies you think a ship regularly traveling to the ass-end of nowhere needs. Our med bay looks well stocked, but I'd prefer you get whatever you need or want."

"Roger," Mercer said. "I raided the stores at home for medical supplies. We'll be as well stocked as a hospital."

Dax keyed in a message on his personal comms. "I love the initiative. I just sent you the ship's banking details. Get whatever you think we need. We'll meet you at the docks in a few hours. *Fortuna* out."

Dax and Burn grinned at each other like idiots, while I tried not to get overwhelmed by the feeling of being an outsider again. I missed the camaraderie of a tight group. Every time I thought there was a chance on the *Fortuna*, new people arrived to remind me I didn't belong.

"I should go get the cargo hold ready. And the report on Kottke," I said quietly and escaped the bridge.

43

___

LACY

I CHOSE to remain in engineering while Dax and Burn docked at the spaceport on Justin. Listening to the engines as we landed soothed my nerves. I wasn't sure I was up to several more days of Finn-level abuse.

Both Dax and Burn had assured me that things would be fine, but I was still fragile from experiencing how close Dax's crew was. No matter how much I wanted to be a part of it, I was still an outsider.

The engines wound down, then stopped. We were here. I checked the gauges and other instruments. Everything looked within the proper parameters. I made a mental note to remind Dax that we should fuel up.

With nothing else to procrastinate on, I sighed and left my happy place.

Burn was waiting for me at the door to the cargo hold. "Any weird rituals we need to be aware of here?"

I laughed. "Not every place has them, Burn. But no, as far as I know, it's business as usual here. Plus, we're not picking up cargo, are we?"

Burn shook her head. "Mercer and Orion are shopping for the ship."

"Then as long as the vendors are paid, there shouldn't be any problems." I opened the door to the cargo hold.

It was empty and it was really too bad that we weren't picking up cargo to fill it. "Actually," I said slowly. "What do you think about hauling cargo to Kottke?"

"Like what?" Burn looked curious, but didn't dismiss the idea out of hand.

"I don't know. But there's got to be something that they like. Or want. Or need. Whatever. We won't stand out as much if we're actually delivering something." Why create a fake backstory when we could use a real one?

"That's pretty smart," Burn said. "Want me to look into it?"

"Burn, Lacy. Open the cargo hold for the guys. They're waiting on the dock." Dax spoke through the intercom.

I slapped my hand on the button to open the external door. "Talk to Dax about it. I'll find the cargo master and ask. Oh, and tell him we'll need to fuel up."

The cargo ramp hit the deck with a slight thud that shimmied through the entire hold. Light flooded in and I squinted against the sudden brightness. I could just make out two figures—one tall and slender, the other taller and built like a tank—standing in the entry.

I assumed the bigger guy was Orion only because of the way Dax had described him.

Not willing to wait around for permission, I raced down the ramp. "Burn's up that way. She'll get you situated."

Ignoring their startled expressions, I dashed by them and lightly jumped the last foot from the cargo hold to the dock.

I'd never been to Justin before, but the spaceports on

the outer edges tended to be pretty small and very similar. The cargo master's office should be right near the center of the spoke. It wasn't in the station proper, so I didn't have to worry about security and ID checks.

I skidded to a stop outside the door and checked the time. They were still open. Barely. I rapped my knuckles against the door.

"Yeah?" A burly dude with graying curls and a wrinkled face looked up from his desk. "Help you?"

"Yeah. You got any cargo going to Kottke?"

"Kottke?" His bushy eyebrows raised further, practically getting lost in the shock of hair hanging over his forehead. "What business you got on Kottke?"

"Well, none," I admitted. "But we're flying by with an empty cargo hold and the captain asked me to check if there's anything that needs to go. Never know when you'll need a little extra cash." Out here, everyone understood the need for a cushion.

"Huh." The cargo master rubbed his chin. "How much room you got?"

I estimated about half of our space. I didn't want to appear desperate or too big.

He keyed something into his computer and I cheered on the inside. No grousing about not going through proper channels.

"Well, looks like I've got a shipment of livestock feed that needs to get down to the planet. Last ship couldn't take it all. Told the folks on Kottke it'd be there next week, but if you can take it, they'll be mighty happy to get it early."

"We'll take it."

"You need to check with your captain?"

"Naw, he trusts me." It was true, I realized. The new

guys might not and Burn was still deciding, but Dax? He trusted me.

The cargo master laid out the terms of the contract and I agreed. It would probably be enough to cover our fuel costs here, even with the extra burn the added weight would cause. And it gave us a legit reason to be on planet other than "Hey, have you seen my sister?"

"All right. Sign here and here." He pointed to a couple of places on a cracked tablet screen.

I scrawled my signature where he indicated and provided our dock number.

"It'll be delivered in a couple hours," he said. "You folks leavin' today?"

"Tomorrow, probably," I said. "How long is the transit to Kottke?"

"Half a day, give or take. You leave by mid-morning, you should be rollin' in late afternoon. Wouldn't recommend landing there after dark. Runway's shit and they usually don't light it real good. Locals get pretty unfriendly after dark too. You get what I'm saying?"

I nodded to show I understood. "Thanks for the help," I said. "And the cargo. Appreciate it."

"Miss," he called before I left the office. "I wouldn't recommend you go anywhere alone down there."

"Just me or my crew too?" I asked.

"Anyone, but especially just you. It's a hard life down there. And they make it harder for some."

A shiver ran through me. Is that what had happened to Layla? I thanked him again and wandered back to *Fortuna*.

No. I had to believe that my sister had been taken because of her research. Because of her obsession. I chewed on my lip. His warning ratcheted up my fear and worry.

Lost in my dark thoughts, I ran into Dax at the bottom

of the ramp. He grabbed my shoulders and kept me from tumbling to the ground.

"Oh hey," I said.

"Oh hey," he echoed. "Burn said you had something to ask me?"

Ask, tell. Practically the same thing, right? "We've got some cargo for Kottke. It'll be delivered later this afternoon."

"What the hell?"

I looked up then, past Dax, and noted for the first time the two men, and Burn standing behind them. If the call earlier was anything to go on, Mercer was the one who'd spoken. He glared at me, his lips pursed in disapproval. He might have been good-looking with his tawny skin and his dark eyes, but his sour expression made him look like an asshole.

Burn was doubled over in laughter. The other guy, the big one who looked like a tank, just watched the interaction with a half-smile.

"I told you," Burn wheezed out between laughs.

Dax sighed and crossed his arms over his chest.

I mimicked him, but it wasn't nearly as effective. "Burn and I were talking about cargo and it got me thinking. Why not take cargo down to Kottke? It gives us a legitimate reason to be there. We'll be delivering livestock feed. Shouldn't take up more than a third of our cargo space. Decent price. Enough to cover the fuel bill, probably a little more."

The rest of the crew had gotten closer as I spoke, and now they crowded behind Dax. I hated feeling like I was under a microscope.

"It'll be delivered this afternoon. Cargo master said it's best to take it tomorrow. Apparently the landing pad is in bad shape and they don't always light it well."

"Why not?" Burn asked.

"Salvage, probably."

The four of them stared at me in confusion.

I sighed. "Say a ship crashes at night. People might come out and pick the wreck clean. And when they get billed, they argue that the shipment never arrived. They refuse to pay for goods they didn't receive. It's hard to prove a negative."

"Diabolical," Burn whispered.

It was. Also kind of awful. "I think that gives us a sense of the kinds of people we'll be dealing with down there."

"They do that on purpose?" Orion asked.

I shrugged. That was not a question I wanted to answer out here in the open. "Can we please get on the ship? I promise, I'll answer your questions there." There was already the chance that we were drawing too much attention.

"You're just going to let her make decisions about our cargo and our schedule?" Mercer still sounded pissed.

"Let's get back on the ship, everyone," Dax said, bypassing Mercer's question.

I appreciated his support.

Burn was the first one to tramp back up the ramp. Orion followed.

Mercer kept glaring at me, so I stepped around him. I'd answer their questions but not out here.

"I can't believe this," Mercer muttered, but he followed me onto the ship.

Dax brought up the rear. Once he stepped into the cargo hold, Burn hollered "clear!" She slapped the button to bring the ramp in and close the external door.

44

———

DAX

THE CARGO HOLD door had barely closed when Mercer began demanding answers.

"What the hell, Dax? She just gets to make decisions for the ship?" He gestured at Lacy, who stood close to the door that would take her to the crew quarters. I didn't think he was a danger to her, but I was glad she was near an exit.

Burn stood between her and Mercer, and that was where he directed his ire next. "And you, Burn. Just laughing like a loon. Last I heard, you voted to leave her on the mining station, too. Now here you are aiding and abetting."

Burn stopped laughing and glared at Mercer. "Calm the fuck down, dude."

I had to get control of the situation. I couldn't openly side with Lacy, though I was impressed with her logic. Showing up with cargo made a lot more sense than just showing up and poking around.

I hooked two fingers into my mouth and whistled. It echoed in the empty cargo hold and more than one person winced.

Oops.

"Stand down, "I demanded. "Let's act civilized here. First, introductions. Lacy, meet Mercer and Orion. Mercer, Orion, meet Lacy."

Lacy nodded at them.

I glanced over at Burn. "You all know Burn." Burn smiled and waved, her middle finger extended. I sighed and rubbed my eyes.

"Second, yes. Lacy was a stowaway. Yes, she tried to steal our ship."

Lacy muttered, "I did steal it." Given the way everyone glared at her, they'd all heard her comment too.

Did she not get I was trying to help her?

"But," I said, holding up my hand to forestall any comments, "she's made amends. She's secured us valuable cargo and has been teaching Burn and me the ins and outs of this new business. And I gotta tell you, we were in over our heads here."

"You trust her?" Mercer asked. "Finn said she'd served on Orpheus Blazer's ship."

"Yes, I trust her." I had my own thoughts on what her role on that ship had been. If I was right, things could still blow up in our faces. So I kept my suspicions to myself. "In this, yes, I trust her." I flicked my eyes over to her. Hoping that she knew that this wasn't the only way I trusted her.

Her gaze met mine briefly and I hoped she'd gotten my message.

"What about you, Burn? Finn said you were against her too."

Hands wrapped around the railing, Burn leaned forward, eagerly watching Mercer. "You've talked to Finn? He's awake? How's he doing?"

Mercer shoved a hand into his hair, his features pained.

"Yeah, shit, sorry. Called to check up on him on our way here. He woke up two days ago. I couldn't talk to him, but the doctor said he was groggy, in pain, and pissed that you'd left him there."

His tone turned soothing. "Based on his injuries, you guys made the right choice. He's had two surgeries. They're keeping an eye on one of his legs, just in case they need to do another. You made the right choice." He nodded at me and at Burn, then turned to Lacy. "Still not sure about you, though."

"What's his prognosis?" I asked Mercer.

He whistled low. "Best guess, two to three months. Maybe less if he's an ideal patient. But you know Finn. He's never been an ideal patient."

"No kidding," Orion muttered. It was the first time he'd spoken. And while he wasn't the most talkative guy, that seemed unusual for even him. I'd check on him later, but for right now, we needed to hash out the Lacy situation. None of us could afford to be distracted when we made the rescue attempt.

"Thanks for the update, Mercer." I meant it. I'd hated to leave Finn there, but without a qualified medic onboard, I'd been afraid we'd lose him.

The cargo hold was silent for a moment as we all thought about Finn.

"So, your girl, she handles the cargo?" Orion asked.

I ignored the "my girl" part, although I wished it were true. "Lacy has been teaching us as much as she can since we left Harrier, but there's a lot to learn. So, yes, she's in charge of the cargo for now."

"Until we drop her off somewhere." Mercer again.

My breath hitched. "Yes," I said though I felt like I'd been punched in the stomach.

"And what is it you do?" Mercer asked her, slipping into his snooty, high-society voice.

"I'm a mechanic," Lacy answered calmly.

"And you let her near our ship?"

"Look," Lacy said, cutting me off before I could defend her. "This shit is getting old. I've already done this whole song and dance with Finn." She stepped forward next to Burn and addressed Mercer and Orion from the platform on the stairs.

"You don't like me? Fine. You want me off the ship? Great. You can have that—after you help me rescue my sister. Burn and Dax gave me their word. They promised you would help too. If not, why don't you get back on your little red ship and get the hell out of here. I don't need your shit endangering my sister."

She took a deep breath and continued. "Tonight we'll get the cargo. Tomorrow we'll head to Kottke. Hopefully we'll have Layla free within twenty-four hours. After that, as soon as you find an acceptable planet, we'll be off your ship. A week max. That's all you have to suffer my presence for."

She glared at Burn and me. "Take care of the cargo when it gets here." Then she whirled around and stomped through the door to the rest of the ship. The door slammed behind her.

Thattagirl.

"Yep, I like her," Orion said.

My eyes widened as my gaze whipped toward him.

"Yeah, me too," Burn said. "You were kind of rude to her, Mercer."

What was even happening here? I choked back a laugh when Mercer's jaw dropped.

"What the hell, Burn? Finn said you didn't like her either." Mercer sounded as confused as I felt.

"I didn't, and then I did. And wait 'til you hear about the treasure!" With that, Burn followed Lacy through the door.

"Treasure?" Mercer asked incredulously.

I rubbed my forehead. "It's a long story."

"But treasure? Finn didn't mention anything about treasure."

I was as tired of the questions as Lacy was. I studied the members of my squad. My best friends. Men I considered family. "Look, Lacy had the right of it. Are you in or out? Anything else threatens the mission."

Mercer studied me. I let him. The man had saved my life more than once. I considered him a brother. "You've got it bad, don't you, Dax?"

I started. "What?" That was not the diagnosis I'd expected.

Behind him Orion nodded. "He's right. I've never seen you like this before."

"It's not—" I started to deny it, but he was right. And I was tired of hiding. "Yeah, maybe I do. So what?"

"Are you sure you're thinking clearly?"

I gritted my teeth. I understood why he was asking and maybe someday I'd appreciate his concern. And I would for sure remember this when he finally brought a woman around, but I still hated having to justify my feelings.

"Yes, I'm sure. She's been upfront with us about everything." Except maybe that last secret I thought she was keeping. "She's made connections for us and earned us more money than I'd hoped for right out of the gate. We got off to a rocky start, but things have smoothed out."

"You believe this story about her sister?"

I nodded. "I do. I've seen the videos and I agree with her logic."

"Videos?" Mercer asked.

"Yeah, if you're in, you can hear all about them. If not, I'd rather respect her privacy."

Orion and Mercer looked at each other. Orion shrugged. "I'm in," he said.

"Are you sure?" Mercer asked.

"It's Dax. Of course I'm sure. If he trusts her, I trust her." His smile broke through the new beard he was sporting. "Plus, I want to hear about the treasure."

"It's not as exciting as you think it is," I warned. I still didn't believe it was out there.

Mercer threw his hands up. "Fine, I'm in too. I'm not letting you idiots go down to a backwater planet without backup." He paused. "So tell us about this treasure."

I shook my head. "Nope, that's Lacy's job. While I wait for the cargo to be delivered, you two head back to the spaceport and grab dinner for all of us. Noodles if you can find them."

Orion nodded. "What kind?"

"Spicy garlic. Or whatever they have, I guess." Maybe Lacy would accept the noodles as a peace offering.

"What, we're out of heat-and-eats?" Mercer joked.

"No. But while we're on station, we might as well eat real food."

Mercer stared at me. "You're not going to leave without us, are you?"

"Despite whatever Finn might have told you, I'm not abandoning my crew. That's you guys."

"C'mon, Orion," Mercer said and stomped toward the exit.

I crossed to the steps so I could lower the ramp. "Drinks too," I called out behind them.

Mercer raised his hand and flipped me off, while Orion laughed.

45

———

LACY

Dɪɴɴᴇʀ ᴡᴀs an awkward meal of spaghetti and garlic bread, with fizzy fruit-flavored drinks. I hadn't been expecting it, so it was a nice change of pace. And the garlic smelled much better than the aroma of livestock feed that had drifted through the ship until the filters kicked in.

Dax didn't seem to enjoy dinner, because he spent most of the meal glaring at Mercer, who, at one point, muttered, "What? They're noodles."

Now we were all crammed onto the bridge around the holo table. All eyes were on me as I zoomed in on the little dot that was Kottke. "We are here," I said, pointing to the small dot that represented Justin on the screen. "Based on the information from the cargo master and *Fortuna*'s calculations, it will take us about ten hours to reach Kottke."

I zoomed in further and the screen switched to a satellite image that I'd been able to find on Justin's network. "This was taken a year and a half ago, but as far as I can tell, Kottke isn't really growing." The majority of the image showed dry dusty land. There was a cluster of buildings near the upper right, maybe twenty of them, and then other buildings scattered about the landscape in ones and twos. What looked like dirt roads connected them.

"Looks unpleasant," Dax said. He reached up and zoomed in further, but the picture turned grainy.

"Yeah, it's mostly sandy desert, from what I was able to find. I prefer my sand on the beach," I joked.

"Good to know." Dax wasn't looking at me, but there was something in his tone that made me tingle.

"Any industry?" Mercer asked.

"Not exactly." I'd dug up everything I could find during our transit to Justin and I had some thoughts about their industry, but I'd build up to that. "Most of the people and businesses are in and around the spaceport, Crash City." I pointed to the cluster of buildings.

"Sounds like a great place," Burn muttered.

"Right? Crash City is home to a couple of bars and restaurants. A place I think is a general store, maybe, and some rundown hangars and ship-repair shops. Those are most likely chop shops."

"For the crashed ships?" Burn asked.

"Yeah, probably. Most estimates put the population around a thousand permanent residents. I'm not sure how many live in or around Crash City, versus the outlying properties. From what I can tell, it's mostly subsistence farming and some hard-scrabble mining."

"For what?" Dax asked.

I shrugged. "Not enough info. The most common beliefs are either gold flakes or some type of gemstone." Personally, I thought most of the expensive trade goods came from crashed ships, though I could be wrong. I wasn't a geologist.

"Is that the treasure Burn mentioned?" Orion asked. He stood a few feet behind the rest of us. He was a big guy, probably at least six foot three or four. He was definitely taller than the rest of the crew, so he could probably see over them. He was solid too. It'd be easy to find him intimidating, but so far I'd experienced nothing but kindness from him.

"Treasure? What? No, that's . . . I'll explain that shortly." Flustered, I tried to remember where I was. I skimmed my notes. "The original settlers were prospectors who thought they could terraform it. The process created an atmosphere, but didn't do much to the planet itself."

"When was that?"

"Hundred and fifty years or so ago."

"And it's still that unsettled?" Mercer sounded surprised. Then again, with the accent that he put on and off, it was likely he came from one of the big planets at the center of the system. Where everything was built up, because there was no more available land on the surface.

"It's at the ass end of nowhere," Burn said before I could reply. I wondered if that was what her home planet was like. "No plants, no industry. Why the hell would anyone want to settle there?"

I agreed.

Dax grimaced. "I've been to a few places like that. No central government?"

I shook my head and switched the screen again. This time it showed a closeup of the city, including a control tower and the landing pad. No buildings that looked like they housed a government. "None that I can find."

Dax stepped back and leaned against the ship's main console. "No industry. No government." He looked at me. "You're thinking crime?"

Glad someone else had come to the same conclusion, I nodded. "It's the only thing that makes sense to me."

"Walk us through it," Mercer said, without even a please or thank-you.

"No central government is a good start. No one to keep an eye on what you're doing. It's possible that it's run by a crime family, maybe more than one, but it's so small I can't see it supporting several. The control tower looks to be in good shape and that takes funds, especially if you're bringing things in and out. Then there's the warning the cargo master gave me about folks not being that nice. And finally, the few export records I was able to find read more like a parts catalog than farm products or ores."

"I'm guessing you learned all about a life of crime while you served on the ship of the most notorious outlaw—"

"—Scoundrel—"

"What?" Mercer's question, but everyone was staring at me.

"He's really more of a scoundrel than an outlaw. Maybe a rogue? I don't know exactly. He has his own code which, sure, is mostly in the gray area, but the law isn't always right."

"How long were you part of his crew?"

Crap. I tended to get a little defensive whenever anyone went after my dad. "Does it matter?" *Please say no.*

"I guess not. But those are some really interesting ideas you have there. It almost sounds like you believe them." Mercer stared hard at me.

"Let's just say I don't *not* believe them and leave it at that. Anyway, now that we've established that Kottke's main industry is probably crime, how should we approach this?" Hopefully that would be enough to distract them from my oversharing.

"Wait," Burn said. "What about your sister? And the treasure?"

With a few flicks of my wrist, the image of Kottke disappeared and was replaced by one of my sister.

"This was one of my sister's last videos." I paused, closed my eyes, then opened them and took a big leap. "She's spent her entire life researching the *Queen of Stars.*"

"She found it?" Orion spoke at the same time as Mercer. "It doesn't exist."

"See, treasure!" Burn bounced on her toes.

"It's fake," Mercer said. "She's feeding us a line."

"My sister believes it's real. She has years and years' worth of research. One of her last entries mentioned going to meet someone who claimed that an escape pod from the *Queen of Stars* had landed on their home planet. And that they had proof."

More talking over each other. I just waited them out. Finally, they quieted down. "You don't think your sister was, um, stupid enough to meet some stranger, do you?" Orion asked gently.

I wasn't so sure about that, but I wasn't going to blame Layla. "I think she took all possible precautions," I said carefully. "From her records, she met them in a public space, on a public station."

"This is neither," Mercer snapped.

"Well aware," I snapped back. "It took me a while to figure it out. She said she met this person on a forum for speculation about the fate of the *Queen of Stars.* She was skeptical, but they sent her enough of a teaser that she believed them. They set up a meeting on Causeway, as far as I can tell, but I don't think she made it there. I think she ended up here, on Kottke."

It had taken me days and days to come up with this theory. No, it wasn't just a theory. I had painstakingly pieced together her last few days.

"The person who posted on the forum? I did some

digging through the forum and her records. His name is Johnstone Farrow. Some of his postings refer to a hot, dry, desert planet. And," the piece de resistance, and the reason I knew my sister had decided to meet him, "one of the original crew on the *Queen of Stars* was named Gaylord Farrow."

The bridge exploded in chaos as everyone spoke at once.

46

DAX

After Lacy's briefing, we'd returned to the mess because it had more room. More room to move, more room to think. After several hours of wrangling and more pots of coffee than I wanted to count, we had a plan. Or most of a plan.

Mercer and Orion had argued for more time to refine our strategy. While extra time never hurt, I didn't think waiting another day would do us much good since we had no idea what we were facing down there.

It wasn't just that, though. Lacy was already a bag of nerves and another delay when her sister had been missing for weeks just might break her.

I'd ordered everyone to bed with instructions to meet again in the morning. Then I locked the ship down tight and grabbed a few hours of sleep myself.

The next morning, Burn waltzed into the mess right on time. Mercer and Orion trailed after her. Both looked freshly showered and alert. Good.

"This is the mess," she said, doing a little spin and gesturing around the room. "But you already knew that.

Fresh food there, prefab food there." She pointed in opposite directions. "Coffee there." She stopped her spin and glared at them. "If you take the last cup, make a new pot. We're back in civilization now." She reached for a mug. "Oh, and Lacy makes weak-ass coffee. Beware."

I choked back a laugh. Lacy's coffee was the worst. If she were staying on board, we might need to get two pots, because she drank as much coffee as we did, but complained that ours was like tar.

"That's because motor oil belongs in the engines, Burn, not in a mug," Lacy snarked as she followed them into the room. She didn't look nearly as rested as the others. She'd probably been up all night worrying about her sister.

"Here, sit down." I stood and pulled out the chair next to me.

When she sat, I gave her shoulders a squeeze. The others stared at me, but I ignored them. I knew how freaked out I would be if one of my sisters was missing. We were so close, and still, anything could happen.

With a final squeeze, I stepped away from the table and toward the coffee. Orion had just pulled a mug off the shelf, and I plucked it from his hand. "It's her favorite," I said, already reaching past him to fill it two-thirds with coffee. Then I doctored it the way she liked it, with a flavoring she'd bought on Rigel Naught.

"Gotcha," he said with a wink.

Good thing my hands were full or I would have flipped him off. I grabbed a shelf-stable pastry from the dry goods storage and the last piece of fresh fruit from the chiller. "You need to eat something," I said, setting breakfast down in front of her.

"I'm not hungry," she said.

I grabbed my own breakfast, a bready, bacon and cheese–filled heat-and-eat and sat down next to her. "I don't care." I pushed the plate toward her while everyone else took a seat around the table.

Despite the stress of the moment, I smiled. My team was on the ship. I'd missed this, eating with them most mornings.

Lacy took a sip of coffee, but didn't touch the food.

"Look, Lacy, I get it. You're stressed out," Burn said. "But if you don't eat, you might pass out. If you pass out, we might have to abandon the mission. And even if we don't have to abort, you'll be out of commission, and we might not recognize your sister. So I think you should eat, so we have a better chance of rescuing her. But that's just me."

"Fine," Lacy said with an exasperated sigh. She didn't dig in the way the rest of the team did, but she took reasonable bites.

Thank you, I mouthed to Burn.

She rolled her eyes and made kissy motions at me.

I finished my coffee and after enjoying the clatter of silverware and the sounds of a full dining room, I steepled my hands and studied my team. "Once we launch, we'll have about ten hours in transit. I want to use that time to check our gear and prep for the mission. Mercer and Orion, you'll be in charge of the equipment, while Burn and I pilot the ship. We'll rotate through so you can gear us up as well."

Lacy swallowed the last of the pastry and looked at me. "What about me?"

"You're in charge of the engine room and the cargo. Whatever we need to make this look legit."

We'd hammered this all out last night, but it was good to go over it again.

"Pick the least military-looking clothes you have," Lacy said. "We're just traders, not soldiers. I picked up coveralls for everyone that say *Fortuna.* Unless you don't want to advertise."

"No names." Everyone agreed.

"Then try to look more like Blazer than space corps."

I winced, but knew what she was saying. The man was famous—or infamous—for his high boots, dark trousers, vest, and gun belt.

"We'll do our best," I said before anyone could argue. My clothes didn't look anything like that, but I'd find something. Burn would probably look like a supermodel, though.

"Finally, I'll need you guys to kit Lacy out with protective gear." Neither Burn nor I had body armor—I hadn't even thought it was something we would need aboard—but the guys had brought some for us. Now we just had to cobble together something for Lacy.

"Any questions?"

When no one responded, I continued. "Great, we launch in an hour."

The breakfast conversation turned to regular topics and my three team members caught each other up on what they'd been doing since leaving the corps. I listened with half an ear, most of my attention on Lacy. When she finished her meal and pushed away from the table, I followed.

We walked side by side in silence to the crew quarters. When we reached the captain's quarters, I grabbed her hand and pulled her inside with me.

"I love what you've done with the place," she quipped.

I was glad to see that hint of humor return.

As she turned in a circle to study the room, I did the same. My quarters were twice the size of the crew cabins, which meant not only a bigger bed, but more furniture.

There was a bigger desk in an alcove, almost like an office. A bigger bathroom. And a bigger closet.

And all I'd brought with me was a duffle bag full of clothes. They barely made a dent in the closet space. "I keep wondering if I should let someone else take it."

"You're acting captain, right?" she asked, her gaze on me.

"Yeah."

"Then it's yours. If anyone argues, they can step up and captain the ship."

She was right, I realized. While I was making the decisions, or at least guiding them, the captain's quarters should be mine. If someone else wanted the job, that was fine. Or if I decided to follow Lacy, they'd need a new captain.

Would I do that? Could I do that?

This wasn't the time for that kind of decision. Our focus, my focus, had to be on Layla.

I led Lacy over to the desk and gestured for her to take a seat. She took one of the visitors' chairs and I took the other, shifting so I faced her.

"To what do I owe the honor of being in your cabin?" Her voice was stronger now. Seeing her so quiet at breakfast had unnerved me. She glanced over at the bed.

Ignoring the big, fluffy, soft elephant in the room, I kept my gaze on her. I'd imagined her in my bed more than once, but as much as I'd enjoy spending the entire transit cocooned in my cabin with her, we couldn't afford to be distracted.

"I wanted to talk to you in private. I know the team has been a lot to deal with, and I'm sorry about that."

"You don't have to apologize for them. You're not the one being an asshole. At least not anymore." Her grin was warm and open.

I took her hand, rubbing my thumb over the back of it. "I'm sorry about being an asshole."

"I accept," she said. "I'm sorry about stealing your ship."

I laced my fingers with hers. "Are you, though?"

"Okay, I'm 90 percent sorry. But without it, I'm not sure where I'd be now. If I'd be about to rescue my sister."

"That's what I wanted to talk to you about."

"The rescue?" Eyes full of worry, she tugged her hand free and stared at me.

"You don't have to come with us, if you don't want. You can stay safe on the ship. Or even up here."

She surged to her feet. "You think I'm a liability?" Her voice rose and I was grateful we were having this conversation here, rather than elsewhere on the ship.

"No, not at all. I just want to make sure you're safe. I . . . You're important to me. I don't want you hurt."

"I don't want you hurt either, Dax." She offered me her hands and tugged me to standing. "I appreciate you worrying about me, but I'll be okay. I promise. Plus, I can help. I know it."

Her arms slid around my waist and she lay her cheek against my chest. I closed my arms around her.

"What if we don't find her?" Lacy asked quietly. "Or worse, we do and it's . . . it's really bad?"

I rested my cheek against the top of her head. I'd been expecting this moment for a while. It hadn't been a question of when it would happen, but if she would share it. I rubbed my hand up and down her back.

"I'm not going to feed you a line of bullshit just to make you feel better. There's a chance that we won't find her. If that happens, we'll regroup, explore other leads. I told you we'd help you find your sister and we will."

She sniffled. "What if they've hurt her? Or k—killed her?"

Fuck, she was breaking my heart.

"Don't borrow trouble. Right now, we don't know anything. When we arrive at Kottke, we'll go down, we'll ask some questions—"

"And get some answers," she broke in.

"—and get some answers. Then we'll work out the next steps to getting her back."

My hand continued to rub soothing circles over her back. She wasn't the only one who had considered the possibility that Layla had been injured or killed. But until we had proof, I was hoping for the best.

If the worst had happened, I'd burn it all down if Lacy asked me to.

"Thank you," she said. "I know I haven't said it often enough. Or maybe even ever. But thank you. For helping me. For getting me this far." She raised up on her tiptoes and pressed her lips to mine.

Though I worried for a moment, this kiss wasn't about gratitude. It was about connection.

I embraced that, embraced her. And tried to tell her with my body and with my lips, the feelings I hadn't even dared to admit to myself yet.

47

———

DAX

"Kᴏᴛᴛᴋᴇ Tᴏᴡᴇʀ ᴛᴏ ɪɴᴄᴏᴍɪɴɢ ᴄʀᴀꜰᴛ. Identify yourself."

"This is it," I said to Burn. "Kottke Tower, this is *Fortuna*. Permission to land?"

"State your business, *Fortuna*."

Burn rolled her eyes. "Gee, they're friendly."

I was glad the outgoing comms were off. "Real welcoming." Toggling the comms back on, I said, "Got some livestock feed from Justin to deliver. Then top up on fuel, check for any outgoing cargo, and get a cold drink, not necessarily in that order."

The pause on the other end was long. Too long?

"Thought that feed wasn't getting here for a few days," the suspicious voice in the tower said.

"We're just passin' through, checked in with the cargo master on Justin to see if there were any short-hop jobs. He had this one." My palms were sweaty and I wiped them on my jumpsuit one at a time and wished Lacy was up here on the bridge with us.

Since the bridge couldn't hold all of us comfortably, I'd made the executive decision that only Burn and I would be here for the landing. Lacy was in engineering, while Mercer and Orion were in the jump seats in the cargo hold.

"Someone will meet you at the landing zone for the cargo."

"How about that drink? And the fuel?"

There was a laugh on the other end. "The drinks'll be a lot cheaper than the fuel. But if you need it, you can fill up at the port."

"Got any recommendations for where to get that drink?" I asked.

The voices on the other end quieted. "Go to Greenfield. Any other place, well, that'll cost ya."

Sure, that wasn't suspicious. "Copy, thanks."

Back in their professional but unfriendly tone, the tower personnel said, "*Fortuna*, you're cleared for landing. Look for the big red lights. You can't miss 'em. And if you do . . . well, you won't be leaving here any time soon."

"Roger. Thanks. See you boys on the ground."

"Kottke Tower out."

I toggled off the external comms and flipped on the internal ones. "We're cleared for landing. They definitely warned us away from landing anywhere but the official zone."

The others acknowledged that.

"They also directed us to a specific bar and indicated that going anywhere else would cause problems for us."

Mercer spoke up. "So, we go to one of the other ones?"

That wasn't my take, but I was new to all this. "Lacy, what do you think?"

"I think we go where they tell us. We don't want to draw attention to ourselves, at least not yet."

"They didn't bat an eye when I said we were looking

for some cargo. That might also be why they pointed us to that bar."

Burn spoke. "We've got the big red lights, kids. Hold on to your asses, everybody, cuz we're about to land."

I flipped off the comms and took control.

THE CARGO MASTER on Justin was right. The landing zone on Kottke looked like crap, but the landing went better than I'd expected. After securing the ship, Burn and I hustled to the cargo hold to join the others. We met Lacy on the way.

"Why aren't you in the body armor?" I said, studying her outfit with a frown. She was wearing a flight suit that looked like a cross between her coveralls and a spacesuit. It had obviously seen better days. Grease streaked across the front and over most limbs. How the hell did she think that was going to provide any protection?

"It didn't fit. You're all taller than me. And wider."

Burn sniggered and Lacy glared at her. "Shut up."

"You think that will protect you?" I wouldn't hesitate to leave her on the ship, rather than risk her out on this backwater planet.

"It'll be fine, Dax." She rolled her eyes. Then she tugged at the zipper at her neck, slowly undoing it a few inches.

"Whoa, now." Burn threw a hand up to cover her eyes. "No one said anything about a strip show."

"I think I liked you better when you didn't like me," Lacy said. She tugged the zipper down a few more inches and rolled the fabric out.

"What am I supposed to be looking at?" The outside of the suit was gray, while the inside was black.

"None of your gear fit me, but this flight suit does. I lined it with the material from a couple of your gear bags."

Burn dropped her hand and reached out to touch the material. "Smart. How did you get it to stay in place? Do you sew?"

Lacy looked horrified. "No. No sewing. I used a bonding agent we use for short-term ship repairs. We'll have to get more when we're someplace that isn't here."

I still wasn't happy that Lacy didn't have a full set of body armor—I'd rectify that as soon as possible—but it was a clever solution. The gear bags were made of heavy-duty ballistic material. It wasn't battle-rated fabric, but it was tough enough to handle transport, which had been known to include crashes and accidental weapons fire. It would stop energy weapons and knives and if she was very, very lucky, it might stop a projectile weapon.

"Do you remember that guy in our company who could not fucking keep his laser from firing prematurely? His gear bag was beat to shit, but those shots never caused any harm." Burn paused, then added, "I always felt bad for his girlfriend."

I closed my eyes and gave a quiet laugh. That damn guy had been the laughingstock of the entire platoon until he got on the battlefield. There he'd been a fucking deadeye. But he wasn't safe to be around when we were training.

"What about your head?"

"I lined a hat with the material, too. It's in my bag."

"You should be wearing it." My drill sergeant voice slipped out.

"Easy there, Sarge." Burn put her hand on my arm. "Lacy is perfectly safe while she's on the ship."

"Are you sure you don't want to stay onboard?"

She tugged the zipper back up to her neck and glared at me. "We're not having this conversation again."

The cargo door opened, and Mercer popped his head out. "You guys comin' or what? Got some guy outside who says he's here for the cargo. Got a hover cart and everything."

"On our way." Burn hurried toward the door.

When Lacy turned to follow her, I put my hand on her arm to slow her down. "I just want you safe," I said quietly.

Her hand covered mine. "I know that, Dax. But I can't sit here and worry about my sister *and you*. I have to be out there looking for her."

"Fine. At least tell me why you're covered with grease." The ballistic material, once she'd explained it, made perfect sense. The dirt and grime didn't.

Her smile was bright. "Hiding in plain sight." I held the door to the cargo hold open for her. "You guys scream ex-military, even with the too-long hair and the personal gear."

I ran my hand through the offending extra length.

"I don't look like that," she said, like it explained everything.

"So?"

"If I look like a regular person, but I'm hanging around with a bunch of mercenaries—"

"We're not mercenaries," I interjected with a frown.

"—they're going to wonder who I am. Am I someone who might be worth money? I don't want to become another kidnapping victim. So, I look like a mechanic." She shrugged.

"And?" I still wasn't sure what she was getting at.

"A bunch of mercs are going to need a mechanic, right? Tada. Here I am." She raised her hands. "The really brilliant part, I think, is that we're on such a backwater planet, that they probably think that if you had to hire a girl mechanic, you're a crappy bunch of mercs."

Burn looked up from the floor of the cargo hold and laughed. "That's pretty damn brilliant."

Lacy beamed a smile at her. "I know, right?"

"You can't know that they're going to think that," I argued.

Lacy smirked at me. "Uh, yeah, I can."

Burn nodded.

"What are you arguing about?" Orion asked.

I scowled at the two women and shook my head. "Lacy thinks that anyone seeing that we have a female mechanic will think that we're a really crappy mercenary team. Burn agrees with her. I said they're wrong. No one is going to think that."

Orion was still pondering his response when Mercer stepped out from behind him. "That's probably the first smart thing your girl has said since I met her."

She scowled at him.

"I don't like that assumption, but if we can use that to our advantage, fine." I descended the steps, Lacy behind me.

"Where's the bag?" Mercer asked her.

"Bonded to the clothes." She didn't explain further.

He nodded.

I was surprised, but thankful. Maybe he was warming to her.

"Burn and I should be in charge of the cargo," Lacy said. "Lull them into a false sense of security. You guys go and melt into the shadows or something."

I looked down at my khaki cargo pants and lighter shirt. They weren't quite desert camo, but there wasn't going to be much fading into the darkness.

There weren't many places to hide in the cargo hold. I

stationed Mercer back in the hall outside of the hold. No single team member was more important than the others, but we'd just gotten the medic on board so I wanted to keep him safe and healthy for the moment. We might need him for Layla.

Orion, the man mountain, crept as far as he could into an alcove on the far side of the hold. He wasn't hidden by a longshot, but you'd also have to look right at him to really see him.

As requested, I found a shadow near the external door, so I positioned myself there, ready to protect Lacy if there was trouble.

She glared at me and tried to shoo me back. I shook my head.

Lips pressed together, she finally nodded, then turned her back on me with a flounce. I stifled a laugh.

After one last look around the hold to ensure everyone was in place, she said, "Show time!"

Burn opened the external cargo hold door, and then, with slow and steady steps, she descended the steps and crossed to the stacks of feed bags.

"Hi. Are you here for the cargo?" Lacy said brightly.

There was a long pause. I imagined whoever was at the door was ogling her. My jaw clenched.

Burn took a step closer to Lacy, which didn't reassure me.

I wished I'd considered a spot with a direct line of sight to the door. Knowing Lacy wasn't fully protected, I'd rather be the one dealing with the cargo. Why had I gone along with this?

Oh, right, because she had the most experience.

I hated that.

"Yup," a deep voice said.

"Great," she said with far more cheer than necessary. "It's right over there."

"You ladies alone?" The second voice was even sleazier than the first.

I was hating this plan more by the second.

"Captain's busy. You need any help with that cargo?" Burn asked in a flat voice.

"Just being friendly. Don't get your knickers in a twist." A hearty laugh.

I clenched my hand around the butt of my blaster.

"Oh, don't you worry, boys. It's not my panties in a twist. It's my trigger finger with an itch."

My jaw dropped at Burn's response.

"You don't have to be such a bitch about it," the second guy said. "We were just bein' friendly."

"I don't get paid to be friendly," Burn said. "Load your hover cart and give her the tablet to confirm payment." She gestured toward Lacy with her chin.

If Burn wasn't careful, she'd blow the whole "bad mercenary" charade.

Lacy counted off the bags of feed as they loaded them. "Fifty-nine on the cart, fifty-nine on the invoice. Just need your signature to complete the transaction, gentlemen."

"How about you let me buy you a drink instead?"

"Time is money, gentlemen," Burn said and took another step closer. "And I don't want to waste any more time waiting for my money."

I blinked in surprise. Burn had always been a badass, but this was next level. The mercenary queen.

I'd buy her a drink myself to thank her for protecting Lacy like this.

Lacy made a small sound of pain as the tablet was wrenched out of her hands. I assume the asshole signed it, because then he said, "See? Happy now?"

"Perfect," Burn said. "Now get off my ship."

"Thought you said the captain was busy."

She raised a brow. "Mmhmm. Busy watching you two."

Weapon held casually in her hand, she stared at them. Finally, after some grumbling, the hover cart and the two men tromped down the ship.

Lacy was quick to close the ramp. "Burn, you were amazing."

"I really was, wasn't I?" A wide smile broke across her dark face. "That was so fun."

Applause echoed around the cargo hold. Orion stepped out from his alcove, clapping. "You're a bad bitch, Burn."

Burn holstered her weapon and practically skipped across the now-empty cargo hold. "Damn, Orion, I've missed you." She launched into his arms.

He caught her easily and swung her around. "Missed you too, squirt."

Orion gently set Burn back on her feet and she leaned into him. "Now do we get to go fuck some shit up?"

"I think we've created a monster," I said with a smile. Burn had always been an adrenaline junkie. Stirring those guys up had probably been a rush. "But to answer your question, yes. Now we go fuck some shit up."

48

———

LACY

I'D SPENT the walk from the ship to the center of Crash City looking around in wonder. I hadn't been on a planet in years. Kottke was so bright. It was late afternoon, but the way the sun reflected off the sand made it seem like the middle of the day. I'd forgotten what outside—real outside—was like. I obviously needed to get out more.

The landing zone and our ship were on the outskirts of town, but since the town was so small, the walk had only taken a few minutes.

While I gawked, Dax and Burn had been getting the lay of the land. I would've walked right into the side of a building if Dax hadn't stopped me.

"Are you ready for this?"

I met his concerned gaze and nodded. "Ready."

We were stopped in front of Greenfield, the bar the control tower had "recommended." Like most of the buildings in town, it was low and squat and made of wood that had bleached after so many years in the harsh sun. It looked sad and old, not welcoming in the slightest.

"You remember the plan?" Dax rested his hand on my lower back.

"I remember." It was just the three of us, nice and casual. Mercer and Orion had already made their way here to do reconnaissance. We'd split up so we didn't look like a scary group. *Fortuna* was the only ship at the spaceport, so it was obvious where any newcomers were from.

I exhaled slowly. Now that we were face-to-face with the plan, I realized how out of my depth I was. Even with Burn and Dax at my back, my nerves were jangling. Thank god I had stolen *their* ship. Doing this alone would be even scarier.

"Deep breath. You got this," Dax murmured. He gave me a squeeze and then his hand was gone.

I could do this.

The door swung open with a creak. Crossing the threshold, we transitioned from bright day to gloomy night. Conversation stopped, but the clink of glassware continued. Once inside, I stepped to the side and let my eyes adjust. Burn and Dax entered right behind me. The door swung closed with a groan.

Despite feeling everyone's eyes on me, I kept to the plan and walked in like I did this every day.

"Beer?" Burn asked.

Dax and I both nodded and she peeled off toward the bar.

The inside was bigger than I'd expected, with more than two dozen tables and a bar that ran the length of one side of the building. Maybe a third of the tables were in use, including the one where Mercer and Orion sat.

Dax ignored them when we walked past. He chose a table on the other side of the room, near the wall. He grabbed the seat that gave him the best view of the whole space.

My shoulders tensed as I settled across from him, exposing my back to the room. I scooted my chair around so I had at least a limited view.

"Drinks?" A waitress in black cargo pants and a tank top appeared at our table.

"Got drinks taken care of." Dax pointed to Burn standing at the bar. "But you got anything to eat?"

The waitress curled her lip. Her voice dropped to a whisper. "If you want food poisoning, order anything that says fresh. Something fried is your best bet. That or a sealed snack bag if you want to splurge."

Wow. *That* all sounded delicious.

I let Dax do the talking since she didn't look at me the whole time. He ordered fries, which I planned to stay away from, and a few bags of chips. Hopefully the snacks would be edible, since I was hungry and would need to absorb the alcohol if the beer was drinkable.

"Be right back with those, handsome."

She turned and deftly sidestepped past Burn, who was juggling three glasses of beer. I grabbed two and set one in front of Dax. She nodded in thanks before taking the chair next to him. "Ooh, you got the handsome treatment. Think she really thinks so or is it part of the service here?"

Dax shrugged, but he looked embarrassed.

"Probably both," I said. "Guys probably tip better if they think she's into them. Plus, how many actually good-looking men come in here every day?"

Burn looked around the room. "Looks like one or two locals, but I think we broke records bringing three of them in today."

My eyes had adjusted to the dim light and I could see Dax's cheeks turn red.

I burst out laughing.

"Well, that got people's attention." His voice was a quiet rumble. His eyes were sharp, taking in everything happening behind me.

"They all looked when we entered the room, but no one's paying much attention to us now," Burn added.

"Give it a few more minutes," I said. "Maybe something will look promising." Speaking of promising, my beer smelled like beer, but I wasn't brave enough to try it first. "Have you tried this yet?"

Burn shook her head. "Too busy juggling. And also too afraid. I can't decide if this place is just your average spaceport bar or if there's something more sinister."

"Me too!"

Dax just shook his head at both of us.

I was going to go crazy if I didn't have something to do. And drinking was doing something, so . . . I picked up my glass and sniffed again. Still smelled like beer. "If this kills me, please still try to rescue my sister."

"We will," Burn said. She lifted her glass and we clinked.

I looked at Dax expectantly. He sighed in exasperation, but lifted his glass. "Cheers."

"Cheers," I repeated. "Here goes nothing." I took a baby sip of the beer. It tasted . . . good. Like, surprisingly good. A bit hoppy, with little bursts of freshness. I took another small sip.

Same results. I lowered my glass and stared at it.

The waitress dropped three bags of chips on the table, then reached past Burn to place the fries in front of Dax. "Everything okay with your drinks?"

"Yes," I said. "No. Maybe?"

She finally tore her gaze away from Dax and looked at me. "What do you mean?"

"I mean, it's a good beer. I didn't expect that?"

She laughed. "So you want to know if it's poisoned or something?"

"Well . . . yeah."

"Not today," she said, absolutely straight-faced.

I looked at her in horror and set my beer down so fast it sloshed.

"That's a joke. The owner's grandfather always wanted to make beer, so a few years ago they cobbled together a brewing apparatus for him. He's been tinkering since." She grimaced. "Some batches are better than others."

Practically every planet made beer, but a good, small-batch alcohol could fetch a nice price in the right markets. "Do you sell it off-planet? Are you looking for someone to ship it?" The words flowed out of me so quickly, I worried that there was some kind of truth serum in it.

"You looking for cargo?" The waitress got a speculative look in her eye.

I put my drink down and dialed back my enthusiasm. It wouldn't do to oversell our hand. "Wouldn't hurt. Delivered some feed and wouldn't mind an outbound load."

The waitress looked at all three of us one by one. "If you're serious, I can let some people know."

We all nodded. Dax let me continue the conversation. "Saw the hangars. Got anyone who sells spare parts? This lot," I gestured at Dax and Burn, "decided to go 'exploring' and I'm worried a few of our parts are gonna fritz out. I'd rather have spares with me, if I can, rather than need a part and not have it."

"Sure. I can put the word out for that too." There was a gleam in her eyes that told me that she got a cut of any business she sent their way.

"Thanks."

The waitress took off and instead of returning to the bar, she headed toward the back room.

"Well, we've started the ball rolling." I reached for a bag of chips. My beer was half gone and I really needed to slow down.

"You went off script." Dax sounded disapproving.

"I know," I said. "I was nervous. It seems to have worked, though."

He was still frowning but he nodded.

"Let's call it a win then," I said.

He crossed his arms over his chest and looked everywhere but at me. I tried not to take it personally—he was probably keeping an eye out for trouble—but it still felt like he was mad at me.

I raised my glass and put a smile on my face even though I wanted to scowl back at him. "Pick up your glass and take a sip. Or a pretend sip. We're supposed to be having a good time."

"She's right," Burn said.

"Thank you." I could really get used to having her on my side instead of against me.

Dax unwound enough to take a drink. "You're right." He raised his glass again, then paused, staring over my shoulder.

I turned my head and caught a glimpse of checkerboard plaid in my periphery.

"You the ones looking for parts?" A gruff older man stepped closer to our table and I got a better look at him. He wore grease-streaked overalls over the plaid shirt. His hands were streaked with grease. His nails were short and blunt and I bet if we shook hands, I'd feel calluses similar to mine.

"Yep," Dax said.

His abruptness didn't seem to deter the old guy. He grabbed a chair from a nearby table, flipped it around and straddled it, resting his arms on the top of the back.

"Whatcha need?" he asked Dax.

"Ask her." Dax pointed at me. "Tell him what we need."

Although the command made me bristle, these were the roles we were playing. I pulled a datapad out of my pocket and powered it up. It was an old one that we'd scrubbed clean of any usable data. We weren't taking any chances on this planet.

During the transit from Justin, I'd created a list of parts, starting with common ones that any ship might want to have on hand and then ending with the ones specific to *Fortuna*. I read it off, keeping one eye on the list as I scrolled through it and the other on him to watch his reaction.

"That all you got?" he asked when I finished.

"There's more. I just didn't want to waste your time if you can't handle it."

"Girlie, you're wasting my time right now. Give me the whole dang list. I got work to do." He pulled out a beat-up tablet and set it on the table.

"Sure, sorry." I transferred the file to his datapad with a flick of my finger.

He scrolled through it once or twice, then tapped his fingers on the screen. "I can cover about 90 percent of that." He quoted a number I found reasonable and a time of a couple hours from now, so I agreed.

"What about the rest?"

He rubbed his jaw. "That's some pretty specialized stuff, and well, we're not a real specialized planet. Can't you get those parts at your next stop?"

Valid question and I pretended to give it the

consideration it deserved. "If we were going somewhere civilized, sure. But they," I jerked my thumb at Dax and Burn, "think we'll do better sticking to the edge of the system for a while. We don't need any of those parts right away, but I don't want to be caught without it either. Can anyone else here help us out?"

He rubbed his jaw again. "Well . . ." He drew the word out and the wait nearly killed me. "You may be able to get the parts on-planet, but I wouldn't recommend it."

"Bad stock?"

He frowned and shook his head. "Bad guys." He pointed his finger at me. "If you're determined to look for those parts, you be sure and take your crew with you. Between the four of them, you should get there and back safely. If you decide to go. Which you shouldn't."

The old man was a lot sharper than I'd figured, since he'd put Mercer and Orion with our group. And more honest than I'd expected, since he seemed to be trying to steer us away from the guys who ran the chop shop.

"I'll take them with me," I said. "I'll need someone to carry the heavy stuff."

"This ain't no joking matter, girlie. The men who might have the parts you want didn't get them legally, if you get what I'm sayin.' You don't want to be messing with them."

"In and out," I promised. I leaned close. "Is our ship safe?"

He was quiet a long moment. "Long as you and your crew don't go missin', it should be fine. So make sure you don't."

"Thank you," I said.

"I ain't done nothin'," he said. "Just business. You get those parts before dark. You want to be in your ship when night falls around here."

I nodded.

"It's the big hangar on the edge of town," he said. "I can't stop you, but I wish you'd reconsider." Standing abruptly, he shoved his tablet in his pocket. Over my shoulder, Burn and Dax watched him go.

49

LACY

AFTERNOON HAD FADED into evening by the time we received the supplies from the man in the bar and had stowed them away.

"I didn't expect you to actually buy anything." Burn had helped me carry a load down to the engine room. Now she watched me put the parts away in their assigned places. "I thought the list was just for show."

There'd been some argument when the rest of the team realized that I truly intended to purchase the supplies. The price had been good, even sight unseen, and I'd rather have the spares to rig a solution than only have a broken part. Compared to what they had earned from the delivery of the stupid shooters, what I'd spent was just a drop in the bucket.

I latched the storage unit so supplies wouldn't go flying during sudden moves. "Oh, I was serious," I said. "Everything on the list were parts and supplies I'd prefer to have on hand in case of emergency. Floating in space because a part broke and you couldn't repair it?" I shook my head.

"Thanks for the nightmare fuel," Burn said.

"You shouldn't have to worry now. The ship has spare parts to cover almost everything. All you'll need is a qualified mechanic to replace them."

Burn's hand on my shoulder stopped me when I would have walked past her to the exit. "Lacy, about that . . ."

I didn't let her finish. "Please don't distract me right now, Burn. We're so close to finding my sister and I'm hanging on by a thread."

"Okay." She frowned. "But we need to talk."

"Sure. We can talk. After." I looked at her hand. She removed it reluctantly. I really didn't need the reminder that I wasn't the ship's mechanic. Finn was. Finn, who had months of rehab ahead of him.

Dammit, *Fortuna's* engine room felt like mine. But it wasn't and I had to remember that.

Burn followed me back to the mess, where everyone was supposed to meet. "Are you ready for this?"

Was I ready to go on a raid to try to rescue my sister who may or may not be on this planet? Absolutely not. I'd never admit that to anyone on this team, though.

"Sure," I said brightly.

"Liar." Burn's gaze held sympathy. "You can stay behind, you know. We can loop you in via comms."

Jaw set, I shook my head. "No. I have to be there when you find her." My dad would never forgive me if something happened to Layla because I didn't go. I wouldn't either.

"It's okay to be scared," she added. "No one on the team would think less of you. This is our job. We're used to it. This is way out of your comfort zone, I bet."

The shock of Burn being nice to me was too much. "I'm terrified," I admitted, although I hadn't intended to.

"Of what?" she asked.

"Everything. What if my sister is there? What if she isn't? What if someone gets hurt?" I shook my head trying to snap out of it. "I feel so useless."

"You're not useless. You're smart. Strong. You wouldn't have gotten this far otherwise."

I snorted.

"No, really," she said. "You stole a ship, delivered highly explosive cargo, and got the strongest man I know to fall in love with you. And I'm starting to like you."

My mission anxiety had been replaced by a whole other type of anxiety. "Wait. What did you say?"

Footsteps rang in the corridor outside the mess. We both turned, leaving our conversation hanging.

"We're a go for the mission," Dax said.

"Yes!" Burn pumped her fist.

My stomach churned with a mess of emotions. This was really happening. "When do we leave?"

"Within the hour." Dax and the guys stood just inside the room. Clustered together—big, muscular, and mean looking—they could easily be a recruiting ad for the space corps. Or an ad for a blockbuster movie about the space corps.

Dax broke away from the others. My breath hitched at his approach, Burn's words circling in my head. I was vaguely aware of Burn stepping away, but my attention was hyper-focused on Dax.

He cupped my cheek, and I leaned into it. "Are you okay?"

"Getting there," I said.

"Want to sit this one out?"

My laugh was probably closer to hysterical than I would have liked. "I thought about it, but no. The waiting would be worse. And I need to know, regardless of the outcome." I reached up and put my hand over his. "What's the plan?"

He caressed my cheek a moment longer. When he turned to face the team, he kept my hand in his.

"Orion and Mercer did a little recon when they came back from the bar earlier. Guys?"

"There are a bunch of shops situated around the landing pad selling parts," Orion began. "Some of them may even be small chop shops, but it appears the majority of the work is being done in that big hangar right outside of town."

Mercer picked up the story. "We cased the place on our way back. There are a few guys guarding the doors. Probably more inside. They're well-armed but not trained. We can take them, easy."

Standing there tall and confident, I believed him.

"How do you figure?" Dax asked.

"The big guy here," Mercer pointed at Orion, "stumbled up to the wall to take a leak and set off the alarms. The 'guards' surrounded us, but let us go since we were drunk."

"Seriously?" I looked from Mercer to Orion. They both appeared dead serious. "Oh. Ew."

Both men laughed. "Okay, so we weren't really drunk and Orion pretended to take a whiz. We wanted to test their reaction times."

Mercer shook his head, a pitying look on his face. "Those guys were outclassed. One of them tried to beat up Orion—show him who was boss—but he broke the guy's nose with a love tap."

I covered my face with my hands. "Oh my god." I dropped them and looked at Dax and Burn. "Is that how you normally do recon?"

Dax's smile widened and little flutters filled my belly. "You'd be surprised what falls into official strategies."

50

———

DAX

Nighttime on Kottke was a dusky gray. There was no wind and the air smelled and tasted like dust. Their moon tonight was just a sliver and most of the businesses didn't have external lights. Even the spaceport appeared to have shut down for the night. *Fortuna* was only a shadow behind us. It all lent credence to the cargo master's warning to not be out at night.

Our target, the hangar, was one of the few exceptions. It wasn't well-lit on the outside, but light snuck out of the cracks around the windows and doors, and between the metal sheets on the walls.

We'd donned gray camouflage and our body armor for this incursion. Not a perfect match, but it should help us blend into the shadows.

I led the way from the ship. Burn was directly behind me and Lacy was tucked in front of Orion and Mercer who brought up the rear. I hated having Lacy out here with us, but I'd made her as safe as possible. I could only hope that it was enough.

Moving slowly, carefully, we finally made it across town

to the hangar. The air pulsed with loud, raucous music and even louder bangs of metal-on-metal.

I raised my hand to signal a stop. We were only fifty feet from the main door. The double doors didn't appear locked and would probably be easy to breach, but the recon from earlier indicated that there was another door, less used, to our right. The primary entrance would likely have more eyes on it, so we'd decided to try the other door.

Keeping Lacy by my side, I used hand signals to direct my team to their positions around the secondary entrance.

Orion was responsible for the breach. Quiet was best, but he'd use brute force if needed. Mercer would provide backup for him. Burn was stationed slightly farther away, so she could take care of anyone or anything that got past Mercer. I'd protect Lacy until it was safe to enter.

Flashing my fingers, I counted down. Three. Two. One.

Orion put his hand on the doorknob.

I tensed, ready for action. All my senses were on alert and I was terrifyingly aware of Lacy behind me. If things went to shit, the only thing I was concerned with was getting her to safety. That single-minded focus should have concerned me, but I didn't have time right now to consider what it meant.

When Orion turned the handle, it squeaked. A tiny sound that nevertheless held us all motionless. He pulled and metal scraped on metal. My breath nearly stopped.

He paused and we all waited.

And waited.

And waited.

When nothing happened, Orion tugged on the handle and the door pulled free.

Orion paused, one hand on the door handle, the other

holding his weapon, while the team slipped into position behind him.

Mercer nodded and Orion eased the door open all the way. The light was brighter and the noise was louder, but nothing else seemed to be happening.

"Step in just enough to look around and then report back." I didn't want to stand here silhouetted by the open door for very long. We needed to be either in or out.

"Roger." Orion handed the edge of the door to Mercer, then hefted his weapon. He disappeared from view.

Orion was back in the space of a few heartbeats. "About what we expected. I counted three guys and they're pretty heads down over whatever they're working on. They'll be easy to take down. Biggest obstacles are the piles of junk and parts. Might be people I can't see behind them. They could make a hell of a racket if we get tangled up in them."

"Thoughts?" I asked the team.

Used to making fast decisions in stressful situations, we quickly decided that it was a go.

Orion, back on point, stepped through the doorway again, with Mercer and Burn close on his heels.

"Stay behind me," I told Lacy. "We don't know what we're facing."

She nodded.

I stepped through the door with sure, steady steps. I was all that stood between the bad guys and Lacy.

Snap out of it. I couldn't allow my concern for her to be the very thing that put her in danger.

Orion directed us to our positions with a series of hand signals. I circled to the right, angling my body between the room and Lacy. I pointed to a place for her to stand that would keep her in the shadows and out of the line of fire.

My target was crouched in front of a piece of machinery that looked like it belonged in the engine room. Lacy could probably tell me what it was and what it did, but that wasn't why we were here.

Steps light, unhurried, I approached my target. I raised my weapon and, with one smooth motion, brought the butt down on the back of his head. He collapsed to the ground and hit his toolbox. It rattled, sounding like a bomb going off. I pivoted on the balls of my feet, checking to see if the noise had attracted any attention.

Nothing.

I turned back to the downed bad guy, intending to tie him up, but Lacy had already taken care of it. His wrists and ankles were tied with a complicated series of knots. I gave them an experimental tug. They held and seemed secure. "Nice work," I said with a nod of approval.

"Thanks."

"We need to gag him," I whispered, "and then put him out of sight."

"Already on it." She pulled a roll of duct tape from her pocket and slapped a couple strips over his mouth and beard, then wrapped another piece around his head to hold everything in place.

Damn, that was going to hurt when he tried to take it off.

"You'll need to move him, though," she said. "I can't do it without making a lot of noise."

"Got it." I hefted the guy by his collar and dragged him into the shadows where I'd hidden Lacy. He was scrawny, but unconscious, he was dead weight. I tucked him behind a stack of crates. He should be out for a while.

I rejoined Lacy. "Anything from the rest of the team?"

She nodded and pointed down the aisle to where Burn was flashing the all-clear signal. I flashed a response back.

"Same plan as before." My hand cupped her cheek briefly. "Stay behind me and stay out of danger."

Lacy nodded, then stooped to pick up a long wrench. "Okay, ready."

I studied her choice of weapon. It suited her. "Okay. Just remember, quietly."

Lacy rolled her eyes. "I'm new, not stupid."

"I know. I just worry."

Surprise flared in her eyes. She grabbed my hand with her free hand and squeezed my fingers. "I worry about you, too. Now let's get to Burn."

We moved through the hangar as quickly and quietly as we could, keeping a wary eye out for threats. The cavernous space distorted sound and with the racket coming from near the front of the building, we might not hear anyone who came up on us. Plus, the haphazard aisles and the ship parts scattered about the place offered any number of hiding places.

Burn was in sight, only fifteen feet away, when Lacy gasped.

I whirled around, raising my weapon as I did so. There was no one there except Lacy. "What's wrong?"

"It's . . ." Instead of answering, Lacy approached a nearby rolling tool chest.

"Burn, watch our backs," I whispered before following Lacy to the workstation. "What's wrong?"

Transferring the wrench to her left hand, she plucked an item off the top of it. "This is mine." Though still quiet, her tone was somewhere between a growl and a whine. "She was here, Dax. My sister was *here*!"

"Lacy, baby, what is it? What did you find?" My heart was in my throat. What had caused such a visceral reaction for her?

Lacy turned slowly, her hand clenched around the base of a gray, plastic . . . I peered closer. A toy shark?

"My sister gave this to me." She thrust it toward me. As she did, the head of the bobblehead shark started vibrating and the mouth started chomping at me.

What the fuck?

"Lacy, that could be from anywhere. Lots of people like toys." I scanned the top of the tool chest for any other signs that Lacy's sister had been here. Maybe a great big sign that said *Layla Dupree was here.* But there was nothing.

"Look, I can prove it." She tucked her wrench under her arm and twisted the shark around. She pointed to the lettering on the toy's display platform. "Right there."

Emblazoned was a word: MAKO.

"My sister did that. It's the figurehead for *Mako.* It lived on the console of my ship." Her eyes widened. "That bitch! She stole my ship!"

I bit the inside of my lip to keep from laughing. Now she knew how it felt. Still . . . it looked like proof that we were on the right track. Now we had to learn what it meant.

She grabbed my arm. "Dax, if this is here, it means *Mako* might be here too. I've got to find my ship."

Before she could dart past me, I wrapped my arm around her waist. When she started to struggle, I pulled her closer. "Shhh. You can't go rushing out into the hangar before we've had a chance to clear it. We'll ask the team if they've seen her, okay?"

Wide eyes met my gaze. "I've got to find them, Dax. Layla and *Mako.*"

She was killing me. "We will, baby. We will."

This woman had me making promises I wasn't sure I could keep.

"Let's go show Burn what you found. She's getting worried."

Lacy took a shaky breath in, a calmer breath out. "Okay. You're right. I'm okay. You can let go now."

I didn't want to ever let her go, but I did.

Before Burn could say a word, Lacy thrust the bobblehead shark at her. "My sister was here, Burn. This is proof."

Concerned, Burn looked at me before responding.

I gave her a subtle nod. It wasn't 100 percent, but the handwritten MAKO on the side certainly made it seem less circumstantial.

"That's great, Lacy. What is it?"

"It's the figurehead from my ship, *Mako*. Which means my sister has been using my ship. Did you see her while you were clearing the hangar?"

"Um, nothing that said *Mako*. What does it look like?"

"Exactly like the *Fortuna*," Lacy said. "Unless they've stripped her for parts. Then she would look more like that." She gestured toward a ship that looked uncomfortably like a skeleton, only a few structural metal pieces left.

Burn winced. "Nope, I didn't see anything that looked like our ship."

We had to find her sister. Even more so now than before. If Lacy had lost her beloved ship, she deserved to have her sister returned, alive and well. And I'd do my damnedest to make sure that happened. After this conversation, I thought Burn would too.

Mercer and Orion approached our position, hauling a conscious but tied-up worker with them.

"Thought it'd be easier to get some answers this way." Orion's deep voice sounded menacing. The bound guy shivered.

Good. That might make this easier.

I maneuvered the entire team into the shadows, keeping Lacy behind me.

I hoped the interrogation would go easy, that the man would tell us what we wanted to know quickly and without bloodshed. I didn't want Lacy to witness this. Didn't want her to see this side of me, of the team. I thought I'd left this behind when I'd left the corps, but for her, I'd get my hands dirty again.

Mercer and Orion had let the man fall to his knees, so I crouched in front of him. "We have some questions. You're going to give us the answers. If you don't, if you try to call for help, it will not go well for you. Nod if you understand."

His head bobbed up and down.

"Good. Let's get started." I pulled down the gag. "Who owns this place?"

His mouth opened wide. When Orion nudged him in the back of the head with his weapon, the guy reconsidered his plan to yell.

"The Farrows and the McMillers."

"And what do they do?"

He opened his mouth, closed it. Orion prodded him again.

"Hey, man, stop it!"

I gave him a look.

He scowled at me. "They're entrepreneurs."

That was a nice, bland term for a bunch of criminals. "And?"

"What do you mean 'and'?" the guy asked.

"It's not a difficult question," I said. "What's their business?"

"Selling," he said quickly. When I looked at him,

unimpressed, he hurried to add, "They sell everything. But, uh, mostly ship parts. Like these."

"How do they get the ships?"

"I dunno. They just do."

I was pretty sure he was lying.

Tired of squatting, I stood, stretched, then pointed at the skeletal ship. "Where'd they get that one?"

If anything, the guy got even paler. "Crew got in a bar fight, so it was confiscated."

That was a pretty broad answer. I didn't trust it. "Who confiscated it?"

"The town."

That wasn't . . . unexpected. This place seemed to run on nothing but dust and despair. Of course, they would all be a part of it.

"Where did you get this?" Lacy pushed past me, shaking the shark toy at the man.

Dammit, Lacy.

I bounced on my toes, ready to sweep her away, but the guy lurched backward. Whether to get away from the shark or the wild-eyed woman wielding it, I wasn't sure. Orion blocked his way, forcing him to stay in place.

"That's . . . that's not mine. It's Bert's." His gaze darted around, like he was looking for Bert. Or for an escape.

She bent forward and glared at him, all while shaking the shark. "No, it's mine. Where is the ship that it came from? Where is the crew?"

If anything, his eyes got wider. "It wasn't our fault. No one told us that ship was off limits. Farrow was pissed when he learned that the team had taken it in. I don't know what he did with it. Really, I don't."

Lacy growled, low and deep in her throat.

Holy shit.

I looked at Burn, then Mercer and Orion. Their eyes

were as wide as the mechanic's, but their expressions held respect.

"And the crew?"

"There was just one." He held up his bound hands in a protective gesture and his voice wavered as he stared at the shark. "Bert thought she was a cop, but the way Farrow whisked her away, everyone else thought she was a hooker."

Based on Lacy's expression when he said that, if MAKO had actually been a shark, this guy would have been chum.

I put my hand on her shoulder and gently urged her upright. "Easy there, tiger . . . uh, shark. You got the answers you wanted."

I looked at the man on the floor, surprised he hadn't pissed himself in the face of Lacy's fury. "Anything else we should know?" I glanced from him to Lacy, the message clear. If he didn't answer me, he'd be answering to her.

The words tumbled out.

"Ship came in late in the day, so we figured we'd strip it in the morning. We got on board and the ship started sending out some kind of signal. We freaked out, man. We just strip the ships, nothing more complicated than that." His gaze begged me to believe him.

I did. That explained Lacy's data chip.

"What happened then?"

"I don't know. Our computer guy did a trace, but said it looked like a data dump, rather than a call for backup. McMiller hired some guys to track the signal, but we never heard from them. Guess they didn't find it. Old Man Farrow was pissed."

And that explained the guys who'd come after her. But I knew that those weren't the answers she was looking for.

"Where's this compound?"

The guy swallowed hard and looked like he was thinking about not answering.

Lacy must have thought so too because she shook the shark at him again, a sneer on her face.

"Just a few miles out of town. Can't miss it. Head west on the main road and you pretty much run into it."

Well, shit. It wouldn't take the team and me that long to run that far, but I wasn't sure that Lacy would be able to keep up. Leaving her behind wasn't an option.

"Where *exactly* are they holding her?"

"I don't know. There's the main house and a couple of outbuildings. Probably one of those. I've only been there once!"

This was going to be like a needle in a haystack. And we only had tonight to figure this out or I was pretty sure we were going to become the next ship to disappear.

"Anybody got any more questions?" Maybe one of them would think of something I hadn't.

Lacy nodded, gripping the shark tightly. "You got any working ships in here? Small ones?"

He swallowed hard but considered her question. "Naw, we strip them pretty quick. Most of us live in town and don't have ships. There's a shuttle in the corner that might work. Doors are a bit twitchy."

"Which corner?"

He pointed to a section closest to the front of the hangar that we hadn't cleared.

I leaned close to Lacy so I could whisper in her ear. "You got any more questions?"

She shook her head.

"What about keys or whatever it takes to fly it?" I asked him.

She turned her head, her lips curving into a smile. "I can hotwire it."

The pure confidence in her voice was a turn-on in an otherwise tense situation.

"All right, let's roll." I nodded to Mercer.

He pulled the guy's gag up and stuffed it back in his mouth, just in time to stifle his squawk of outrage. "Sorry, man." He pulled an auto-injector out of the med kit he wore on his hip. He pressed it against the mechanic's neck and the other man slumped in Orion's grip.

"What did you give him?" Lacy asked.

"A light sedative," Mercer said. "He'll be fine. But since we can't have him following us . . ." He shrugged.

Orion picked the mechanic up and carried him deeper into the shadows, tucking him into a corner.

"Time to go," I said, when he rejoined the group. "Burn, you and Orion take point. Make sure no one is between us and the shuttle. If they are, knock them out like everyone else."

I looked at Lacy. "We need to be out of here before they wake up."

"Got it." She unzipped the top of her suit and tucked the shark in. Then she transferred the wrench to her right hand. "I'll need one of these tool chests when we're at the shuttle. Hopefully there will be one close by."

"Got it." We'd deal with that when we were closer.

"Everyone ready?" They nodded. "Let's go."

Lacy was in the middle of the group again. As she started walking, Mercer leaned close. "You better be as good as you say you are."

"Oh, I am." Lacy followed Orion and Burn without a backward glance.

51

LACY

My hand clenched the wrench and my shoulders twitched with every sound in the hangar. The loud music continued to pulse, echoing around the space. Hyperaware of every movement and every shadow, I tried not to crowd Burn. For years in my teens I'd begged my dad to let me come on his missions. He'd laugh his ass off now, if he knew how much I wasn't enjoying this. My nerves were not made for these operations.

Burn stopped a few feet in front of me. Orion slipped into the shadows and Mercer followed him.

When they returned, Mercer gave the all clear. "I knocked out the two guys who were nearby. We'll need to make a wider search to make sure." He smirked at me and I wanted to punch him in the nose. "Your turn. The shuttle is just around the corner, not too far from another set of doors. Get it running."

I gave him a plastic smile. "Get me that tool chest."

Burn led the way, keeping her body between me and whatever was ahead of us. There were plenty of places for people to hide in here. I hunched over and tried to make myself as small a target as possible as we hurried to the shuttle.

When we reached it, the side doors were both wide open. I plastered my body against the side, while Burn cleared the interior.

I barely waited for her to whisper "Clear" before I scrambled inside and made my way to the cockpit.

"Can you start it?" Burn asked as she clambered in after me.

"Let's find out." I studied the console, noting the location of the controls. I'd worked on this model of shuttle before, but they weren't common on Elegium Station. Too small for interplanetary work and too old in some crews' eyes. That age could come in handy.

I pressed the ignition button. Maybe we'd get lucky.

Nothing.

"So you can't get it running?"

Was that disappointment or a challenge in her voice? I couldn't tell and I didn't have the time to worry. "Shhh."

I slipped MAKO out of my suit and set it on the console so I could work unencumbered. Sliding out of the pilot's seat, I dropped to my knees so I could access the panels under the main console. I popped the panel off with my multitool and flicked on the tiny flashlight I'd brought with me. Turning my head so Burn could hear me, I said, "I need you to hold this over my shoulder so the light shines right here." I wiggled the light so it flashed over the section I needed to have illuminated.

"Little busy here watching your ass, Lacy."

"Do you want me to get this thing running?"

"Yes." Her tone implied it was a stupid question.

"Then figure out a way to do both." The actual work

was a one-person job, but working under these less-than-ideal conditions required extra hands.

She took the light from me with a deep sigh. "Fine."

"Thank you."

After ensuring that the light was angled where I wanted it, I lay flat on my back and scooted closer to the control panel. I stared up at the tangle of different-colored wires.

They were color coded for a reason, but experience had taught me that some mechanics were lazy and didn't always match the colors up correctly after a repair. Who knew what kind of chaos I'd find in a chop-shop ship.

I ran my fingers over each one to figure out which system each wire was connected to. As I feared, it was a mess.

A perfect fix was out, but I was pretty sure I could create a workaround.

"Are you done yet?"

I ground my teeth together to keep from making a snarky reply. "Not yet. Tell Mercer I need wire strippers and snips from that tool chest."

"You need what?"

"Wire cutters or something that can cut through wire. And wire strippers. They'll have a series of holes on the blades to pull the plastic off the wires."

The light bobbled as Burn passed my request on to Mercer. While I waited, I mapped out the wires for the most crucial systems to have a working, flying shuttle.

"Are these what you want?"

I held out my hand and she carefully set the tools in my palm. I pulled them closer and, surprisingly, they were exactly what I wanted.

"Perfect. Tell Mercer he did good." Maybe being a people doctor helped him recognize ship doctor tools.

I took a deep breath, then got to work. I stripped and

twisted wires, made and tested connections until I was satisfied. The whole time, I ignored Burn's increasingly concerned questions or answered with single words or grunts.

I patted the underside of the console. "Okay, baby, if you get us through this, I'll make sure to fix you up right." The shuttle didn't deserve to be left here with people who treated her so badly. We could fit her onto our ship.

I slid out. "Okay, we're good to go."

"Good. The boys are getting antsy." Behind her words were the faint sounds of a fight.

I understood, since I was feeling the same way.

I smoothed my hand over the shuttle's console again, then tried the ignition. After a cough she sprang to life. More of a stutter than a purr, but I could fix that later.

"Good girl," I crooned. "Get the guys on board and have someone open a door for us," I told Burn, while continuing to pet the shuttle.

She nodded and raced to the open shuttle door. "Somebody open the door. Everyone else, get onboard!"

Pounding feet and the sounds of a scuffle came from behind me, but I was too busy familiarizing myself with the controls to worry about them. Either Burn had my back or she didn't, but my job was getting us out of here on the shuttle.

Burn appeared in the space just behind the pilot's and copilot's seats. "Go now!"

I eased the shuttle a few feet off the ground, prayed there wasn't anything in the way, and aimed for the slowly opening hangar door.

The shuttle glided forward more smoothly than I'd expected and I gave her another approving pat. "Such a good shuttle."

I kept a slow, steady hand on the throttle. We were

airborne, but I had no idea how she would fly until I put it to the test.

Burn dropped into the copilot's seat next to me.

"Everything okay?" I asked. *Please don't let there be a problem.*

"So far. Orion and Mercer are in the back keeping an eye out from the side doors. Dax is opening the door for our departure."

My heart leapt into my throat. He could handle himself, but that didn't stop the worry. It just increased my need to not screw this up.

"He's a professional. This is what he does." It was like she read my mind.

"I know. It doesn't make it any less worrisome."

"If the two of you are going to make this relationship work, you're going to have to get used to this."

"Get used to stealing a shuttle and sneaking out of a hangar in the middle of the night to meet up with more bad guys? I didn't think you guys wanted to be that kind of cargo runners." I had to keep this light, so I could function through the tension riding me.

Burn laughed like I wanted her to. "Well, true. But given our backgrounds, I don't think we'll be able to escape exciting situations like this every once in a while."

"That's good to know."

"We don't want to be anything like Blazer," she continued. "He gives a bad name to all the other ex-military who want to go into a nice private cargo business."

My hands tightened around the wheel. Had Burn noticed? If she did, hopefully she'd chalk it up to nerves. "He probably thinks he's doing the right thing."

She snorted. "Being known as a scoundrel across the galaxy isn't an endorsement."

Fuck it. "What exactly do you think he does?"

Burn sneered. "Whatever the fuck he wants. That's the problem. He wheels and deals and makes governments look like asshats."

"Governments *are* asshats," I muttered, scanning the distance between us and the door. There was a surprising lack of activity around us. Please let that be a good thing.

That startled a laugh out of her. "But starting rebellions and selling arms to both sides isn't a great look."

Had my dad actually done that? Not that I knew of, but I didn't track his escapades that closely. He appreciated profit *and* underdogs, and you never knew which one would come out on top.

"Look, I don't know who's right or who's wrong," I said, still concentrating on piloting the shuttle. "But did you ever consider what those people might be rebelling against? Maybe they can't feed their families on what the companies pay them. Maybe they just want to decide their own lives."

"You flew with the guy," Mercer commented from the back. "Are we supposed to believe that you don't agree with him?" The guy from the rich family, with his charming take on the world.

Why were we having this conversation now?

"It was a job," I lied. It was family. "Did you agree with everything the space corps did?"

Silence met my words. Not just from Burn, but from Mercer and Orion in the back too.

All of the sudden, I realized how alone I was with three heavily armed and highly trained professionals.

Dammit. This was why I tried to distance myself from my dad. Not because I didn't agree with him—although I didn't believe in everything he did—but because he'd raised me with a completely different set of rules and beliefs compared to most people. And they didn't always like that.

I didn't take the words back. That would be cowardly and I'd been raised to stand up for my beliefs. "Just because something is wrong doesn't mean it isn't the right thing to do."

That was Dad's motto. Maybe it was mine, too? I didn't really know.

"I'll think about it," Burn said. "Can we get out of the hangar now?"

More than happy to end this conversation, I steered toward the open doorway. I was still tense. The conversation, thinking about my dad, worry for Dax, making our escape path. I was going to need a drink when this was all over.

"How fast should I be going for Dax to get onboard?"

"A little slower than this." Burn spoke first but the others echoed her response.

"Okay. I'll slow down when we get through the door." It was coming up quickly. I kept my speed and my course steady through it. Dax gave me a thumbs-up as we passed him.

I immediately dropped my speed. We were practically hovering in place. "Do you have him?" Worry for him crept into my voice.

Quiet murmurs from the back practically begged me to turn around, but I kept my focus on the controls. A couple of grunts and then Burn's voice. "We got him."

"Good." I released my breath in a whoosh. Knowing Dax was safe on board significantly lowered my stress. Now only one of the people I cared about was still in danger.

Dax and Burn traded places. I glanced over at him, checking for injuries. "You're okay?"

"I'm fine," he said. "No need to worry."

"I wasn't worried," I shot back so quickly it was obviously a lie.

He reached over and cupped the back of my neck. The warm, steady weight of his hand eased the last of my tension.

"Can I go faster now?"

"Do it. Not sure how long it will be 'til someone sounds an alarm. We need to get in and out with your sister as quickly as we can."

I nodded, hating that we were going in mostly blind.

Upping our speed, I kept a close eye on the gauges. I didn't expect problems with the shuttle, but I was prepared for them.

Cooler night air rushed in as we covered more ground.

"Can't we close this door?" Mercer asked.

I ignored him until Burn asked the same thing.

"That mechanic said the doors were wonky. I can take a look later, but the priority was to get her running."

"Think the shuttle was there for parts or repairs?" Burn asked.

"Parts, probably." The wind carried Mercer's words up to me.

I was instantly offended on behalf of the shuttle. "It's okay, baby. Ignore the mean man. He doesn't know what he's talking about."

"Do you honestly think that works?" That was Orion.

I couldn't prove that it didn't. "Would you rather be flying in an angry shuttle?"

"Seriously, you're talking to this piece of shit shuttle?" Mercer again.

Asshole.

I'd never admit it, but I was starting to enjoy the

sniping with Mercer. He was like the brother I never wanted.

"We could call it the shittle," Burn said with a laugh.

"It's okay, baby," I whispered again. I had to believe that the shuttle would take us to the compound and the team would find my sister. When we found her, we needed to have a way back to our ship. "I believe in you."

52

LACY

"I think we're getting close," Dax said. He pointed at the growing pinprick of light ahead of us.

The last ten minutes had been spent mostly in silence, only broken when somebody had pointed out a light or checked behind us for tails. It had been both stressful and amusing to glance back and see Mercer leaning out the door to look behind us, while Orion had a death grip on his belt with one hand and gripped the shuttle's door frame with the other.

"Should I approach head-on?" I looked over at Dax.

He gave his answer serious thought. "Pull to either side when we get closer. Whichever one looks less bright."

I opened and closed my hands around the controls, releasing the tension. "Then what?"

When the silence ticked on, I asked, "Do I just fly by? Are we landing? Going up to the front door?"

Ever since we'd approached the hangar, unsure of what we'd find, we'd been improvising. Which was fine, sometimes plans fell apart. But the closer we got to Layla, the more winging it was stressing me out. I wanted a solid plan, one that would guarantee success.

"If it's dark enough, we'll land and proceed into the compound. If it's too bright, continue past and we'll find a better place to set down."

"Daylight's a few hours away." Midnight had come and gone while we were in the hangar. Sunrise on Kottke was in six hours and I didn't know if it would be the gradual kind of sunrise or the hello, wake up kind. Six hours to find Layla, get back to the ship, deal with any surprises, and get off-planet.

Easy, right?

Dax's hand landed on my thigh. "We'll get her out, Lacy. Trust me."

"I do." It was true. I trusted Dax. I even trusted his team. I just didn't trust the universe to not fuck with this rescue even more. If Layla wasn't at the compound . . . Well, I didn't know what I would do, but I doubted it would be pretty.

"We're getting closer." Dax swiveled in his seat. "Douse any lights." He leaned closer to the windshield.

My gaze danced from my controls to the growing lights ahead of us. As we neared, the single light broke apart, becoming distinct light sources.

"Circle right," Dax said abruptly.

I nodded and eased the controls right to take us in a wide circle. The area below us looked more like an abandoned ranch than a compound. I slowed down and dropped closer to the ground.

"Are the sensors reading anything?" Burn leaned over my shoulder.

"No sensors." I felt everyone's gaze snap to me.

"What the hell does that mean?" Burn asked.

"It means that someone really fucked with the wiring

on this shuttle. I got it to start, but I don't know what else they did down there." Someone had messed around under the hood of the shuttle a lot. Like, *a lot* a lot. "The way this baby was wired, there's a chance I could turn on the sensors and the horn could go off."

"Shuttles have horns?" Burn sounded truly curious.

"Usually, no, but with what they did to the ignition, I can't say this one doesn't."

"Okay, people, focus." Though Dax kept his voice quiet, the command in it was unmistakable. "We have visual and that's it. So keep your eyes peeled."

"Will do," Burn said before she disappeared back into the belly of the shuttle.

"I'm not seeing anything but the buildings," I whispered. "Do you think it's a trap?"

Dax shook his head. "No. I think they're complacent. This is, after all, the ass-end of nowhere. They're surviving mostly on luck. Ships go missing on the edges all the time. If they were closer to the core planets, I think someone would have noticed and shut them down."

I flicked my gaze over to him. "Someone like your team."

"Exactly." His nod was sharp. "I think your sister is an outlier. This Farrow, whoever he is, he was looking for information, not a ship to strip for parts. Based on what that mechanic said, Farrow was pissed they were treating her like business as usual. I think they want her research."

"Then she's only safe until they get it." My stomach clenched at the implications.

"Lacy, if your sister is half as stubborn and creative as you, she's keeping them on their toes and they don't have that research yet. Have faith."

His words didn't eliminate all my worries, but I was able to breathe again.

He pointed toward a fence. "Set down over there."

"I don't think the fence is going to provide much cover." Not if we were landing inside it.

"The tree next to it will help," Dax said.

Trusting the former marine's tactical instincts, I eased the shuttle down to the ground. We were a hundred feet from the closest building in the compound. There was a high-pitched whirr from the engine but it settled down almost immediately.

"Shh," Mercer growled from the back of the shuttle.

"Shh yourself," I snapped.

I powered off the shuttle and crossed my fingers that she would start up again after we rescued Layla. "Thank you," I whispered to the ship and ran my hand over the controls.

"That's really disturbing," Mercer said.

"You're really disturbing." I swiveled around just in time to catch Burn give him a shoulder check.

Dax unfolded from the copilot's seat and stood between our two chairs. He braced his hands on the ceiling and stretched. I leaned back in my seat to enjoy the view. The man looked good in everything, including combat armor.

"What's the plan, boss?"

"I counted half a dozen buildings as we flew over. Anyone get something different?"

Well, shit. I hadn't been counting buildings. Then again, I'd been concentrating on flying. Fortunately, everyone else knew that was a thing and they all agreed with his count.

"We work our way in toward the main house, starting with there." He pointed to the one structure we could see. "One of the buildings is probably the barracks. We want to avoid that if possible. Any questions?"

"Teams of two?" Burn asked, a gleam in her eye.

A sharp nodded from Dax. "You and Orion take point. Mercer and I will be right behind you."

I could do math and I had a bad feeling about where this was going. "What about me?"

"You stay here and keep the shuttle ready. We'll get your sister and then get the hell out of here."

"Nope. No way in hell! She's my sister!" I was getting damn tired of arguing about this. I thought Dax understood.

"That's why it's better if you stay with the shuttle. That way we can keep both of you safe," Orion said kindly.

"That's exactly why I should go. All she's going to see if you go without me is another group of strangers kidnapping her again."

"We're rescuing her," Orion protested.

"She doesn't know that, does she?" I crossed my arms over my chest and glared at them, ready to take them all on. Not my wisest decision ever, but I wasn't going to back down. "I crossed half the fucking galaxy for this. Got you cargo in exchange for this."

"Stole our ship for this," Burn added.

I glared at her. "Not exactly."

She just gave me that lopsided smile of hers.

"Are you doing this because you want the glory?" Mercer asked.

I sputtered and wanted to take a swing at the asshole. I didn't because I knew that was stupid and we didn't have time to waste. "I'm doing this because she's my sister and I want her to know that she's safe."

"Enough," Dax said and we all stopped talking. "The longer we stand around here arguing, the higher the chance that we're caught." He pinned me with his gaze. I could tell he wasn't happy, but I knew that I was right. Layla and I had the same upbringing. *I'd* be leery of a new group of people breaking me out. It would feel like a trap.

"You're with me," Dax said. "Stay between me and Mercer."

"How about you and Burn?" I tried to bargain.

His glare turned harder.

Burn snickered.

"You want to come, you abide by my rules." Dax didn't say anything else until I'd nodded. "Stay between me and Mercer. Do what I say, when I say it, no questions asked."

This all sounded very familiar and I had a flashback to my dad giving me the very same lecture. It was almost like he'd kept some of that military training. Who knew?

"Fine," I grumbled. It wasn't the most graceful acquiescence, but I didn't care.

We were finally here. After trying what felt like forever to get them on my side, we were finally doing this.

Soon my sister would be safe and we could leave this backwater planet.

53

DAX

IT WAS the middle of the night and the compound was quiet. Which, sure, middle of the night. But this didn't feel like any raid that I'd ever been on before. Was that because it was the first one to occur out of the corps? Or was it because of the constant struggle to keep worry for Lacy from overwhelming everything else?

I hated that she was out here, though Mercer and I were keeping her as safe as possible. She wasn't dressed for a mission like this and she definitely wasn't trained for it.

Ahead, Burn signaled for a stop and I passed it on behind me. My body tensed, waiting for Lacy to run into me. Surprisingly, she was proving adept at stealth. Maybe Blazer had taught her some moves. Rumor had it that he'd been military before he became a criminal.

Weapon ready and my body tense, I waited for the all-clear. It wasn't long—mere seconds, really—but it seemed like forever since the life of someone I'd come to lo—Someone I'd come to care deeply about was in danger.

After we'd rescued Lacy's sister and were out of

danger, I wasn't letting Lacy out of my sight. Possibly not out of my bed either, if she was amenable.

Shoving the badly timed thought away, I refocused on the mission. Based on the plan we'd hastily cobbled together before leaving the shuttle, Burn and Orion would fan out, clearing any guards around the first building. Orion would also scan with the infrared goggles. He and Mercer had only picked up the one pair, so we were relying on him.

Burn and Orion drifted back to our little group. "No guards," Burn reported quietly.

Orion flipped the goggles to the top of his head. "Not many signatures either. One lone figure in the first building. A few in the next building. I think that's serving as the bunkhouse. And two in the main house."

"So she's here?" Lacy whispered. "Right there?" Pointing at the building in front of us, she started to head toward it.

I grabbed her wrist and dragged her back. "Not yet."

Her jaw set mulishly, but I stared her down. Finally, with a big sigh, she nodded.

"We'll check here," I decided. "Then circle around to the main house, if she's not here. I want to avoid the bunkhouse if at all possible."

We slid from shadow to shadow, approaching the small outbuilding at an oblique angle, keeping clear of the small, dark windows.

We reached the door without incident. As Burn had noted, there were no guards. It didn't make any sense if they were keeping a prisoner here, so I directed Orion to make another circuit of the building.

"No guards," he confirmed when he returned a few minutes later.

Signaling for Burn to watch my back and for Mercer to watch Lacy, I eased the door open and slipped inside. Orion followed me in. "What do you see?" I asked.

He scanned the room before us with the heat-sensing goggles. "Not here, but . . ." He trailed off and rescanned the room. "Look for a basement."

A basement definitely sounded more like where you would keep a prisoner than the main house.

I would never say it around Lacy, but I did wonder about the outcome of our mission. What were the odds that Layla was still alive? If they believed she knew the location of the *Queen of Stars* and its mythical treasure, how safe was she?

I shoved those thoughts away. We would deal with whatever we found after the fact.

As Orion and I stepped deeper into the building, looking for a way downstairs, the other three followed us in.

I drifted to Lacy's side. "We think there's a basement. Orion's looking for the door."

She nodded, her lips pressed tightly together. It took courage to face this and I wanted to let her know how proud I was of her. And how worried.

"Here," Orion called softly. He stood off to the far side of the room. His weapon was still in his dominant hand while he ran his hand around the doorframe with his other hand.

"Open it," I instructed. I placed my body between Lacy and the door. She tried to shift to see around me, but I moved with her.

"We don't know what's down there. It could be dangerous." I touched her arm. "We're so close. Let's not rush the last steps."

She clenched her fists and nodded abruptly.

I checked on my team. Burn watched the main door, while Mercer stood just inside the doorway. Orion laid small charges on the door's hinges, then motioned the rest of us back. He took up a position a few feet from the basement door and pressed the detonator.

The explosives discharged with a little *zzt*, a tiny yellow spark, and a puff of smoke. Burn covered Orion while he peeled the door out of the frame. He used it to shield them both while Burn peered into the stairwell.

"One flight of stairs, looks like it goes straight down."

"If they've been keeping her in the dark this whole time . . ." Lacy stalked forward.

I put my hand out to stop her. "Just a few more minutes," I cajoled.

"Fine," she said through clenched teeth. "But let's get moving."

Trying to explain why we needed to be methodical about this would just set her off, so I signaled Burn to go ahead. Orion leaned the door against the wall.

"Mercer, follow Burn. Orion, you've got topside." He'd block any trouble that came at us from the outside. "Let us know if we have any problems."

"You got it, Dax."

I gave him a nod, then herded Lacy toward the stairs. Mercer stopped on every stair, sweeping the space around and below us. It felt like hours later, but was probably just a few minutes when we arrived at the basement.

The stairs spit us out into a big room, similar to the one upstairs, laid out mostly the same.

We approached slowly. As we neared, the shadows started to resolve into . . . "Light," I whispered.

Behind me, Lacy flicked on her flashlight, quickly clicking it to red so it didn't ruin our night vision.

"Is that a . . . a room?" Burn asked.

Lacy flicked the flashlight over that side of the basement. Each flicker revealing another flash of what I was coming to understand was a glassed-in room.

A cry of distress behind me. "Lacy, give Burn the flashlight. Burn, go check it out."

She nodded briskly, grabbed the light, and made her way to the cell.

"Let Burn go first. Please."

Her agitation filled the space around us. I had to ignore it in order to do my job and keep us all safe. I looked around the room and peered into every dark corner.

After spending a long minute studying the cell, Burn returned.

"Is it her?" Lacy asked anxiously.

"It's a woman. She's laying on the bed, looking the other way. I think she's pretending to be asleep."

"She's alive?"

Burn nodded.

A weight I hadn't realized I was carrying dropped away. Lacy's sister or not, finding a dead woman in the cell would make this whole experience a hell of a lot worse.

"Now can we go?" Lacy grabbed my arm and tugged. I looked at Burn for her opinion.

She handed me the flashlight. "If it's her sister, might do her good to see Lacy."

True.

"Let's go." Lacy tried to race forward, but I stepped in front of her. "We do this together."

"Fine." Impatience and thanks warred in her voice.

Burn trailed us, while Mercer kept a lookout near the stairs.

"You ready for this?"

"Yes." She raised her hands like she was going to shove me out of the way if I didn't move, so I stepped to the side.

This close, I could make out details of the room. There was a bed, a small desk. A wall in one corner partitioned off what I assumed was the bathroom. There was even a small fridge unit and a reheater. It looked like a cozy room. If you ignored the fact that it was a glass cell.

It looked like it was built into the basement. What the hell kind of place was this?

For all her eagerness, when we reached the glass, Lacy's resolve seemed to waver.

"Want me or Burn to do this?" I asked quietly.

"No," she said shakily. "I can do it. Just give me a minute."

I nodded and gave her space. Just a little.

She took another breath and visibly pulled herself together.

"Layla?" Her voice was little more than a whisper.

Could the other woman even hear her?

"Fuck off, I'm sleeping."

Apparently so.

Burn snickered. The woman in the cell definitely sounded like she was related to Lacy.

Lacy knocked on the glass. Softly at first, then with more force. "Layla?" Her voice wavered as she spoke her sister's name. When the woman didn't respond, she pounded on the glass. "Layla!"

The woman stiffened, then rolled to her side to face us. "Lacy?"

"Oh my god, Layla!" Lacy pounded on the glass wall again.

I stepped closer. "Shh. They might hear us."

She nodded, then placed both her hands on the glass. "Layla!" she said a little more softly.

The other woman rolled to sitting and I got my first clear look at her. She appeared tired and thinner than what I remembered from the videos. There were no visible marks on her face, but that didn't mean she hadn't been hurt.

"Is it really you, Lacy?"

I clenched my jaw at the tremor in her voice.

"It's me, Layla."

The woman stood from the bed. She wore loose trousers and an oversize shirt. Her feet were bare. Remembering the stylish woman in her videos, I didn't think the clothes were hers. She walked slowly over to the glass and pressed her hands against it. "I was starting to think you wouldn't come."

Lacy pressed her palms over her sister's. Now that they were closer, I could see the resemblance. Her sister —I should probably start thinking of her as Layla— pressed her forehead against the glass. Lacy did the same.

After a moment, Layla lifted her head and looked at Burn and me. She recoiled and took a step back. "Where's Dad?" she asked as she tried to peer past us.

"What?" Lacy stepped back from the glass and looked at her sister in concern.

"When I sent you the data log, I thought you'd go to Dad."

Lacy hunched over. "Um, no. I came myself." Burn coughed. "Well, I came with a ship." Lacy pointed to us in quick succession. "Dax, Burn, and over there, Mercer. Orion is upstairs keeping watch."

"Why didn't you get Dad?" Layla sounded seriously confused. And the way she kept asking for their dad gave me a bad feeling. Was I right in my suspicions?

"It didn't cross my mind. The data chip was delivered

and the next thing I know, guys were breaking into my place wanting a map."

Layla gasped. "Oh no! I thought once the data was out of reach, they'd stop looking."

"Who's your dad?" Mercer sidled up and asked the million-dollar question.

Layla looked at him in confusion. "Didn't she tell you? Orpheus Blazer."

54

DAX

"What the fuck, Lacy?" Mercer yelled. Then he snapped his mouth shut and glared at her.

Burn looked just as surprised. Then she looked at me. "Did you know?" she asked, hurt in her voice.

I shook my head. "Not for sure. I'd started to wonder."

"You said no more secrets," Burn said to her.

Lacy dropped her head and sank into herself. "I know. It's just . . . Everyone thinks he's this criminal and he's . . . He's just our dad. And it hurts listening to people bash him all the time. It's easier to keep it to myself."

"You said you were on his crew," Mercer said.

"Yeah, I was. As a mechanic. Everything I told you was true. The only thing I left out was my dad's name." Now she lifted her chin belligerently. "It's not like any of you introduced yourself and said, 'And my dad is Mr. Blah Blah.' Can we just get Layla out of here?"

Mercer, the only one on the crew with family as famous, or maybe infamous, as hers, looked like he wanted to argue.

"Later." My tone brooked no argument.

"Open the door, Mercer," I said when no one showed any signs of moving. "You'll want to step back, Miss Blazer."

"Dupree," Layla said. "We both use our mom's name because of assholes like you." After dropping that little bomb, she disappeared behind the privacy wall.

Mercer pulled a thin strand of detonator cord from his pack. With careful, precise movements, he broke off a small piece and carefully crafted it into a shaped charge. He affixed it to the door, near the lock, and placed a tiny detonator in the ball of explosive.

Then he pulled out a small tablet from his pocket and linked the detonator to his control.

"That's not too big, is it?" Lacy asked him as she studied the charge.

"What, your daddy didn't teach you explosives?" His tone was snide, but there was a hint of something. Understanding?

"Don't be a dick, Mercer. I don't want to come this far to lose my sister to your fuckup."

Mercer lost his glare and his gaze thawed slightly when he looked at Lacy. "Relax, sweetheart. It won't hurt your sister."

She stepped close and stood on her tiptoes so she could look him in the eye. "If anything happens to my sister, I will hold you personally responsible. Do you understand me?"

Her voice was cold and the threat was clear. Whatever she'd done to tamp down her Blazer side was gone now.

Mercer understood that. He nodded.

Lacy brushed past me and took shelter behind the stairs. I nodded at Burn, directing her to go stand with Lacy. She nodded back and slid out of the way. She stationed herself at the base of the stairs and kept an eye out for any unexpected visitors.

"You got this?" I asked Mercer.

He nodded. "Yep. It's under control. You got that?" He jerked his chin toward Lacy and Burn.

I exhaled. "I have no fucking clue."

He smirked at me, then sobered. "Get clear. Layla?" he called to the woman in the cell.

She popped her head out from behind the wall. "What?"

"You ready? It'll be a ten-count as soon as I'm clear of the door."

She swallowed but nodded. "Big explosion?"

"Shouldn't be. Just enough to pop the lock out, but you never fuck with explosives."

She took a deep breath. "Got it. Get me out of here, please." She ducked back behind the wall.

"Stay safe, man." I slapped Mercer on the shoulder and cleared out, taking up a position next to Lacy. She was shaking with nerves. I wrapped my arm around her.

Mercer backed away from the cell as far as he could and still keep the detonator in range.

He spoke loud and clear. "Ten.

"Nine."

"Eight."

"Seven."

"Six."

"Five."

"Four."

"Three."

"Two."

"One."

Lacy tucked her head against my chest and dug her fingers into my shoulder.

There was a *pop* and a puff of smoke. Lacy turned her head at the muffled sound. Mercer stepped up to the door and grabbed the handle. When he pulled, the door opened easily.

Lacy pulled out of my arms and raced toward the open cell. "Layla, are you okay?"

Mercer blocked the open doorway with his arm. "The point was to get your sister out of the cell, right?"

Lacy glared at him but stopped trying to enter the glass room. Seconds later her sister stepped out. She walked through the small cloud of smoke and coughed. "I'm here. I'm fine."

Lacy wrapped her in a hug, then stepped back to study her. "You look awful. Are you sure you're okay?"

"Rude." Layla elbowed her in the side. "You see how you look when you've been locked in a cell for two weeks. I'll be a lot better when I get out of here, I promise. Can we leave now?"

I nodded. "Burn, we clear on your side?"

She lifted her chin. "Clear."

"Orion, we clear up top?"

There was a crackle of static.

"Orion?"

This time he responded. "Yeah, boss, we're clear."

"Problems?"

"Naw. Just had to duck out of the way. There have been some lights, but no one has come in."

I didn't like the sound of that. I liked being trapped down here even less.

"Roger. We're on our way up."

Lacy wrapped her arm around her sister's waist. "I've got you." Layla gave her a tired smile and leaned against her. That smile was so like Lacy's.

But her rescue meant that Lacy's time on the *Fortuna*

was limited. I didn't want her to go, but didn't see any way she could stay. My team wouldn't accept a Blazer—a Dupree—as a member of the crew. Would they?

Burn took the stairs first. She paused nearly at the top, her legs the only thing I could see. Then she scrambled up. "We're clear, Sarge. C'mon up."

Lacy and Layla moved slowly to the stairs. Without shoes, Layla was cautiously taking each step.

I didn't blame her, but we didn't have time for this. Faster would be better. We'd been lucky so far. I didn't trust that it would last.

I secured my weapon and approached them. "Go," I told Lacy. "Burn will guard you. I'll bring Layla up."

Lacy looked at me uncertainly.

"I promise," I said.

"Are you okay with this?" Lacy asked her sister.

"Do you trust him?"

Lacy nodded without hesitation.

Layla's eyes widened. "Okay, then I trust him too. Let's go."

Consent given, I wrapped my arm around Layla's waist and placed the other under her knees. I swept her into my arms easily.

"Go," I told Lacy again. "We'll be right behind you."

After a last searching look, she hurried to the stairs and up them. "Burn, keep an eye on Lacy. You've got the rear," I told Mercer.

He nodded somberly. "Go."

"I could have made it," Layla said, after I barely missed knocking her head on the overhead beam.

I smiled. She said that in the same snotty tone that Lacy used sometimes. They were definitely related. "Not fast enough."

"Yes, I—"

I gave her a look. She stopped talking, but the mulish set of her jaw—something else she shared with her sister—told me that it wouldn't be for long.

I was right.

"What's going on between you and my sister?"

"What?" Distracted, I almost lost my footing. When I righted us and was able to look down at her, she was staring at me with a knowing expression. "Nothing." I was not having this conversation. Not right now and not with her.

"Yeah, right. You just happened to almost break our necks because nothing is going on."

"I didn't almost break our necks," I countered through clenched teeth.

She laughed and clapped her hands like a little kid who's just learned a secret.

Dammit. It wasn't a secret. It was . . . complicated.

"I never thought she'd go for the military type," Layla continued when I didn't respond.

I didn't think I reacted, but she must have seen something in my expression, because she continued. "She didn't tell you about our upbringing." She studied me again. I wished that I had my face shield because she was scary perceptive. "Oh. She didn't tell you who our father is."

I fought to keep from having a reaction—I wanted to have this conversation with Lacy, not with her sister—but I couldn't help pressing my lips together.

"This is going to be so much fun!"

We broke through the top of the stairs. "What's going to be fun?" Burn helped steady me as I stepped onto the ground floor.

"The fireworks between my sister and my rescuer."

Burn smirked.

Well, crap. That wasn't good.

Mercer stepped out of the stairwell and I moved closer to the door. Orion stood in the doorway, facing out. Lacy hovered next to me, her gaze constantly checking on her sister.

"Our ship is in town, but we have a shuttle here," I told Layla. "There's a lot of gravel outside, so one of us will have to carry you."

"I can do it," Lacy said.

"No, you can't." Layla and I spoke in unison.

Lacy glared at me. "It's not that I don't think you can," I said to her. "You can do anything you put your mind to. But I need you free to get the shuttle started while the rest of us catch up."

I thought she was going to argue, but she surprised me. "Fine. That makes sense."

I studied our small group, trying to figure out the best way to break the team up.

"Burn, you're with Lacy. Orion, watch our six." I looked at Mercer and Layla. "Mercer, I need you to carry Layla this time. I'll provide cover."

Mercer gave me a pitiful look and placed a hand on his lower back. "I'd really like to help, boss, but my back." His lips twitched and I knew he was full of shit. He'd been carrying a full pack today and never once had he complained about "his back."

Dammit. I didn't want to carry her again. The woman saw too much.

I narrowed my eyes and glared at him. "I won't forget this."

He just laughed.

I looked at Layla. "Do you get airsick?"

She looked startled. "What?"

"Airsick, motion sick, seasick. Do you get any of those?"

Both she and Lacy stared at me like I'd lost my mind. "Noooo," she said slowly.

"Great. I apologize in advance, but this is going to be a bit uncomfortable."

"What are you talking about?" Lacy asked.

"I need to carry her over my shoulder."

"What? No!"

Surprisingly, it was Orion who stepped forward to reassure her. "It's the most efficient way to carry a wounded soldier—as long as it won't cause additional problems," he told her. "And it will let him keep his gun arm free."

"I'm not wounded," Layla exclaimed.

"Without shoes, you'll be hurt soon enough."

Her mulish expression amplified her resemblance to Lacy. "Fine. But put me down as soon as possible."

"Agreed."

"Do you get sick?" Lacy placed a hand on her sister's shoulder and looked closely.

"I never have before," Layla said gamely. "Can you imagine Dad's reaction if I got motion sick?"

They both laughed.

"Time to go, people."

Everyone nodded.

Lacy and Burn were the first at the door. Burn peered out.

"It's clear, Sarge," Burn said as she completed her scan.

"All right, team, let's go!"

Orion pulled the door back and Lacy and Burn raced into the dark night.

55

———

LACY

I was sucking in air by the time we reached the shuttle and I wasn't sure that I would ever lose the tension in my shoulders. I put my palm on the outside and rested a moment, trying to catch my breath.

"You can rest when you're dead," Burn hissed from behind me. "Get your ass in the shittle and get ready to boogie."

"Shuttle," I gasped, in between breaths.

"I. Don't. Care," Burn ground out. "Get. In. There."

"I'm going, I'm going." I hauled myself through the open door and stumbled into the cockpit. After we were off this damn planet, I was going to sleep for a week. Then I'd figured out what to do with the rest of my life, since I was pretty sure that Layla's big reveal had nuked my relationship with Dax and the rest of the crew.

Practically on autopilot, I ran through the pre-flight checklist, saying each step out loud so I wouldn't forget one. I didn't want to miss a step, especially since this was a new-to-me shuttle that had been tinkered with by people who probably didn't know what they were doing. We'd gotten here in one piece. Now I had to make sure we got back to *Fortuna* safely.

I was tired, stressed out, and probably running on pure adrenaline by now, but there was some exhilaration there too. We'd found Layla and she was okay. Or, at least, she seemed okay.

As I ran through the checklist, there was a thump on the roof of the shuttle. I froze. It was followed by the sound of scrabbling up there. "Um, Burn, I think something just attacked the shuttle. Can you take care of it?"

Her laughter rang through the shuttle. "That was me, you idiot. I'm up here watching their backs."

My cheeks flamed and I was glad that I was alone in here. "Oh, uh. Okay. Thanks."

That actually helped ratchet down part of my stress level. Knowing that she was watching my sister's back—and Dax's—made me feel a lot better. I was able to run through the rest of the pre-flight checklist a lot quicker knowing that there was another layer of protection for the people I loved.

Loved?

Well, shit. There went my concentration again.

Only having done this a million times before helped me make it through the last of the checklist. All the while, my brain was scrambling to make sense of the emotions I'd just admitted.

Love. *Pfft.*

Sure, that might be what I felt for Dax, but I'd probably blown it all to hell when I didn't tell him that I was Blazer's daughter.

A pang in my heart confirmed my suspicions.

"We have incoming," Burn said.

Heart in my throat, I asked, "Ours or theirs?"

"Ours."

"Good." I flipped the ignition switch and was rewarded with a smooth purr from the shuttle. "We're all set here." Lowering my voice, I patted the console. "Thank you, baby."

When we left Kottke, I wasn't leaving her to the mercies of those bastards. She deserved better. And Dax and his team could use a shuttle for *Fortuna* in their cargo business.

"Be ready to launch when I give you the word," Burn said.

I kept my hands on the controls and strained to hear anything happening in the back. All I heard, though, was the rush of blood in my ears and my breathing, which had slowed but wasn't anything approaching normal. My dad always said he got "in the zone" on missions. Apparently, I didn't get that gene.

Waiting sucked. After what felt like forever, someone boarded the shuttle. I heard movement, but no one spoke. "Burn?" I kept my voice low, but there was no disguising the anxiety in my voice. "Was that ours?"

"Yep."

Ugh. I hated this.

There were more footsteps behind me. "Please let that be them, please let that be them," I muttered under my breath before I turned around.

"Them who?"

I jumped at Mercer's voice. "You asshole!"

He laughed.

"Where's my sister? Is she on board?"

"She's fine," he said, "just a little green around the gills. Dax is strapping her in. At least she missed him when she puked."

A rush of sympathy for my sister filled me. "But they're okay?"

"Yes, they're okay. I'm fine, too, thanks for asking."

Turning back to the controls, I rolled my eyes even though he couldn't see me. "What about Orion? Is he on board?"

"Yep, next to Dax," Mercer said.

Out of the corner of my eye, I saw Burn swing down from the roof like a gymnast, uncurling and landing with her feet just inside the door. "We've got incoming."

"Bad guys?" With everyone on board, that was the obvious answer.

Mercer slid into the co-pilot's seat. "Time to go."

I pulled back on the controls and the shuttle hovered over the ground.

With slow and steady movements, I aimed the shuttle toward town. "Let's see how fast you can go, baby," I whispered. The quicker we got back to *Fortuna*, the quicker we could be airborne and off this backwater planet.

Shots pinged the outside of the shuttle and my heart jumped into my throat.

"Why doesn't this thing have weapons?" Mercer snarled next to me.

I glanced over at him. "Because it's a shuttle. You want weapons, you buy 'em. I'll install them."

"You could do that? Give our little shittle some claws?"

"Yes. But only if we're in one piece. So shut up and let me fly."

More shots pinged the outside of the ship. "Aren't you going to do something?" I yelled over my shoulder at Dax.

"Burn and Orion will take care of it." He sounded way too calm for me.

I took a moment to glance back. Burn and Orion were each hanging out one of the open doors. They were firing at whoever was following us. Burn was laughing like an idiot, the same way she had when we'd picked her up from Pangaea.

"You guys are crazy," I muttered.

"Get higher," Mercer said. "They might have more trouble hitting us."

I increased our altitude and aimed for town. And hoped our ammunition outlasted our pursuers.

56

DAX

Burn, Mercer, Orion, and I hung out the open doors of the shuttle as Lacy circled the landing zone twice to see what kind of welcoming party was waiting for us. But, like the compound, there was nobody out there.

I levered myself back inside the shuttle and looked at the others. "I didn't see anything, did you?"

Mercer shook his head. Burn said, "No, Sarge," and Orion kept looking another minute before he returned inside and pulled up the infrared goggles. "Nothing."

"That's really fucking weird, isn't it?" Burn asked. "I keep waiting for the other shoe to drop."

"He said he didn't want to hurt me." Layla spoke for the first time since she'd puked outside the compound. Head back against the seat cushion, she didn't open her eyes or look at us.

I dropped back into the seat next to her, gently so I didn't jostle her. "What? Who said that?"

"Johnstone Farrow," she said in a deep voice that weirdly suited the name, because that was exactly how you'd expect that name to be said.

"The guy you met from the forum?"

That got her to crack an eye open. "You know about the forum?"

"I know all about your files," I said. "Your research project."

She opened her second eye. "Lacy really does trust you."

Burn sat on the other side of her. "So have you found the treasure?"

"So you all know then?"

Mercer and Orion nodded.

"Fucking perfect," she muttered in the exact tone Lacy would use. "No, I haven't found the ship yet."

Burn's face fell. "Dammit!"

"But I'm close. I know it. Farrow knows it now too."

"You gave him your research?"

"No!" She sounded offended I would even ask. "He said he had journals from the original crew. Said his family had been on an escape pod from the *Queen of Stars* that landed here on Kottke."

"And you believed him?" There was Mercer's cynicism.

Layla shot him a dark look. "No. Do I look like an idiot? I vetted everything he said. Questioned it all. But he had information that, well, the only place he could have gotten it was from someone who'd lived it."

"Hey, so I'm glad you all are having a nice reunion with my sister, but can I land this thing yet?" Lacy called from the cockpit.

"Shit, yeah, sorry. Go ahead and land. There's no one out there," I said.

"Strap in, everybody," Lacy instructed.

Mercer and Orion took their seats, but everyone was still focused on Layla. "Why did you say that he didn't want to hurt you? Did he hurt you?" I felt sick at the thought.

"No," she shook her head. "He treated me okay. He was really apologetic. Said his dad got overzealous. I guess finding the ship has been the family's, I don't know, quest, forever."

Lacy interrupted again. "Touching down in five, four, three, two . . . one."

The landing jostled a bit, but I'd had a lot worse in the service. Even Layla looked calm. That made sense, given her—their—upbringing.

"Now that we're back, could someone open the cargo hold for me?" Lacy stepped out of the cockpit and into the main cabin.

"Why?" I asked.

"So I can fly the shuttle inside." She made it sound like the obvious answer.

"We're not taking the shittle with us," Mercer said.

That was my gut reaction too, but Lacy always had a reason. "Why do you think we should?" I asked.

She gave me a small smile. I'd apparently asked the right question.

"You're going into the cargo business, right?"

When we all confirmed that was still the plan, she continued. "With a shuttle, you'll have access to more ports. Smaller ones that *Fortuna* can't dock at, but you can remain in orbit and send your shuttle down."

"I thought you said it was in bad shape," Orion said.

Lacy shrugged. "Yeah, the guys in the chop shop messed her up. But she can be fixed."

"She's the best mechanic you'll find," Layla interjected. "Let her do it. She'll get it good as new. Better even."

Lacy's cheeks pinked at the compliment. "Look at it this way. You basically get a free shuttle; you'll just need to pay for parts." When no one said anything, her face fell. "Well, and you'll have to pay your mechanic."

She returned to the cockpit without another word.

Layla stood. "You're all a bunch of assholes. So she didn't tell you who our dad was. Big fucking deal. News flash, she's not Orpheus Blazer. She's Lacy Dupree. Mechanic. Pilot. Best sister in the galaxy. And you don't deserve her. Especially you." She poked me hard in the shoulder as she passed me to join her sister in the cockpit. "Now can we please get off this fucking landing zone and onto the ship before they turn us all into scrap?"

After she disappeared into the cockpit, Burn said, "Damn, I wish my sister had defended me like that."

Orion patted her shoulder gently. We all knew about her fucked-up childhood.

"Layla's right," I said.

"About getting in the air?" Mercer grumbled.

"Yeah, that, too."

I stood, my mind whirling with all the thoughts that Layla's passionate defense of her sister had stirred up. She was right. I had an amazing woman and I was letting her slip through my fingers.

Winning her—and wooing her—would have to wait.

Mostly.

Nothing said a little shuttle that needed some TLC couldn't be a courtship gift.

"Help me get the cargo hold open. We're keeping the shittle."

I sᴀᴛ in the shuttle in *Fortuna's* cargo hold and contemplated my life choices. Trying to get Dax and the crew to let me stay for the low price of a free shuttle was possibly the stupidest thing I'd ever done. Topped only by breaking into and stealing *Fortuna* in the first place.

"So, are we getting out or what?"

I looked at Layla in the copilot's seat. She looked like shit. Dark circles under her eyes. Her hair ragged and unkempt. "I'm so glad you're okay." I reached out to grasp her hand. I needed confirmation that she was really here. That I wasn't imagining this.

"I'm really glad you came for me." She wiped a tear away with her other hand. "Though I'm still kind of surprised you didn't get Dad."

I laughed, but it came out watery. "If those guys hadn't broken into my apartment—"

"I'm so sorry about that!"

I waved away her apology. "I might have brought Dad into it, once I figured out what was going on. But I didn't even look at the chip until I'd stolen Dax's ship." Yes, that had definitely been a mistake. "Seriously, though, this planet would be burning if Dad had been here."

Layla released my hand and wiped her eyes again. "You're right." She looked away from me. "That would have been a tragedy."

"What the hell, Layla? They kidnapped you!"

"An escape pod from *Queen of Stars* landed here, Lacy." She turned back to face me, her usual enthusiasm in her eyes. "I need to learn more about it."

The thought of her returning here made me physically ill. And reminded me we had to get the shuttle lashed down so we could take off. "Are you sure it wasn't a trick, Layla? A trap to get you here and steal your research?"

She shook her head. "Stone said it wasn't. I believe him."

"Stone? You mean Johnstone Farrow? The guy from the forum? You're just going around calling your kidnapper by his first name?" My voice rose with each word. This was insane, right?

My sister pressed her lips together. "His father was the one who had me kidnapped. Stone, I mean Johnstone, was keeping me safe from him."

"Mmm hmm." I didn't buy that for a second, but I had just gotten my sister back. I wasn't going to ruin this moment by arguing.

While she was avoiding my gaze, hers fell on MAKO. "Oh, you rescued him! I'm so glad."

Okay. I lied. I was totally going to ruin this moment by arguing with my sister. "Speaking of, where the hell is my ship?" I snatched MAKO off the console and held him close.

She winced. "I don't know. I'm so, so sorry. Dad said I should ask you if I could borrow her, but I was sure you wouldn't mind. I didn't expect all this to happen." Her gaze dropped to the figurehead in my arms. "You found him. He wasn't with the ship?"

I shook my head and tightened my grip on the little shark. "He was in a chop shop, Layla. Do you know what they do there? They chop ships into little pieces!"

She gasped. "Oh no! You saw her there?" She grimaced. "Was it terrible?"

I sighed. "I didn't actually see her. I found this on a tool chest and the mechanic I questioned said that you and the ship had been taken to the compound. But I didn't see the ship when we flew over. *Mako's* gone." Tears welled in my eyes, the day's emotional roller coaster taking its toll.

"That sucks. But you said you questioned someone. Like interrogated? Like torture?"

I laughed at the memory. "I threatened him with my very vicious shark." I thrust it toward her and shook it so the mouth moved.

"You're lying! That would never work."

"It did," I said primly. "You can ask any of the crew. Let's get out of here and I'll tell you all about it in my room."

Layla nodded and followed me out of the shuttle. When I saw Burn waiting for us, I tensed.

"Lacy," she started.

I didn't want to hear anything she had to say. I didn't need—or want—to hear how terrible a person I was. Or how horrible my family was.

"You'll want to strap the shuttle down for departure," I told her. "Once that's done, you can tell Dax he's free to take off."

Without waiting for a response, I crossed the cargo hold and led Layla to my room.

58

———

DAX

WE LEFT Kottke as sunrise was breaking over the planet. It painted the desolate landscape in stunning pinks, rich oranges, and fiery yellows. We cleared their airspace without reaching out to their control tower. No point in letting them try to deny us.

"Sure looks better from up here," Orion said.

I agreed.

The four of us were on the bridge, celebrating a successful mission and planning our future. Except I didn't feel much like celebrating.

"She's pissed," Burn said.

I didn't have to ask for clarification, even though there were two more women on board.

"Are you really just going to let her leave?" Burn asked.

"Why wouldn't he?" Mercer asked. "It was what the three of you agreed to, right?"

Burn scowled at him. "Sure, but things change."

"You just want her to stick around for the treasure."

Burn stuck her tongue out at him.

I was surrounded by toddlers.

"Tell me you don't want to go on a treasure hunt."

Orion's cough sounded an awful lot like a laugh.

"It's not real, Burn. They never sent the ore ship. There is no treasure. It's just a fairy tale," Mercer said.

"Layla thinks it's real and I believe her."

"Treasure aside, what are you going to do, Dax?" Orion's serious tone sobered the atmosphere on the bridge.

"I'd like her to stay. I'd like you all to agree to bring her onto the crew."

Burn's half-smile gave me hope that she would agree. Mercer and Orion, though, were inscrutable.

"And if we don't?" Mercer asked calmly.

Was I really doing this? Yeah, I was. "Then I'm going to beg her to let me come with her."

Burn's squeal nearly deafened me.

Mercer glared at me. "You'd give up all this for—"

I cut him off. "For love? Yeah, I'd give this all up for love."

"That sounds like an ultimatum," Mercer said. "You know how I feel about those."

"I do." Mercer's family had gotten the shock of their lives when, in response to an ultimatum, Mercer had joined the space corps.

This was different.

"It's not an ultimatum. I'm not forcing you to choose anything. *I'm* choosing. And I choose her."

There was a gasp from the doorway. Lacy stood there, shock on her face. Behind her, Layla wore a huge smile.

"What? How?"

"I may have 'accidentally' turned the intercom on," Burn said.

"You . . ." I had no words. "Thank you."

I looked up at Lacy, who was still staring at me. "What

do you say? Want to join me? Wherever that ends up being?"

She studied me a long, *long,* moment. "Yes," she said finally, her eyes shimmering with unshed tears.

Relief flooded through me.

Then she was in my arms and I was holding her as if I'd never let her go.

Her lips found mine in a frantic kiss that lasted not nearly long enough, when she remembered we had an audience and pulled away.

"What about my dad?" she asked, her voice suddenly serious.

I swallowed hard. "If you promise to protect me from him, I'm totally fine with your dad." I paused, thought about it. "But I don't want to join his crew."

"Neither do I." Her arms tightened around me and her head rested against my chest. "We'll figure it out. I still have my apartment on Elegium Station. I think."

The nearby throat clearing surprised me. "What if you didn't have to?"

"Didn't have to what?" I looked at Mercer, since he'd been the one who'd spoken.

"What if you didn't have to figure it out? You've got a crew and a perfectly good ship. Why would you want to leave?" Mercer asked.

"Both of us?" I asked the second-most important question of my life.

Mercer looked at Orion, then at Burn. All three nodded. "Both of you."

I looked down at Lacy, who was gazing up at me. "What do you think?"

"I think we go for it."

Her smile was prettier than a sunrise on Kottke.

"Um, hi. Yay," Layla said. "Congrats and all that, but what about me?"

Lacy shifted in my arms so she could look at her sister. "What about you? I figured we'd drop you off at whatever planet you wanted. Unless you wanted us to deliver you to *Eternal Nocturne*. Since you don't have a ship."

The bite Lacy put on the last word told me that she and her sister hadn't quite worked out Layla's loss of *Mako*.

Layla's eyes widened and she frantically shook her head. "No need to drop me off at Dad's. I'm sure I'll figure something out." She made a big show about looking around innocently. "What about here? Can I stay here?"

Lacy made a sound I couldn't interpret and buried her face in my chest.

Did she want me to say yes? Or no?

59

LACY

I CLOSED the door to my room quietly. After the crew had agreed to let Layla stay for as long as she liked—I was pretty sure Burn had voted so she could hunt for treasure —Layla had taken a shower and fallen asleep on my bed. We'd caught up on the most surface level things while she showered. I knew sleep—and probably food—would be the best thing for her. They would give her the strength to tell us about her ordeal.

Though what she'd shared already was as curious as it was worrisome. I needed to know more about this Johnstone Farrow and his family, but that wasn't my most pressing need. While Layla slept, I had my own issues to take care of. I'd left a note on the pillow next to her because I didn't want her to wake up and not know where she was or where I was.

Hearing Dax confess his love for me over the ship's intercom had been shocking. And life-changing. Getting to stay on the ship? It was like a dream come true. But I hadn't wanted him to feel pressured by the audience to make that choice.

I tiptoed down the crew quarters' hallway and made my way to the bridge.

I knew that was where Dax would be. He wouldn't relinquish it until we were well and truly safe.

The door to the bridge was open a crack. I squared my shoulders and took a deep breath. I could do this. I'd done it a hundred times since the moment I'd stolen this ship. Somehow, this time felt more important than all the others. Even the times when I'd begged him to help save my sister.

He'd come through in spades for me. I loved him for that and a hundred reasons more.

I rapped on the door before I could chicken out. "Dax?"

"Come in, Lacy."

His deep voice carried so much emotion, it sent shivers through me.

I stepped onto the bridge. The lights were low, most of the illumination coming from the controls rather than the light fixtures. The dark of space loomed ahead of us through the front screen. I imagined the planet behind us and smiled. We'd done it.

"Close the door," Dax said.

As soon as I had, I crossed to him and he pulled me down onto his lap. "How's your sister?"

"Sleeping."

"That's good. Did Mercer check her out?"

I nodded. That had been a battle, since my sister had insisted she was fine. "He threatened to make it a condition of her staying onboard."

"It wouldn't stick, not without a vote, but it was a good play."

It had been. "I'm glad he did. I would have worried."

We sat in silence for a moment.

"How did no one know that Blazer has kids?"

I froze, the secrecy so ingrained in me, I could barely speak. Then I relaxed and settled against Dax's chest. "Loyalty."

"What do you mean?" Dax looked puzzled.

How to frame it in a way that he would understand? Not that he didn't understand loyalty, but how would he understand my father? "If Mercer had a kid and asked you not to mention it, would you tell anyone?"

He looked offended. "Of course not."

"Why?"

"What do you mean?"

"Why wouldn't you mention it?" I persisted.

"Because he asked me not to."

"And?"

"Because he's my friend. He's my family."

"And if it was Burn? Or Orion? Or me?"

"Of course not!" He looked so offended.

"That's why. My father's crew is very tight knit. Most of them have been with him from the start and he trusts them."

"What about newer crew members?"

Of course he'd caught the distinction. Should I tell him the rest of it? I *had* promised no more secrets. "New crew are given the same expectations. And of course, the threat of a violent and painful death if anyone talked about us."

Dax choked. "That would do it. Is he going to threaten me?" he asked conversationally.

"I . . . honestly? Yeah, he probably will."

His arms tightened around me. "Will you protect me?"

"Always."

"I love you, Lacy Dupree."

"I love you too, Dax Cooper."

His fingers tangled in my hair and my hand curved around his neck.

I tugged him down for a kiss, needing his taste like I used to need oxygen. His lips met mine in a fiery tangle of need.

His hands slid down my neck, my back, and left trails of tingles the entire way down. They curved around my upper thighs as he lifted me so I could straddle his lap.

I pulled away slightly. "The intercom isn't on, right?"

He glanced over at the console, his lips curving into a grin. "Nope. No intercom." His mouth captured mine again.

The kiss was a blur of sensation. Until persistent knocking on the door broke into the moment.

Dax pulled back from the kiss and yelled at the interloper. "What?"

Burn's voice sounded like she was holding back laughter. "Uh, hey, Dax, if Lacy's up there with you, you might want to tell her that her sister is awake and hanging out in the mess. Mercer got her some food and she said she was up for talking."

My cheeks flamed. I looked at Dax. He indicated that it was my decision. "Thanks, Burn. We'll be right out."

"Oh no, don't rush on our account," she practically purred. "I can't wait to ask your sister all about your childhood. I'm sure she has the *best* stories."

"Fuck. That's sister-level evil," I said.

Dax just laughed.

"We better get down there." I pressed my lips against his one more time.

I smoothed my shirt and patted down my hair for probably the hundredth time as Dax and I made our way to the mess hall. It was a short distance that we would usually cover quickly, but I was moving slowly.

Like he could read my mind, Dax held his hand out to me. "Ready?"

"Nope, not in the slightest." I put my hand in his, grateful for the contact, the support.

He pulled me forward and into the dining hall.

Conversation stopped. Layla sat at the table, a bowl of soup and a glass of juice in front of her. Her eyes widened as she looked from Dax to our clasped hands to my face. I gave her a little half smile. Her eyes got even wider, then she smiled. *He's cute,* she mouthed.

I tried to will away my blush but I don't think it worked. My gaze swept the room as I tried to get a sense of everyone's mood.

Burn lounged casually in a chair angled between the door and the table. If I didn't know better, I would say that she was in a defensive, protective position.

Orion was at the stove ladling up another bowl of soup. And Mercer sat closer to my sister than I would have expected for someone with such disdain for our family name.

"You're awake. How are you feeling?" I released Dax's hand and swept across the room to Layla. She was already looking so much better than when we found her.

"Better," she said. Her voice was still a bit husky and she reached for a glass of water. "Your, uh, friends here have been telling me how you tracked me down."

"It was a group effort." I looked at the three crew members, wondering what the hell they'd told my sister.

"Burn said you were very insistent that you go after me right away."

I nodded. That wasn't so bad.

"After you stole their ship." My sister said the last absolutely dryly.

"Dammit, Burn!"

Burn burst into a belly laugh. "See, I told you she stole the ship. Why didn't you believe me?" She wiped tears from her eyes.

"Lacy would never do anything to harm a ship. Why do you think you ended up with that piece of shit shuttle in the hangar?"

"You mean the shittle," Burn said. She couldn't stop laughing.

"I didn't steal the ship." Dax laid his hand on my shoulder and I felt his laughter. "Okay, I stole the ship. But I was only able to do it because he left the factory preset codes intact."

Layla's mouth dropped open. "But that's . . . that's an amateur move."

Laughter broke out around us. I turned my head and sweetly said, "See, I told you so."

"Dammit, Burn."

Burn raised her hands. "Hey, I left that part of the story out. I was trying to make you look good, Dax."

"If I go down, I'm taking you with me." I gave Dax a sweet smile and he laughed.

I turned back to Layla. "Are you up to talking about what happened?"

She shrugged. "I think I've told you most of it. There's something down there that I need to know."

I took her hand gently. "It's too dangerous for you to go back. Even if I want to go back and kick their asses some more."

Layla smiled. "I'd pay to see that."

"Don't worry," Dax said. "They'll be punished soon enough."

Eyes wide, I looked at him. "What did you do?"

Dax nodded toward Mercer. "He called some old buddies in the corps. Told them to start exploring missing ships and people in this region. And he may have mentioned that Kottke was a good place to start."

My hand flew to my mouth to cover the laugh. "That's not as much fun as what I was thinking, but probably more effective in closing them down for good."

The trill of a message interrupted the conversation.

Burn looked at her comms. All the blood drained from her face and her communicator dropped to the floor.

"Are you okay? What's wrong?" Mercer got to her side quickest.

He picked up her comms and tried to give it back to her. When she refused, he looked at the screen, then her. "Shit."

She nodded and turned away, but not before I saw a tear slide down her cheek.

Mercer cleared his throat. "Can I share this?" he asked gently.

A sound of distress escaped Burn, but she nodded.

"Aunt Bernice. I hope you get this message in time. Mother has decided that it's my turn to bring honor to the family name." Mercer paused and swallowed hard. "She's marrying me to the preacher's oldest son. Save me. Please. Your niece, Alia."

"She's thirteen fucking years old," Burn said in a sad, tired voice. "He's in his thirties."

My stomach roiled. That was horrible.

"We have to go," Orion said.

Everyone nodded, even Layla and me. There was no question.

"Clear the table," Dax said. "We've got work to do."

READY FOR BURN'S ADVENTURE? **Stolen Chances** *is coming Spring 2026. Sign-up for my newsletter for all the latest updates.*

ENJOY THIS BOOK?

Reviews and ratings encourage other readers to try out a book and I'd love your help spreading the word!

If you could take a quick moment to rate or leave a review for this book on your favorite book site, I'd be forever grateful!

ACKNOWLEDGMENTS

The acknowledgements are almost harder to write than the actual book. Almost. What if I forget someone? If I did, please accept my deepest apologies and know it wasn't intentional!

Writing *Stolen Stars* in first person was a huge, scary decision that I second-guessed practically every other day. So huge thanks to my friends and family who read bits and pieces and assured me that yes, it did work.

Thanks to my mom, who insists on editing the drafts even though she only needed to read it for fun. You can take the professor out of the classroom, but apparently can't take the classroom out of the professor.

As always, there are so many people to thank:

Christine, my friend and critique partner who is always willing to read my pages, even when I give her a ridiculous deadline.

Shelli, for sharing book signing tables and years of encouragement.

Michelle, who took a chance on this book because we're friends, even though science fiction isn't "her thing."

Eilis, who put up with my pushing deadlines on this book. Sorry – and thank you!

Katherine at Grand Gesture Books, who took a chance on an indie author and was the first bookstore to carry my books! Seeing my books on your shelves was a dream come true!

We Be Book'N, Beguiled Books, and the Yakima Book

Co for adding the Stroke of Midnight series to their shelves!

The P&T Mastermind for chats and encouragement.

And to the readers…you have no idea how much I appreciate you. Thank you!

ABOUT THE AUTHOR

Once she stopped being stubborn and learned to read, Heather always had a book in her hand. Or in her bag. Or under the pillow.

Anne McCaffrey, Nora Roberts, Agatha Christie, and Tamora Pierce. Heather devoured anything and everything, from sci-fi and fantasy novels to historical romance and Harlequins. Her favorites, though, were the stories that combined swoony romance with fantastic adventures. Now she creates her own worlds and plays "what if…?"

Heather lives in Seattle with her husband and two cats. When she's not writing (or working at her day job), she can be found reading, traveling, or enjoying a quiet cup of tea–sometimes all at once!

Find her online at heathergreye.com or on social media

www.ingramcontent.com/pod-product-compliance
Lightning Source LLC
Chambersburg PA
CBHW021409310726
48971CB00005B/1260